A DEVONSH

LAWFUL DUTY

MICHAEL CAMPLING

Shadowstone
Books

Published by Shadowstone Books
ISBN: 978-1-915507-14-3

We must find our duties in what comes to us, not in what we imagine might have been.

— GEORGE ELIOT, *DANIEL DERONDA*

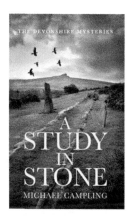

PROLOGUE

1992

EXETER

STANDING OUTSIDE THE ICEBOX NIGHTCLUB, Lynsey Clifford fumbled in her handbag for her cigarettes and lighter. The box of Marlboros was almost empty, but she had a couple left, and that would see her through until the morning. Tomorrow was Sunday; she could have a lie-in and then walk to the shop and stock up. As well as cigarettes, she'd buy a magazine, a loaf of bread and a pint of milk, then back to her flat for a mug of strong coffee and a mountain of toast: a sure-fire cure for the hangover she was bound to have.

She lit up her Marlboro and breathed deep, filling her lungs then tilting her head back to send a plume of smoke into the cool September air.

That was better. Lynsey looked out over the river, watching the glimmering reflections on the water's surface. *It's pretty*, she told herself. But beneath the gently shimmering reflections, the undulating water appeared even darker than the night sky, and the thought of its murky depths sent a chill to her stomach.

Lynsey's long dress was thin and did nothing to shield her against the cold, but she'd be okay. In the club, it had been too hot, too muggy, the atmosphere laden with the scents of stale sweat, cheap perfume and spilt beer. She looked around while she smoked her cigarette, imagining the smoke warming her from the inside out. There was no one in sight. She was completely alone and that, too, was okay.

It'll be winter soon, she thought. *Endless rain and short gloomy days.* All the more reason to make the most of the crisp autumnal evening. Lynsey allowed herself to revel in the moment, savouring the solitude, the sensation of the night air stroking her skin, the stillness.

Earlier, the cobbled streets of Exeter's quayside had been buzzing, crowds of young people chatting and laughing as they wended their way past the grand old buildings and headed for the club, urged on by the promise of a drink and a dance.

Some had been drunk, some tipsy, but most had been behaving themselves and trying to look reasonably sober. If the bouncers thought you'd had a skinful, they'd turn you away, and that would spell an early end to the evening. Once the pubs threw you out at eleven, there was nowhere else to go but home, and where was the fun in that?

Lynsey sighed. She'd be going home on her own tonight. Tony was being a prick. He'd brought the lads along, and they'd all had too much to drink, the whole gang of them downing lager as if their lives depended on it. As far as he was concerned, he was out with the boys.

Acting like teenagers, she thought. *It'd be pathetic if it wasn't so funny.* Tony was the same age as her, for God's sake, and at twenty-three, it was about time he grew up. Some of her old university friends were settling down, sending out wedding invitations and talking about mortgages, but she was nowhere near that state of affairs. And so long as she stayed with Tony, she'd get no closer to married life.

It's time to move on, she decided. *It was fun for a while, but it's run its course.* She'd break the news to Tony soon, maybe even tonight. Sometimes you had to rip the plaster off, get the pain over and done with. Then you could forget about the past and move on.

Lynsey mentally rehearsed what she'd say to him. The problem was, she never knew how Tony would react when he'd been on the beer. He could be needy, wheedling and begging for affection, but she'd seen a darker side to him too: fists clenched, eyes dark with anger, his teeth bared. Jealousy and rage; it was a bad combination.

All it took was for a man to talk to her in the pub, or even to look at her in a certain way, and Tony would barge in, all puffed up and full of testosterone, draping his arm heavily over her shoulders, claiming her as his own.

I should've dumped him months ago, Lynsey told herself. To Tony, she was a possession, a prize to be shown off. Even now, he might be wondering where she'd got to. He had a habit of haunting the edge of the dance floor, his gaze fixed on her, his eyes narrowed, watching her every move. No more. She'd see him in a minute, and she'd give him the bad news straight away. But all that could wait until she'd finished her smoke.

Lynsey strolled toward the river, walking right up to the quay's edge. Below her, the dark water lapped against the ancient stone wall. A shiver ran over her skin and she used her left hand to rub her right arm, her fingers sliding over the smooth bare skin. Staring down at the water made her dizzy, so she looked back up at the sky. That last drink had been a mistake; she didn't feel herself. Usually by now she'd be ready to dance the night away, but something wasn't right. All she wanted to do was go home and go to sleep.

From behind her, she heard footsteps grating on the cobbles, and she half turned to see a figure emerging from the club. *It'll be Tony,* she thought. *Come to check up on* me. It was time for her to face the music.

Lynsey took one last look at the river. Her cigarette was finished, so she held it out over the water and let it go. The tip flared for a moment, then the cigarette hit the surface and went out. She'd thought it would make a fizz, but there was nothing, not even a splash. The bright point of heat and light had been extinguished without a sound.

MONDAY

1

1992

Timothy Spiller guided his Volvo 340 into a parking space and switched off the car radio. They'd been playing "It's Probably Me" by Sting, the theme tune to the latest Lethal Weapon film, and Spiller smiled to himself. Life in the police just wasn't like that.

He climbed from the car and shut the door with a gratifying clunk. That was Swedish engineering for you. Solid. Reliable. He hadn't quite got used to the car yet, but he was enjoying every minute behind the wheel. The Volvo might have a fair few miles on the clock, but compared to his old Datsun Cherry, it was a dream to drive.

With his fingertips, Spiller brushed a streak of dirt from the dark blue bodywork, then he headed across the car park. *That was daft,* he told himself. His first day in a new job, and he'd have to shake hands with his colleagues, but here he was with muck on his hand.

He pulled a handkerchief from his pocket and wiped his fingers. You only had one chance to create a first impression, and he intended to make it a good one.

Pocketing his handkerchief as he went along, Spiller

gazed up at the utilitarian building of brick and glass: Heavitree Police Station, his new place of work. His heart beating a little faster, Spiller strode up the steps and let himself in through the glass door. He was here. At last, he'd made it.

The uniformed sergeant behind the counter had the look of a seasoned officer, his years on the beat etched in the lines on his brow. Not a hair on his grizzled head was out of place, and his white shirt could've been used to advertise Persil. He regarded Spiller with a raised eyebrow and an indifferent smile.

"Yes, sir, how can I help you?"

Spiller stood tall. "Good morning, Sergeant. I'm Tim Spiller. I'm the new Detective Constable. It's my first day."

"Ah." The sergeant plucked a clipboard from beneath the counter and studied it, tapping a plastic biro against the page as he read. Brightening, he offered a smile and a nod. "Right you are, Tim. Welcome to Heavitree. I'm Colin, Colin Goodwin, but call me Skip; everyone does."

He offered his hand for a shake, and Spiller took it. "Thanks. Nice to meet you, Skip."

"Listen, Tim, they're expecting you upstairs today, but..." He glanced at his watch. "It's barely eight o'clock, so there's hardly anyone in CID. DCS Boyce is in, he always starts early, but I don't think you want to disturb the detective chief superintendent on your first day."

"Oh." Spiller tried not to let his disappointment show. "Never mind, I'll wait. I expect everyone else will be here in a minute."

"Maybe," Goodwin replied without much conviction. He regarded Spiller for a moment, and his expression softened. "On the other hand, it's quiet at the minute, and I expect DCS Boyce will be ensconced in his office, so I suppose I could take you up and show you around."

"If it's not too much trouble—but don't you have to cover the desk?"

Goodwin waved Spiller's question aside. "My shift's almost over. Phil will be here in a minute. I'll leave him a note."

"Okay. I'm ready when you are." Spiller put his hands in his pockets in a show of nonchalance, but he had to stop himself from bouncing on the balls of his feet.

At last, Goodwin emerged from a side door and indicated a stairway at one end of the lobby. "It's this way."

"Yes, I've been here before, for my interview."

"Of course you have. It must've been while I wasn't on duty. I never forget a face."

Spiller didn't doubt Goodwin's claim. He knew a dyed-in-the-wool copper when he saw one, and as he followed Goodwin up the stairs, he said, "Have you been here long?"

"Oh yes. Donkey's years."

"I bet you could tell some tales," Spiller said.

Goodwin halted and turned to face him, his eyebrows lowered. "What do you mean by that?"

"Nothing really. But when you've been at a nick for a while, you get to know who's who, both in here and out there. I expect you've seen a few familiar faces in the cells over the years, haven't you?"

Goodwin nodded slowly, then he resumed his journey up the stairs in silence.

Oh dear, Spiller thought. *I've touched a nerve there.* Perhaps Goodwin had previously been accused of gossiping or telling tales out of school. A desk sergeant saw almost everything that went on in a station, and the job came with a great deal of responsibility. One thing was for sure, Spiller did not want to be on Sergeant Goodwin's wrong side. One way or another, he'd have to make amends.

But perhaps Goodwin wasn't the type to take umbrage for long; by the time they reached the second floor, his businesslike demeanour was back.

"This is your new home from home," Goodwin said, opening an unmarked door and striding inside.

Spiller followed, gazing around the CID Office in awe. The last time he'd seen it, the place had been a hive of activity, but with the desks unoccupied, the room seemed enormous.

"Ah," Goodwin said. "Sorry, sir, I didn't see you for a second."

With a start, Spiller spotted a smartly dressed man in the corner of the room and recognised him immediately. This was Detective Chief Superintendent Mark Boyce, the man who'd interviewed Spiller before accepting him into CID. In a pale blue shirt and dark blue tie, Boyce looked immaculate, his hair neatly combed and his charcoal grey trousers neatly pressed. He was filling the kettle at the sink, and he kept his attention on the task as if judging the correct amount of water to the nearest millilitre. Apparently satisfied, he set the kettle down carefully and switched it on, then he ran his gaze over Spiller, his eyes bright.

"This is your new DC, sir," Goodwin went on. "Tim Spiller."

Spiller stood to attention. "Reporting for duty, sir."

Boyce smiled. "Ah, Timothy. Good to see you again, and you've arrived bright and early. Excellent. I'll be with you in a moment."

"Yes, sir. Thank you, sir."

Goodwin leaned a little closer to Spiller and lowered his voice. "Call him Super. He prefers it."

Spiller nodded.

"Right, I'll leave you to it," Goodwin muttered. He nodded to Boyce and raised his voice to add, "See you tomorrow, sir."

"Yes. Thank you, Sergeant." Boyce consulted his watch, and Goodwin took this as his cue to leave.

Spiller stood awkwardly, but Boyce beckoned him over.

"Tea?" Boyce asked. "Milk and sugar, that's right, isn't it?"

"Yes, sir, but I can make my own cup of tea."

Spiller made his way over to join his new boss, who was already bending to hunt through a cupboard in search of a clean mug.

"Success," Boyce said, straightening his back and brandishing a mug. "I'll do the honours on this occasion, but I don't make a habit of brewing up for the whole of CID."

"No, sir. Of course not, sir. I'm sure you're far too busy for that."

Boyce made a noncommittal noise, and Spiller sensed he'd said the wrong thing. In the silence, the kettle clicked off, its job done.

"It's not that I've too much on my plate," Boyce went on as he made their drinks. "I have plenty to do, but I'm not one of those officers who sit in an ivory tower. I like a tea break as much as the next man, so you'll see me out here, grabbing a drink the same as everyone else. But I have a routine. That's the secret to this job, Tim: routine. Make a plan and stick to it. No matter how many tasks land on your desk, you can only tackle them one at a time. Bit by bit, we get the job done."

Boyce consulted his watch and then removed the teabags from the mugs, adding the milk and sugar quickly, his movements deft and precise. That done, he handed Spiller a mug and waited expectantly.

"Thank you, sir." Spiller took a cautious sip. "That's very nice, sir. It hits the spot."

"The trick is to time the brew. Too long and it's stewed, too short and it's barely tea at all." He paused, studying Spiller thoughtfully. "Why didn't you listen to Sergeant Goodwin?"

Spiller had a mouthful of tea and almost choked on it. "Sorry, sir?"

"I heard what he said. There's nothing wrong with my hearing. He advised you to call me Super, knowing full well that I hate it, but you ignored him. Why? Were you simply being cautious?"

"No, sir." Spiller composed himself. "I noticed he didn't follow his own advice. He always referred to you as sir, so I guessed he might be having a bit of fun at my expense."

Boyce laughed. "By God, Tim, you're sharp as a tack, I'll give you that. We'll make a detective out of you yet."

"Yes, sir. That's what I'm here for."

"Good man."

They sipped their drinks in silence for a while, Spiller's gaze roaming the room while Boyce stared into the middle distance, his mind elsewhere.

The door opened, and both men breathed easier as a besuited man strode into the room.

The new arrival greeted Boyce, then acknowledged Spiller with a nod. "You must be my new DC. Tim Spiller, am I right?"

"Yes, sir."

"Tim was here early, raring to go," Boyce said. To

Spiller, he added, "This is Detective Superintendent John Chisholm. He'll set you on the straight and narrow. You'll be seeing more of him than you will of me, although..." Boyce looked from Chisholm to Spiller. "I'll be keeping an eye on you, Tim. I'm not going to hold your hand; if you need that, you're in the wrong job. But I can see your potential, and I'll be having a chat with you now and then, just to see how you're doing."

"Thank you, sir. I appreciate that."

Boyce nodded. "Gentlemen, I'll leave you to it." He took a sip of his tea and then marched across the room, disappearing into a corner office and closing the door firmly.

Chisholm strolled over to his own large desk at the far end of the room, then he shrugged out of his jacket, hanging it on the back of his chair.

"First things first, Tim," Chisholm said. "Milk and two, and leave the bag in. I can't stand weak tea in the mornings." He sat down and frowned at Spiller. "When you're ready, in your own time."

"Sorry, sir. I'll get right on it." As quickly as he could, Spiller made a mug of tea. He'd kept a keen eye on Boyce earlier, so he found everything he needed without difficulty. But when he splashed milk on the counter, he searched in vain for something to mop it up.

"Leave it," Chisholm called out. "You can get a paper towel from the loo later. Bring my tea over, will you? I've got a tongue like the bottom of a budgie cage."

Mumbling an apology, Spiller hurried over to Chisholm's desk, a mug in each hand. As he waited, Spiller felt the colour rising to his cheeks, but Chisholm didn't seem to notice. He was too busy rifling through the stacks of cardboard folders cluttering his desk.

"Pull up a pew," Chisholm said. "Any one will do, but that purple one is good."

Spiller hesitated. The only purple chair in the office was noticeably newer and smarter than the others, its upholstery pristine.

"Go on," Chisholm went on. "I haven't got all day."

Setting down the mugs, Spiller grabbed the chair and sat beside Chisholm, leaning forward, ready to absorb the gems of information that were surely about to come his way.

"Ta." Chisholm grabbed a mug and took a gulp. "Not bad, Tim, but let's crack on. This is my desk, and it's where I'm to be found. If you need anything, come and ask. I *could* have an office of my own, but I politely declined. I want to be here, where I can see what's going on, and I won't stand for any monkeying about. Save that for the pub after work. You are coming out for a drink tonight, aren't you? First day and all that."

"Thank you, sir, but—"

"Guv," Chisholm interrupted. "Call me guv or guvnor, I'm not fussy. DCS Boyce likes to be a bit more formal, but that's his prerogative. Out here, we're all in the trenches together. But you're not trying to wriggle out of a night in the pub, are you?"

Spiller adjusted his position on the chair. "I appreciate the invitation, but my wife's expecting me home for dinner."

"It's your loss, but don't make a habit of turning us down. I want to see you fitting in, Tim. It's good to chew the fat, especially after a crappy day, and there are plenty of those. But let's not dwell on that. Where are you from, Tim?"

"Telford, guv."

"Ah, I thought you were from somewhere up there. You sound like a Brummy."

"It's not far from Birmingham."

"I know, Tim. I know. You were in uniform up there, yes?"

"That's right, guv, but CID is always where I wanted to be."

"Not a university lad, then?"

Spiller shook his head. "My parents wanted me to go to college. I tried business studies. They run a shop you see, and—"

"I don't need your whole life story. You're here, and that's good enough for me. Welcome to CID."

"Thanks, guv. I'll do my best to hit the ground running."

"You're damned right, you will." Chisholm clapped his hands together. "Moving on, let's get your induction over with. First, health and safety. In the event of a fire, I advise you to leave the building. You'll know there's a fire on account of all the smoke and flames and such, but what you won't hear is the ringing of bells. The smoke detectors in here don't work for some reason, which is just as well, as some of us like to have a fag now and then without sloping off to the outside world. Do you smoke, Tim?"

Spiller shook his head firmly.

"Just as well. Boyce does not approve."

"Me neither," Spiller said. "But the smoke alarm, if it's broken, isn't that—?"

"Dangerous?" Chisholm interrupted. "Maybe, but if you want a safe job, go and work in a..." Chisholm waved a hand in the air. "Forget that. Nowhere's safe these days. We went out to a stabbing last year. The victim was a lecturer. Teacher training. Knifed by a disgruntled student."

Chisholm puffed out his cheeks and exhaled. "It makes you wonder, doesn't it? What chance have the kids got when the only people who might actually want to be teachers are unhinged?"

Before Spiller could reply, the door opened and a group of three men walked in, chatting. Spying Spiller, they exchanged fleeting glances with each other before greeting Chisholm.

"Gather round, lads," Chisholm called out, and the trio assembled around Chisholm's desk.

"Lads, this is our new DC, Tim Spiller."

Gesturing to each of the new arrivals in turn, Chisholm said, "In no particular order, DC Adrian Cove, DI Oliver Nicholson and DS Patrick Reilly. A merry band known to all as Ade, Ollie and Paddy. We're missing DC Jenny Hoggarty, who's on holiday if you can imagine such a thing." Chisholm spread his arms wide. "I mean, who'd want to miss all this?"

Spiller joined in the brief chorus of hollow laughter.

"We're a small team and a tad top-heavy," Chisholm went on. "DCS Boyce is doing his best to get us some more manpower, or person-power, or whatever you want to call it, but government cuts being what they are, we'll all have to pitch in and make the best of it." Looking to Spiller, he added, "All clear?"

"Yes, guv," Spiller replied. "Good to meet you all. Is Detective Chief Inspector Wendell not in today?"

A murmur ran around the group.

"Brian will not be gracing us with his presence today," DS Reilly said. "The DCI has been unavoidably detained."

Given Reilly's name, Spiller had expected an Irish accent, so he was surprised to hear the flat northern vowels of a Yorkshireman. A good few years older than Spiller, and sporting a thick moustache, Reilly had a hangdog expression and a relaxed posture that somehow made his suit seem scruffy. But he had a friendly twinkle in his eye, and Spiller warmed to the man.

Standing next to Reilly, DI Nicholson had the look of a harassed middle manager. Clean-shaven, his cheeks pale and slightly saggy, he wore a V-necked pullover beneath his jacket.

Glancing nervously at the others, Nicholson said, "The DCI has been suspended pending the investigation of an allegation."

"A bullshit allegation," Chisholm snapped. "He's been made a scapegoat, pure and simple. It's total madness, is what it is, and it leaves us short-handed. That means you'll have to get stuck in Tim. In at the deep end, sink or swim."

Spiller nodded. "That's fine by me."

This seemed to entertain the others, and the mood in the room lightened.

The only one who hadn't spoken so far, DC Adrian Cove, stepped closer to Spiller, his arm outstretched for a shake. "Welcome aboard, Tim. I reckon you'll fit right in."

"Thanks."

Spiller guessed that he and DC Cove were about the same age, although Cove's moustache was even fuller than Reilly's and it made him look older.

Maybe I ought to grow a moustache, Spiller thought, but he'd tried before, and he couldn't quite carry it off. Unlike Cove, whose thick dark hair had only been restrained with the aid of hair gel, Spiller kept his mousy hair short, and his one and only attempt at growing a beard had ended in a sparse and unconvincing affair.

"Right then." Chisholm made a shooing motion with his hands. "That's enough standing around, ladies. Let's get to work. Morning briefing in..." He glanced at the clock on the wall. "Twenty minutes. You've got time to grab a drink, and Tim here is a dab hand at hot beverages, aren't you, Tim?"

Spiller opened his mouth to reply, but the others talked over him.

"Cheers, Tim, black coffee, no sugar."

"Tea, one sugar."

"Same for me."

The three made for their desks, but Nicholson stopped short.

"Hey, who the bloody hell's nicked my chair?" Wheeling around, Nicholson clapped his eyes on Spiller. "That's my chair, son, and not to be taken."

Spiller almost fell over his feet in his rush to stand up. "Sorry, sir. I didn't know."

"I had to fight tooth and nail to get that chair," Nicholson said. "It's ergonomic. I need it for my back."

"Right." Spiller pushed the chair toward Nicholson. "Apologies, sir. It won't happen again."

Spiller risked a sideways glance at Chisholm, but the man was all innocence, shaking his head as if amazed at Spiller's nerve.

"See that it doesn't." Nicholson took the chair and wheeled it to his desk in silence.

"Okay, Tim," Chisholm said. "Take the desk facing Ade. Make yourself at home and see if you can coax that old computer into life. If you look carefully, you'll find a hole for a key. Wind the clockwork up tight and you should get an hour out of it before the spring runs down."

Spiller managed a chuckle.

"Please don't laugh at the guvnor's jokes," Adrian Cove called from across the room. "It only encourages him."

"Don't you listen, Tim," Chisholm said. "You laugh as loud as you like. Okay, what else do you need to know? The loo is down the corridor, the stationery is in that cupboard in the corner, and that concludes your induction. Now, you've just got enough time to make those drinks before the briefing, so I'd get my skates on if I were you."

Chisholm went back to sifting through his papers, and Spiller knew what he had to do. Plastering a smile on his features, he pulled himself up to his full height, and with as much dignity as he could muster, he headed for the kettle.

2

WITH AN EFFORT, Lynsey opened her eyes. The blindfold was tight, the fabric pressing hard against her skin, its edges digging into her cheeks and forehead. It flattened her nose and made breathing difficult, so she opened her mouth and gasped for air.

Lynsey tried to free her arms, but the ropes had left her wrists and ankles raw, and struggling only made the pain worse. She was tied to some kind of bed, and she could hardly move a muscle.

She thought of calling for help, but she'd tried that before, and he'd pushed her down and threatened to cut her throat. His voice had been little more than a whisper: a low, guttural growl intended to frighten her. Lynsey had tried not to react, but it hadn't been easy. The man's sinister, soft voice had sent a shudder of revulsion through her whole body. She'd been tempted to provoke him, to make him shout and yell. Anything would've been better than his insidious whispers. But she hadn't dared. She'd heard the anticipation in his voice. He hadn't been making idle threats; he *wanted* to cut her throat.

Lynsey almost wept, but she'd run out of tears some time ago. She had to make herself strong and focus on surviving. It was the only way she was going to come out of this alive.

How long had she been here? It felt like forever. Her whole body ached from being held immobile, but she could deal with the pain; the fear was so much harder to bear. What was he going to do to her? So far, he'd touched her only to tie her up, and she'd only been dimly aware of that. He must've been giving her something, because she'd been dazed and confused ever since she'd been taken.

The last thing she remembered clearly was getting into the taxi on Saturday night. After that, her memories were shot through with holes.

What happened? How did he do this to me? Lynsey forced her mind to focus. She recalled standing by the water. A man had come out and tried chatting her up. He hadn't been much to look at, but at least he'd been polite. He'd offered her a cigarette, but she'd said no. She'd told him she wanted to be alone, and he'd gone back inside.

There were other memories of that night, but they'd become twisted and disjointed. She'd tried to piece them together, but they seemed somehow unreal, as though they'd happened to someone else.

She recalled Tony making a fuss when she'd broken up with him, and she remembered heading home. The bouncer had said something about calling her a taxi, but she'd told him not to bother. A couple of minutes later, a minicab had pulled up alongside, the driver calling out her name, so she'd assumed the bouncer had phoned for a taxi after all. She hadn't wanted to get in, but she'd felt unsteady, her thoughts sluggish, and she'd found herself climbing into the back seat. But what then?

Had somebody else got in the car with her? A dark memory lurked at the edge of her consciousness, but she couldn't capture it. Something had happened. Something...

A sudden noise made Lynsey tense, her breath trapped in her chest. It had sounded like a shoe scraping across the floor. He was there, in the room with her. He must've been watching her while she slept.

Straining her senses, she picked up another sound. He was sniffing, blowing his nose.

"It's cold in here," Lynsey said with as much confidence as she could muster. "Why don't you do something about it?"

There was no reply. The silence pressed down on her like a physical presence, smothering her with its weight, making her want to scream. But then came the same rasping whisper as before, the man's voice almost inaudible: "It's not that bad. Do you want a blanket?"

"What I want is to get out of here."

He sniffed again. "Not yet."

"Why do you keep sniffing? And why don't you talk properly? Is there something wrong with you?"

He didn't deign to reply, and the silence stretched out until Lynsey could bear it no longer. "How long was I asleep?"

"Hours. All night."

"What? Did you put something in my water? It tasted funny."

"I might've slipped you a little something. No sense in you getting upset, wearing yourself down."

Lynsey let fly with a string of curses.

"Now, now," he said. "That's no way for a nice young lady to talk."

"Piss off."

"I'll go when I'm good and ready, not before. We need to have a chat first."

"If you're telling the truth, I've been here for two nights, so it must be Monday. They'll be missing me by now, wondering why I'm not at work."

"Possibly. Let's talk about work, Lynsey. You have something I need. Where is it?"

"Not this again. I told you, I have no idea what you're talking about."

"But that's not true, is it? You were the last person to see that document, and now it's missing. We want it back."

"That's tough because I don't have it."

"Then where is it?"

Through clenched teeth, Lynsey said, "I don't know."

"Yes, you do. You've taken it, Lynsey."

"No. My boss thought I took it, but he was wrong. I tried to tell him, but he wouldn't listen. I didn't even know what it was. I'm just an assistant. I do admin."

"Don't play games. You're not stupid, Lynsey. You work in the accounts department. You knew perfectly well what you were looking at."

"No. There's tonnes of paperwork, but I understand hardly any of it. You've got the wrong person. You may as well let me go."

Footsteps. He was close now, standing over her. She could sense his nearness.

"Lynsey, why must you keep on lying like this?"

"I don't... It's not..."

He sighed, his breath washing over her cheeks.

"Please," she said, her voice faltering. "Please let me go. I haven't seen your face. I don't know who you are or where I am. You could... you could take me somewhere and let me go. Please, I'm begging you."

"There's no need to beg. I'll let you go eventually. But first, you need to tell the truth."

Some spark of defiance kindled in her stomach. "I have told you the bloody truth. There's no point going on, asking the same questions over and over. Let me go or my father—"

"Oh yes, your father," the man interrupted. "He'll be very distressed, won't he? Did you give the document to him? Is that why we couldn't find it in your flat?"

"No. I haven't given anything to anybody."

"I don't believe you."

"That's your problem. Whatever it is you want, I haven't got it."

"That is a shame," the man murmured. "This isn't going to get us anywhere. Maybe we need to pay a visit to your dear daddy."

"Go ahead. He's not frightened by the likes of you. And when he finds out what you've done, he'll hunt you down. He'll find you and make you pay."

"I don't think so." Footsteps again. The man was moving away from her. He paused and she heard the jangle of metal, the sound of a key sliding into a lock.

"We'll be sending a message to your father soon, and we'll be giving him a little something; something to prove you're still alive."

"What... what do you mean?"

He chuckled darkly. "Don't worry, I'm not going to start chopping off fingers. Nothing so messy. I'm going to give him a photograph, that's all. I took it this morning while you were still asleep. Just you and today's paper. That ought to get the message across."

"Bastard," Lynsey hissed, her voice rising as she went

on, "You're getting off on this, aren't you? You're sick, a filthy little pervert. You're..."

Lynsey let her voice fade. The door had closed quietly, the lock turning with a metallic click, the bolts sliding home with a grim finality.

"This can't go on," she whispered. "They'll be missing me already. Someone will come looking, and they'll find me. They have to."

3

As SOON AS Detective Superintendent Chisholm made for the briefing room, DC Spiller followed. He could've waited for the others to take their places, but he was not going to follow along like a lost lamb. Yes, he was the new boy, and his colleagues had mucked him around a bit, but that was not going to be the way of things.

It was time to make a stand. The centre of the room was filled with a rectangular arrangement of tables, and Spiller marched straight to the front and took a seat. He'd be close to Chisholm and he'd have a clear view of the whiteboard. Perfect. Tim placed his notebook on the table and opened it at a blank page, his pen in his hand.

The others filed in and took their places. The seat next to Spiller was taken by DC Adrian Cove, and he too, had his notebook and pen at the ready. Lowering his voice, Cove tilted his head closer to Spiller and said, "If you miss anything, make a quick note and ask me later. I'll fill you in."

"Thanks, but I should be all right."

"Okay, but I remember what it was like on my first day, so the offer's there."

"Cheers," Spiller said. "Good to know."

The last to arrive was DI Nicholson, and as he sat down, he looked pointedly at Spiller. "Someone's keen."

Spiller sent him a smile. "I should hope we all are, aren't we?"

A few of the others chuckled, and Chisholm said, "Quite right, Tim. That's the spirit."

Nicholson looked put out for a second, but he laughed it off. "He'll be after our jobs next."

"Not for a good while, sir," Spiller replied. "I've got a lot to learn, especially from the more experienced officers such as yourself."

Mollified, Nicholson said, "Fair enough. You've got your head on your shoulders, I'll give you that."

"Okay, end of chit-chat," Chisholm announced. "Let's get this done."

Chisholm whisked through several cases, moving briskly from one to another, assigning tasks and asking for progress reports, all without the aid of notes.

Spiller scribbled hurriedly in his notepad, the furrows in his brow deepening as he tried to keep up. The others, meanwhile, hardly wrote anything, nor did they refer to their notebooks as they reeled off information when asked. They were all clearly on top of their game, but Spiller's mind was a whirl.

"Last but not least, we're going to follow up on a missing person," Chisholm said.

A chorus of groans ran around the room.

"Now, now, lads," Chisholm chided them. "Many an important case has started off as a MisPer, which is why it's an excellent job for a new DC to cut his teeth on."

Spiller looked up with a start.

Chisholm grinned at him. "That's right, Tim. You're the lucky chap holding the winning ticket. You'll work alongside DS Reilly. He'll show you the ropes. All right, Paddy?"

"Yes, guv," Reilly replied, though he didn't look too pleased about it. "Another MisPer. Just what I've always wanted."

"You'll like this one," Chisholm said. "The missing person is one Lynsey Clifford, and she was reported missing by her father, Francis Clifford."

"The businessman?" Reilly asked. "The guy with all the scrapyards?"

"The same," Chisholm replied. "Mr Clifford rubs shoulders with the great and the good, so he's what we might call a big cheese, although not to his face and not in front of the Chief Constable if you get my drift. Mr Clifford has his fingers in a lot of pies, and he also has deep pockets when it comes to local charities, including a drugs awareness campaign we're involved in ourselves."

"Blimey, does he walk on water?" Nicholson asked with a grin, but if he'd hoped for a laugh, he didn't get one.

"As far as we're concerned, yes," Chisholm said. "Mr Clifford is to be treated with all the respect due to an upstanding member of the public. He's on our side, and we'd do well to keep it that way. Is that understood, Tim?"

Spiller nodded. "Yes, guv. I'll do my best."

Chisholm let the silence hang in the air for a moment, then he hooked his thumb toward the door. "Let's get cracking."

There were a few mutters of "Yes, guv", and then everyone stood and headed back to the main office.

When Spiller exited the briefing room, he found DS Reilly waiting for him.

"Get your coat," Reilly said. "We're going for a drive."

———

DS REILLY DROVE a convertible Ford Escort, and when he accelerated out of his parking space, Spiller's head was thrown back against the headrest. Involuntarily, Spiller's hand groped for something to hold on to, and Reilly didn't miss it.

"Don't worry, lad," Reilly said as he pulled into the road and worked his way rapidly up through the gears. "The XR3i might have a bit of poke, 103 horsepower to be exact, but I can handle her."

"You don't use a pool car, then?"

Reilly's horrified glance spoke volumes.

"Fair enough, Sarge." Spiller put his hands in his lap and tried to look relaxed.

"Call me Paddy, or we'll get nowhere. But no Irish jokes, mind; I've heard them all. My dad was from Dublin, but I was born in Scarborough, and that's all you need to know."

"Nice. I went to Scarborough on holiday when I was little. I remember the model ships. They staged a sea battle on the pond. It wasn't bad."

"Peasholme Park." Reilly drove in silence for a while, then: "Aren't you going to ask?"

"Ask what, Sarge, I mean, Paddy?"

"Where we're headed."

"No. Lynsey's father reported her missing, and the guvnor says we're to treat him with kid gloves, so I'd say we're going to meet the man himself, probably at his office.

You mentioned scrapyards, but I doubt whether a high-profile businessman works on the site. He'll have an office near the city centre."

Reilly chuckled and tipped him a wink. "Spot on, lad. We'll be there in ten."

Nine minutes later, according to Spiller's watch, Reilly pulled the Ford to an abrupt halt outside a grand, red brick building on Southernhay West. The building boasted four floors, and with its tall sash windows and impressive wooden door, the place had the look of a townhouse from a more prosperous age. These days it housed only office workers, a gleaming painted sign above the door advertising *Clifford Salvage and Demolition.*

As they exited the car, Spiller almost informed Reilly that he'd parked on a double yellow line, but he stopped himself in time. His reaction to Reilly's driving must've made him seem overcautious; fussing over a parking restriction would only make matters worse.

Reilly strode up the steps and into the building without pausing to press the polished brass doorbell, and Spiller hurried after him.

Inside he found Reilly in conversation with a receptionist: a woman beyond middle age whose doughty demeanour said she was less than impressed.

"Do you have some identification?" she asked.

"Of course, madam."

Reilly flashed his warrant card, and the receptionist studied it, then she cast her icy gaze at Spiller.

Spiller produced his warrant card without being asked. "Good morning, ma'am. I'm Detective Constable Spiller of the Devon and Cornwall Police. We're sorry to trouble you, but we're here to see Mr Clifford."

"Yes, so this gentleman has already said, but without an appointment, it's quite impossible."

"Mr Clifford will want to see us straight away," Spiller insisted. "It's about his daughter."

The receptionist's face fell. "Is she all right?"

"We'll discuss that with your boss," Reilly replied. "Are you going to show us the way, or shall we go and look for him?"

"One moment, please." The receptionist made a call, and a minute later she was leading them up the stairs to the top of the building. She halted outside a white wooden door, but before she could knock, it was opened from within and a silver-haired man appeared in the doorway, his face creased with worry.

"Gentlemen, come in," he said. "I'm Francis Clifford. Thank you for coming so promptly." He nodded to the receptionist. "Thank you, Margaret. Perhaps some tea for these officers." He glanced at Reilly. "Or would you prefer coffee?"

"Coffee would be appreciated, thanks," Reilly replied.

"The same for me, please," Spiller said. "Thank you, Margaret."

"You're welcome, sir," Margaret said, her tone a little less frosty. She headed back down the stairs, and Clifford gestured to his office, urging the two men inside.

Reilly strolled in, taking a look around, and Spiller followed suit.

The office had clearly been designed to portray a certain image. The single desk, made from polished dark wood and topped with green leather, was large and sturdy, and the bookshelves were crammed with matching sets of hard-backed books. The plain burgundy carpet was deep underfoot, and the walls were adorned with gold-framed watercolours of verdant landscapes. Everything in the room spoke of solid reliability and good, old-fashioned integrity. Mr Clifford was a man of substance, not some flash-in-the-pan business tycoon with ideas above his station.

"Please, have a seat," Clifford said as he took his place behind the desk.

"Thank you, sir," Reilly replied. He made himself comfortable in a seat facing Clifford, and Spiller took the remaining chair, getting out his notebook and pen as he sat down.

Clifford, meanwhile, seemed to be having difficulty composing himself. He ran his hands through his hair repeatedly, all the while taking slow breaths as if to calm himself.

"Are you all right, sir?" Spiller asked gently.

"No," Clifford snapped. "Of course I'm not all right. What kind of daft question is that? My daughter is missing, for God's sake."

"Yes, sir, that's why we're here," Reilly replied, casting a glance at Spiller that said, 'Let me do the talking'.

Spiller took the hint, sitting upright and waiting with his lips shut tight.

"Now, sir," Reilly went on, "when did you first notice that something might be wrong?"

"*Might?*" Clifford demanded. "There's no *might* about it. Lynsey is missing."

Reilly nodded. "I hear what you're saying, Mr Clifford, but how old is Lynsey?"

"Twenty-two, no, twenty-three." Clifford pinched the bridge of his nose. "Christ, I don't know whether I'm coming or going."

"It's a distressing situation, sir," Reilly said. "But

Lynsey is an adult, so she may have her own reasons for taking off. That's often the way these things turn out, but we'll do everything we can to find her as soon as possible. Remember, for all we know, Lynsey is safe and well. Don't imagine the worst. Try to stay calm and help us to help you. To begin with, we need to know when you first became aware that something was wrong."

"Yes, of course. Forgive me, gentlemen. I don't mind admitting I'm worried sick." Clifford ran a hand over his mouth. "This morning, at about 8 o'clock, I called Lynsey to ask her something. I was hoping to catch her before she left for work, but there was no reply. I redialled several times, but there was no answer. That's very unusual, but I thought she might've gone to work early, so I waited for a while and called her work number. One of her workmates answered, but she said she hadn't seen Lynsey. I left a message asking Lynsey to call me as soon as she got in, but the call never came. At about nine o'clock, I tried again, but she still hadn't arrived at work. That was when I began to worry."

Spiller was busy making notes, and without looking up, he said, "What time does Lynsey usually start work?"

"8:30," Clifford replied. "And she's always punctual. She takes her job very seriously, and she's never late."

"Where does she work?" Reilly asked.

"Lynsey works for the County Council in the finance department. She's training to be an accountant, but at the moment, she's working as an assistant."

Spiller paused to look up at Clifford, taking in the man's gold watch and cufflinks, his silk tie. Reilly, it seemed, was doing the same, and Clifford wasn't immune to their scrutiny.

"I know what you're thinking," Clifford said. "Why is

the daughter of a wealthy man taking an entry-level job and earning public sector wages?"

"It had crossed my mind," Reilly admitted.

"It's probably not relevant, but Lynsey wanted it that way. She's always been independent, and she wanted to start from the bottom and work her way up. I've offered to help her more times than I can count, but she always turns me down. My daughter is determined to make a life for herself, and when she sets her mind on something, there's nothing anybody can do to dissuade her."

"That's good," Reilly said. "It helps to build a picture of Lynsey, and we'll get into more detail in a minute, but tell us what happened after you'd called her office."

"At first, I thought she must've taken to her bed, maybe with the flu or something, although she's rarely ill. But I couldn't figure out why she hadn't called her manager to let him know, so I cancelled my appointments and drove to her flat. I'll give you her address in a second, but I can tell you, she isn't there. The place seemed... abandoned."

"What gave you that impression?" Spiller asked. From the corner of his eye, he saw Reilly purse his lips in disapproval, but he couldn't sit there and say nothing. His mind was teeming with questions, and he had to ask at least some of them.

Clifford looked down for a moment as if picturing the scene. "It's a small flat, and whenever I've visited, it's always been tidy, but this morning there were dirty dishes piled in the sink and laundry on the floor. In her bedroom, there's a chest of drawers, and they'd all been left open, and her bed was a mess. It looked as though she'd grabbed some clothes and left in a hurry, like she'd run away."

"Could that be a possibility?" Reilly asked.

Clifford looked as though he'd been slapped. "No. No.

Lynsey wouldn't just disappear without a word. She'd never do anything so hurtful. I know I said she was independent, but she's always been thoughtful and caring. We're close. We're a close family. If there was something wrong, she'd tell me or my wife, but there was nothing. We spoke last week, on the phone, and Lynsey was... she was happy."

"That's a good sign," Reilly said. "What day did she call?"

"I called her. It was Thursday—in the evening. We didn't talk about anything in particular. It was just a chat, a catch-up. Lynsey was fine. If she'd been upset, I would've known."

I wouldn't be so sure, Spiller thought. When he'd been Lynsey's age, his calls to his parents had concealed more than they'd revealed. Putting that thought to one side, he said, "When did you last actually see your daughter?"

"The Sunday before last. I took Lynsey out to lunch. The Double Locks. It's by the canal, but I expect you knew that."

"I certainly do," Reilly said. "Was your wife there as well?"

"No, it was just the two of us. It's something we do sometimes. A sort of tradition. We, er, we had a nice time." Clifford's voice faltered and he cleared his throat.

Reilly paused before asking his next question. "Does Lynsey live on her own?"

Clifford nodded.

"No flatmate or lodger?" Reilly went on.

"No. It's a one-bedroom flat. It's on Raleigh Road. Number twelve. It's near Magdalen Road."

"I know it," Reilly said. "Some nice houses down there. Lynsey can afford the rent on her salary, can she?"

"She *could*, but I own the building, and I don't charge

her rent. Lynsey lives in the top-floor flat, and she keeps an eye on the other tenants. Before you ask, I knocked on all the doors and asked at the other flats, but no one's seen Lynsey since Saturday afternoon."

"Who saw her and when?" Spiller asked.

"Carol. Carol Whitaker. She has the flat beneath Lynsey's. Flat 2. She was going out on Saturday when she saw Lynsey coming home with some groceries. There's a small convenience store on the main road. Lynsey often goes there, I believe. She's mentioned it on more than one occasion, but she always calls it the shop. I think it's a SPAR."

"We'll check it out," Reilly said. "Do you have a recent photo of Lynsey?"

"Yes." Clifford picked up one of the two silver picture frames on his desk and handed it to Reilly. "This was taken a couple of years ago, on her twenty-first birthday."

Reilly studied the photo, then he handed it to Spiller. "Slip that out of its frame, would you, Detective Constable?"

"Certainly." Spiller undid the clips on the back of the frame and released the photo. It showed an attractive young woman with straight, dark hair. She was beaming for the photographer, her brown eyes alight with happiness. The photo showed only her head and shoulders, but she appeared to be wearing a cream-coloured top with thin straps over her bronzed and athletic shoulders.

Spiller gazed at the photograph sadly, hoping this young woman was all right.

"Does Lynsey have a boyfriend?" Reilly asked.

"Yes. Tony Carter. They've been going out for months."

The corner of Clifford's lips turned down, and Reilly seemed to notice.

"You don't approve?"

"It's not that. Not exactly. Tony's a nice enough lad, but he's..." Clifford tutted as if scolding himself. "It's not for me to cast aspersions. Like I said, he's nice enough. We've met a few times, and he seems like a decent bloke, but I don't know him well."

"Can you give us his contact details?" Reilly asked.

"I don't have his address, but we probably have his phone number at home, so I can find it for you later. Oh, and I know where he works. He's an estate agent at Berkley's. He's based at their office on Dix's Field."

"We'll pay him a call," Reilly said. "Any other close friends we should know about?"

Clifford held out his hands and let them fall to his desk. "I can't keep track of them. I think Lynsey has a fairly wide social circle, but there's no one significant, as far as I can tell; no one who stands out." He looked thoughtful. "My wife might be able to tell you more." Plucking a business card from a polished metal container on his desk, Clifford offered it to Reilly. "My home number is on here. Give Diana a call, and she'll tell you about Lynsey's friends."

"Thank you, sir." Reilly took the card and studied it briefly before pocketing it. "We'll want to have a chat with Mrs Clifford in person, but that can come later."

"You must do whatever you need to do, but please don't disturb my wife more than necessary. Diana's nerves have been a little frayed recently, and after today..." Clifford's sentence ended in a small sigh.

"We understand, sir," Reilly said. "We'll be sensitive, and we'll chase up a few other leads first."

"Thank you. I appreciate that." Clifford hesitated. "Would you be able to call me later and let me know what you've found out?"

"Of course," Reilly replied. "We'll keep you in the loop as much as we can. In the meantime, please try not to worry yourself. I've seen this kind of thing before, and there are all kinds of reasons for a person to drop off the radar once in a while. Lynsey might call you at any moment, so please bear that in mind. If she does get in touch, let us know as soon as you can."

Reilly rummaged in his jacket pocket and retrieved a business card of his own. He passed it to Clifford who took it without comment.

"We'd like to take a look at Lynsey's flat," Reilly said. "I take it you have a key."

"Yes. Hold on a second." Clifford opened a desk drawer and pulled out a long metal box, laying it on his desk before opening it. Spiller counted ten rows of small compartments with five to a row, and it looked as though they all contained keys.

While Clifford ran his fingers over the compartments in turn, Spiller said, "How many buildings do you own, Mr Clifford?"

"Oh, far too many." Clifford looked up and brandished a key ring labelled *12 Raleigh Road*. It contained at least half a dozen keys, and he handed the whole bunch to Reilly. "Do you need someone to come with you?"

Reilly shook his head. "We can handle it on our own. At this stage, we'll have a preliminary look around, but we may need to revisit the flat later. Can we hang onto these for a while?"

"Yes, I don't see why not, so long as you bring them back when you're done."

"That's very helpful, sir," Reilly said. "We'll head off now and see what we can find out."

He stood and Spiller copied his example.

"We'll be in touch," Reilly went on.

Clifford rose and shook their hands in turn, but he didn't say a word. The man looked drained and a little lost, as though he'd been keeping his act together during their conversation and now had no idea what to do.

Reilly and Spiller took their leave and made their way swiftly back to Reilly's car.

"Lynsey's flat?" Spiller asked.

"Lynsey's flat," Reilly replied. "Hop in. We'll be there in five."

Spiller didn't doubt it.

4

IN PREPARATION for his transfer to Exeter, Spiller had spent a couple of days driving around the city, trying to master its haphazard layout. He'd driven along Magdalen Road a couple of times, but this was his first visit to its offshoot, Raleigh Road, and he paused on the pavement, looking around while Reilly locked the Ford Escort.

Joining him, Reilly said, "It's not bad here, is it?"

"Good-sized houses," Spiller replied. "Quiet but handy for the city centre."

"Are you looking to rent?"

"To start with. We're in a little flat at the moment, but it's temporary. It's tiny, and it's driving my wife mad. We can't stay there long."

Reilly's surprise was obvious in his voice. "Are you married?"

"Yes. For almost a year."

"Well, well, you're a dark horse. You've kept that quiet."

"It's not that," Spiller said. "Nobody asked. There hasn't been time."

"That's the guvnor, for you. He might come across as a bit of a joker, but he doesn't hang about. Get used to it."

"Suits me. I like to get things done, myself."

"In that case, lead on." Reilly held out the bunch of keys he'd been given by Francis Clifford. "Let's see how you work."

Spiller took the keys without a word. His mouth was suddenly dry. This was it, his chance to give a proper account of himself as a detective, and he'd better not make a mess of it.

Spiller headed for the front door of number 12, sorting through the keys as he went along. Three of the keys had small plastic tags attached, and he guessed they were for the individual flats. From the others, he selected a key that looked a little more well used than the rest, its metal tarnished.

"This looks like the key for the shared entrance. It's branded Yale and so is the lock, and that tells me something else."

"Go on."

"Mr Clifford kept the originals and gave copies to his tenants. That suggests he's a careful man."

Reilly tilted his head from side to side. "Maybe, but don't go getting all Sherlock Holmes on me, lad. Let's stick to what we can see and what we can't. In other words, pay attention to what's here and what might be missing."

"Okay. That makes sense."

Squaring up to the front door, Spiller tried the key he'd selected, smiling as the lock turned smoothly.

Reilly mimed applause. "What's next?"

"Up to Lynsey's flat?"

"Not so fast. Check the hallway, especially if there's any mail lying around."

Spiller nodded and led the way in. The hallway was surprisingly wide, its walls decorated with woodchip wallpaper and painted with magnolia emulsion, but the floor still boasted its original ceramic tiles.

At the far end of the hallway, a man's bike with drop handlebars had been leant against the wall. Closer to hand, a door was labelled with self-adhesive lettering: *Flat 1.*

On the opposite wall, a narrow shelf held an assortment of envelopes and fliers. Reilly scooped up all the mail together and began rifling through.

Spiller peered over Reilly's shoulder. "Anything?"

"One." Reilly waved an envelope. "It looks like an electric bill. Addressed to Flat 3 but in the name of Clifford Property Management. I guess Daddy pays the bills as well as the rent."

"What's the date on the postmark?"

"Last Friday. It probably arrived this morning, but I doubt whether it can tell us anything else." Reilly tossed all the mail back onto the shelf. "Let's move on. Top floor. I hope you're fit."

"I try," Spiller said. "But there's never enough time." He set off up the stairs, taking them as quickly as he could. Spiller tried to hide it, but he was soon breathing hard. Behind him, Reilly kept pace easily.

"Oh dear," Reilly said. "It's a good job it's me with you and not Boyce. The Detective Chief Superintendent likes us to keep trim. Me, I play footy. Five-a-side. The guvnor's on the team, and we're always on the lookout for new talent if you fancy a kickaround."

"Thanks, but I've never been into football. I like rugby. I used to play, but not anymore."

"Not since you got wed, eh?"

"Yeah, although that wasn't why I stopped. I decided to concentrate on my career for a while."

"All very well, but take my advice, Tim. You need an outlet in this job, something to work off all the nervous energy, or you won't go the distance. Believe me, I've seen plenty of good coppers give up the ghost. Either they leave or they stop putting the effort in, hanging on to the job by the skin of their teeth, one eye on their pension. You don't want to end up like that."

"I won't." Spiller reached the final landing, and he halted in front of a wooden door. Unlike the others they'd passed, this one wasn't painted gloss white but a deep blue, the uneven brush strokes allowing streaks of white to show through.

"Being the landlord's daughter has its perks," Spiller said. "I'll bet Lynsey painted this herself, making it her own."

"Either that or someone hired a useless decorator. Go on, Tim. Open it up."

Spiller tried the key labelled with a 3, but it wouldn't turn.

"Jiggle it," Reilly said, and Spiller did as he suggested.

"No good." On a whim, Spiller tried one of the unlabelled keys and it worked first time. "That's odd. Maybe Lynsey changed the lock."

Reilly shrugged. "You might be right, but let's not play guessing games. Mr Clifford might've labelled the wrong one. Perhaps he isn't quite as careful as you thought. Anyway, let's have a gander."

They made their way inside, shutting the door behind them. The door gave directly onto the lounge, and Spiller found himself copying the way Reilly scanned the room, looking high and low, his sharp gaze darting from one detail to the next.

As Clifford had said, the place was untidy, and Spiller could see that this might not be the usual state of affairs. Yes, there were cushions, magazines and items of clothing on the floor, but other parts of the lounge were neat and ordered. The mantlepiece held a collection of ceramic ornaments, dogs mainly, and they were perfectly aligned in a row.

On the wall by the window, a macrame pot holder contained two variegated spider plants, one above the other, and Spiller recalled something his wife had told him. Sheila was the font of all knowledge when it came to houseplants, and she'd said that spider plants tended to become thin and straggly, drooping all over the place unless they were kept in check. But these specimens were healthy and well cared for.

Reilly pointed to an open doorway. "You take the kitchen, I'll take the bathroom, but mind what you touch. Anything important, give me a shout."

"Got it."

In the small kitchen, Spiller found much the same picture. There were dirty dishes in the sink, and an assortment of packets scattered over the work surface, but the small jars in the spice rack were all aligned with their labels showing. Beside them on the wall, a rack held a neat row of stainless-steel utensils. Spiller ran his eyes over the herbs and spices. Sheila was a keen cook, but she restricted herself to bay leaves, dried mixed herbs and an occasional sprinkling of paprika; all other flavours came courtesy of a stock cube.

Lynsey Clifford, on the other hand, seemed to have more exotic tastes, and she'd invested in garam masala, turmeric and chilli powder, as well as dried basil, thyme and oregano.

Spiller opened the small fridge and squatted down to examine its contents: eggs, milk, bacon and a packet of cheddar. In the salad drawer there were a few carrots and a red pepper. On the glass shelf, Spiller found a plastic container and pulled it out. The stewing steak looked reasonably fresh, and according to its sell-by date, it was to be used within two days. It may well have been bought on the previous Saturday; the day Lynsey had been seen returning with groceries.

Very strange, Spiller thought. *Who would buy half a pound of steak if they were planning on running away?*

It was hardly conclusive, but according to her father, Lynsey's salary wasn't high. The meat might well have been the most expensive item in her shopping basket, and she wouldn't have wanted to waste it.

Spiller replaced the meat and stood up as he closed the fridge. A quick look through the cabinets revealed nothing of interest, so he went in search of Reilly.

The bathroom was at the end of a short hallway, and he found Reilly inside, holding a small brown bottle up to his eyes and studying the label.

"Valium," Reilly said. "Prescribed in Lynsey's name." He looked to Spiller. "She's a bit young to be taking tranquillisers, isn't she?"

"I'm not sure. Perhaps she suffers from anxiety."

Reilly made a noncommittal sound and thrust the bottle back into the cabinet. "I don't know, I sometimes think they hand these things out like sweeties. Far too many pills end up on the streets. It's ridiculous."

"I'll follow that up if you like."

"Knock yourself out."

Spiller pulled out his notebook, then he retrieved the pill bottle and noted down the details. "Anything else?"

"Nope, unless you want to know what kind of shampoo she uses. It's that one off the telly if you're interested." Adopting an American accent, he added, "Did you just step out of the salon?"

Reilly laughed at his own performance, but Spiller didn't react. His gaze was fixed on the matching set of plastic bottles ranged across the edge of the bath.

"Lighten up, lad," Reilly muttered. "Come on."

Reilly made for the door and Spiller followed, but he couldn't help thinking about all those toiletries. The bewildering range of shampoos on offer in any branch of Boots meant little to him, but in his limited experience, women liked to look after their hair, and they often took great care in choosing a brand. It seemed odd for Lynsey to have left home without her favourite hair products.

In the bedroom, there were clothes all over the floor, and as Clifford had mentioned, the chest of drawers looked as though someone had rifled through it in a frenzy. All the drawers had been left open, and their contents were a jumbled mess, underwear and sweaters muddled together and overflowing. The wardrobe was in a similar state of disarray, with clothes left hanging lop-sided from their hangers.

By the bed, Spiller spotted a hardback book lying open and face down. He picked it up and studied the cover. It was a copy of *Far From the Madding Crowd* by Thomas Hardy. On the flyleaf was an inscription: *For Lynsey on your sixteenth birthday, with all my love, Mum xxxx.*

The novel looked as good as new, and it was the only book Spiller had seen in the whole flat. Lynsey was not an avid reader then, but she'd kept this book in her bedroom.

It might well have been a treasured gift, not something to leave behind, nor to throw on the floor in a way that would damage the spine.

A deep sense of unease settled on Spiller's shoulders. He exchanged a look with Reilly and knew he was arriving at the same conclusion.

"She didn't run away," Spiller said.

"No. To my eyes, this place has been ransacked."

"Nothing broken or knocked over though, no sign of violence."

"Even so, I don't like it," Reilly said. "We need to get the SOCOs in here fast. You take a last look around, I'll find the phone and call it in."

"Will do," Spiller said, but Reilly was already marching from the room.

Spiller made his way carefully around the bedroom, stepping over the discarded clothing, and his heart beat faster. Someone had been through the whole flat, searching for something, but what had they been looking for? And what had become of Lynsey? Had she escaped or had someone taken her? If so, why?

Spiller found no answers as he checked the wardrobe and peered beneath the bed, but his gut told him this case was about to go up a gear. The stakes were about to get as high as they could. He had no idea what might've happened to Lynsey, but she wasn't going to turn up of her own accord.

Lynsey was in danger, and he'd do everything he could to find her. But what if they were already too late?

Standing in Lynsey's bedroom, Spiller made a vow. Whether Lynsey was dead or alive, he'd make sure she got justice. *This is the job*, Spiller thought. *And I'll get it done.*

5

Francis Clifford stared at the contract on his desk, but the rows of dense text swam out of focus. He'd read the same paragraph at least five times before, but he'd gleaned nothing from it. Why was he still here, trying to work? He should be at home, trying to comfort his wife.

But he knew why he'd stayed in the office. Diana was in pieces, and when her mood hit a low, he couldn't be around her. Nothing drove him to distraction faster than the weakness he saw in others.

Someone tapped on his office door and Clifford pushed the contract away, glad of the distraction. "Come," he called out, and the door opened, Margaret sidling in. Normally, Margaret strode into his office like she owned the place, but not today. She knew something was wrong.

"What is it, Margaret?"

"I'm sorry to bother you, sir, but a courier has just arrived, and he brought this." She held out a white envelope.

"He said it was urgent. He was most insistent."

Clifford beckoned her to come closer, and Margaret obeyed, sliding the envelope across his desk.

"Thanks, Margaret, you can go."

Margaret nodded in acknowledgement and made for the door.

Clifford was halfway through opening the envelope before he realised there was no name or address on the outside.

He pulled out the single sheet of paper it contained, and something fell onto his desk. It was a small square of curiously glossy card, and when he turned it over, his blood ran cold. The Polaroid photograph clearly showed a young woman, blindfolded and tied to a bed, and what little he could see of her face was bleached white by the light from a flash. His mind shied away from the truth, but there was no use in denying it; the girl was his only daughter. Lynsey.

Against his will, Clifford's gaze went to the accompanying sheet of paper. The message was written in stark block capitals:

NO POLICE OR SHE DIES.

A noise must've escaped from Clifford's lips, because Margaret froze in the doorway, then turned on her heel.

"Mr Clifford, are you all right?"

"Yes, thank you, Margaret. I... I just had some bad news, that's all."

Her eyebrows lowered in concern, Margaret moved closer. "Is there anything I can do to help?"

"No." Clifford opened his desk drawer and slid the photograph and message inside. "Although... you'd better cancel my appointments for the rest of the day. Something's come up."

Margaret was watching him carefully, but she showed no sign of leaving.

"It's something to do with those policemen, isn't it? Has something happened?"

"No, it's nothing to worry about." With an effort, Clifford made his voice neutral. "Margaret, who brought that envelope? You said a courier, was it one of the regulars?"

"No, sir. I didn't recognise him at all. He was one of those motorcycle types, and he kept his helmet on the whole time. I barely got a look at him."

"Did he say what company he was from?"

Margaret shook her head. "I tried asking him what the letter was about, but he wouldn't say. He was in a rush, and he was rather brusque, rude, even. He just kept saying it was very urgent and must be given directly to you without being opened." She bowed her head a little. "I gave in, I'm afraid. It seemed like the only way to make him leave. I hope I didn't do the wrong thing."

"No, you were right to bring this to my attention."

Clifford pushed himself to his feet, but the floor swayed beneath him and he pressed a hand against the desk to steady himself.

"Oh dear," Margaret murmured. "Mr Clifford, I hope you don't mind me saying this, but you don't look well. You don't look well at all."

"I'm fine. It was a dizzy spell. I must've stood up too quickly." Clifford took a breath. "I'll be leaving early today, Margaret. In fact, I'm going home now. As soon as you've cancelled my appointments, you can take the rest of the day off."

"Oh, but—"

"I mean it, Margaret," Clifford interrupted. "Once you've cleared my schedule, go home or do some shopping, whatever you want. You'll still be paid, naturally."

"Very well, Mr Clifford. Your only important meeting this afternoon was with Councillor Jeffries, but I'll speak to his secretary. Should I make another appointment? You know what they're like at the council, they like plenty of notice."

"Yes, fine. Fix something for the end of the week."

"Certainly. I'll do that right away." Margaret hesitated. "Mr Clifford, are you sure there isn't anything else you need? You're very pale. Whatever this bad news is, it's obviously knocked you sideways. Is there anyone you'd like me to call?"

"No. No calls," Clifford snapped.

Margaret's face fell. "As you wish, sir."

Regaining his composure, Clifford held up a hand. "I'm sorry, Margaret. I didn't mean to bite your head off. The thing is, there's been a setback with one of our projects, but you mustn't breathe a word of this to anybody. We've got to keep it under our hats. If anybody asks, everything's fine and I've popped home to spend some quality time with my wife, okay?"

"Of course. I never spread gossip. Never."

"I know, Margaret, and I appreciate that, I really do. But whatever happens, and whoever asks, even if it's those detectives, everything's normal. I'm serious. If word gets out and our competitors sniff trouble, they'll swoop in and tear this firm to pieces. Do you understand, Margaret?"

Margaret nodded, her expression resolute.

"Good. Well done. And you needn't worry, Margaret. I'll take care of this. I'll take care of this myself."

6

SPILLER MARCHED through Lynsey's flat and found Reilly finishing his call.

"Got it, guv," Reilly was saying. "What about the door-to-door?"

Reilly listened, nodding. "Cheers, guv. Appreciate it. Will do." He paused, glancing at Spiller. "Yeah, he's fine. No problem at all."

Placing the receiver back in its place, Reilly turned his attention to Spiller. "The guvnor's on it. He's got Ollie ringing around the hospitals, and he's drafting in some uniforms. They'll start the door-to-door, so you never know your luck. Somebody might have seen or heard something."

"Won't they need the photo of Lynsey?" Spiller asked. "We ought to get it photocopied."

Reilly looked faintly amused. "We're not trying to see if she's been here; this is where she lives. Her neighbours know what she looks like. It's strangers we're looking for, especially if they came and went in the dead of night."

"I suppose so, but wouldn't it be better if—"

"Never mind what you've seen on Miami Vice," Reilly interrupted. "Flashing a photo has its uses, but not here and not now. Come on, we'll go downstairs and talk to her immediate neighbours. If there was any rough stuff up here, they'll have heard it." He raised a warning finger. "You contradicted me just now, and that's fine when it's just you and me, but I don't want any of that in front of a witness. Let me do the talking, Tim. All you have to do is watch and listen, okay?"

Without waiting for a reply, Reilly made for the stairs and Spiller trailed after him.

At the next landing, Reilly rapped on the door of Flat 2, and it was opened a moment later by a young woman with a mop of blonde curly hair.

"Police," Reilly said, showing his warrant card. "Can we have a word, love?"

"Er..." The young woman's gaze darted from Reilly to Spiller and back.

"It's all right, Carol," Spiller said. "It is Carol, isn't it? Carol Whitaker? We got your name from your landlord, Mr Clifford. He gave us a key to Lynsey's flat."

"Right. Yes, I'm Carol. What is it you want?"

"A few minutes of your time, if you don't mind," Spiller said quickly before Reilly had a chance to speak. He could almost see the need for action coming from DS Reilly; the man was like a coiled spring and it was unsettling Carol no end.

"You're not in any trouble, Carol, but we do need to speak to you," Spiller went on. "It would be best if we talk now and get it over with."

"I suppose that'd be all right," Carol said. "Is it about Lynsey? I saw Frank, I mean, Mr Clifford earlier. He asked if I'd seen her. He looked upset. Is something wrong?"

"We'd better talk inside," Reilly replied. "It's important."

"Come in, then." Carol stood back and ushered them inside.

Like the flat above, the door gave onto the lounge, but the room was smaller than Lynsey's and less well furnished. The floor was covered in hard-wearing carpet tiles in a dull shade of dark brown, and the beige curtains were thin. Like the entrance hall and the stairwell, the walls had been papered with woodchip and painted magnolia.

One corner had been given over to a small dining table and a couple of chairs. On the table, an empty wine bottle had been pressed into service as a candle holder, and streaks of molten wax had solidified into ridges down its sides. Beside the candle holder, a small wooden bowl held some potpourri, though it was doing little to dispel the scent of mildew that hung in the air. A brass ashtray crowded with butts showed that Carol was a smoker, but at least the place didn't reek of cigarettes.

"Have a seat." Carol indicated the two-seater sofa. It was covered with a colourful throw, but its misshapen cushions said it had seen better days.

"Thank you, miss."

Spiller lowered himself cautiously onto the sofa, its springs complaining as they sagged beneath his weight. Spiller leaned forward rather than trust the backrest, and he was glad when Reilly chose to perch on the sofa's arm.

Carol pulled one of the chairs from her dining area and sat facing them, her hands in her lap.

Spiller whipped out his notebook and pen. "Is that Whitaker with one T?"

"That's right."

"Have you lived here long?" Reilly asked.

"Oh, it must be three years now. Longer than Lynsey. She's only been upstairs for about a year. Before that, we had a bloke named Jim. He was all right, but he played music at all hours. Blur mainly. And he brewed his own beer. The place smelt like a brewery. As soon as you opened the front door, it hit you."

"So you were pleased when Lynsey moved in," Spiller suggested.

Carol half shrugged. "Lynsey's nice enough."

"You don't sound too sure," Reilly said. "Is that because she's the landlord's daughter?"

"Not really. To be honest, I don't really know her that well." Carol hesitated. "Is she all right?"

"That's what we're trying to establish," Reilly replied. "At the moment, we don't know where Lynsey is, and we'd like to make sure she's not in any bother. Anything you can tell us might help, so don't hold back. What's she like?"

Carol shifted uncomfortably on her chair. "She's a bit up herself, if you know what I mean. Like she thinks she's better than other people; better than me and my mates, at any rate."

"So you weren't friends," Spiller said, "but was there more to it than that? Did you fall out?"

"No, nothing like that." Carol's hand went to her chest. "Don't get me wrong, we got on okay. We said hello when we passed on the stairs, but we didn't hang around together. I tried to be friendly at first. I invited her in for coffee, but she said she was busy, so I asked her again one night. I had a couple of friends around, so I invited her in for a glass of wine, but she said she was going out. She went out a fair bit. I suppose she could afford it."

"Did she ever say where she went?" Reilly asked.

Carol thought for a moment then shook her head. "I don't think she went to the pubs around here. All I know is, she'd come home late sometimes. I'd hear her on the stairs, and it'd be one or two in the morning, so she must've been out at a club or something. Sometimes I'd hear a car outside and voices calling out, like maybe her friends were dropping her off."

"Did you ever meet any of her friends?"

"No, but I talked to her boyfriend a few times. Tony." Carol smiled as if at a secret.

"A nice-looking lad, is he?" Reilly asked.

Carol stifled a giggle. "He's all right. He's got something, but he's punching above his weight with her."

"I understand he's an estate agent," Spiller said.

Carol looked impressed. "Oh, I didn't know that. He doesn't act like an estate agent. He's more rough and ready. A man's man."

"I presume Tony visited Lynsey fairly often," Reilly began. "How do you think they got on?"

"The same as any couple. You'd hear them talking, having a laugh, singing along to the music. He's got a nice voice, Tony. Deep. He can carry a tune."

"You said they're like most couples," Reilly said. "Most couples have rows. Did they ever argue?"

Carol smiled wistfully. "Now and then. If they raise their voices and I haven't got the telly on, I can hear every word they say, but it's nothing bad. You know, they're making something out of nothing. The usual."

"Go on," Spiller said gently.

There was a pause before Carol replied. "I don't want to give you the wrong idea, but Tony's a bit of a lad. Sometimes, it sounded like she'd want to go out, but he'd be watching the football on the telly. I'd hear the cheering and all that, and when somebody scored a goal, he'd raise the roof and she'd moan at him. Other times, she'd want him to stay in with her, but he'd want to go out with the lads. That never ended well. She'd yell at him, and he'd storm off, slamming the door. Then she'd put some music on, and once or twice, I heard her crying. I would've gone up, but she wouldn't have wanted to talk to me."

Reilly sent Spiller a meaningful look, and Spiller put Tony Carter's name at the top of his to-do list.

"This is all very helpful," Spiller said. "When did you last see Lynsey?"

"Like I told Mr Clifford, it was Saturday, about five o'clock. I passed her by the front door. I was going to work, and she was coming in with a carrier bag. I think she'd been to the shop around the corner. They sell all sorts. It's a bit pricey, but it's handy when you've run out of milk or whatever."

"How did Lynsey seem?" Spiller asked.

Carol shrugged. "Happy, I guess. She said something about it being Saturday night at last. It sounded as if she was looking forward to going out and having fun."

Reilly sent Carol a smile. "How the other half live, eh? There she was, getting ready for a night on the town while you were heading out to work."

"Yeah, but that's the way of things, isn't it? She comes from money, but I never held it against her. If I had a few quid, I'd wear designer jeans and get my hair done somewhere decent. Good luck to her."

"Where do you work, Carol?" Reilly asked.

"I work at a pub: The Mount Radford on Magdalen Road. I'm usually behind the bar. The money isn't great, but it'll do until something better turns up."

"I know the Mount Radford," Reilly said. "It's a nice pub. What time did you get home?"

Carol puffed out her cheeks. "Nearly midnight. I was knackered. I went straight to bed."

"Did you hear Lynsey coming home?" Spiller asked.

"No, I was dead to the world, although..."

Carol frowned, looking down at her hands. Spiller leaned even further forward, watching her intently, and from the corner of his eye, he saw Reilly doing the same.

Finally, Carol looked up. "I'd almost forgotten. I was half asleep and I wasn't sure if I imagined it, but I think I heard voices. It might've been Lynsey." She brightened. "And there was definitely a car. I heard the door slam, and then it drove away."

"If I hear a noise in the night, I always look at my watch," Spiller said. "Did you do that, Carol?"

Carol started to shake her head but changed her mind. "I went straight back to sleep, but I did get up a bit later. I was thirsty, so I went to the kitchen and there's a clock. It was about three in the morning, so the van must've been a bit before then."

"The *van?*" Spiller asked. "A minute ago, you said you heard a car."

"Oh yeah. I don't know what I was thinking. It's not like I saw anything. I didn't look outside."

"Van doors can be quite loud," Spiller said. "Sometimes the doors slide along the side and that makes quite a distinctive sound."

"I know what you mean, but I don't remember. Sorry."

"That's all right, love," Reilly said. "What about other noises from upstairs on Saturday night? Did you hear anyone moving around up there?"

"No, not since the afternoon. I thought she might've

gone away for a bit. It's been quiet as the grave." Carol shivered. "It's nothing like... I mean, something hasn't happened to Lynsey, has it?"

"Let's not get ahead of ourselves," Reilly replied. "We don't know where Lynsey is, but there could be lots of good reasons for that. It would help a lot if you could keep an eye out for her. If you see Lynsey, or you hear anything from upstairs, give us a bell, okay?"

Reilly pulled a business card from his pocket and handed it to Carol. "You do have a phone, don't you?"

Carol nodded, studying the card. "If she turns up, I'll go and knock on her door, make sure she's all right."

"No, don't do that," Reilly said firmly. "Call us, Carol. If Lynsey is in some kind of trouble, we'll deal with it. You'd be better off steering clear."

"If you're sure, but it seems a bit..." Carol's eyes grew round. "Should I be worried?"

"No, love, but you should be careful," Reilly said. "Better safe than sorry. You do keep your door locked, don't you?"

"Always."

"There you go then." Reilly stood, straightening his jacket. "Right, we'll leave you in peace, Carol. Thanks for your time. You've been a great help."

"Yes, thank you, Carol." Spiller rose from the sofa, glad to be free from its clutches. "Look after yourself."

"Yeah." Carol stood, Reilly's business card held in both hands at waist height. "I'll see you out."

Carol escorted Spiller and Reilly to the door. Reilly warned her that a team would be visiting Flat 3 to take fingerprints. He assured her it was nothing to worry about, then they took their leave.

There was no answer when they knocked on the door of

flat 1, and when they stepped out onto the pavement, the curtains were closed at the ground-floor windows.

"Maybe they've gone away," Spiller said.

"Maybe. Of course, we probably have the key on that bunch Clifford gave us."

Spiller wrinkled his nose. "We can't let ourselves in though, can we? We've no grounds for a search."

"Just testing, Tim. Anyway, the uniforms will catch up with them when they start the door-to-door. If there's still nothing doing, we can pop back later. In the meantime, we'll get out of here."

They climbed into the car, but Reilly didn't start the engine. He stared out through the windscreen, his hands on the wheel and said, "You had a lot to say when we were talking to Carol. What were you playing at?"

"Sorry," Spiller replied. "I didn't mean to step on your toes."

"I'm not bothered about that, but what was all that stuff about van doors?"

"I was trying to jog her memory." A sinking feeling stirred in the pit of Spiller's stomach. He had an idea where he'd gone wrong, but no doubt his colleague was about to set him straight.

"You don't ask leading questions like that, lad. Never. People might think they have good memories, but they don't. Start putting ideas into their heads, and you'll get nowhere. Even if you turn up something useful, it'll never stand up in court. Defence lawyers can smell that kind of thing a mile off, and they'll run a coach and horses through it, believe me. I've seen it happen far too often."

Spiller wanted to say that it was Carol who'd first mentioned a van, but there were times when you had to stay quiet and accept what was coming.

Reilly turned to Spiller and looked him in the eye. "You're keen, lad, that much is obvious, but you need more than that. If you want to get on in CID, you have to be smart, and you have to be patient. And another thing. We might not stand on ceremony in our nick, but just because we don't bow and scrape, it doesn't mean we take no notice of rank. I'm a DS and you're a DC. Never forget that."

"No, I won't."

Reilly sighed. "Bloody hell, you look like you've lost a pound and found a penny. Listen, Tim, this is nothing personal. You seem all right, and I reckon you'll fit in, but this morning, when you said you have a lot to learn, you were dead right. You're new, and we'll all cut you a bit of slack, but not too much and not for too long. So the next time I tell you what to do, take heed, lad. All right?"

Spiller nodded. "Yes, Detective Sergeant."

"Paddy."

"Sorry. Yes, Paddy."

"Right." Reilly started the engine and pulled out into the road. "Now I reckon it's about time we had a word with Tony Carter, don't you?"

"Definitely," Spiller said. "I don't like the sound of him at all."

"We'll keep an open mind, but..." Reilly glanced at Spiller. "You probably know what I'm going to say, don't you?"

"When there's foul play, the perpetrator is often someone known to the victim."

Reilly laughed under his breath. "I was going for, *It's always the boyfriend*, but it amounts to the same thing, lad. It amounts to the same thing."

7

In Exeter's Rougemont Gardens, Francis Clifford sat on a park bench and stared out over the rolling stretch of manicured lawn. When someone took a seat next to him, he didn't turn to look at them; he didn't need to. The man sitting next to him exuded a certain presence.

Barry Leeman, Clifford thought. *The name doesn't suit him.* To Clifford, the name conjured a jolly shopkeeper or a friendly bus driver. Not that he'd say anything of the sort to Leeman's face; he'd seen what happened to people who didn't treat the man with proper respect.

"A nice afternoon," Leeman said. "Hardly a cloud in sight."

"Yes," Clifford intoned, his gaze directed dead ahead.

"Not so nice for you, I suspect," Leeman replied. "You wouldn't have called otherwise."

"True, but this problem is of a different nature. It's altogether more serious and more sensitive."

"I see." Leeman paused. "Any complications will be reflected in the price, I'm afraid."

"That doesn't matter. Money is no object. I'll pay any price."

"Now that is interesting, but I wonder if that's a promise you can afford to keep. I've heard whispers. Your business isn't quite what it once was."

Clifford couldn't help himself; he risked a fleeting sideways glance. "No, that's not true."

"Now, now, Francis." Leeman leaned sideways, his shoulder pressing against Clifford's.

The closeness of the man turned Clifford's stomach, but he couldn't object.

Lowering his voice to a throaty whisper, Leeman added, "Let's not lie to each other, Francis. We'll never get anywhere unless we tell the truth."

Clifford squared his shoulders, hoping Leeman would get the message and back off, but it didn't work.

"You're too close," Clifford muttered. "You'll draw attention."

"From whom? There's no one around. I could slit your throat and walk away, and nobody would be any the wiser; except for you and me, of course. But let's hope it doesn't come to that. Now, the truth if you please. How's business?"

"I've had a run of bad luck," Clifford admitted. "There have been a few deals that didn't go as planned, but that's the way of the world. It's a cut-throat business."

"So's mine." Leeman chuckled darkly. "But at least we're on the same page now." Leeman moved back, giving Clifford some room. "Tell me, what appears to be the problem?"

"It's all in here." Clifford pulled a folded envelope from his inside breast pocket and laid it on the bench between them.

Leeman let out a hiss of exasperation. "That's not how we do business, Francis. You don't hand things to me. This isn't a spy film."

"I don't have time to do it any other way. There's everything you need in there. I'll get up and walk away. After that, we'll make any arrangement you want."

Clifford felt his temper flare. How badly he wanted to grab Leeman by the throat and shake some sense into him. But he settled for fixing the man with an angry glare. "Someone has my daughter, Barry. They have her, and Christ knows what they might do to her. She's twenty-three, for God's sake."

Sitting perfectly still in his pristine black overcoat, his legs crossed, and his hair immaculately arranged into a side parting, Leeman was apparently unmoved. His clean-shaven cheeks remained immobile, and behind his gleaming spectacles his dark eyes were devoid of emotion.

"I'll get her back," Leeman stated. "But what about the perpetrators? What shall I do with them?"

"Make them pay. Make them suffer, then get rid of them. But they can't just disappear. I want them to be found. I want to send a message."

"Risky. Costly too."

Clifford spoke slowly, emphasising every word, "I don't care."

"Understood." Leeman smiled. "Right, you'd better be off. Don't let me keep you."

"Fine." Clifford rose stiffly and strode away. He didn't look back until he reached the gate that gave onto the street, and by then the bench was empty. Barry Leeman was nowhere in sight. It was as if he'd simply vanished.

8

"HERE WE ARE," Reilly said. "Dix's Field." He swerved the
Ford into a parking space, and they climbed from the car.
Spiller paused on the pavement to scan the uniform row of
red brick buildings. The ground-floor windows were
arched, and each wide front door was crowned by an
ornate fanlight.

Each house had tall sash windows at the upper floors,
some of them equipped with a wrought-iron balcony, their
railings echoed by the fence set in front of the houses. The
overall effect was impressive, as though the individual
houses made up a single and rather grand mansion.

Across the road, an area of grass boasted a row of
mature trees, and Spiller caught a glimpse of a church spire
at the end of the street. To his eyes, the place looked like
something from one of those costume dramas Sheila liked
on the telly.

"Odd name," Spiller said. "Dix's Field. I suppose it was
named after some local bigwig."

"Don't know and don't much care. We're heading

down the road." Reilly set off along the street. "It's not quite so posh where we're going."

Spiller fell into step beside Reilly and soon saw what he meant. The road became wider, fine old houses giving way to boxy buildings made from dull concrete and aluminium-framed windows.

Reilly marched up to a retail unit, its windows advertising dozens of houses for sale or rent. Across the front window, a sign read *Berkley's Estate Agent*.

Reilly paused before opening the door. "I'll take the lead. If I want you to chip in, wait until I give you a nod, okay?"

"No problem," Spiller replied. "But..."

"What?"

Choosing his words carefully, Spiller said, "I don't want to get in your way, Paddy, but I hate to hang around like a spare part."

"I know where you're coming from, Tim, but just because you're not asking the questions, it doesn't mean you're wasting your time. You're learning on the job, and that's always the best way. Besides, two heads are better than one. Listen carefully, and you might pick up something I miss."

"Okay, Paddy. You're the boss."

"Quite right."

Reilly led the way inside, and a middle-aged man rose swiftly from his seat, striding around his desk to meet them, his hand extended for a shake.

"Good morning, gentlemen. I'm Malcolm, the senior property consultant here at Berkley's. What can I do for you today? If you're looking to buy, I've got a couple of beauties I could show you." Lowering his voice to a stage whisper, he added, "They've only just come on the market, so I'm not supposed to show anyone yet, but I can see you have a keen eye."

"Sorry to disappoint," Reilly said, sounding distinctly unapologetic as he showed his ID, "but we're here on police business."

Malcolm's face fell and a small sigh escaped from his lips. "Tony."

Reilly nodded.

"What's he done this time?"

"The usual," Reilly replied.

"Parking tickets? Again?" Malcolm shook his head. "I've told him a dozen times, but he thinks he can park anywhere he pleases. It's up to him to pay the fines. We're not liable, as I'm sure you know, so you'll have to do what you have to do." He smiled sadly. "When and if he turns up, that is."

"Tony not in today?" Reilly asked.

"No, he called in sick. A tummy bug, apparently, but a heavy weekend is more like it."

Reilly tutted. "Youngsters, eh? They don't know they're born. Could you scribble down Tony's address for me?"

"Yes, but..." Malcolm frowned. "If you're dealing with his parking fines, you'll have his details already, won't you? Aren't they all on a computer?"

"Of course, sir, but it'll save time if you help us out, and we'll be grateful for your assistance." Reilly fixed the man with an implacable stare.

"I suppose it'll be all right." Malcolm went to his desk and wrote on a pad, tearing off a page and walking slowly back to join them.

Reilly held out his hand, and after a brief show of reluctance, Malcolm presented him with the sheet of paper.

Reilly glanced at the address, then passed it to Spiller. "Thank you, sir. All that remains is to get your surname and phone number and so on. My colleague will take your details."

Spiller took his cue, stepping forward smartly as he pocketed the piece of paper and whipped out his notebook.

"Let's start with your full name, sir."

"Malcolm Barr. Barr has two R's."

Spiller wasted no time in obtaining the man's name, address and phone number, and he recorded every detail diligently. When he was done, he glanced at Reilly and received a nod that said, 'Over to you.'

"Before we go," Spiller began, "I've a few more questions for you, Mr Barr. How's Tony as an employee?"

Malcolm hesitated. "I hope I didn't give you the wrong impression earlier. Tony can be a bit careless, but he's good at his job. He's a natural salesman, and he can turn on the charm when he wants to." Malcolm smiled as if at a private joke, and Spiller sensed a thread he could pull at.

"Who does he turn on the charm for? The ladies, perhaps?"

"Well, he is good with our female clients. We sometimes joke that I'll handle the husbands and he can handle the wives."

"And how does Tony *handle* the wives?" Spiller asked.

Malcolm's composure slipped. "Oh, I didn't mean to imply there's anything inappropriate. It's just that Tony's young, and he has a way with the ladies. He gives them a smile and a bit of flattery, that's all."

"I see." Spiller made a note, mainly to let Malcolm know this was a serious matter.

"When we arrived, you assumed that Tony had done something wrong," Spiller went on. "Why was that?"

"No reason."

Spiller gazed at the man, his pen poised, waiting.

Malcolm's professional demeanour vanished. "Okay, it's not just the parking. I've had some complaints about Tony. The ladies like him, but he doesn't always know where to draw the line."

"What kind of complaints?" Spiller asked.

"From husbands mainly. They think he gets over-familiar with their wives, and they're probably right."

"What about your female clients?" Reilly said. "Do they complain?"

Malcolm nodded. "A few of them. I've spoken to Tony about it. I've warned him often enough. I've told him someone might talk to the police if he made a nuisance of himself, but he doesn't listen. I must admit, I wondered if that's why you were here."

"I see," Spiller said. "Define making a nuisance."

"Oh, I don't mean anything awful. He might lay his hand on a woman's back as they go through the door, for instance, but nothing worse than that."

"Are you sure about that?" Reilly asked. "What about when he's in the car with a client? Does his hand ever slip onto a woman's knee?"

"Er, no, not as far as I know. No one's ever said anything like that."

"And what about his absence today?" Spiller said. "Is Tony really ill, do you think?"

"I doubt it. He sounded hungover to me." Malcolm attempted a world-weary smile. "Still, we were all young once. We've all thrown a sickie after a night in the pub."

"Not all of us," Spiller stated. "Personally, I don't drink when I've got work the next day."

From the corner of his eye, he spotted Reilly staring at

him, but Spiller pressed on. "But we're not here to talk about my principles, Mr Barr. We're looking at Tony Carter and the way he carries on."

"Yes, although you haven't really said what he's supposed to have done."

Spiller looked to Reilly and received a nod. "Mr Barr, we're looking into the disappearance of a young woman."

"What?" Malcolm paled. "You're not suggesting it's something to do with Tony, are you?"

"Not at this stage," Reilly said. "But there's a connection between the woman in question and Tony Carter, so we need to talk to him."

"Who... who's missing?" Malcolm said, his voice faint. "Not his girlfriend, surely. Not Lynsey."

"Do you know Lynsey?" Reilly asked.

Malcolm shook his head. "We've never met, but he talks about her all the time. I think they're pretty serious."

"What gave you that impression?" Spiller said.

"I don't know. The way he talked about her, I suppose. He seemed to go out with her every weekend, and sometimes in the week as well. I know Tony thinks the world of Lynsey. If anything's happened to her, he'll be devastated."

"All the more reason for us to be cautious with the information we release," Reilly said. "We don't want to cause alarm, so please do not contact Tony until we've had a chance to talk to him ourselves. Don't say anything to anybody. We don't want rumours flying around the place; that would do more harm than good."

Malcolm nodded vaguely, but he didn't seem to be taking Reilly's words in. "So is it Lynsey you're looking for or not?"

Reilly left a pause before replying. "Mr Barr, I'll spell

this out for you. We're looking for a young woman who's been reported as missing, but we're not releasing her name at this stage, and speculation isn't helpful. Think of that young woman's family and what they're going through. Do you have children, Mr Barr?"

"Yes. A boy and a girl. They're grown up now, but they're still…" Malcolm's voice trailed away. "Those poor parents. It's your worst nightmare."

"Exactly," Reilly said. "So you'll understand why we must keep this between ourselves for the time being. Remember, we might find the young woman at any moment, but we can't afford to sit around and wait. We're talking to everyone who knows her, so we need to meet with Tony Carter right away. Hopefully, we'll be able to eliminate him from our enquiries. Is that all clear to you?"

"Yes, perfectly."

"Good. Then we'll be off." Reilly caught Spiller's eye and nodded towards the door. To Malcolm, he said, "Goodbye, for now. We'll be in touch. If you see Tony before we do, give us a call." Reilly handed out a business card and they took their leave.

Outside, Reilly headed back to the car at a brisk pace. "We'll go straight to Carter's house," he said. "With a bit of luck, we'll catch him while he's still worse for wear."

"What if he really does have a stomach bug?" Spiller asked.

"Do me a favour." They walked on for a few paces, then Reilly sent him a sideways glance. "Do you really not drink on a work night?"

"Never."

"You'll have a drink after work tonight though, eh? We've got to christen you, bring you into the fold."

"Thanks, but I'd better get home after work. Sheila's making a Lancashire hotpot."

"It'll keep. That's the whole point of a hotpot. It might come from the wrong side of the Pennines, but you can't go wrong with a hotpot. The longer you leave it, the better it'll be."

"I don't think Sheila would see it like that."

"Get on with you," Reilly said. "She married a copper; she must have nerves of steel. She'll understand you having a pint after your first day. Besides, it'll be good for you. You'll get to meet everyone, and that always helps. Shake a few hands, let them see what you're made of. Make the right friends now and it'll help you down the line."

"Is that what you did?"

"Me? Nay, lad. I'm not made for glad-handing folk. I speak as I find, and they don't always like that down here. I dare say they think I'm a brash northerner, but that can't be helped. I had my card marked a long time ago. I've been a DS for a long while now, and that's the way it'll stay until I get my pension."

"You never know," Spiller said. "The guvnor seems to think highly of you. He put you in charge of the new boy, so he must trust you."

"Chisholm is one of the good guys. We get on fine, him and me, but he's not the only senior officer in CID."

Reilly's tone had grown more sombre as he'd spoken, and Spiller took this as a signal to ask no more questions. Still, he couldn't help but wonder about Reilly. He seemed like a good copper, and it sounded as though he wasn't without ambition, so what was holding him back? Was it as simple as he said? Had he rubbed too many people up the wrong way? If so, who had Reilly fallen out with and why?

I'm overthinking it, Spiller told himself. *It's nothing to do with me.*

Reilly interrupted his thoughts by asking for Tony Carter's address.

"37 West Grove Road," Spiller said without breaking stride, and without retrieving the note Malcolm had given them.

Reilly smiled. "Good lad. We call that patch St Leonard's."

"On account of the church?"

"That's right. Do you *attend*, if that's the right word?"

Spiller shook his head. "Sheila's more that way inclined than me. I don't really go in for all that, but I've been trying to find my way around and they're useful landmarks, churches. There was one at the end of Dix's Field. What's that called?"

"Southernhay Church. United Reform."

"I take it you don't go."

Reilly seemed to find this amusing. "The job's my religion. Pick one and stick to it, that's what I say."

Spiller thought for a second. "What about DCS Boyce? I'll bet he goes to church."

"Oh, I wish I could tell you that you're wrong, lad, but you're spot-on. Every Sunday he's there with his good lady wife. Mind you, if we need him on the job, he'll be at his desk before any of us. First to arrive, last to go home, that's his motto, come hell or high water."

"That's good," Spiller said. "It sounds like he's got his finger on the pulse."

Reilly looked as though he was going to say something, but they'd arrived back at the car. "Jump in. The sooner we get to Carter's gaffe, the better."

Five minutes later they were marching up to the front door of 37 West Grove Road.

The terraced houses were compact and neat: two-storey buildings with a single bay window on each floor. Most of the small front yards had been laid to flagstones or concrete, but some residents had added potted plants to brighten them up.

While Reilly rang the doorbell of number 37, Spiller stood back on the pavement to check the upstairs window. The curtains had been opened, and as Spiller watched, a face briefly appeared at the window's edge before ducking back out of sight.

"He's in," Spiller said. "At least, someone is."

"I might have to send you around to cover the back," Reilly replied. "I'd take the motor, but you can't drive down the back of this street. It's on foot or nothing." Reilly cocked his ear. "Hang on, I can hear someone coming down the stairs."

They waited in silence, but not for long.

"Bugger it!" Reilly muttered. "He must've slipped out the back. How's your running?"

"Not bad. Which way shall I go?"

Reilly pointed to the end of the street. "Go that way and turn left, then left again down the backs of the houses. I'll get the car and head him off. All right?"

Spiller nodded and broke into a run, unbuttoning his jacket as he went. He seemed to be racing along, his arms pumping and his feet flying, but he was already sweating, his heart beating hard against his ribs. Maybe he'd let his fitness slip more than he'd realised.

An engine roared, and he glimpsed Reilly's Ford as it shot past, its tyres squealing as the car swerved to a halt at the end of the road. The road was a dead-end as far as cars were concerned—the only way to continue was a narrow alleyway that ran at right angles to the road—but Reilly knew what he was doing. He performed a rapid three-point turn, then the Ford sped back the way it had come. Spiller ran on, making for the alley's mouth and turning left.

He spied the opening of the path behind the houses, but before he could reach it, a man emerged, running hard. The man was younger than Spiller, taller and more athletic too, and there was nothing wrong with his reactions. He saw Spiller and headed in the opposite direction, putting on a burst of speed. He was getting away.

Spiller urged his legs to move faster, but the younger man had already reached the end of the alley, turning right and disappearing from view.

Oh no, you don't, Spiller thought, and from somewhere he found an extra gear. Sweating profusely, thighs burning, Spiller hared to the alley's end and found himself on the pavement of a long, straight road. The man was some distance away and running hard.

Spiller gave chase, gasping for air as he ran, his throat parched and his tongue dry. He did his level best to maintain the pace he'd set, but still, the younger man was putting more distance between them. "Stop!" Spiller called out. "Police!"

If anything, the young man increased his speed. Where the hell was Reilly?

As if in answer to his call, the Ford Escort streaked past, Reilly gunning the engine. In a second, it overtook the young man, then it pulled across in front of him, mounting the kerb at an angle and screeching to a halt, the driver's door flying open.

Reilly jumped out of the car and the young man swerved to avoid him. Reilly might've been a good few years older than his opponent, but he was ready. He seemed to know exactly what the young man was going to do, and he intercepted him without hesitation, grabbing him by the arm and spinning him around, making his opponent the victim of his own momentum. The young man collided with the side of Reilly's car, and before he could react, Reilly pulled the man's arms behind his back and wasn't about to let go.

Spiller caught up with them just as Reilly was applying a pair of handcuffs.

Reilly sent him a quizzical look. "Are you all right, lad?"

Spiller made do with a nod; he was too busy breathing deep to talk.

"Okay." Turning his attention to the young man, Reilly added, "You are Tony Carter, yes?"

"I'm not saying anything," the man snapped. "I want a solicitor."

"We all want something," Reilly replied. "It wouldn't hurt you to say please."

"Are you having a laugh?"

"Not yet, no. Maybe later, when you get sent down for twenty years or so. That might make me crack a smile."

"What am I supposed to have done?"

"We'll get into that at the station," Reilly replied. "DC Spiller, could you take care of the driver's seat, please? We need to make room for our special guest."

"My pleasure." Spiller released the catch and tipped the seat forward, then he stood back to give Reilly some room.

"I'd say mind your head as you get in," Reilly said while he manhandled his captive into the back seat. "But it's a soft top, so you'll be all right. Although you've been in the wars already, haven't you, son?"

With the man safely installed, Reilly pushed his seat

back into place. To Spiller, he said, "Make sure you've seen that shiner he's got. It takes a while for a black eye to come up like that, and we don't want him saying I did it."

Spiller leaned in to see. "Oh yes. That is a nice black eye you have, sir. Been in a fight?"

The man scowled, turning his head away.

"No conversation, some people," Reilly said. "Right, back to the nick and we'll see what Mr Carter has to say for himself, presuming this is Mr Carter, of course."

"Ready when you are," Spiller replied, and as he climbed into the passenger seat, he smiled. Now this was his idea of police work.

9

SITTING in the driving seat of his BMW 5 Series on St Leonard's Road, Barry Leeman almost smiled. There were times when the police were almost competent, and all he had to do was tag along. What was more, they really could be very entertaining. The way this pair had chased after Tony Carter—it had been a treat to watch.

He'd pay good money to see clowns like those two any day of the week. Especially the younger one, all earnest enthusiasm and dogged determination, still smiling even though he'd just run himself ragged. He was new, and he might turn out to be fun.

Paddy Reilly, on the other hand, had a way of putting a dampener on things. He was too contrary for his own good. On the plus side, Reilly played by the rules most of the time, and that made him predictable. Predictable was good. Predictable was useful.

Reilly was good at his job, but he wasn't the sharpest tool in the box. He hadn't noticed Leeman tailing him from Carter's place of work, and he hadn't even noticed the BMW as it drove onto West Grove Road and stopped on the opposite side of the street. Of course, Leeman had parked more thoughtfully than Reilly, so he'd been able to turn his car around with ease. He'd simply reversed to the junction, tucked his car around the corner and waited for Reilly to go racing past.

He'd followed at a reasonable distance, certain that Reilly had his mind on the chase, then he'd parked to enjoy the show.

Now all he had to do was follow Reilly's vulgar little car to the police station, and he'd take it from there.

It was all a little too easy.

10

IN THE INTERVIEW ROOM, Spiller watched while Reilly unwrapped two new cassettes and placed them in the recorder. On the other side of the table, the man who'd finally identified himself as Tony Carter sat with his arms folded, staring straight ahead as if oblivious to their presence.

The cassette recorder emitted a beep. "Bingo," Reilly said. "DS Reilly and DC Spiller present, interviewing Mr Anthony Carter at 11:15 am." He clapped his hands together. "Right, let's begin, Tony. Is it all right if I call you Tony?"

With a show of reluctance, Carter looked at Reilly, then he nodded to the recorder. "What's all that about?"

"Oh, it's high tech, is this," Reilly replied. "We've only been using it since January. Consider yourself privileged."

"Lucky me, but what's it for? What am I supposed to have done?"

"We'll come to that," Reilly said. "Why did you run, Tony?"

Carter shrugged a shoulder. "I like running. It's good for you."

"In your jeans and your woolly jumper?" Reilly asked. "Not exactly dressed for it, were you, lad?"

"I can wear what I like, can't I?"

"Oh yes." Reilly sat back in his seat. "You legged it before we had a chance to introduce ourselves, so you didn't know we were police, did you?"

"No. How could I?"

"Who did you think we were?"

Carter let out a humourless laugh. "No idea, but I reckoned you were bad news. I wasn't far wrong."

"That's just rude, lad. Where are your manners? I'll have you know we're a couple of upstanding officers of the law."

"How come you shoved me against your car, then? That was police brutality, that was."

Reilly shook his head. "Nothing of the sort. That was what we call minimum necessary force to detain. Besides, you were a danger to the public, running about like that. You could've had some poor old dear off her feet."

Carter's only reply was a rolling of his eyes.

"Do you drive a van, Tony?" Reilly went on.

"Are you joking? Do I look like I drive a bloody van? I've got an Audi Quattro, mate."

Reilly made a show of being impressed. "I bet that goes, doesn't it?"

"It can, but I stick to the speed limit. If I get banned, I'd lose my job, so I take it easy."

"Glad to hear it," Reilly said. "You didn't go to work today though, did you? Heavy night, last night, was it?"

"I might've had a couple."

"More than that, I reckon," Reilly said. "You're looking a bit rough."

Carter tutted in contempt. "So what?"

"So, I'm interested in what you've been up to," Reilly replied. "When we knocked on your door, you reckoned someone was after you. Maybe that's something to do with that black eye."

"Nope. You're barking up the wrong tree, mate."

Reilly smiled. "I'm not your mate. I'm a detective sergeant conducting a lawful inquiry. Now, how did you come by that shiner?"

"It was some bloke the other night. He took a dislike to me, gave me a thump."

"Did you report it?" Spiller asked.

"No. It was nothing."

"It looks nasty to me," Spiller said. "Do you know the man's name?"

Carter shook his head.

"What was the disagreement about?" Reilly asked.

"I dunno. I don't remember. It was late and I'd had a few pints."

"We've all been there," Reilly said. "But tell us the details and we'll move on. Where and when?"

Carter sighed. "Saturday night. Outside The Icebox. It's a nightclub by the quay. Some bloke reckoned I looked at him the wrong way or something. I told him to bugger off, so he thumped me."

Reilly sucked air over his teeth. "Harsh. But you're a big lad. I expect you gave as good as you got, didn't you?"

"No. It was one punch and that was an end to it. I let it go. I don't go looking for trouble."

"That's a sensible attitude," Spiller said. "But I'm not sure I believe it."

"That's your problem. It's what happened."

"Was there anyone who can back up your story?" Spiller asked.

"No. It was outside. There was just me and him."

Reilly drummed his fingers on the table as though deep in thought, letting the silence in the room build.

"Is this really what you want to talk about?" Carter went on. "I told you, it was one punch. Haven't you got anything better to do?"

"You would not believe the amount of work waiting on my desk," Reilly replied. "But as of now, you are my number one priority."

Carter lowered his eyebrows as this statement sank in.

"Who was with you on Saturday night?" Reilly went on.

"I dunno. There were a few of us. It was a lads' night out."

"It wasn't just the lads, though," Reilly said. "There were some girls too."

"I suppose so. What about it?"

"It's an important detail," Reilly replied. "Tell me who you were with that night."

"Seriously?"

Reilly nodded, his gaze locked on Carter.

"All right, I'll try. There was my mate Wayne, and Eddie and—"

"Full names, please," Spiller interrupted.

Carter licked his lips. "Wayne O'Neill, Eddie Appleton, Keith Osborne. Is that good enough for you, or do you want me to spell them out?"

"That's fine for now," Spiller replied. "But once again, you're steering clear of mentioning the women. We need their names too."

"Why? I told you, it was me and the lads. There were a few girls hanging around, but so what?"

"So stop beating about the bush and give us their names," Reilly said.

"Okay, I give in. No need to get narked." Carter smirked. "Let me think. There was Ashley—that's Ashley Hawkins. She goes out with my mate Keith, so we might've talked to her a bit. She was with her friends, Mel Parker and Lynsey Clifford."

"Tell me about Lynsey."

"Why? What's she got to do with—"

"Come off it," Reilly interrupted. "You are Lynsey's boyfriend, aren't you?"

"Yeah. Well, I was."

"*Was?*" Spiller said. "Why do you use the past tense?"

"Because she dumped me, that's why. What are you getting at?"

"We're asking the questions," Reilly intoned. "And we want to know about Lynsey Clifford."

"Hang on, is she okay?"

"You tell me," Reilly said.

Carter shifted in his seat. "I haven't seen her since Saturday night. Has something happened?"

"You sound worried, Tony," Reilly replied.

Carter pulled a face as though Reilly had said something ridiculous. "Me? Never."

"So you weren't bothered when Lynsey gave you the elbow?" Reilly asked.

"Plenty more fish in the sea."

"But you and Lynsey had been going out for a long time," Spiller said. "You must've been upset when she broke it off."

"Not so much. It's not like I'm a teenager."

Spiller nodded thoughtfully. "Did you have a key to Lynsey's flat?"

"No, I did not."

Spiller heard the resentment in Carter's tone and knew

he'd touched a nerve. "You would've liked a key, though, wouldn't you?"

"We're not going out anymore, so it's beside the point, isn't it?"

"Nevertheless, I'd be grateful if you'd answer the question," Spiller said.

"All right, it would've been handy, but she didn't want it that way. End of story."

Spiller saw the glint of anger in Carter's eye and chanced a bluff. "You used to have a key to Lynsey's flat, but she changed the lock, didn't she?"

Tony blinked in surprise, but he recovered quickly. "Are you accusing me of something?"

Spiller's smile was serene. "I'm not accusing you, Tony. I simply want to know what happened. Did Lynsey give you a key and then subsequently change the lock?"

"Well... it was kind of like that, but you're making it sound as if I did something wrong, and it was nothing really."

"Enlighten us," Reilly said.

"Lynsey gave me a key a while back, but about a month ago, I..." Carter paused to run his tongue over his lips. "I went around to her place after work. I thought Lynsey was going to be in, but I'd had a few pints after work, and I'd forgotten about her class. She goes to step aerobics once a week, and I'd got the days muddled up."

"So you used your key and let yourself in," Spiller suggested.

"Well, yeah. To be honest, I needed a slash, so I went in. I didn't think she'd mind, otherwise, what was the point in me having the key?"

"I take it that Lynsey *did* mind," Reilly said.

"Yeah, but it was..." Again, Carter broke off, his cheeks flushing.

To Spiller, the man seemed to have gone from looking guilty to being merely embarrassed. Softening his tone, Spiller said, "Go on, Tony. Tell us what happened."

"I needed a coffee to sober myself up, but I dropped the jar of instant, and it went all over the floor. It sounds daft, but when I tried to clean it up, I used a wet cloth and made even more of a mess. I looked for a mop, but when I opened the broom cupboard, a load of stuff fell out. I dare say I lost my temper a bit, and that's when..."

"Lynsey came home," Spiller said.

Carter nodded. "She wasn't too pleased. After that, she changed the lock and said she didn't want any uninvited visitors."

"Lynsey gave a copy of the new key to her father," Spiller said. "Did you know that?"

"No, but it's no wonder. He owns the place and, well, you know..."

"What do we know?" Reilly asked.

"She's daddy's golden girl, isn't she? Lynsey can do no wrong, not in his eyes."

"Fathers and daughters, eh?" Reilly said.

"Tell me about it."

Carter's lopsided smile said he didn't give a damn, but there'd been a hint of bitterness in his voice.

"Did you get on with Lynsey's father?" Spiller asked.

"Yeah. Well enough. He's a decent bloke."

Spiller nodded in acknowledgement. "What about her mother?"

"We haven't spoken much, but she seems nice."

Reilly sent Carter a conspiratorial smile. "I saw her once at a fundraiser. She's a good-looking woman."

"Yeah."

"Fancy taking a pop at her, did you?"

"What are you on about?" Carter spluttered.

"You know what I mean," Reilly insisted. "The older woman. You wouldn't be the first young man to—"

"This is ridiculous," Carter interrupted. "I don't know where you're getting this, but it's a load of..." He glanced at the cassette recorder before adding, "old rubbish."

Reilly grinned. "Is it? I wouldn't put it past you, Tony. Not satisfied with the daughter, you have a go at the mother. But that would be awkward wouldn't it? Much easier, though, if Lynsey was out of the way."

"For God's sake," Carter muttered, an edge of anger creeping into his tone. "It's like a bloody nuthouse in here. Why don't you start making sense?"

"No need to lose your temper," Spiller said. "We're—"

"I'm not bloody well losing my temper," Carter snapped. "It's you two, you're winding me up. Why are you going on about Lynsey's mum all of a sudden? And what's all this stuff about the flat?"

Reilly glanced at Spiller. "Tell him, Detective Constable. Give him the bad news."

"Certainly, Detective Sergeant." Spiller locked eyes with Carter. "I'm sorry to have to tell you this, but Lynsey Clifford is missing. We're very concerned for her safety, and you may well be the last person who saw her."

Carter stared at each of them in turn, his expression blank, his eyes dulled by confusion.

"Do you have anything to say about Lynsey's disappearance?" Reilly asked. "Can you tell us where she is?"

"I don't..." Carter looked down, shaking his head. "She can't... Not Lynsey. Not my Lynsey."

"When did you last see her?" Reilly asked.

"I told you," Carter replied, his tone uncertain. "Saturday night."

"You'll have to do better than that," Reilly said. "Place and time."

"It was outside the club, just after half past twelve. I wondered where she was, so I went out looking for her. She was outside, by the water, just standing there by herself."

"Was this before or after you got thumped?" Reilly asked.

"Before."

"You sound very sure of that," Spiller said. "Earlier, you claimed you didn't remember what time you were assaulted."

"I know it happened afterwards, because I went on a bit of a bender after she chucked me." Carter looked crestfallen as he recalled the memory. "I found her outside, and she said she wanted to break up with me. I tried talking to her, but she didn't want to know. She said it was all over."

"I bet that hurt," Reilly said. "I bet it made you angry."

"No. I wasn't angry with her. With myself, maybe, for mucking it up, but not with Lynsey."

"We talked to Lynsey's neighbours," Spiller said. "There were reports of arguments."

Carter's cheeks had been pale, but now they coloured. "Who said that? It was that stupid cow downstairs, wasn't it? Carol. Poking her nose in. She's got a bloody nerve, with the way she carries on."

"We're not at liberty to disclose who gave us the information," Spiller replied. "But I take it you don't get on with Lynsey's neighbours. Why is that?"

"I don't really talk to them, but I know when

something's going on under my nose. Lynsey never saw it, and I never told her, but you might want to ask Carol about all the blokes who come and go."

"We'll decide who we want to interview," Reilly said. "Right now, it's you we're talking to. And I'll remind you that your ex-girlfriend is missing. You don't seem too worried about it."

"Of course I'm worried, but I don't know what else to tell you."

Reilly slammed his hand against the table, and Carter flinched.

"Start with the truth," Reilly growled. "Lynsey dumped you, so you lost your temper. You got rough with her, and she lashed out to defend herself. She punched you in the eye, but it wasn't enough to stop you. You went too far, didn't you, Tony?"

"No, this is bullshit."

"You told us you were outside when you got hit," Reilly said. "You also said there was no one else around, but now it turns out that Lynsey was outside. Was she with this other bloke, is that it?"

Carter clenched his jaw, the muscles in his cheeks twitching.

"Was Lynsey cheating on you?" Reilly went on. "Had she found someone else?"

"No. But..."

Spiller offered an encouraging nod. "Go on, Tony. Tell us what happened."

"After she chucked me, I went back inside. I needed a drink, and the lads were getting the tequilas in, so I had one or two. After a bit, I told them what had happened, and someone reckoned there'd been a bloke sniffing around Lynsey all night. He'd even been outside with her."

"Do you know the man's name?" Reilly asked.

"Mank, that's what they call him. I don't know his real name, but I've seen him around."

"And you had reason to believe he'd been chatting up your girlfriend," Reilly said. "What did you do about that?"

"Nothing."

"Are you sure about that?" Reilly asked. "You didn't confront him?"

Carter gestured angrily at the table as though it were to blame for his troubles. "Look, I'd had a few drinks, all right? I saw the bloke walking out, and I might've gone after him to have a word. I don't recall what I said, but it must've put his back up, because he thumped me, but that was it. My mate came out and picked me up. He told me to leave it, and that was that."

"Where was Lynsey during this altercation?" Reilly asked.

"I don't know. I didn't see her around. I figured she'd gone home."

"So you left her on her own outside at night," Spiller said. "Weren't you concerned about her?"

"What was I supposed to do? She'd told me to leave her alone."

"You could've made sure someone was with her," Spiller replied. "A friend perhaps."

"Yeah, but I wasn't thinking straight. Besides, Lynsey's not daft. She can look after herself."

"Apparently not," Reilly said.

Again, a silence built up as the two policemen regarded Carter in silent approbation.

"Look, I don't know what Lynsey did after she chucked me; I wish I did. I wish she hadn't broken up with me. But

I've told you what happened, and there's no point banging on about it. You ought to be out there looking for her."

"We're taking care of all that," Reilly replied. "How would Lynsey normally get home after a night out?"

"If I was with her, we'd walk."

"That'd take you about fifteen minutes," Reilly said. "Which way did you go?"

"It depends on who was there. We'd sometimes walk her friends home."

"Very chivalrous," Reilly muttered. "But if it was just the two of you, did you ever go for a stroll?"

"Not really. We just went back to her place."

Reilly leaned forward and lowered his voice as if sharing a conspiracy. "There's Bull Meadow Park on the way home, isn't there? You didn't make a habit of popping in there for a quickie in the bushes, did you?"

Carter pulled a face. "We're not kids. We didn't need to muck about like that."

To Spiller, Reilly said, "Make a note. We'll organise a search. Bull Meadow Park."

"Got it," Spiller replied. "What about the quayside? We could call the divers in."

Reilly nodded. "Good thinking. I'll arrange that."

"Hang on," Carter blurted. "Are you saying...? You don't think...?"

"We don't know what to think," Reilly replied. "But you can help us out, Tony. Can you do that? For Lynsey's sake, can you tell us where she is?"

"No. The last time I saw her was outside the club when she chucked me. I swear."

"Let's say we believe you," Spiller began. "Would Lynsey have walked home on her own?"

Carter frowned. "No. Thinking about it, she would've taken a taxi. She was careful about that."

"We'll check the taxi companies," Spiller said. "Might she have taken a bus?"

"Not from the quay," Reilly replied. "Not at that time of night. And before we start looking at taxis, we need to talk to this Mank character. Are you sure you don't know his real name, Tony?"

"All I know is, it's best to steer clear of him. That's what everybody says."

"But you confronted him because he'd been talking to Lynsey," Spiller pointed out. "That seems careless, Tony."

"I'd had too much to drink. It was a stupid thing to do, and I've regretted it ever since. So..." Carter broke off, chewing his lower lip.

"What's up?" Spiller asked. "What were you going to say?"

"I was just thinking, if you talk to Mank, do me a favour. Don't tell him what I said about him. Don't mention me at all, okay?"

"You're scared," Reilly stated. "Why is that?"

Carter shook his head. "I'm saying nothing."

Reilly grunted in disapproval. "Help us out here, and we won't forget it."

"I've said all I'm going to say."

"That's not good enough," Spiller shot back. "I don't believe a word you've said, Mr Carter."

"I've told you the truth. Lynsey dumped me and told me to stay away, so I went inside and had a few drinks. I was by the bar all night. You can ask anybody. Loads of people saw me there."

"When did you leave?" Spiller asked.

"Me and the lads left at chucking out time. Two in the morning. We went straight home. We walked."

"That's a fair walk," Reilly said. "Why didn't you call a taxi?"

"I'd had too many. Throw up in a taxi and they charge you a tenner, sometimes more. I didn't want that. Better to walk it off. I had my mates with me, so we were all right."

"We need phone numbers and addresses for your friends," Spiller said. "We'll need to talk to them."

In a rush, as if he'd decided to get it over with, Carter reeled off contact details for his friends, and Spiller jotted them all down.

Reilly thanked him, then said, "Do you ride a bike, Tony?"

Carter stared at him. "No. Why?"

"There's a man's bike in the hallway at Lynsey's place," Reilly replied. "Is it yours?"

"Of course not. I take the Quattro, or I walk."

"What about your friends? Any of them keen cyclists?" Reilly said.

"No. They've all got their own cars."

"Do any of them drive a van?" Spiller asked.

Carter shook his head. "This again. No, definitely not. Is that it? Only, I've had enough. I want to go home. I'm done."

In the silence that followed, Spiller studied Carter and saw a look in the man's eyes that he couldn't quite fathom. Was Carter filled with regret at his drunken evening, troubled by the realisation that he'd landed himself in the firing line for no good reason, or was he haunted by guilt?

"Now you really do look worried," Spiller said.

"I'm worried about Lynsey."

"So are we, son," Reilly said. "If you know anything that might help us find her, you'd better tell us now."

"I've said everything I can. I really want to go. I'm allowed to go, aren't I?"

Spiller waited for Reilly to pass judgement. Personally, he would've liked to hold on to Tony Carter until they'd had time to check out his alibi, but they didn't have sufficient grounds to detain him.

Sure enough, Reilly sat back, his weary smile signalling the end of the interview.

"We're not stopping you from leaving," Reilly said. "We might need to talk to you again, and we'll be having a word with your friends, but don't even think about cooking up a story between you, because we will find out. If anybody lies, we'll be coming after you and your pals, okay?"

"We don't need to lie. We didn't do anything wrong."

"We'll see," Reilly replied. "But we've gone as far as we can for now. Let's leave it at that."

Reilly announced the interview was over and stopped the tape.

"Is that it?" Carter asked. "Can I go?"

Reilly held out his hands. "You could've left any time you wanted."

"You should've said that before we started."

"I wasn't obliged to, and you didn't ask." Reilly jumped to his feet. "Come on, Tony. We're done for now. I'll escort you off the premises."

Carter stood uncertainly. "What about Lynsey? What are you going to do?"

"We'll find her," Spiller replied, standing up. "We're doing everything we can."

"Whatever's happened, it wasn't anything to do with me," Carter said. "I told you the truth. Honest."

"I hope so, Tony." Reilly extended his arm and guided Carter toward the door. "Listen, we might call on you again, but don't leg it next time, okay?"

Carter nodded dumbly as he made for the door, his fingers pressed against his brow as if to ward off a headache.

"It's not your lucky day, is it, son?" Reilly said. "I'll tell you what, I'll see if I can rustle up a patrol car to take you home."

"You're all right, I'll walk," Carter replied. "I need some air."

"Suit yourself, lad."

Spiller and Reilly accompanied Carter to the main entrance, then they stood for a while, their hands in their pockets as they watched him trudge away.

"We didn't have enough to arrest him, did we?" Spiller asked.

"Unfortunately not," Reilly replied, "and to be honest, there isn't much point in talking to his mates; they'll say anything to keep their friend out of trouble. But never fear, there's a long way to go yet, but we'll get there. And there's no time like the present. Let's go." Reilly set off for the car park, and Spiller fell into step beside him.

"Next stop, the quayside," Reilly said.

"Are we going to the club?"

"We certainly are. But we won't get far on an empty stomach. There's a nice little cafe down there, so we'll kill two birds with one stone. We'll grab a bite and see what we can see, okay?"

"Sounds like a plan."

"Good, because I, for one, am in dire need of a strong cup of coffee."

11

Spiller had been to the quayside once before, but he hadn't set foot in The Riverside Cafe. It was an intriguing little place that seemed to be part of an antiques centre. In the cafe, the air was redolent with the aroma of freshly toasted bread and the hint of frying bacon.

DS Reilly placed his order—coffee and a sausage sandwich—then he patted Spiller on the back and went to find a table.

I suppose that means I'm paying, Spiller thought, but that was okay. Reilly was gradually accepting him, and that was worth the price of a hot drink and a snack.

Spiller ordered a cappuccino and a bacon sandwich for himself, then he paid up with a smile and went to join Reilly at a table by the window.

"It's all right in here, isn't it?" Spiller said. "Is it your regular?"

Reilly shook his head. "I'm keeping that treat in reserve. As a rule, I eat whenever and wherever I can. This place is okay, but we're not here for the ambience." He nodded to the window. "See what's over the road?"

Spiller peered out at the stone buildings on the other side of the street. They had an industrial look, as though they'd once been warehouses, but they boasted a pair of garish signs, one proclaiming the curious name *Mambo,* the other *The Icebox.*

"So that's the place," Spiller said, "Will there be anyone there at this time of day?"

"We'll soon find out. We'll pop over after our coffee."

As if on cue, a waitress delivered their drinks and sandwiches. They thanked her, but before tucking in, Reilly looked askance at Spiller's drink. "Cappuccino? It's all froth and no coffee."

"I like it," Spiller said. "It would be a dull world if we were all the same."

"Simpler though." Reilly took a drink of coffee and winced. "On the other hand, you might've made a good choice there, Tim. This stuff has been sitting in the pot for so long it could've come over with Raleigh."

"I can get you another." Spiller made to stand, but Reilly waved him back down.

"Don't worry about it. What doesn't kill us makes us stronger." Reilly devoured his sandwich, washing it down with gulps of coffee, and Spiller had to eat quickly to keep up.

"So what do you think of our nick, so far?" Reilly asked.

"It's all been a bit of a whirl," Spiller replied. "I was expecting to be trawling through paperwork for ages before I went out on a case."

"In any other nick, you might be right, but the guvnor has his own way of doing things."

"A baptism of fire."

Reilly grinned. "Kind of, but try to take it as a good thing. He must reckon you can cope with it."

"Fair enough." Spiller finished his coffee in silence.

Reilly watched him for a while, a quizzical expression on his face, but he couldn't keep quiet for long. "Is that it? *Fair enough?*"

Spiller nodded. "If he thinks I can do the job, that's good enough for me."

"Well, you did all right when we were interviewing Carter, so I'll tell you what, Tim. We'll head over to the club and see if we can't find someone who was there on Saturday night. This time, I'll ask a few questions, then I'll hand it over to you. See if you can push a bit further *without* asking any leading questions. All right?"

"Sure. Thanks, Paddy. I won't let you down."

"You'd better not. Let's go."

Reilly led the way from the cafe, marching to the main entrance of The Icebox and hammering on the door with his fist.

It wasn't long before a young man answered the door. Dressed in faded jeans and a T-shirt, he eyed them warily. "What do you want? We're closed."

"We know," Reilly replied, showing his warrant card. "We're police. Got a minute?"

The man seemed to renew his grip on the edge of the door. "That depends. I'm not the owner or anything. I work behind the bar, I was just stocking up."

"Were you working on Saturday night?" Reilly asked.

The man nodded.

"Then you're just the fella we need to talk to," Reilly went on. "What's your name, son?"

"Freddie."

"Have you got a surname?"

"Hall. Freddie Hall."

"Now we're getting somewhere," Reilly said. "Let's pop inside for a bit, eh?"

"I don't know. Maybe I ought to call my boss. He doesn't—"

Reilly held up a hand to cut him off. "Never mind about that, son. You're not in any trouble, and we haven't come to see if you're watering down the drinks, although I wouldn't be surprised if you were. We're tracing the movements of a young woman, and we have reason to believe she was here on Saturday night."

"We get lots of girls in here, especially on Saturdays."

Reilly gestured meaningfully toward the doorway. "Inside, Freddie, there's a good lad."

Freddie looked distinctly displeased, but he stood back and ushered them through to the bar. The windows were shuttered, and the place was gloomy, the overhead lights fighting an unequal battle against the room's darkest corners and alcoves. The black background of the carpet didn't help, despite its lurid pattern of swirling maroon lines.

Spiller looked around as he walked into the bar, the carpet clinging to the soles of his shoes with every step. A lot of beer had been spilled in this room, as the smell made very plain.

The place might look better at night, Spiller decided. With the neon signs switched on and the seats full of lively young people, the bar might seem passable. In reality, it was tacky to the point of being grim, the tables stained and chipped, and the vinyl-covered barstools worn and patched up with tape.

Moving over to the bar to take advantage of the one decent source of light, Reilly asked Spiller to show the photo of Lynsey.

Spiller obliged. "Have you seen this young woman recently?"

Freddie narrowed his eyes, one hand on his chin as he examined the photo, then he shook his head. "No. Sorry."

Spiller didn't believe him for a second; the man had been putting on a show.

Perhaps Reilly felt the same, because he said, "That is a shame. What do you think, DC Spiller?"

"I think, DS Reilly, that Mr Hall ought to look again." Turning his gaze on the barman, Spiller hardened his tone. "I'll remind you, sir, that wasting police time is an offence."

"I'm not wasting anybody's time. I don't know her."

"We didn't ask whether you know her or not," Spiller stated. "We asked if you've seen her recently. It's a simple question, Freddie. Do yourself a favour and answer it properly."

Hall looked at Spiller as if seeing him anew, and Spiller was secretly pleased to have made an impression.

"Okay, okay," Hall said. "No need to get uptight. I already told you, we get a lot of girls in here." He glanced at the photo again. "But, yeah, she comes in here. I think so, anyway."

"What about on Saturday night?" Spiller asked. "Did you see her then?"

Hall nodded slowly. "I reckon so."

Why didn't you say that in the first place? Spiller wanted to ask, but he knew the answer. In his days as a uniformed constable, he'd learned that most people didn't willingly talk to the police. The idea of becoming a witness and appearing in court filled ordinary people with dread. Only criminals didn't care one way or the other.

Aloud, Spiller simply said, "Was Lynsey here on her own?"

"No, she was with her usual crowd. They come in every so often."

"So you *have* noticed Lynsey before?"

"I might've done."

"Any particular reason?"

Hall looked slightly abashed. "Well, you know, she's a looker, isn't she? She's not like most of the girls we get in here. She's posh. Upper class."

"And what about her friends?" Spiller asked. "What are they like?"

"They're just the same as everyone else. They have a few drinks and a dance. The blokes get a bit loud by the end of the night, but they don't cause any trouble."

Spiller studied Hall's expression. The young man was getting twitchy, fidgeting with his hands. What was he holding back?

"There was something different on Saturday night, wasn't there? Something out of the ordinary," Spiller said. "Let's not muck about, Freddie. Tell me what happened."

Hall screwed up his features. "I don't really—"

"Come on," Spiller interrupted. "Tell us what you know."

"Look, there might've been a little trouble that night. There was one bloke with his eye on that girl, and he's a bit rough, that's all."

"I'm not hearing a name," Reilly said.

Hall shook his head, but Spiller fixed him with a look, making it clear he was prepared to wait all day if necessary.

"Bloody hell," Hall mumbled. "Don't tell him I said anything, okay? But it was a guy they call Mank. His real name's Dennis. Dennis Mankowich. He comes in here a lot."

"You said he had his eye on Lynsey," Spiller said. "What made you think that?"

"He was acting a bit weird. Like I said, he's in here all the time, but he doesn't usually mix with the other punters. He has his own little group. They're family. They just sit there, drinking. They're a miserable bunch, but you don't want to get on the wrong side of them." He hesitated. "On Saturday, though, Mank kept staring at that girl, a fat grin on his face like he fancied his chances. It was enough to make you laugh. I mean, she'd never be interested in a bloke like Mank. Apart from anything else, he's an ugly sod."

"Any idea where we might find Mr Mankowich?" Reilly asked.

"No. I couldn't tell you."

"Okay." Spiller sent the young man a smile. "During the evening, did Lynsey seem to be with anyone special?"

Hall blinked as though genuinely puzzled. "You mean, like a boyfriend?"

"Exactly."

"Yeah, she usually has her bloke in tow."

"Do you know his name?" Spiller asked.

"Tony," Freddie replied, his expression sour.

"You don't think much of him," Spiller stated.

"He's okay, but he's not..." Hall's lips moved as he searched for the right words. "Put it like this: she's out of his league. The bloke reckons he's cool, flashing the cash around, but he's not all that. Do you know what I mean?"

"Ideas above his station," Spiller suggested.

"Yeah, that's about right."

"One last question from me, but it's an important one," Spiller said. "Did you see or hear of anything that might've made you concerned for Lynsey's safety?"

Hall's eyes flashed in alarm. "Why? What's happened to her?"

"That remains to be seen," Reilly put in. "Answer the question, Mr Hall."

"Okay, but I didn't see anything like that. I was busy behind the bar."

"Even so, you looked in her direction once in a while," Reilly said. "A pretty girl like that; who wouldn't?"

"I might've."

Reilly chuckled conspiratorially. "Nobody would blame you, son. Admit it, you've taken a shine to her yourself."

Hall looked down for a moment. "I might've looked at her a couple of times."

"How did she seem?" Spiller asked.

"Fine. Most of the time. Later on, I thought she looked a bit mopey, but she'd been on the gin and it takes people that way sometimes, doesn't it?"

"Oh yes," Reilly replied. "Any idea when she left?"

"Before the end of the night. I didn't see her go, but she suddenly wasn't there. Her mates stayed until we kicked them out."

"Even her boyfriend?" Reilly asked.

"No. I think he left just after Lynsey. He was pretty far gone that night. I remember thinking she'd have her hands full."

"There's a funny thing," Reilly said. "Your memory's getting better by the minute."

Hall looked shamefaced. "Look, I wasn't trying to hide anything, but the boss doesn't like us to go blabbing about the customers. He says it's bad for business, and what he says goes. If he finds out I've been talking to you, I'll get the sack. You backed me into a corner, so I've tried to help, but I've told you as much as I can."

Hall's voice had risen as he spoke, and Reilly made a downward motion with his hands. "Calm down, son. You're not going to get in any trouble. We're almost done here, but there's something else we need to talk about."

Hall seemed to deflate. "Go on."

"There was a fight on Saturday night," Reilly began. "And—"

"I don't know anything about it," Hall interrupted.

Reilly heaved an exaggerated sigh. "Don't play silly buggers, lad. We've already talked to Lynsey's boyfriend, and he told us what happened. We'd like to hear your side of the story, that's all."

"I really didn't see anything. I didn't even know about it until it was all over. I heard the guy got punched, but it was outside, and it wasn't a big deal. Gaz sorted it out."

Spiller raised his eyebrows. "One of your bouncers?"

"Doormen. Gary Murphy. He's good. Nobody messes with him."

"We'll need to talk to him," Reilly said. "We need names, addresses and phone numbers for anyone working that night."

"Seriously?"

Reilly smiled. "Deadly. Do you have a pen and paper, or would you like us to provide them?"

"I'm not sure if I—"

Reilly didn't let him finish. "You can do it here or at the station, Freddie. What's it to be?"

"All right, I'll sort it out, but I don't know the numbers by heart. They're on a pinboard in the office. I'll have to go and write them down in there."

"Go on then," Reilly said. "Off you pop. Addresses too, mind. *Real* addresses. No mucking about."

Hall trudged away, grumbling to himself.

"Shall I go and keep an eye on him?" Spiller asked Reilly.

"No. Give him a minute. He'll be back. He's not as daft as he looks. Freddie's figured out which way his bread is buttered."

"Okay. Maybe I could take a look around while we wait."

"Relax, lad. You're like a cat on a hot tin roof. You need to pace yourself in this game." Reilly paused, cocking his ear. "See, he's coming back already."

Sure enough, Hall reappeared, carrying a page torn from a spiral bound pad. Handing it to Reilly, he said, "There. That's everyone I can think of."

"Thanks." Reilly took the list and scanned it before handing it to Spiller.

"Yes, thank you for that," Spiller said as he read. As well as his own details, Freddie had added phone numbers and addresses for the bouncers, Gary Murphy and Greg Taylor, and he'd done the same for a DJ by the name of Joe Edmonds.

But something wasn't right. Spiller watched Freddie from the corner of his eye. The man was nervous, the muscles around his mouth twitching, and his gaze kept flitting from Reilly to Spiller. He had the air of a man who'd pulled a fast one and was waiting to see whether he'd get away with it.

Spiller looked to Reilly and saw that he, too, was studying Freddie. Had he come to the same conclusion?

As if in answer to Spiller's unasked question, Reilly tutted. "Do you expect me to believe this, Freddie? Were you behind the bar on your own on a Saturday night?"

Hall ran his hand over his chin. "Oh, I forgot the barmaid. That would've been Lucy. Lucy Proctor. Do you want her number as well? Only I'll have to go back to the office and get it."

Spiller opened his mouth to say yes, but Reilly didn't give him the chance. "Does she ever go outside while she's working?"

Hall shook his head.

"What about when she collects glasses or empties?" Reilly asked.

"We don't allow glasses or bottles outside. Gaz and Greg make sure of that."

"Never mind then," Reilly said. "I doubt whether your barmaid would've seen anything useful, and the same goes for your DJ, but we'll be talking to your bouncers—sorry, doormen." Reilly paused. "We've got enough to be going on with. We'll head off unless you want to ask anything, DC Spiller?"

"Actually, I do have a question," Spiller said. "It's about this Mank character. Did he stay until closing time, or did he leave earlier?"

Hall shook his head.

"That wasn't a yes or no question," Reilly pointed out. "When did Mankowich leave?"

"I have absolutely no idea," Hall stated, then he pressed his lips together tight.

Reilly and Spiller stared at Hall for a second, but there was no point in expecting anything more; the young man had clammed up.

"I think we're done here, don't you?" Reilly said.

"For now," Spiller replied. "We'll be in touch, Mr Hall."

They made for the door, leaving the young man staring after them, his expression almost as gloomy as the bar.

Back out in the sunlight, Reilly nodded to Spiller. "You did all right, Tim. Not bad at all."

"Thanks, Paddy." Spiller took a deep breath of fresh air, glad to have escaped from the cloying smell of stale beer. "It was interesting what he said about Carter, wasn't it? Especially if he was right, and Carter left about the same time as Lynsey. Carter claimed he'd stayed until closing time."

Reilly nodded. "Carter was loud and making a nuisance of himself. A barman would've pegged him as a troublemaker, and he definitely would've noticed when he left. He was probably glad to see the back of him."

"I'm also interested in the mysterious Mr Mankowich. Have you heard of him?"

"Something tells me the name ought to ring a bell, but I've been racking my brain, and I can't remember why. I've a good memory for names, and I have an inkling we've had dealings with a Mankowich before."

"I can check on the PNC when we get back to the nick," Spiller suggested, referring to the Police National Computer.

"We'll give it a shot, but you don't want to rely on computers too much. They might not lie, but they don't give you the full picture. It's people we're dealing with, not facts and figures."

"So what's the alternative?"

"You'll see," Reilly replied with a grin. "When I can't put my finger on a case, I use CID's secret weapon."

Spiller tried to conceal his impatience. "Which is?"

"It's like the adverts say, Tim: I know a man who can."

12

In the Riverside Cafe, Barry Leeman smiled at the waitress as she brought him his tea and began unloading her tray onto his table. "Thank you, but I don't need the milk. I drink it black."

"Oh, sorry." The waitress plucked the jug of milk and put it back on her tray. "Would you like a slice of lemon with your tea?"

Leeman shook his head. "It's fine as it is, thank you."

"Right. If there's anything else, give me a shout."

"I will." Leeman maintained his smile until the waitress was back behind the counter, then his expression turned to stone as he gazed out of the window.

There they were, Reilly and his new colleague, emerging from the nightclub. Leeman sipped his tea as he watched them stroll along the quay. When they were sufficiently far away, he took a last sip and got to his feet. The waitress was eyeing him from across the cafe, looking faintly alarmed.

"Got to dash," Leeman called out to her. "Lovely tea.

Shame I can't stay." He tossed a pound coin onto the table as a tip, then he marched for the door.

Across the road, he passed the door to The Icebox nightclub without stopping, then he turned into a narrow alley that ran alongside. The place had to have a back entrance, and he soon came to a tall wooden gate set into the wall. It was locked, and though he could reach the top, it had been festooned with barbed wire.

Never mind. Looking for exits and entrances was never a waste of time; you never knew when you might need to beat a hasty retreat.

Returning to the main entrance, he found the front door unlocked and slipped inside. It was dingy, the furniture draped in shadows, and that was excellent.

Silently, he went to the bar, listening to the activity coming from behind it. Glass bottles clinked and rattled, and a male voice sang softly, the inane lyrics belonging to some dreadful pop song or other.

Leeman risked a peek. The young man squatted on his haunches, intent on his task as he filled a shelf with bottled beers. Leeman considered joining the young man behind the bar, but it looked cramped back there, and he liked to have space to work.

There was no alternative. The mountain must go to Mohammed. Leeman cleared his throat loudly, and the effect was immediate.

"Bloody hell!" The young man spun around and stood up, his right fist clenched and ready. Good. This was going to be fun.

"Who the hell are you?" the young man demanded. "You shouldn't be in here. Out!"

Leeman offered him a gentle smile. The young man had a handsome face. What a pity.

"I said *out!*" The young man leaned forward, pointing to the door. "Now! Before I—"

Leeman never found out what the young man was threatening to do. Reaching up with both hands, his movements too fast to follow, he grabbed the young man by the shoulders and pulled his head down hard, slamming his face into the bar.

The cartilage in the young man's nose snapped with a satisfying crunch, and when Leeman lifted the poor fellow's head, he saw eyes dulled by pain and blood pouring from the man's nose and lips to streak his smooth skin.

"Oh dear," Leeman said smoothly. "Now, let's have no more shouting. Instead, we'll talk in a more civilised way, and then nothing like that needs to happen again. Okay?"

The young man swallowed hard and tried to speak, but Leeman placed a finger against the man's bruised and bleeding lips.

"Hush now."

Leeman pulled a clean tissue from his pocket and offered it, but the young man simply stared at him, his eyes welling with tears.

"Take it." Leeman waved the tissue in the air. "You need it, my friend."

The young man took the tissue and held it over his lips, gasping in pain.

"What's your name?" Leeman asked gently.

"Freddie. But please, don't—"

"Now, now," Leeman interrupted. "You're going to be okay. I know it hurts, but you're young and fit. You'll be right as rain in no time, believe me. It looks worse than it is."

"What do you want?" Freddie asked, his voice wavering.

Leeman sighed, contented. "There. We've come to the point already. Isn't that wonderful?" Without waiting for a reply, he said, "Those policemen—what did they want to know? Who were they looking for?"

Conflicting emotions clouded Freddie's expression, but fear won the day. Leeman could see it in the young man's eyes. He could smell it coming off him. It was almost beautiful.

"They asked about a girl," Freddie mumbled. "Lynsey. And her boyfriend."

Leeman watched Freddie carefully. Sadly, the silly boy was holding something back. Leeman took a breath and let it out slowly, then he placed his hands on the bar and leaned in, his eyes boring into Freddie's.

"There's something else, Freddie, something you're not telling me, and I find that very disappointing. Very disappointing indeed."

"They asked about Mank, but I didn't tell them anything, I swear."

Leeman raised an eyebrow. "Mank?"

"You don't know him?"

Leeman shook his head, and Freddie let out a shaky breath.

"I thought... I thought maybe you worked for him."

"Do I look like I work for the kind of lowlife who hangs around in a dump like this?"

It was Freddie's turn to shake his head.

"I don't associate with criminals or thugs or..." Leeman looked thoughtful. "What shall we call them? I know, ne'er do wells." He laughed quietly to himself. "I am a freelance contractor, Freddie, a specialist. One of my areas of expertise is the extraction of information. It can be a messy business, drawn out and painful, or it can go easily. I assume you'd prefer the latter, so you're going to tell me everything you know about this Mank person, including where to find him."

Freddie ran his tongue over his bloodstained lips, and then he began to talk.

Two minutes later, Leeman put his hand in his pocket and pulled something out. Freddie flinched, but Leeman had only a black leather wallet in his hand. Tossing a few ten-pound notes onto the bar, he said, "Freddie, go home. Get yourself cleaned up, and then go out and buy yourself some new clothes. You need to smarten yourself up because you'll be looking for a new job. You don't work here anymore."

"But I can't just—"

"You can and you will," Leeman interrupted. "Telephone whatever reptile runs this place and tell him you're done. Make an excuse if you like, but tell him you have no choice which, incidentally, happens to be true. If I see you around here again, I will be displeased, and you don't want that."

Leeman stepped back and looked around the room. "You don't want to be stuck in here, Freddie. At best, it's what I can only describe as a shit hole. Move on." Focusing his cold gaze on Freddie once again, he added, "Do you understand?"

"Yes. I don't even like it here." With trembling fingers, he picked up the money from the bar.

"What do you say?" Leeman intoned.

"Erm, thanks?"

"Good lad. Manners cost nothing." Leeman sent the lad

an avuncular smile, and then he walked out and kept moving, heading back to his car.

The fresh air awakened his appetite, and he considered his options for lunch. He could afford the time. Dennis Mankowich would not be hard to find.

13

Back at Heavitree police station, Spiller and Reilly pulled up their chairs and gathered around the desk of Detective Superintendent John Chisholm.

"Dennis Mankowich," Chisholm murmured. "I wondered when that little tosspot would surface again."

Reilly sent Spiller an I-told-you-so look. To Chisholm, he said, "There wasn't much on the PNC: a couple of arrests for GBH and three for common assault, but nothing stuck. He's never seen the inside of a courtroom."

"Don't I know it," Chisholm muttered. "I had him for GBH a couple of years back. It was a sure thing. The victim was a young doctor. The poor sod was on a night out with a few mates from the hospital when he saw some bloke taking a beating. The doctor stepped in and tried to help the guy on the ground. Mank was the one doing the kicking, and he did not appreciate someone trying to spoil his fun. In front of half a dozen witnesses, he turned on the doctor and beat the hell out of him, then he walked away."

"Bastard," Reilly said. "How come he didn't get sent down?"

"I thought we had him," Chisholm replied. "You couldn't ask for better witnesses than doctors and nurses, but Mank had an even bigger crowd who swore blind he'd been at a darts match on the other side of the river. We'd have taken it to court, but one by one, our best witnesses changed their stories. It was dark, they said, so they couldn't be sure who they'd seen. Somebody had got to them, and that was the end of it."

His tale over, Chisholm grimaced.

"Is he part of a gang?" Reilly asked.

"Worse; he's part of a family. The Mankowich clan are from the arse-end of Eastern Europe, Christ knows where, but they've made themselves very cosy around here. We've had a dozen of them through the custody suite, and we've managed to send one or two down, but it's never easy with that lot."

Spiller frowned at the tone of Chisholm's condemnation, and it didn't go unnoticed.

"Don't look at me like that," Chisholm said. "I've got nothing against people who come to this country legally. Good, hardworking people, most of them. But there are bad people all over the world, and if some of them come over here, I for one am not going to roll out the red carpet. A criminal is a criminal, no matter where they're from, and I treat them all the same. Got it?"

Spiller had the sense to stay quiet, but he nodded in what he hoped was a contrite manner.

"What happened to the doctor?" Reilly asked.

"He was okay in the end. He had a concussion and a couple of broken ribs. He needed a few stitches, but he made a full recovery. I think he moved away to Norfolk. You can't blame him."

"There was an address for Mank on the computer, but

it was from a couple of years ago," Spiller said. "What are the chances he's still there?"

"Buddie Lane," Chisholm replied. "Have you ever heard of a more inappropriate address for a mindless thug?"

"You couldn't make it up," Reilly said. To Spiller, he added, "It's in St. Thomas. A residential area. Lots of semi-detached houses and not much else. A nicely anonymous kind of place."

Chisholm folded his hands in his lap. "You could take a trip over there, but I doubt he'll be at the same address. From what I recall, he was renting the house from an uncle, so he might well have moved on. But before we go knocking on any more doors, what's the bigger picture? What are we looking at, Paddy?"

"At this stage, I'm not too sure," Reilly replied. "We're no nearer to finding out what happened at Lynsey's flat. The uniforms have been door to door, but they haven't found anything very much. A couple of neighbours thought they might've heard a vehicle door being slammed shut, but nobody bothered to look outside, so we've got no eyewitnesses."

"I don't like it," Chisholm said. "Ollie drew a blank with the hospitals, and I've had him tracing Lynsey's financials, but it's not good news. Her last cash withdrawal was early Saturday evening, and there's been nothing since, so she hasn't used her cards or taken out any cash."

"How much did she take out on Saturday?" Spiller asked.

Chisholm pointed at him. "Good question, Tim, but it was only twenty-five quid. Enough for a night out, a bag of chips and a taxi home, but not enough to live on, not for long at any rate. By the end of the night, she wouldn't have had enough for a train ticket."

"Unless she prepared everything in advance," Reilly suggested. "But then why would she go out with her friends if she was planning on running away?"

"It could've been a smokescreen or one last fling," Spiller said. "A way of saying goodbye to her old life before she headed off for a new one."

Chisholm shook his head. "This isn't *Play for Today*, Tim. People aren't half so dramatic as they make out on the telly. If Lynsey wanted to take off, there was nothing stopping her. She has resources, she has a family with money. She'd have done it properly. She wouldn't have stranded herself at Exeter St David's in the dead of night, shivering on the platform with no money and no bags, waiting hours for the next train." Chisholm paused. "Assume the worst. We're looking at murder or kidnapping, possibly with a sexual motive."

"I'm with you there, guv," Reilly said. "One hundred percent."

Chisholm looked to Spiller. "You've seen her flat, what do you think, Tim?"

"I agree."

Chisholm waited for a moment as if expecting more, but when nothing was forthcoming, he seemed secretly pleased.

"Right, lads, here's a few questions for you. If someone's taken her, where did they do it? If it was at her flat, why didn't the girl downstairs hear anything? The sound of a vehicle door slamming doesn't amount to much. That could've been anybody. If she was taken in the street nearby, why did none of the neighbours notice?"

"I don't know, guv," Reilly admitted.

"We haven't found out who lives on the ground floor

yet," Spiller said. "I can look into that, guv. Mr Clifford ought to have the resident's contact details."

"Didn't you get those when you spoke to Francis?" Chisholm asked.

Reilly tilted his head, abashed. "Sorry, guv. I didn't think of it at the time, but we'll chase it up."

"Good, but that's not like you, Paddy. You normally dot every I and cross every T."

"I slipped up. I won't make excuses, but at that stage, we were looking at a bog standard MisPer. Things have changed."

Chisholm nodded. "You said her flat might've been searched. Have forensics come up with anything?"

"Not as far as I know," Reilly replied. "There's a lot for them to go through, but it's about time they got their arses in gear."

"I'll see what I can do," Chisholm said. "At least we have Mankowich's prints on file. I'll tell them to be on the lookout." He paused. "Let's keep our powder dry as far as Mank is concerned. Don't go to his address yet. Let's see what kind of case we can build. Show Mankowich's photo to Carter and see if he'll confirm that Mank hit him. Make sure you get Carter's statement on the record. But first, talk to Francis Clifford's wife. You said Francis was vague about his daughter's friends; her mum might have more of an idea."

"Yeah, he said as much," Reilly replied. "Mothers and daughters can be close."

"Maybe, although I met Diana Clifford at a charity do, and I happen to know she's not Lynsey's mum," Chisholm said. "She's Francis Clifford's second wife, and quite a bit younger than him."

"How much younger?" Spiller asked.

"A gentleman doesn't inquire," Chisholm replied. "Regardless of her age, she's sharp as they come, so she might be able to give you some insight into Lynsey's state of mind. Paddy, you know the drill. Was Lynsey unhappy about anything, had anybody been bothering her, was she okay for money, did she have problems at work?"

Spiller surreptitiously took out his notebook and began making notes. Seeing the others watching him, he said, "I don't want to miss anything. There's nothing wrong with my memory, but this is my first proper case. I want to do it right."

Chisholm seemed to think this was entertaining, so Spiller kept his head down, scribbling away at top speed.

"Get the names of Lynsey's friends, as many as you can," Chisholm went on. "Trace them, talk to them, find out what they saw. If there's a history of arguments between Lynsey and Tony Carter, we need to know about it. Did he ever lose control, did he throw crockery, did he get a bit handy with his fists? We need chapter and verse."

Looking up from his notes, Spiller said, "Is Carter our prime suspect?"

Chisholm shook his head. "You're jumping the gun, Tim. If Lynsey turns up dead, we'll set up a team and go all out to catch her killer. If that happens, your role will change, but we'll cross that bridge when we come to it." To Reilly, he said, "Is there anything you need, or are you all set?"

"I'm good to go," Reilly replied. "I'll visit Mrs Clifford right away." He hesitated. "I'm happy for Tim to tag along. From what her husband said, Mrs Clifford is in a bit of a state, and Tim has a nice touch with the ladies."

Spiller blinked in surprise. "Have I?"

"Yeah. You were good with Carol Whitaker," Reilly said with a grin. "You calmed her down. It's what comes of being a happily married man. You could give lessons. Most of us are between wives at the moment."

"Cheeky sod," Chisholm muttered. "I've been married for years."

"How many years, exactly?" Reilly asked.

Chisholm pulled a face. "How the hell should I know? When my good lady wife tells me it's our anniversary, I believe her. We go to the Berni Inn, we have prawn cocktail, a nice T-bone steak and black forest gateau. Throw in a bottle of plonk and all is well with the world."

Reilly mimed applause. "Here he is, folks, the last of the great romantics."

"Bugger off, you two," Chisholm said. "Go and do your job and leave me to do mine." He plucked a sheet of paper from his in tray and began reading.

Reilly and Spiller stood, but as they wheeled their chairs back into place, Chisholm added, "Watch your step with Diana Clifford."

There was something in his tone that made Reilly and Spiller stop and turn to look back at Chisholm.

"She's very glam, is Diana," Chisholm went on, the sheet of paper in his hands apparently forgotten. "But make no mistake, she's nobody's fool, and like her husband, she has friends in high places. Put a foot wrong, and we'll all be getting hauled over the coals. I do not relish that prospect, not one bit."

"We'll be careful," Reilly said.

"You better had be," Chisholm replied, and it seemed to Spiller that Chisholm's cold gaze had settled on him.

Unsure how to respond, Spiller contented himself with a nod of acknowledgement, then he put the chair back where it belonged and fell in behind Reilly as he made for the door.

14

LYNSEY SAT on the edge of the bed and hung her head. The blindfold was still on, and her wrists and ankles were still bound together, but at least she wasn't tied to the bed anymore.

Her trips to the toilet were becoming routine. He'd release her from the bed then lead her, still blindfolded, into a small, stinking bathroom and tell her to get on with it. She'd hear him lurking nearby, but her bodily needs overpowered the bitter sense of humiliation.

This time, though, had been different. After the bathroom, he'd given her a bottle of water and a sandwich. She'd wanted to throw it in his face, but the smell of bread and cheese had been too tempting, and she'd devoured it in seconds.

Afterwards, he hadn't told her to lie down. Instead, he'd tied her hands and feet, linking her bound wrists to the rope around her ankles. It was better than being on the bed, but she couldn't lift her hands to her face, and she definitely couldn't remove her blindfold. She'd tried, but it had been useless.

Lynsey stood on shaky legs and took a tiny step forward. There was just enough give in the rope around her ankles to allow her to shuffle along the floor. Slowly, she made her unsteady way across the room until she met a wall. The wall was rough, like unplastered bricks, and very cold to the touch. The whole place was damp, as if she might be in a cellar or an outbuilding.

Slowly, she sidestepped until she met a door. It was solid metal and felt sturdy, though rust or loose paint flaked beneath her fingertips. She found the handle and turned it, listening with bated breath as the mechanism squeaked, but the door didn't open. She pushed and pulled the handle with all her might. Something metallic rattled on the other side, but the door barely budged a millimetre.

Bloody hell! Lynsey tried again, but it was no good. He'd warned her not to shout or hammer on the door. He'd said no one would hear apart from him, and he'd be back to deal with her if she made a noise. But maybe he'd been bluffing. Maybe he'd just been trying to frighten her into submission.

To hell with that!

Lynsey tipped back her head and yelled for help, shouting louder than she thought possible. She called out over and over until her voice cracked and tears flowed down her cheeks. And when she could shout no more, she listened, her head resting against the door.

There was nothing except the distant sound of a dog barking. Something, at least, had heard her. But as she listened, a door slammed somewhere. She heard nothing for a few long seconds, but then slow footsteps grew closer and closer.

Lynsey backed away.

It was him.

15

"I'M GLAD YOU'RE DRIVING," Spiller said. "These lanes all look the same to me."

"You get to know your way around," Reilly replied. "But God help you if you don't know how to reverse around a bend. There's a lot of single-track roads, and if you meet a tractor coming the other way, you won't have much choice."

"I can handle a car."

"Good. Anyway, if I'm not mistaken, there's a right turn coming up any minute now."

The address of Francis Clifford's house had meant nothing to Spiller, but Reilly had assured him it was on the edge of the city, not far from Pennsylvania Road, and he seemed to know where he was going. A lane opened on the right, and Reilly braked as he threw the Ford Escort into the junction, changing gear and accelerating away. The leafy lane was winding, the bends blind, but Reilly took it all in his stride, sending his car speeding along the tarmac.

Spiller said nothing, but he was quietly impressed.

Perhaps it was time he brushed up his own driving skills after all.

They met no oncoming traffic, and it wasn't long before Reilly pulled into the driveway of a large house.

"What do you reckon?" Reilly asked as they climbed from the car.

Spiller ran his gaze over the house. The walls had been painted a pale shade of blue, its windowsills and cornerstones picked out in white. The windows were small, their panes subdivided by diagonal strips of lead, and the house was topped with terracotta tiles.

"I think," Spiller began, "that it looks out of place. It ought to be by the sea."

Reilly sent him a sideways glance as though he didn't quite know what to make of this. "It must've cost a packet, that's for sure. The salvage business must be booming."

"Maybe, but I wouldn't want to have his mortgage, not with interest rates being what they are. They say there could be a recession on the way."

"No, John Major will sort it out, don't you worry."

"I didn't have you down as a Tory, Paddy."

"Why not? Someone's got to take law and order seriously. Major's all right. He's an ordinary bloke like you and me. He never went to university, you know. He left school at 16."

Spiller heard the enthusiasm in Reilly's tone and let the matter drop. He'd never had much time for the Conservative Party himself, but he needed to fit in, and politics was a topic best left until he was more sure of his place in the team.

"Anyway, let's focus on the job in hand," Reilly went on. "Remember, I'm taking the lead, but you can chip in as we go, okay?"

"No problem."

Together, they strode up to the front door. Reilly rang the bell, and a few seconds later, the door was answered by a tall, slender woman wearing a long plaid skirt and a pale pink poncho. Her auburn hair fell to her shoulders in loose curls, and she arched a perfectly shaped eyebrow as she looked down at them in silence, her disapproving gaze making it clear they weren't welcome.

Reilly smiled. "Hello, Mrs Clifford. Sorry to bother you."

"Is that so?"

As if taken aback, Reilly nodded dumbly, and Spiller stepped in.

"I'm Detective Constable Timothy Spiller of the Devon and Cornwall Police, and this is my colleague, Detective Sergeant Patrick Reilly. We're here to talk about Lynsey."

A flicker of interest registered in Mrs Clifford's eyes. "Is there any news? Have you found her?"

"Not yet, I'm afraid, Mrs Clifford," Reilly replied. "We're doing our best, and we're pursuing a number of lines of inquiry."

"That's all very well, but why are you here?"

"We need to get as much background information on Lynsey as possible," Reilly said. "The more detail we can get, the better. It'll help us to put together a picture of Lynsey's life."

"I don't see what good that'll do. It would be better if you spoke with my husband." She stepped back and took hold of the door's edge as if to swing it shut.

"Mrs Clifford, you *can* help," Spiller said, injecting as much urgency into his voice as he could.

Mrs Clifford stared at him, her hand still on the door's edge. "How so?"

Spiller held her gaze. "We don't yet know what's

happened to Lynsey, but someone within her social circle will have seen or heard something that could help us find her. They might not have realised the significance of what they've seen, but we can piece it together, and then we can bring Lynsey home."

Mrs Clifford eyed Spiller for a moment, then she opened the door wide. "You'd better come in."

"Thank you," Reilly said, and they stepped into the house.

From the outside, Spiller had expected an entrance hall of grand proportions, but the house was old and the hallway was narrow and dim, the only light coming from a small leaded window beside the front door.

"Coffee?" Mrs Clifford asked.

"Please," Reilly replied. "If it's no trouble."

"No trouble at all. This way."

She led them toward the back of the house and through a painted wooden door. Spiller stepped through and his eyes went wide. If the hallway had hinted at a bygone age, the kitchen went all out to compensate. The room was an extension to the house, the ceiling sloped, and Spiller guessed that it ranged across the entire back of the building. Three large skylights bathed the modern fitted kitchen in a warm glow, and the place exuded a sense of light and space.

If only Sheila could see this, Spiller thought. It was a dream kitchen, but while Sheila would turn the place into a whirlwind of activity, delicious smells filling the air, this room looked as though it had never been used. It was almost clinical in its sterility. There was not so much as a bowl of fruit to break up the monotony of its polished granite worktops.

"It'll have to be instant," Mrs Clifford said. "I've run out of the real stuff, and I haven't been to the shops today, for obvious reasons."

"Instant is fine for us," Reilly said. "Thank you."

Mrs Clifford didn't reply. She simply produced three mugs from one cupboard and a jar of coffee granules from another. She spooned coffee into the mugs and filled them with water directly from a tap.

Seeing Spiller's surprise, she said, "It's boiling water. I'd have been happy with a kettle, but Francis insisted we have all the bells and whistles. Milk? I've no sugar, I'm afraid."

Before Spiller could reply, Reilly said, "We'll take it as it comes, thanks."

Mrs Clifford passed their drinks, and Reilly took a sip before smiling appreciatively. "Gold Blend. Just like the advert."

"I don't watch the television." Mrs Clifford averted her gaze from Reilly as though she'd lost interest in him, and Spiller found himself the object of her attention. "You said I can help," she went on. "What do you want to know?"

"To begin with, and I'm sorry if this sounds insensitive, but we'd like to know about Lynsey's state of mind," Spiller said. "How has she been recently?"

Mrs Clifford shook her head. "I know what you're hinting at, but there's no way Lynsey has harmed herself. She would never do anything like that. She's a strong young woman, and she knows her own mind. She'd never put Francis and me through that much pain."

Spiller nodded thoughtfully. "I hear what you're saying, Mrs Clifford, but we all have our troubles. Has there been anything bothering Lynsey? Any difficulties with her friends or her boyfriend?"

"Not as far as I'm aware." She paused. "Have you talked to Tony Carter?"

"We have," Reilly replied. "According to him, Lynsey broke up with him on Saturday night."

Mrs Clifford's expression froze.

"Is that a surprise to you?" Spiller asked.

"Yes. It's the first I've heard of it. I've met Tony, of course, but I thought he was a permanent fixture. I don't know what else to say."

"What were your impressions of Tony Carter?" Reilly said.

The corner of Mrs Clifford's lips curled downward in a display of disinterest. "We didn't interfere in Lynsey's choices."

"With respect, Mrs Clifford, that's not an answer to the question," Reilly pointed out. "What did you think of him?"

There was a pause before Mrs Clifford replied, and Spiller detected a faint flush of colour in her otherwise creamy complexion. Was that due to the way Reilly had pressed her to answer, or did she harbour some feelings for Tony? She was, perhaps, ten years or so older than her stepdaughter, but in the scheme of things, that wasn't an insurmountable age gap. And Diana Clifford had looked after herself, that was plain to see. Spiller suspected he wouldn't have to look far before he found a pair of Reeboks and a yoga mat.

"Well, how shall I put it?" Mrs Clifford began, "Tony isn't quite what I would've hoped for in a son-in-law. He and Lynsey seemed very fond of each other, but I often felt they were mismatched. They come from very different backgrounds, and that doesn't always work out. Lynsey was never spoiled, we made sure of that, but I can't deny she had certain privileges. She likes to stand on her own two feet, and I applaud her for that, but let's be honest: she's never wanted for anything. Tony, on the other hand, hasn't had the best start in life. His father was a brute."

"Did you know Tony's father?" Reilly asked.

"Heavens, no. It was just something I heard. I suppose Lynsey must've told me about it."

"Does Lynsey confide in you a lot?" Spiller said.

"Not especially. She's always been an independent young woman."

Reilly raised his eyebrows. "I'd have thought you had a lot to talk about. After all, you and Lynsey are quite similar in age."

Now there was a definite rush of blood to Mrs Clifford's cheeks. "What are you implying, that I married a man old enough to be my father, is that it?"

"What my colleague is trying to say, is that Lynsey might have found you more relatable than an older person," Spiller said quickly. "Perhaps she valued you as a role model. You say that Lynsey's strong-minded and independent; I imagine that many people might say the same about you."

Mrs Clifford made a dismissive noise in her throat, but her gaze softened as she regarded Spiller. "Are you married, Detective Constable?"

"Yes. For about a year."

"Children?"

Spiller shook his head. "Not yet. One day, maybe. I hope so, anyway."

Mrs Clifford sighed. "I said the same once, but it wasn't to be. Now that I have Lynsey in my life, I've been given a chance. I may not be her biological mother, but Lynsey is very special to me. She still feels the loss of her dear mum. I don't know if Francis told you, but his first wife died five years ago. Cancer. We do our best to keep her memory alive. I can never take her place, and I'd never try. I don't have the mother and daughter relationship I dreamed of, but it's as close as I'll ever get."

"I understand," Spiller said softly. "I'm sorry about our earlier questions. We ought to have been more sensitive. I can only apologise."

"Yes, the same goes for me," Reilly put in. "Apologies."

Mrs Clifford had grown downcast, but she took a sip of her coffee and seemed to rouse herself. "You're only doing your job, and you're looking for Lynsey. That's all that matters."

"We'd like to talk to Lynsey's friends," Spiller said. "Might you be able to give us some names?"

"Yes, I think so. I'll try, anyway. I might only know first names or nicknames, but I'll see what I can come up with. Leave it with me and I'll give you a call."

"That would be very helpful," Reilly said, "but it would be even better to have some names right away. Do you happen to know if there was anyone she usually went out with?"

"There was Mel and Ashley; they were mentioned a lot. I can't recall their surnames, but I do know that Mel was a friend from work. They were in the same department at County Hall. I believe Ashley works in a supermarket. I think it was Safeway, but that's not much help, is it?"

"It's all very useful," Spiller replied. "We should be able to find them, but if you remember their surnames, we'd be grateful if you could give us a call."

Mrs Clifford nodded slowly, and for the first time, sadness crept into her expression. "You will find Lynsey, won't you? If we don't see her soon, I... I don't know what we'll do. We're going spare."

"We'll follow every lead," Reilly said. "You've given us some valuable information, and we'll do everything we can." Reilly hesitated. "There's something I have to ask."

"Go on."

"As far as you know, was there anyone who might wish Lynsey harm?"

"No. Of course not. Lynsey gets on with everyone. She's a good person."

"How about you and Mr Clifford?" Reilly said. "Do either of you have any enemies?"

Mrs Clifford shook her head firmly, but Spiller saw a flash of emotion in her eyes.

"Are you sure about that, Mrs Clifford?" Spiller asked. "Your husband runs a business, and he must have rivals."

"What could that possibly have to do with Lynsey? Francis keeps his work and his family separate. He would never do anything that might put Lynsey in harm's way. He dotes on that girl."

"Nevertheless, someone may be using Lynsey as a way to hit back at Francis," Reilly said. "I know it's unpleasant to think about, but we have to consider every possibility."

"You'll have to ask Francis. But you've talked to him already, haven't you?"

Reilly nodded. "Yes, but our inquiry has progressed since then. We'll need to talk to your husband again soon."

"Will you let us know if you... if you find anything?"

"We will," Reilly said. "But I think we'd better get going, Mrs Clifford. The sooner we hit the streets, the sooner we'll find Lynsey."

"Of course. I'll see you out."

Mrs Clifford led them to the door, closing it behind them as soon as they'd stepped outside. She didn't say goodbye, but Spiller looked back and caught a glimpse of Mrs Clifford, her face framed by the door as it closed. That brief look was enough to see that she was utterly distraught, the tears running freely down her face.

He'd thought her haughty and distant when they'd met, but she'd been holding it together, pouring all her energy into keeping up appearances while her world fell apart. Perhaps she'd been in denial, hoping against hope that the next person on her doorstep would be Lynsey, safe and well. But their visit had robbed her of that meagre comfort.

Diana Clifford had understood the subtext of their questions, with their weasel words such as 'harm' and 'enemies', and a crueller set of possibilities might well have taken root in her mind. Diana Clifford might not be Lynsey's biological mother, but alone in that huge house on the edge of the city, she'd be wrestling with the worst fears a parent can ever know.

As if picking up on his mood, Reilly said, "It's very sad."

"It is. We've got to find Lynsey, Paddy. We've got to."

"We will, lad. Keep the faith. At least the names Mrs Clifford gave us tie in with what Tony Carter said."

"Lynsey's friends, Mel Parker and Ashley Hawkins."

"That's right." Reilly checked his watch. "I don't know where the day's gone, but by the time we get back into town, I reckon County Hall will have shut up shop. That leaves us with a trip to the supermarket, and I can only think of one Safeway in Exeter."

"Sidwell Street."

"Well done, lad."

"I've been in for groceries," Spiller admitted. "It's not bad."

"I can never find a damned thing in those places," Reilly said. "We'd better hope we have more luck with Lynsey's friend Ashley."

16

Barry Leeman parked his BMW on Commercial Road and strolled along the street until he came to The Bishop Blaize. Set back from the main road, the place looked like a couple of houses had been knocked together and turned into a pub. A group of three men were sitting on a picnic bench beside the entrance, pints in front of them, and Leeman made his way to the front door. But before he could open it, one of the men called out to him, "It's closed."

Leeman turned with a smile. The man was heavyset and might once have been strong, but he'd gone to seed. His stubbled jowls sagged, and his bald head showed rolls of fat on the back of his neck. Dressed in a black leather jacket, and with a heavy gold chain around his neck, he fancied himself a man to be reckoned with.

Keeping his tone friendly and polite, Leeman said, "Are you sure?"

The man narrowed his eyes but said nothing.

Leeman gestured to the table. "You seem to have been served."

Next to the heavyset man, a wiry older man jutted his

chin. When he spoke, his voice rasped in his throat and the cadence of his speech carried the remnants of a European accent.

"Didn't you hear him? He said it's closed. Now bugger off."

"That's not very polite. I'm not looking for any trouble, gents. If it's all the same to you, I'll step inside and see what the landlord has to say."

The heavyset man grunted and began getting to his feet. Perhaps the beer had made him clumsy, because he was having difficulty extricating his bulk from the picnic bench's frame.

Leeman turned to face him. This wasn't how he'd wanted to play it, but a thrill ran through him at the thought of the big man crumpling to the ground.

Unfortunately, the third man, the youngest of the three by far, broke into laughter, spoiling the moment.

"Leave the poor guy alone," the young man said. "He didn't mean nothing. He's just after a pint."

"This is nothing to laugh about," the first man growled, finally freeing himself from the bench. "He's got to learn some respect."

The younger man made a downward motion with his hands. "Go back to your pint, Tommy. I'll deal with this." Draining his pint and jumping to his feet, the empty glass in his hand, the young man turned to face Leeman.

"The pub's not open yet, pal. It's too early. Try somewhere else." He grinned, adding, "Before I let Uncle Tommy teach you a lesson."

Leeman studied the young man, rapidly taking in every detail. The man's hair was too long to be tidy, and it carried a sheen of grease, as though he'd inexpertly applied some kind of hair wax. His features were mean and narrow, his skin pale and his blue eyes watery. He'd attempted to grow a goatee without much success, and his black bomber jacket was a size too large for his thin frame, but he carried himself with a certain loose-limbed poise. His posture said he was stronger than he appeared at first glance, and his glassy stare hinted at the likelihood of sudden violence.

It's almost certainly him, Leeman decided. The nightclub barman had provided an excellent description, and this man fitted the bill in every particular. There was little doubt. He was looking at Dennis Mankowich, otherwise known as Mank.

"You know what?" Leeman said. "I've just remembered that I've been here before, and I didn't much care for it. I wouldn't drink in here if you paid me."

The young man covered his confusion with an incredulous laugh. "What's your game, pal? Are you some kind of nutter?"

Leeman considered. "It's hard to say, but it's a distinct possibility."

The heavyset man lumbered forward to stand beside his nephew. "He's taking the piss, Dennis. Don't let him talk to you like that."

Excellent, Leeman thought. He'd definitely found Mank. Aloud, he said, "I didn't mean to cause any offence, gents. I was simply trying to answer your question, but I've spoken out of turn, so let me buy a drink. I can see the place is open for you, at least, so have a round on me." Leeman's hand moved fast, and he was suddenly holding a twenty-pound note. Offering it to Mank, he added, "Please, it's the least I can do."

Mank's gaze flicked to the money before refocusing on Leeman. "I could take your money and then give you a kicking anyway."

"You could," Leeman said. "But what would be the point? I've learned my lesson already. I didn't get to go inside, and I'm twenty pounds down, so I'd say I've lost, wouldn't you?"

"You've lost your mind, mate," Mank said. "You want to get your head seen to."

Leeman nodded. "It has been said."

Mank sneered. "Ah, you're not worth bothering with." He snatched the twenty-pound note. "Go on, bugger off. And don't let me see you around here again, understand?"

"Oh yes. I get the message. You won't see me, I can promise you that." Leeman stepped back. "Well, this must be my lucky day."

"Oh yeah? How do you work that out, pal?"

Leeman simply smiled, then he turned and walked away.

"Nutter!" Mank called after him, and Leeman laughed quietly. He'd be watching Dennis Mankowich, but he'd be true to his word, at first, anyway. At their next encounter, the young man would not see him; not until it was too late. And then there would, indeed, be a lesson handed out. Whether Mank learned anything from the experience was a moot point; he was unlikely to survive it.

17

THE SAFEWAY SUPERMARKET WAS BUSY, packed with shoppers stocking up on the way home from work. A few harried parents dragged kids in their wake, the adults pushing trollies with grim determination while the kids dawdled along the aisles, bored and listless.

Reilly went up to one of the checkouts and showed his ID to the female shop assistant, asking to see the manager. A moment later, a call went out on the Tannoy:

"This is a staff announcement. Would Mr Everett come to checkout three, please, where two gentlemen from the police are waiting to see him. Thank you."

A few shoppers cast glances at Reilly and Spiller, and both men stood with their hands in their pockets, shuffling their feet in an effort not to look like police officers.

"I didn't think she'd say that," Reilly muttered. "I thought they had a secret code for these things so as not to cause a fuss."

"I'm not sure whether that's true," Spiller replied. "But if there are any shoplifters about, they've just had the fright of their lives."

They didn't have to wait long before a middle-aged man in a short-sleeved white shirt and tie hurried toward the checkouts.

The assistant on checkout three tilted her head to indicate Reilly and Spiller, and he leaned in to say something to her. From the stern look on his face, he wasn't best pleased about the unsubtle message on the Tannoy.

That done, he strutted over to meet the policemen, his expression serious and his movements stiff. The word 'uptight' sprang to Spiller's mind, but he pushed the thought aside. It was important to keep an open mind.

"Hello," the man said. "I'm Mr Everett, the manager here. I understand you wish to see me, but before we go on, can I see some ID, please?"

I was right the first time, Spiller thought as they presented their warrant cards.

"Very well. We can talk in my office. If you'll—"

"Actually, we only need to speak to one of your employees," Reilly interrupted. "Her name is Ashley Hawkins. Is she at work today?"

Everett was put out, but he could hardly argue with two police officers, especially not in front of customers and staff. His lips pursed, he nodded. "Ashley's here, but what's this in connection with? Has she done something wrong?"

"Certainly not, sir," Spiller stated firmly, and Everett's mouth drooped as if in disappointment. He'd probably relished the prospect of handing an employee over to the police, and Spiller was determined to burst his bubble, adding, "We believe that Ashley is an important witness, and it's vital that we speak to her right away."

"In relation to what?"

"We cannot disclose that at this time, sir," Reilly said.

"All I can tell you is that we're investigating a serious crime, so if we can find somewhere to speak to Ashley in private, that would be appreciated."

Everett's lips moved as he decided what to say.

"This is an urgent matter," Spiller said. "Time is against us, so if you could take us to Ashley, we'd appreciate your assistance."

"Of course. This way." Everett led them through an unused checkout, releasing the extendable cordon and putting it back in place as soon as they'd passed through. He marched through the store, his gaze raking the aisles. "Ashley will be in the produce department, restocking the shelves."

Amid the rows of fresh produce, a young woman with her blonde hair tied back was busily rummaging among the vegetables. Spying Everett approaching, she renewed her efforts, saying, "I'll get to the bananas in a minute. Someone's messed up the mushrooms."

"Thank you, Ashley," Everett replied. "But these gentlemen wish to speak to you."

Ashley straightened her back and faced them, her eyebrows disappearing beneath her fringe.

Rocking back on his heels, Everett added, "They're from the police."

"Oh." Ashley stared at them blankly. "It's not my mum, is it? Is she..."

"It's nothing for you to worry about," Reilly said. "Ashley, do you know a woman by the name of Lynsey Clifford?"

"Yes, we're mates."

"Good," Reilly replied. "We'd like to chat with you for a few minutes, okay?"

"I'm supposed to be working." Ashley's gaze went to Everett.

"That's all right," Everett said. "You can show these gentlemen up to the break room. It'll be quiet about now, or it should be, anyway."

"Okay," Ashley murmured, "I'll try and be quick." To Reilly, she said, "You'd better follow me."

It only took a minute for Ashley to take them to a small, windowless room above the shop floor. The place was empty, and they sat on plastic chairs, Reilly and Spiller facing Ashley.

"Tell me about Lynsey," Reilly said. "Have you seen her recently?"

"Yeah, we see each other a lot. Most weekends. We go out and have a few drinks."

"Did you go out with her on Saturday night?" Reilly asked.

Ashley nodded. "We went to a couple of pubs in town, and we went to a club after."

"Have you seen Lynsey since then?" Reilly said.

Ashley thought for a moment. "No. We don't usually go out on Sundays, and I've been at work today." Ashley frowned. "What are you asking about Lynsey for?"

"It's a routine inquiry," Reilly replied. "How did things go on Saturday night? Talk us through it."

"I'll try. We started off at The Turk's Head on High Street, then we went to The Prospect."

"That's The Prospect Inn," Reilly explained for Spiller's benefit. "On the quayside."

"That's right," Ashley said. "We stayed there until closing time, then we went to The Icebox."

"Was Lynsey with you all evening?" Reilly asked.

"Yeah, but she didn't stay late. She went home before the rest of us."

Unable to keep quiet any longer, Spiller said, "Any idea why she left early?"

Ashley shook her head. "She didn't say, not to me, anyhow."

"Did she say goodbye before she left?" Spiller asked.

"No. I thought it was a bit off at the time. It's not like Lynsey to go home without telling anyone."

"So it was out of character," Spiller said. "Have you any idea what might have triggered the change in Lynsey's state of mind?"

"I don't know what you mean."

Spiller was about to rephrase his question when Reilly saved him the bother, "Did anyone upset Lynsey?"

"No. We had a few drinks and a laugh, the same as always."

"One witness said that Lynsey might've been unhappy toward the end of the evening," Reilly said.

Ashley appeared to think about this. "I wouldn't say unhappy. She said something about having a bad day at work. Her boss had told her off, apparently. Oh, and I think she might've had a row with her boyfriend, but that happened all the time."

"This would be Tony Carter," Spiller suggested.

"That's right. He gets a bit annoying when he's had a skinful, and he always has one too many."

"Annoying in what way?" Spiller asked.

Ashley wrinkled her nose. "You know, lad's stuff. Shouting daft things, acting full of himself, chatting up the girls, or trying to."

"Let me get this straight," Spiller began, "Tony Carter

was making advances to other girls in front of his long-time girlfriend."

"Yeah, but he's not the only one who does it. I know what my Keith is like."

"This would be Keith Osborne," Reilly suggested. "Your boyfriend."

Ashley's eyebrows rose. "Yeah. He's got what you might call a roving eye, but that's what men are like, isn't it?"

"Some men, maybe," Spiller admitted. "But not all."

Ashley studied him for a moment. "No, not all. But the nice ones are already engaged or married. Are you married?"

"Yes."

Ashley smiled. "You see. Unless you're very lucky, you end up with a bloke like my Keith or Tony Carter. Okay, they're not Mel Gibson, but at least they've got regular jobs, at least they don't—" Ashley broke off suddenly, closing her lips as if biting back her words.

"At least they don't what?" Spiller asked.

"I was going to say, at least they don't cheat, but with Tony, you can't say that. He messes around behind her back. I don't think Lynsey knows, but she's the only one who doesn't."

Spiller and Reilly shared a look.

"Any idea who Tony might've been seeing apart from Lynsey?" Reilly asked.

"I don't like to say."

"You can tell us," Reilly said. "It could be important."

Ashley chewed on her lower lip. "There've been a few, so I've heard, but the most serious one, the one that'd hurt Lynsey the most if she ever found out, is Mel. She's a friend of Lynsey's."

"This would be Mel Parker, Lynsey's workmate at the council," Reilly suggested.

"That's right. You wouldn't think it to look at her, but it's like they say, it's always the quiet ones, isn't it?"

"Ashley," Reilly began, "how sure are you that Tony and Mel were carrying on a relationship?"

"Totally. I've seen them together; more than once, as it goes." She shook her head in dismay. "One time, you'll never guess what they were doing. Only standing outside H. Samuel, looking at the rings in the window. I almost said something, but I thought I'd better not."

"And you're sure Lynsey didn't know?" Reilly asked.

"Of course she didn't. Lynsey thought she'd be getting engaged to Tony herself before too long. She talked about it often enough. It's really sad when you think about it. Tragic."

"Tragic?" Reilly said. "In what way?"

"Well, you know how it goes. When push came to shove, Tony would've dropped Mel like a shot. It was obvious."

"I'm not sure what you're getting at," Spiller said.

"Really? Work it out. Lynsey has money. She might work with Mel for now, but she doesn't need to, not really. Her family are well off. A bloke like Tony isn't going to walk away from that, is he?"

"I couldn't say," Spiller replied. "Earlier, you mentioned that Lynsey and Tony often have arguments. Tell us about that."

"There's not much to tell. It was bickering, really. A lot of fuss over nothing."

"Was there ever anything physical?" Spiller asked.

Ashley frowned. "You've got a funny way of asking

questions. Half the time, I don't know what you're getting at."

From the corner of his eye, Spiller saw Reilly stifling a grin. Spiller took a breath and tried again. "Apologies. What I'd like to know is if you ever saw Tony being aggressive or violent to Lynsey?"

"He didn't hit her. Never. She wouldn't have stood for that."

"Okay, but violence can take other forms," Spiller said. "Did he ever grab her, or restrain her in any way?"

"He might've dragged her off the dance floor or picked her up and run off with her, but that was just mucking around. He didn't... he didn't *hurt* her."

"Did he ever make her do anything she didn't want to?" Spiller asked.

"I don't know. I doubt it. Lynsey wouldn't put up with anything like that. She'd give as good as she got."

"I'll have to ask you to explain that," Spiller said. "Are you saying she could be violent to others?"

Ashley screwed up her features as though tasting something unpleasant. "Don't be daft. I mean, she doesn't mind telling somebody where to get off. She might be posh, but she has a sharp tongue when it suits her."

"Did she tell Tony off?" Spiller asked.

"Yeah, when he deserved it."

"And how did he take it?"

Ashley frowned as if puzzled.

"What I mean is, how did Tony react when Lynsey told him off?" Spiller said.

"I dunno. He just took it. He's always been besotted with that girl. He'd let her walk all over him."

Spiller was temporarily stumped. From what he'd seen of Tony Carter, there was no way he'd accept a dressing down from a woman. But then again, he'd known many a man make a fool of himself rather than lose a girlfriend. Perhaps Lynsey was Tony's blind spot: the weakness he refused to admit, even to himself.

Reilly cleared his throat and said, "Ashley, I'm going to ask you about someone else now. Do you know a man called Dennis Mankowich?"

"Mank. Everybody knows him."

"So I hear," Reilly said. "Did you see him on Saturday night?"

"Yeah, he was at the club. He's there every week."

"Did you see him with Lynsey?" Reilly asked.

"I don't think so." Ashley ran one hand along her upper arm as if warding off a shudder.

"You don't much like Dennis Mankowich, do you?" Spiller said.

"Not really. He kind of stares at you. He doesn't say anything, but it's the way he looks at you. He gives me the creeps."

"Did he ever talk to Lynsey or show an interest in her?" Spiller asked.

Ashley shook her head, then she stared at Spiller, wrinkles appearing at the corners of her eyes.

"There you go again, talking about Lynsey as if something's happened to her. What's all this about? You've got to tell me. I'm not saying another word until I know what's going on."

"Fair enough," Reilly said. "Ashley, I'm sorry to have to tell you this, but Lynsey is missing. We don't know the circumstances, but we're worried, and we're doing our best to find her."

Ashley dropped her gaze as if she could no longer look

at them. "You should've told me. You should've said that in the first place. Why didn't you tell me?"

"I'm sorry, but we had our reasons," Reilly replied. "You're upset, I know, but is there anything you can think of that might help us find Lynsey?"

"I don't know what to say. It's all…" Ashley's voice trailed away and she took several rapid breaths. When she went on, her tone betrayed her rising panic. "Have you tried her parents? Have you checked the hospitals?"

"That's all been taken care of," Spiller said gently. "We're doing everything we can, but we need your help, okay?"

"But what can I do? I don't know anything about it."

"When you were in the club, did you happen to notice if Lynsey went outside?" Spiller asked.

Ashley started to shake her head but changed her mind. "Maybe. I'd been on the Bacardi Breezers, so it was all a bit muddled, but now I think about it, I remember Tony looking for her. He was…" She hesitated. "He gets jealous. If he thinks someone's chatting her up, he barges in and throws his weight around."

"Did Tony go outside to look for Lynsey?" Reilly asked.

"I don't know. I didn't go outside until we all went home. I was having a good time. If only…" Ashley squeezed her eyes shut tight, then she sniffed and dabbed at her eyes with the backs of her hands. "I'm sorry. It's all too much. I can't think straight."

"It's okay, love, you've done very well," Reilly said. "We'll head off, but if you think of anything, or if you hear anything that might help, give us a call, okay?"

Reilly handed Ashley a card and she nodded.

"Take a few minutes, grab yourself a cup of tea," Reilly advised. "Put plenty of sugar in it. You've had a shock."

"I've got to get back to work."

"Never mind about that," Reilly said. "We'll have a word with your boss on the way out."

Reilly stood, Spiller following suit, and Ashley looked up at them. "Thank you. Please find her. She doesn't…" Ashley sobbed, covering her eyes with her hands.

Reilly patted her on the shoulder. "We'll find her, love, don't you worry."

"Will you be all right?" Spiller asked.

Ashley didn't reply, but Reilly nodded to Spiller and then made for the door. Spiller followed, but before he left the room, he looked back at Ashley. She was still sitting huddled, sobbing gently, her head in her hands. Something about the scene struck him as odd, but he couldn't put his finger on it. He gave one last glance around the room, and then he exited quietly and shut the door.

Reilly was already marching away, and Spiller set off to catch up. Something about Ashley still nagged at him, and he replayed their conversation in his head. Something wasn't right, but what was it?

Ashley's distress on hearing the bad news seemed genuine, but before then, there'd been a distinct lack of warmth and loyalty when she'd talked about Lynsey. He'd thought that women tended to look out for one another, but on Saturday night, this so-called friend had barely noticed when Lynsey left the nightclub alone.

Poor Lynsey, Spiller thought. *She was a fish out of water.* He knew what that was like. Lynsey's boyfriend might've cheated on her, and her friends might not have looked after her, but Lynsey had someone in her corner now. *I'll fight for her*, Spiller told himself, *No matter what.*

18

LYNSEY SAT on the bed and bowed her head. She wasn't sure whether the skin on her cheek was broken, but it stung like hell. She'd been lucky, he'd said, to get away with only a slap. If she made a fuss again, there'd be worse to come.

Lynsey sat in silence and shivered. It was getting colder and damper with every minute. It might be nighttime. God knows, she'd been in that hell hole for long enough.

With some difficulty, she lay down on the bed, slumping on her side. She felt drained. Part of her wanted to give up, to sleep. Anything was better than living through this nightmare.

She curled tight, pressing her knees against her chest as she tried to get comfortable, and she realised that, in this position, she could bring her hands closer to her face. She ought to have thought of it before, but she couldn't think straight most of the time, especially after she'd been allowed a drink of water. There was something in it, she was sure.

Forcing herself to concentrate, Lynsey tilted her head forward and tried to push the blindfold away, but it was on too tight, and she couldn't get a proper grip. There wasn't enough slack in the rope.

Still, she could get her wrists up to her mouth. She brushed her chin against the knot. From the way the rope had rubbed her wrists raw, she'd thought it would be rough, but it was smoother than she'd expected. It felt more like a cord. She sniffed at it but detected no odour. It wasn't a natural rope but a man-made fibre of some kind. It triggered a memory.

She'd been on a few sailing trips when she was a teenager, learning how to handle a tiny boat. The ropes had been smooth like this and very strong. The instructors had shown her knots: the special kind that sailors used, each one with its own purpose. Could she remember any of them?

Lynsey nuzzled the rope with her lips. The knot was slim, and she soon found its free ends. She located one of the knot's outer coils with her lips and nipped it with her front teeth, biting hard. She pulled but the knot didn't give.

It won't work, she told herself. *I'm not in a James Bond film.* In a film, the captive would rub the rope against a sharp edge or a piece of glass, but she had nothing. Nothing except her teeth and a long night to kill.

She tried again, gripping the rope with her teeth and pulling, shifting her head, twisting the rope every which way. Had the knot yielded a little?

Yes, Lynsey decided. *I felt it give.* She hadn't loosened the knot, but somewhere inside her, a spark of energy glowed into life. Lynsey redoubled her efforts, biting and tugging at the rope again and again. She'd undo the knot, take off the blindfold and then free her feet. The next time he came back, she'd be ready.

19

LEEMAN LIKED THE DARK. It spoke to something in his soul. Best of all, he loved the deep, ink-black shadows of the night. Over the years, they'd been his friends, and he'd learned to use them well.

Tonight he slipped into the shadow cast by an ugly old building and pressed his back against the stone wall. Ahead of him, Dennis Mankowich swaggered along the pavement. Mankowich had parked his van at the roadside in Buddie Lane. Leeman's BMW had not been far behind.

Mankowich almost certainly didn't know he'd been followed, but that was hardly surprising. Leeman had observed Mankowich for several hours, watching from a variety of vantage points as the man had put several pints away. Sitting outside The Bishop Blaize, Mankowich and his morose companions had taken their drinking seriously.

When Mankowich had finally set off for home, his battered Ford Transit van had been easy to follow. Mankowich had driven sensibly and slowly, making an effort to avoid being stopped by the police. Grudgingly, Leeman had begun to wonder whether Mankowich was as stupid as he'd thought. The man, perhaps, had a level of animal cunning, and that made him dangerous.

Were Mankowich and his cronies capable of orchestrating a kidnap? That was a question Leeman hoped to answer very soon.

Mankowich was some distance ahead now, and Leeman set off after him, keeping to the shadows and searching out hiding places. He needn't have worried. Mankowich clearly knew where he was headed, and he seemed intent on getting there. He didn't pause, nor did he look over his shoulder.

Before long, Mankowich opened a garden gate and marched up the drive toward a modest, detached house. Instead of going to the front door, Mankowich used the side entrance, letting himself in with a key.

Leeman stationed himself on the opposite side of the road and waited. A downstairs light came on, but there was no sign of activity from the upper windows. What was Mankowich up to?

Leeman scanned the street. There was no traffic and no pedestrians. At the other houses, no figures could be seen at the windows. This was a good time to follow Mankowich inside and deal with him. Leeman stepped forward, but as he did so, the side door of Mankowich's house opened, and Leeman darted back into the shadows, just in time.

Mankowich emerged from his house, a white carrier bag in his hand. As Leeman watched, Mankowich strolled along the road in the same direction as before, swinging the bag by his side. He wasn't going back for his van, so wherever he was headed, it must be within walking distance.

This could be it. If Mankowich had Lynsey captive, he'd

be taking her food and water. This was better than Leeman could've hoped for.

As before, he followed, keeping Mankowich in sight while maintaining a reasonable distance between them. His quarry took a left turn into a short road, and Leeman was forced to hang back, but almost immediately, Mankowich turned right. Leeman moved to the corner of the road and spotted Mankowich crossing the street and darting through a gateway, disappearing into the darkness.

Leeman waited a couple of seconds then set off in pursuit. A sign beside the gate showed that Mankowich had dashed into a park, and Leeman hesitated. This wasn't right. Even if there were sheds or outbuildings, a public park would not make a good place to keep a hostage.

Leeman edged forward, his eyes rapidly adjusting to the gloom as he left the lighted street behind. A figure moved ahead, and though he was indistinct, the white carrier bag was a giveaway. Leeman followed carefully, watching where he put his feet. The path was uneven and scattered with gravel. One careless step could announce his presence.

Leeman found himself walking on grass and he relaxed a little. Mankowich had slowed his pace; perhaps his night vision wasn't as good as Leeman's. But no, there was another reason. Leeman heard voices: two men muttered a few words and Mankowich replied in similarly low tones. Who was he meeting? Accomplices in his kidnapping?

Leeman crept closer, sidling up to a lone tree and leaning against its trunk. It was too dark to see the men properly, but the white carrier bag was easy to spot, and it changed hands. Leeman's ears rapidly attuned to the men's voices, and he picked out a few phrases. Bags were mentioned, a tenner each, and Mankowich muttered something that sounded like a threat, his voice dangerously low.

"No worries," one of the men replied. "We'll do right by you, Mank. We always do."

"You better had," Mankowich growled. "I'll see you later."

Mankowich turned and headed back the way he'd come. Leeman stayed stock still. *Keep walking*, he thought. *I'm not quite ready for you yet.* He held his breath and watched as Mankowich swaggered straight past as if he owned the place. A few seconds later, Leeman heard Mankowich's footsteps on the gravel path, and then the sound faded and died.

Satisfied, Leeman stepped out from his hiding place and made a choice. It wasn't difficult.

His left hand in his coat pocket, Leeman approached the two men, making his gait uncertain and his shoulders hunched. The men were both white, their hair cropped close to their scalps, and they faced Leeman, looking him up and down. Their body language said they did not like what they saw.

"What d'you want?" one of them snapped.

"I... I want to buy," Leeman muttered. "What've you got?"

"Nothing for you, pal," the other man said. "Jog on, before you get a kicking."

"You've got to help me out," Leeman wheedled. "Please, lads. I have money." Leeman fumbled in his pocket with his right hand and produced his wallet. "All I want is a bag of H. It's a tenner, right? That's no problem."

The men stared at him in silence.

"Please, I'm desperate," Leeman went on. "I need it. I'm

shaking like a leaf." As if to prove his point, he dropped his wallet, and for a split second, the men's gaze followed it.

It was all Leeman needed. He whipped his left hand from his coat pocket and went to work. The push dagger's smooth handle fitted perfectly in his fist, the blade protruding from between his fingers. Leeman punched it hard and fast into the nearest man's chest, getting in as many strikes as he could. Then he shoved the man hard with his right hand, at the same time sweeping his feet from beneath him. The man fell heavily onto his back, crying out in pain.

The second man had pulled a knife of his own, and he lunged at Leeman, swiping viciously at his face. Leeman leaned back and the man's knife sliced the air, then he stepped close, using his left arm to trap the man's right hand against his body. Leeman pushed down on the man's shoulder while forcing his arm up and back. The man grunted in pain, but he couldn't stop Leeman from forcing him facedown to the ground. Before the man could recover, Leeman punched with the push dagger, stabbing at his victim's kidneys on both sides. Helpless, the man writhed in agony, and Leeman sprang to his feet.

The first man was struggling to get up, but Leeman kicked his hands from under him, and he slumped to the ground, letting out a gargling moan.

It was tempting to deliver a few kicks for good measure, but both men would be dead within minutes, and he hated to waste effort.

"This is a public park," Leeman said. "There's a children's playground for God's sake. What the hell is wrong with you people?"

Leeman stalked away, the men's moans quickly becoming inaudible. It didn't take him long to spot

Mankowich. As expected, the idiot was returning home by the route he'd used earlier.

Leeman waited while Mankowich let himself in at the side door, and this time, lights soon blazed upstairs. It was time to go to work.

Leeman straightened his clothes and smoothed his hair, then he crossed the road. Eliminating the scum from the park had been a somewhat mundane experience, but dealing with Mankowich would be a different matter. *This*, he told himself, *is going to be a pure pleasure.*

TUESDAY

20

THE CALL CAME in the early hours. Instantly awake, Francis Clifford grabbed his bedside phone and sat up, staring into the dark room.

"Yes?"

The caller didn't speak. There was nothing but the background hiss on the phone line, the insistent sound forcing itself into Clifford's consciousness, as loud as any howl of pain.

Beside him, Diana stirred and mumbled drowsily, but she'd taken a sleeping pill and wouldn't wake for hours.

Francis clenched his jaw and waited; he was not a man to be intimidated.

Eventually, the caller spoke, the male voice soft and sinister: "Hello, Francis."

"Who the hell is this?" Clifford demanded. "What do you want?"

"Cooperation, in return for your daughter."

"I'm listening."

"Always the businessman. We knew you'd play ball."

"Who's we?"

A chuckle. "Come on, Francis. Let's not play games."

"Oh, this isn't a game, my friend. I have people looking for you, and when they find you, you'll wish you'd never been born. Your only way out is to release my daughter immediately."

"Save your threats," the caller intoned as though growing bored. "You'll get Lynsey back safe and sound as soon as we get what we want."

"And that is?"

"Information. Lynsey took something that didn't belong to her: a document. She gave it to you. We want it back."

Clifford's mind worked fast. He had no idea what the caller was talking about, but a simple denial wouldn't wash. Better to let the scenario play out while he figured out how to turn the situation to his advantage.

"All right. Where can we meet?"

There was no reply, and Clifford sensed he'd put the caller on his back foot.

"Did you hear me?" Clifford went on. "I'll cooperate. Give me a time and a place."

"That was far too easy," the caller said. "Describe the document to me, Francis."

"Why? We both know what it looks like."

"Do we? I'm not so sure. Tell me what it looks like, and then we'll talk."

"It's just an ordinary document. Plain paper."

He heard a soft shush as if the caller had exhaled into the mouthpiece. Then: "You don't have it."

"I do, and I'm willing to exchange it for my daughter's safe release. All we have to—"

"Don't waste my time, Francis. I'm not stupid. I know you're bluffing. This changes things."

"Yes, it does. All right, I haven't got what you want. Lynsey has not given a document to me, nor has she passed on any information. I can't deliver something I don't have, so you may as well let her go."

"Not yet. There's a plan B."

Clifford steeled himself. "Go on."

"Business hasn't been so good lately, has it?"

"I wouldn't say that."

"We know better. You've been getting in our way, Francis, making a nuisance of yourself. The trouble is, you're still doing things the old-fashioned way, playing golf with the right people, handing out cigars and shaking hands. You've got a lot of friends. Powerful friends."

"People know they can trust me," Clifford said. "There's such a thing as loyalty."

"Yes, and it's a pain in the arse. But the days of the old boy's network are over. The world is moving on, and we can't let you and your cronies stand in our way. So here's what you're going to do."

Francis listened in silence. When the caller finally finished his string of instructions, Francis said, "Yes. I'll do it in the morning. First thing."

"You better had," the caller said. "If you let us down, Lynsey dies. If you call the police, she dies."

The line went dead, and Clifford replaced the handset. Quietly, he got out of bed and went to the en-suite bathroom to splash cold water on his face. That done, he covered his face with a thick towel, pressing it hard against his mouth, and he let out a roar of frustration.

———

FRANCIS CLIFFORD ARRIVED at work on time, as he always did. As usual, he exchanged a few pleasantries with Margaret while he hung up his coat. Keeping his tone light, he asked her to place a call to Samuel Jeffries, then he made for his office, closing the door firmly.

A few minutes later his phone rang, and when he answered, Margaret said, "I have Councillor Jeffries for you, Mr Clifford."

"Thanks, Margaret." Clifford waited for the connection to be made, making his expression dour to suit the conversation he was about to have.

"Francis," Samuel Jeffries boomed. "How are you? I hope you're calling to arrange a rematch. I've been working on my swing, and I'm ready to give you a run for your money."

"No, I'm afraid it's not about golf. Unfortunately, I have some bad news."

"Oh dear. What's the matter? Are you all right?"

"I'm fine. This is purely business." Clifford took a moment to draw breath. "Things have been tight, and we're making some changes. Specifically, we'll be raising our bids on some upcoming projects. It's the only way we can cover our costs."

"Okay, but that won't affect the deals we've already talked about, will it?"

"Unfortunately, it will. It can't be helped."

"I see," Jeffries said. "But you're not going to change your bids too much are you? That would be a disaster."

"Sadly, we will be revising all our bids. They'll be significantly more expensive than—"

"But we agreed," Jeffries blurted. "You gave me your word."

"I know, and I'm sorry, but that's the way it has to be."

Jeffries muttered a curse under his breath. "I didn't think this was the way you did business, Francis. For God's sake, after everything I've done for you... I introduced you to people, I vouched for you, and now you're going to make me look ridiculous."

"I realise this is difficult, but circumstances have changed."

"Bugger circumstances. We have sites that need clearing, and you said you could handle them. The deals were as good as done."

"In principle, yes, but we hadn't agreed terms."

"Nonsense. You gave me your figures, and we shook hands. I thought that was good enough, but now you're trying to gouge the city council, and we won't stand for it."

"I'm not gouging anyone," Clifford protested, but Jeffries wasn't listening.

"If your price is too high, we'll have to use someone else. We always go with the best bid, you know that. We follow the rules."

"Yes, when it suits you," Clifford shot back. "I don't recall you mentioning the rules when I paid for that villa in Tuscany. Did you enjoy your stay, by the way? I hear the pool is excellent."

"I beg your pardon. Are you trying to blackmail me?"

"No. I was happy to pay for your trip. It was an arrangement between friends, and I expected nothing in return. In the same spirit, I'm giving you advance notice of our new bids. I didn't have to warn you. I could've gone ahead without saying a word, but I didn't want to do that."

There was a pause before Jeffries replied. "Francis, I urge you to think again."

"I can't do that, Sam."

"Then we've got nothing to say to each other. And from

now on, it's Councillor Jeffries to you. Goodbye, Mr Clifford."

Clifford slammed the handset back into its cradle, then he stood and paced to the window, staring out at the city.

It had taken him decades to build his business, starting with nothing and fighting tooth and nail for every penny. But he'd brought the whole enterprise to its knees with one phone call.

Clearing the sites for a raft of new developments would've been a massive undertaking, but a necessary one. He needed every single one of those contracts. Without that injection of cash, his business was dead in the water.

Whoever had Lynsey, they must've known the way things stood, and they'd kicked him while he was down. They'd given him no option but to price himself out of the market. He was finished.

But what could he do? Should he go to the police and tell them what had happened?

No. The kidnappers seemed to know his business; they must have their sources of information. Perhaps they were watching him even now. The police would be spotted, and he couldn't risk that. He couldn't do anything that might endanger the life of his only daughter.

Leeman was his last hope. The police were like sledgehammers; Leeman was a scalpel.

He has to find her, Clifford thought. *And fast.*

21

SPILLER TIMED his arrival at Heavitree police station perfectly, crossing the car park at the same time as DS Paddy Reilly and DC Adrian Cove.

"Morning," Cove said with a smile. "You're back for more punishment. Paddy hasn't scared you off completely, then?"

"No, it was a good day. All very..." Spiller searched for the right turn of phrase and settled for, "eye opening."

Cove laughed. "That's CID, all right. *Eye opening*." He paused. "We didn't see you in the pub last night."

"No, I was all-in, to be honest. Another night, I'll come along."

"What he means is, he needs to give the old ball and chain a bit of notice," Reilly said. "Isn't that right, Tim? You need to apply for a pass in advance, or you'll find a note on the kitchen table, *Your dinner is in the dog*."

"That's not true at all," Spiller protested. "We haven't got a dog."

His comic timing had been perfect, and both his new colleagues laughed.

"We're only jealous, Tim," Cove said. "Most of us would kill for a home-cooked dinner and a cosy night in. I was happily married myself once upon a time, but it turns out my wife wasn't."

It was Spiller's turn to laugh, and the three made their way to the CID office, chatting about nothing in particular. But they stopped talking as soon as they entered the room.

Detective Chief Superintendent Boyce stood at the front of the office, deep in conversation with Detective Superintendent Chisholm and a man Spiller had met only once before, DCI Brian Wendell. Both Wendell and Chisholm were nodding along as though listening intently.

Raising a hand to signal a pause in the proceedings, Boyce beckoned to the new arrivals. Reilly, Cove and Spiller joined them, forming a semi-circle, and at that moment, DI Nicholson bumbled in through the doors. Taking in the scene, Nicholson straightened his tie and came to join the assembly without being asked. As the others made room for him, Boyce turned his gaze on Nicholson, and the man seemed to wither under his stare.

Nicholson muttered an apology and seemed about to launch into an excuse, but Boyce cut him short.

"We're all here now," Boyce said. "So let's get started. Before our main briefing, I want to make a couple of quick announcements. Firstly, we have a triple murder to deal with."

A murmur ran around the room, but Boyce swept on before anyone could start asking questions.

"The killings are almost certainly drug related, and all three were in the St. Thomas area. All three victims were known to us, especially one Dennis Mankowich, whom some of you have dealt with in the past."

"Bloody hell," Reilly muttered under his breath.

"Exactly," Boyce said. "Detective Superintendent Chisholm has already attended the scenes and supervised their preservation. Forensic examination of both scenes is underway. As I'm sure you've already worked out, this is going to leave us overstretched, and this brings me to point two." He gestured to Wendell. "You all know Brian, and you know he's been serving out a suspension. Brian was due to come in today to discuss his return to active duty, but since we're up against it, I'm fast-tracking that procedure. I'm confident that lessons have been learned, so as of now, Brian is back at work."

"Nice one," Reilly said. "Welcome back, Bri."

Cove and Nicholson added their congratulations, and Spiller offered an encouraging smile, but he noticed that Chisholm remained tight-lipped. Perhaps he'd already congratulated Wendell, but judging by his pinched expression, Chisholm may have had his own reasons for keeping quiet.

Boyce checked his watch. "Briefing in ten minutes, and we need to start promptly. We've got a lot on our plate, so let's make sure we get off to a good start." With that, Boyce turned and made for his office.

Cove looked to Spiller, "Tea?"

"Yeah, I'll just get myself sorted out first."

"No, I mean, would you like a mug of tea? I'll get them. Milk and sugar, yes?"

"Yes please. Much appreciated."

Spiller settled at his desk and took out his notebook, flipping through the pages in search of references to Mankowich. He gratefully received his mug of tea from Cove, but after only a couple of sips, Spiller got to his feet and made his way to Reilly's desk.

Reilly was hurriedly sorting through a stack of

paperwork. Without lifting his gaze, he said, "Tim. What's up?"

"I was just thinking," Spiller began, "it's a shame we didn't talk to Mankowich yesterday. He was on our radar, but the guvnor told us to hang back."

Reilly looked up sharply, as did Wendell whose desk faced Reilly's.

"What are you trying to say?" Reilly asked. "Are you suggesting that the guvnor knew this was going to happen?"

Spiller felt the blood drain from his face. "No, of course not. I wouldn't dream of it. I was just making an observation, that's all. It's a strange coincidence, isn't it?"

"You need to think before you open your mouth," Wendell said. "Stupid remarks like that do more harm than good. That's how rumours start, and worse."

"I'm sorry, sir," Spiller said, stiffening his posture. "I didn't mean anything by it."

Wendell stared at him for a few seconds, content to let him squirm, then he shook his head. "We'll put it down to your inexperience and forget about it. But take my advice, DC Spiller: use your ears more than your mouth, and you'll be all right."

"Yes, sir."

"And call me Bri." Wendell rose to his feet. "Right, I'm going to have a quick word with the guv before the briefing." He nodded to Reilly then strolled over to Chisholm's desk.

"Don't worry about, Bri," Reilly said. "He's bound to be a bit touchy after what he's been through. But he knows his stuff. We're lucky to have him back."

"Yes. A triple murder." Spiller exhaled, puffing out his

cheeks. "The guvnor said I'd be thrown in at the deep end, but this is..."

"A deeper pool than you expected," Reilly suggested. "Think of it as good experience. Get stuck in and you'll learn a hell of a lot. Come on, let's bag a spot in the briefing room."

Spiller and Reilly found Boyce already sitting at the head of the group of tables, and they sat to one side, their notebooks ready. The others joined them in short order, and when everyone was seated, Boyce began.

"Good, we're bang on time. We received a call just after seven am that a dog walker had discovered two bodies in the Merrivale Road Play Area, a park in St Thomas. Both men had multiple stab wounds. They weren't carrying ID, but they were easily identifiable. Both men have been arrested several times for possession and distribution of drugs, as well as a string of burglaries and common assaults. Their names were Daren Pullock and David Rowse, known as Daz and Dave. A knife was found next to David Rowse, and first indications are that it belonged to him, so he may have been trying to defend himself.

"He was stabbed in the back, in such a way that hit his kidneys. Daren Pullock, on the other hand, had been stabbed several times in the chest. We'll know more later when we get the forensic reports back, and after the post-mortem examination. Also found at the scene was a plastic carrier bag containing twenty-five small bags, each holding a tenth of a gram of a dark brown powder that we believe to be heroin. The colour suggests it's of very low quality, but analysis will tell us how pure it is." Boyce paused. "Any questions?"

A brief silence hung in the air, but not for long.

Spiller took a breath and said, "It's strange that the drugs weren't taken, isn't it?"

"It is notable," Boyce agreed, "but we can't speculate at this stage. The attacker may have been disturbed, or he may have panicked and run for it. It was dark, and the bag was on the ground. He might not even have seen it."

Spiller nodded. "Are we connecting those murders with Dennis Mankowich?"

"Officially, we're keeping an open mind, but there's reason to suspect the murders are linked," Boyce replied. "Moving on to Dennis Mankowich, he was found in his home, and though he had several stab wounds, most of them were superficial. He was found lying on his bedroom floor. His hands were tied behind his back, and his feet were tied at the ankles. Initial findings suggest he may have been subjected to a prolonged attack, possibly with the aim of extortion, although what they were trying to get out of him, and whether they were successful, we can't yet say.

"The end result for Mankowich was the same. His throat was cut, and he bled out. Taken together, the three killings point to gang violence. We could be looking at rival drug gangs, or possibly a fight for supremacy within a gang. Either way, there's trouble brewing, and we need to shut it down."

Boyce stopped to scan his audience. "Now, I can see some jaded looks around this table. You might be thinking, this is what happens to lowlife drug dealers, it was ever thus. But that won't do, not in my team. Whatever we think of Mankowich and his ilk, we can't have these people dishing out their own brand of justice.

"A murder is a murder, and we want these cases cleared up, the sooner the better. With that in mind, we'll deal with the three murders in a single Major Investigation Team, headed by Detective Superintendent Chisholm. We'll be drafting in more officers, but to begin with, the MIT will consist of DCI Wendell, DI Nicholson, and DC Cove."

"Sir," Reilly began, but Boyce didn't let him finish.

"DS Reilly and DC Spiller, you will be brought into the team before long, that's a certainty. We're going to need all hands on deck. Until then, I want you to concentrate on the Lynsey Clifford case."

"Yes, sir," Reilly said. "Understood."

"In fact, I'd like you and Tim to update me on the case, so we'll meet in my office straight away. Everyone else can stay here and get organised." Boyce turned to Chisholm. "John, I'll leave you to get your team sorted. Anything you need, give me a shout."

"Yes, sir," Chisholm said.

Boyce marched for the door, and a murmur of animated voices sprang up in his wake. Spiller and Reilly exchanged dour looks, then they reluctantly got to their feet and followed Boyce from the room.

In Boyce's office, they found him already seated at his desk.

"Sit down," Boyce said. "I'll keep this short."

Reilly and Spiller took the chairs facing Boyce, and he leaned forward to look them in the eye, a sense of restrained energy in his posture. "So, where are we?"

"We're getting through the groundwork," Reilly replied. "Dennis Mankowich was on our list. He was seen hanging around Lynsey on the night she was last seen, and witnesses say he was paying her unwanted attention, but he's out of the frame now. That leaves us with Lynsey's boyfriend, Tony Carter, as our only suspect to date. We know he has a temper, and Lynsey may have wanted to break off their relationship. On the night she went missing, Carter was drinking heavily, and he also has a black eye. He claims it was from an altercation in the club."

"That sounds promising." Boyce looked to Spiller. "What do you think, Tim? Do you see Tony Carter as a suspect?"

"It's too early to say, sir," Spiller replied.

"That's my line," Boyce said. "It's the kind of placeholder comment we give to the press when we want to keep our cards close to our chests. In here, your opinions count for something, so don't hold back. Trust the evidence. What does it say?"

Spiller took a moment to frame his reply. "To my mind, Carter doesn't quite fit the bill. He seemed genuinely surprised when we told him Lynsey was missing."

"That's not hard to fake," Reilly replied. "And don't forget the fact that he legged it when we went to his house."

"He thought we'd been sent by Dennis Mankowich," Spiller said. "Enforcers, coming to settle a score."

Reilly looked doubtful. "Thugs don't knock on the door; they kick it in."

"Could there be a connection between the two cases?" Boyce asked. "Dennis Mankowich was a person of interest in Lynsey's disappearance."

Reilly and Spiller exchanged a look.

"I can't see it," Reilly replied. "We know Mankowich spoke to Lynsey, but there's no other link between them. I think you were right this morning; the murders in the park are drug related, and Mankowich is a dealer. We've no evidence Lynsey took drugs, other than prescription tranquillisers."

"I looked into that," Spiller said. "Lynsey had been prescribed Valium, also known as diazepam. It can be prescribed for anxiety, sleep problems or muscle spasms. People are only supposed to take it for a few weeks."

"Where did you find that out?" Reilly asked.

"I popped into a pharmacist on the way home last night."

Reilly nodded thoughtfully. "Why did Lynsey have it?"

"The label said she could take three a day, so I'm guessing anxiety, but the date was from four months ago, and the bottle was almost full. I don't think she was taking them at all."

"Okay, let's not look for links that aren't there," Boyce said. "Focus on Tony Carter. You think Lynsey's flat had been searched. What was someone looking for? Were they trying to remove incriminating evidence? Or was there something that might've caused embarrassment, such as letters or photographs?"

Spiller frowned and Boyce noticed.

"What is it, Tim?"

"Nothing much, sir. It's just that Tony Carter had been drinking heavily on Saturday night, so if he'd been into Lynsey's flat looking for something, he would've made more mess than we found. Whoever searched the flat was quite careful, methodical even; they only touched certain things. And Tony Carter probably would've been clumsy and noisy, but the downstairs neighbour didn't hear a sound."

Boyce sat back, steepling his fingers. "If it wasn't him, who was it?"

"That, I don't know," Spiller admitted. "To my mind, there's more to this case than we've uncovered so far."

"You might be right," Boyce said. "It's about time we

put out a public appeal. I don't think we can organise a press conference just yet. We'll be making announcements about the triple murder, and we don't want to muddy the waters. But we can achieve a lot if we focus our efforts. Paddy, I want you to set the wheels in motion. Talk to local press, radio and TV. The usual brief: we're concerned for Lynsey's safety, anyone with any information, call us. You'll need to make the usual preparations, and check there'll be enough handlers to take the calls. If it looks like we're getting swamped, I'll draft in a few more people to help. Okay?"

"Yes, sir," Reilly replied. "I'll get onto that straight away."

"Tim, I want you to assist Paddy with this. It'll be good experience. Handling the media isn't always easy, but Paddy knows the score, and he'll help you get your feet wet."

"Thank you, sir," Spiller said. "It's part of modern policing, isn't it?"

"Indeed it is. Like it or loathe it, we need the media more than they need us. Once you've put the word out, what's your next step?"

"We're going to trace everyone who was working at the nightclub on Saturday night," Reilly replied. "After that, we'll head over to County Hall and talk to Lynsey's colleagues, especially a woman called Mel Parker. She's a friend of Lynsey's, and she was with her at the nightclub. She could've been one of the last people to see Lynsey. When we're done there, we have a list of Carter's friends to chase up: people who were there on the night she disappeared."

"That all sounds excellent," Boyce said. "But I've got some bad news. I'm shifting resources around to focus on the murders. As far as your case goes, there'll be no search parties and no divers at the quay. I'm sorry, but I can't give you more resources until we have more to go on. At the moment, we might suspect foul play, but we need more evidence."

"Understood, sir," Reilly replied. "I'd thought as much."

Boyce offered a conciliatory smile. "I'll let you get on, but before you go, a quick word. I know it's disappointing for both of you to be left out of the MIT, but I'll make sure you're involved down the line. In the meantime, Lynsey Clifford is your number one priority. That young woman is still alive for all we know, and our first duty is to preserve life. Remember that."

"Yes, sir," Spiller and Reilly chorused.

"You'd better get to it."

Spiller and Reilly made their exit, both men in a quiet mood. It was hard to read Reilly's expression, but for his part, Spiller's investigative mind was firing on all cylinders. Yes, he'd been dispirited when he'd been excluded from the MIT, but Boyce's parting words had struck a chord. Lynsey Clifford deserved his best efforts, and that was exactly what she was going to get.

22

ALONE IN THE dark and windowless room, Lynsey stood beside the door. It had taken her hours, but she'd untied herself and removed her blindfold. She was bruised and battered, but she was ready, running on adrenaline, her nerves stretched tight. In her hands was a broken piece of wood, a slat she'd pulled from the bed's base, and she held it at shoulder height. It was a poor weapon, neither strong nor sturdy, but it was the best she could do.

And now it was time to use it. Beyond the door, the footsteps grew closer, their familiar rhythm steady. He was confident. Good.

The bolts slid free. A key rattled in the lock, and he stepped inside, a silhouette framed by the doorway.

Lynsey flew at him, swinging the piece of wood with all her might, aiming at his head. He cried out, raising his arms to protect his face, and the wood struck him on the forearm. He yelled a curse at her, but Lynsey swung again and again, raining down blows on him, hitting him on the shoulders, the chest. But he stayed standing. The punch came out of nowhere, his fist slamming into her, connecting with her cheekbone.

Lynsey's world turned white, and she staggered back. Before she could recover, he hit her again, this time in the stomach, and she folded, gasping for air. The piece of wood was wrenched from her grip, and he took hold of her shoulders, pushing her back. The backs of her knees met the bed, and she toppled, landing on the thin mattress.

"Stay down!" he yelled. In the darkness, he loomed over her, a shadowy figure like something from a nightmare, his outline dimly lit by the faint light from the open door. Fear flooded Lynsey's senses, but she couldn't let him win, she couldn't give in.

Lynsey screamed and pushed herself up, hitting out, trying to dig her nails into his face, but he slapped her hands aside and pushed her back. He was stronger than her and faster too. Before she knew what he was doing, she was rolled over and he had both her wrists in one of his hands. A weight pressed hard on her back, as if he was pushing his knee against her spine, crushing the breath from her body. Pain blossomed in her chest, and she gasped for air, her blind rage turning to abject fear.

Lynsey let out a deep sob. She'd failed. It had been her best chance of escape, and it hadn't worked. Sobs shook her shoulders. She'd be punished now. She'd disobeyed and he'd take out his anger on her.

But the weight was lifted from her back, and he let go of her hands. She heard him breathing heavily. There were footsteps, then the door slammed shut.

Lynsey rolled over, tears streaming down her face. Once more the room was pitch black, but he'd gone. She struggled into a sitting position and peered into the darkness. She thought of searching for her makeshift weapon, but he would've taken it away.

"What am I going to do now?" she whispered to the empty room. "What the hell am I going to do now?"

23

REILLY TOOK Spiller on a whistle-stop tour of the local media offices. At each one, they delivered a carefully prepared package: a photo of Lynsey Clifford and a description, along with Reilly's name and the number to call if anyone had seen Lynsey since Saturday night or could provide information as to her whereabouts.

That done, they climbed back into the Ford Escort and Reilly started the engine.

"You tried phoning the bouncers again, didn't you?" Reilly asked.

"Yes, but nobody answered," Spiller said. "I did manage to get hold of the DJ, but he was no help at all. He said he doesn't have time to notice the punters. He concentrates on playing the records, and he has to pack up at the end of the night, so he doesn't go outside until long after all the customers have gone home. Unfortunately, we never got a phone number for the barmaid, so we can't get hold of her yet. We'll have to go back to the club and talk to Freddie Hall."

"If necessary," Reilly replied. "I've already told you, I

don't think she'll have much for us. We'll concentrate on the bouncers. They'll have been at the door, so they should've seen Lynsey leave. We'll make some house calls and see what they say. What about Carter's friend, Eddie?"

"No reply on his phone, but he lives at 7C Barton Court. I thought we could drop in and see if he's home."

"That's over in Whipton," Reilly replied. "We'll get to him later. First, let me introduce you to your new life support system."

"Okay," Spiller replied, stretching the word out longer than he'd intended.

"What's up, Tim? Don't you trust me?"

Spiller raised his hands. "Implicitly."

"Good." Reilly pulled the Ford into the traffic with scarcely a glance at his mirrors, the tyres squealing on the tarmac as the car shot forward.

Spiller gritted his teeth and said nothing during the short journey, only breaking his silence when Reilly parked the car.

"A bowling alley?" Spiller asked. "Erm..."

"You'll see. Come on."

Spiller matched Reilly's brisk pace as they strode across the car park.

It seemed to Spiller that Reilly had a newfound spring in his step, and he couldn't help wondering whether that was a good thing.

Inside the bowling alley, the place was eerily quiet, their footsteps echoing from the hard floor as Reilly led them across the lobby and up a short flight of stairs.

"We're not going bowling," Spiller said. "There must be a cafe in here."

"Not a bad effort, Tim. There's no cafe, exactly, but there's something so much better."

Reilly marched onward, and a few seconds later, he extended his arm. "See?"

"Oh, right. A Wimpy bar. Somehow, I'm not surprised."

They made their way into the brightly lit burger bar, and here, at least, were a few customers to liven the place up.

"It's open, it's cheap and it has everything you need," Reilly stated. "Believe you me, there'll be days when you'll be very glad of this place."

"Maybe, but Sheila usually makes me a packed lunch."

"Now it's my turn to be unsurprised. You can abstain if you want to, but I missed breakfast and I'm famished."

Reilly strode up to the counter where the young man on duty acknowledged him with a nod. "The usual, is it, sir? Large Wimpy burger with fries and a black coffee?"

"Why not?" Reilly replied. "Tim, can I tempt you? I'll pay."

"Oh, well..." Spiller tried to resist, but the smell of fried food was making his stomach rumble. "Go on then, Paddy. I'll have the same as you." To the young man, he added, "But can I have milk with the coffee, please?"

"Sure," the young man replied. "The sugar's on the side there."

"What makes you think I take sugar?" Spiller said.

The young man chuckled. "Do me a favour; don't ask."

"Now then, you two, play nicely," Reilly said. "Let me do the introductions. Tim, this is Ronny. He'll see you right when you're tired and hungry. Ronny, this is our new DC, Tim Spiller, and he's all right. Okay?"

Ronny sent Spiller a brief, businesslike smile and then busied himself with their order. He went about his work with speed and efficiency, and Spiller found himself watching the way the young man worked.

Ronny might have a curiously offhand manner, but there was something about him, and when he delivered their polystyrene cups of coffee and cartons of food, Spiller realised what it was.

Ronny's gaze was sharp enough to cut concrete, and it darted from place to place. It was as if he studied the world in fleeting glances, taking in everything he needed to know in a split second before moving on.

Reilly paid, and Ronny thanked him, but Reilly showed no sign of moving away. He was waiting for something.

"Are you looking for that young woman?" Ronny asked.

"We are," Reilly replied.

"It was on the radio. Lynsey Clifford. They mentioned your name."

"They've broadcast it already," Reilly said. "That is good news. Have you heard anything?"

"Maybe." Ronny's gaze briefly flicked to one side and then back. "I heard Mank got killed. A couple of his dealers too. Is that anything to do with it?"

"Unlikely," Reilly replied. "Separate cases."

Ronny considered this for a moment. "They said Lynsey had been at The Icebox. Mank used to hang around down there."

"A coincidence," Reilly said. "Anything else?"

Ronny shook his head.

"Okay, you know the score," Reilly went on. "Anything comes up, give me a bell."

"Sure."

Reilly scooped up his food and drink, and Spiller did the same, but before he moved away, Spiller said, "What's your surname, Ronny?"

"What?"

"Your surname, what is it?"

There was a pause before Ronny said, "Johnson."

"Thank you. That wasn't so hard, was it? My next question is this: Where did you hear about the murders?"

Ronny twisted his features into a mask of disbelief. To Reilly, he said, "Is he for real?"

"Hold on a minute, young man," Spiller protested. "I asked you a question. Mankowich's name hasn't been made public yet, so I need to know where you got your information."

Reilly nudged Spiller with his elbow. "Tim, Ronny's on our side."

Spiller locked eyes with the young man, but his hard stare was returned in equal measure.

Eventually, Ronny jutted his chin. "Enjoy your meal, *sir*."

"Thank you," Spiller replied. "I will. But—"

"Let's go and sit down," Reilly interrupted, and he ushered Spiller over to the table furthest from the counter. When they'd taken their seats, Reilly unwrapped his burger and took a bite, chewing furiously then washing it down with a gulp of coffee. Lowering his voice, he said, "Tim, that wasn't smart. I told you, Ronny is okay, but you went in with your size nines regardless."

"I was just—"

"You were throwing down a marker," Reilly interrupted. "You wanted to show the kid who's in charge, but that sort of bullshit doesn't wash with lads like Ronny. He's not impressed by authority, and with good reason. He's not had an easy life, and it's largely been people like us who've let him down."

It took Spiller a moment to respond. "I see."

"No, you don't, but if you stick around long enough, you might understand. In the meantime, all you need to know is this: Ronny is a good lad, and he gets around. Just because he's serving burgers, it doesn't mean he hasn't got anything else going on. He's what you might call an activist. He knows a lot of people, and he has a lot of friends; none of them are crooks. They want the streets kept safe just as much as we do, if not more. It's their arses on the line, not ours."

"So what is he, a vigilante or something? I don't like the sound of that."

Reilly sighed in exasperation. "Ronny helps out with community projects, he takes part in campaigns, gets people to sign petitions. He hands out food to homeless people, for God's sake."

"Oh." The wind well and truly taken from his sails, Spiller plucked up a fry and chewed on it. It turned to flavourless mush in his mouth. He tried a sip of coffee, but he'd forgotten to pick up a sachet of sugar and the stuff was undrinkable. He was about to get up and fetch the sugar, but Reilly hadn't quite finished with him.

"Sometimes, Tim, I don't know what I'm going to do with you. You're not in uniform anymore, so stop acting like it. We need to be a bit more subtle than that, otherwise, we may as well go around with helmets on."

Spiller nodded.

"Ronny might give you another chance, but you'll have to earn it," Reilly went on. "How you do that is up to you."

"I'll give it some thought." Spiller hesitated. "And what about you?"

"Eh?"

"Do you give people a second chance too, even if they go in with their size nines?"

"Always." Reilly smiled and took another bite of his burger, not quite finishing his mouthful before adding,

"Unless they're in the National Front. I hate those bastards, don't you?"

"Totally. Without reservation. Bastards, one and all."

"There you go. We've got some common ground." Reilly paused. "What is it with you and all the fancy words? You haven't got a posh accent, but sometimes, and don't take this the wrong way, you come across as a bit stuck up, a bit formal. Did you go to public school or something?"

"No. The local grammar." It was Spiller's turn to hesitate. "My family aren't well-off or anything. My Dad owns a little shop: a convenience store. He wanted me to do better, so they encouraged me to take the Eleven Plus, and I passed. I wasn't fussed about going to the grammar, but Mum and Dad were keen, so I went along with it. Truth be told, my parents could barely afford the school uniform, but they managed it somehow."

"So you had to fit in," Reilly suggested. "And you learned to hide behind long words and fancy phrases."

"I wouldn't put it quite like that."

"I would," Reilly replied. "It's as plain as the nose on your face. Anyway, what did your parents think to you becoming a copper?"

Spiller's smile was wry. "Not a lot. They wanted me to go to college, so I gave it a shot. Business studies. I didn't last long. It wasn't for me, but after I joined the police, things started to look up. I did okay in uniform, but CID is where I want to be, and here I am. I think my mum and dad are coming around to the idea, especially when my dad found out about the pension. He doesn't have one, you see."

"Silver linings." Reilly narrowed his eyes. "Your mum and dad vote Tory, don't they?"

"That's private, Paddy."

"They're Tories and always have been," Reilly stated. "I bet they loved Maggie Thatcher. Her dad ran a shop."

"That fact may have been mentioned," Spiller admitted. "Actually—"

Reilly raised a finger to cut him off, and Spiller turned to see Ronny approaching, a cloth and a spray bottle in hand. Ronny halted at the table next to theirs, and without looking at them, proceeded to spray and wipe the table, putting plenty of effort into the task, although as far as Spiller could see, the table was already clean.

Speaking quietly but firmly, his attention never shifting from his task, Ronny said, "There's a meeting tonight. Green Gables. Back room. Seven o'clock. A few of us want to do something about the druggies. You should come. You might learn something."

"Ah, I can't do tonight," Reilly replied without looking at Ronny. "I've got something on."

"I'll come," Spiller said quietly.

Ronny's gaze flicked to Spiller for a fraction of a second, then he nodded, the gesture so small as to be almost unnoticeable. Without another word, Ronny moved away and began wiping another table.

Reilly looked Spiller in the eye. "Are you sure you want to do that, Tim? There'll be a lot of angry people at that meeting, and they *will* know you're a copper."

"Not necessarily."

Reilly laughed quietly. "It's your funeral. If you go, it won't be on police business, and if there's any trouble, you'll have to keep Ronny's name out of it. If anyone asks, you went of your own accord. If push comes to shove, say you heard a rumour in the pub, but please, for the love of God, don't say anything about a confidential informant. You haven't had time to find one of your own, so everyone will start looking at me, and I do not want that."

"Understood," Spiller said. "I mean... got it."

They finished their meal quickly after that, bolting down their burgers and fries. Spiller had lost interest in his coffee, but he took it with him when they walked out. In the car park, he poured the lukewarm coffee away and posted the cup in a bin.

Reilly watched disapprovingly, but he didn't comment. He simply said, "Right, let's go and track down Carter's mates, Eddie and Wayne, and the bouncers." Reilly grinned. "Sounds like a band."

"It does," Spiller replied. "But probably not a very good one."

24

Spiller and Reilly were caught by roadworks on the way to Eddie Appleton's address. Beyond the line of stationary traffic, a man in a bright yellow coat swivelled a circular sign from *GO* to *STOP*.

Reilly groaned in frustration. Spiller knew how he felt.

I ought not to have thrown that coffee away, Spiller thought. *I could do with something to perk me up.*

Reilly seemed to be feeling the same way, and he fumbled with a packet of cigarettes as the car crawled to a halt.

"Are you going to smoke in here?" Spiller asked.

Reilly glanced at him. "Yes. You're not going to complain, are you?"

Before Spiller could reply, Reilly added, "I've been cutting down out of consideration, but there are limits, you know."

"Okay, but can you open a window?"

"Certainly, your ladyship." Reilly cranked down the window and lit up.

"Those things will kill you, Paddy."

"So I've heard, but right now, this ciggie is the only thing keeping me going, so you'll have to put up with it for a few minutes." Reilly made a point of exhaling his smoke toward the open window.

"Fine." Spiller wound down his own window and breathed deep.

"Cheer up, lad. We're off."

The traffic began to move, and Reilly sent the Ford surging forward, his expression brightening.

When they arrived at Barton Court, Reilly led the way to Number 7, the home of Eddie Appleton. Spiller lagged behind, casting his eye over the properties. Each three-storey building looked as though it comprised several flats, the pebble-dashed living areas separated by red brick stairwells. There were steel-railed balconies on the upper two floors, some of them adorned with laundry hung out to dry.

I wonder if there are any flats for rent. Spiller thought. *They look a lot bigger than where we're living now.*

"Come on, Tim," Reilly called out. "Don't waste your time eyeing up the neighbourhood."

"Who says I was?"

Reilly sent him a knowing grin. "You're an open book, mate. But don't even think about moving here. These flats are all owned by the council. They're for single mums and the like. You won't qualify."

"Right." Thrusting his hands in his pockets, Spiller joined Reilly at the building's entrance, where he was already pressing the buzzer for 7C.

"Hello," someone called out from above, and Spiller looked up to see an elderly man gazing down at them over the railings. The man was in need of a shave and his woolly hat had seen better days, but his smile was broad and genuine when he said, "Are you looking for Eddie?"

Spiller and Reilly stepped back so they could talk to the man without craning their necks.

"Yes, we're police," Reilly replied. "Is Eddie at home?"

The man shook his head. "He's not in trouble, is he?"

"No, it's nothing like that," Spiller said. "We just want to chat with him, ask a couple of questions. It's routine."

The man gave no sign of having heard. "I don't want to cause him any bother," he said. "Eddie's a good lad. He's always helping me out."

"That's good to hear," Reilly called back, raising his voice and enunciating each word clearly. "We only want a quick chat. Do you know where he is?"

"No need to shout." The man rolled his eyes, but he added, "Eddie's working. I saw him go out this morning."

"Any idea where he works?" Spiller asked, pitching his voice at what he hoped was a happy medium.

"All over. He's a handyman. He does repairs for the council." The man scratched his grey stubble. "Come to think of it, you're in luck. I saw him yesterday, and he's doing up a place around the corner. Hill Barton Lane."

"Do you know which number?" Reilly said.

"No, but you'll see his car. It's red. Ladders on the roof rack."

"Doesn't he have a van?" Spiller asked.

"No. It's an estate. Vauxhall."

"Thanks," Spiller said. "That's very helpful. Look after yourself."

"Huh. I haven't got much choice, have I?" With that, the man retreated from view.

"What a sweet old man," Reilly said, his tone laden

with sarcasm. "It's always nice to have such wonderful support from the public."

"He's probably lonely," Spiller replied. "At least he talked to us. There are plenty who wouldn't bother."

"True. Let's hop in the Escort. We'll be there in no time."

"Or we could walk. He said it's only around the corner."

"*Walk?*"

Spiller nodded. "It's good exercise, and we'll get some fresh air."

"Bloody hell, it'll be sackcloth and ashes next. Go on, then. We'll relive our glorious days in uniform. At least we don't have to wear those bloody boots."

"I rather liked my old boots."

"I'll bet you did. Come on." Reilly set off, striding out as if to prove a point, and Spiller walked at his side. Reilly led them around a couple of corners and into a street almost identical to the one they'd left.

"Looks like the old fella did us a favour," Reilly said. "One red Vauxhall Astra estate, complete with roof rack."

Spiller followed Reilly's gaze and smiled. "No ladders, so they must be using them in there." Spiller pointed to a building where the front door had been propped open with a plastic crate.

"It's worth a look."

They marched into the building and paused. The acrid stench of bleach mingled with the smell of fresh paint, and the combination stung Spiller's nostrils.

"So much for fresh air," Reilly grumbled. "It's like the Somme in here. Let's get this over and done with."

From somewhere upstairs came the harsh tones of a song Spiller had heard once too often on his car radio: 'Jump Around'.

"I hate that, don't you?" Reilly asked.

"With a passion," Spiller replied. "But I expect Eddie likes music while he works."

"Maybe it takes his mind off the smell." Reilly extended his arm toward the stairs. "After you, and let's not hang about."

"Fine by me."

Spiller climbed the stairs two at a time. On the first floor, the door was open, this time held in place by a large tin of paint.

Spiller knocked on the door and called out, "Hello. We're police officers. All right if we come in?"

The music stopped abruptly, and male voices could be heard, low and urgent.

Spiller was about to call out again when a man plodded into view. Dressed in faded jeans and a grey T-shirt, he didn't fit Spiller's idea of a handyman. For a start, he was too young and good looking, his hair artfully windswept, the blond highlights emphasising his tan. Designer stubble added to the effect, and Spiller wasn't entirely sure whether the man was wearing eye makeup.

Which boy band is he trying to copy? Spiller wondered, but aloud, he said, "Edward Appleton?"

The man smiled. "Yeah, but it's Eddie." He hesitated. "Did I hear you say police?"

"That's right, sir," Reilly replied, showing his warrant card and making the introductions. "Mind if we come in for a chat? It won't take long."

"No problem."

Spiller and Reilly stepped inside, looking around the bare room. The carpet had been rolled up and the floorboards bore streaks and dribbles of paint, testament to the fresh coat of pale blue paint on the walls.

"What are you up to today, Eddie?" Reilly asked.

"What do you mean?"

Reilly gestured to the room. "What kind of job have you got on?"

"Everything. Cleaning, plastering, painting, putting fresh Artex on the ceiling. Some of these places get left in a real mess. The mould is the worst thing. The stuff we use to kill it stinks." As if to prove the point, Appleton sniffed and wiped his nose on the back of his hand.

"It looks like you're doing a good job," Reilly said. "Are you self-employed, Eddie?"

"Kind of. The council hires a firm, they hire me. The money isn't great but it's regular."

Reilly nodded. "That's the thing with council flats, I suppose. There are always people coming and going."

"That's right." Eddie hesitated. "I guess this is about Lynsey."

"What makes you think that?" Spiller said. "We didn't mention her name."

"No, but it was on the radio. I almost fell off the ladder when I heard it. We couldn't believe it."

"Who's we?" Reilly asked.

Appleton hooked a thumb over his shoulder. "Me and Wayne. He helps me out."

"Is that Wayne O'Neill?" Spiller said.

"Yeah. Do you want to talk to him as well?"

Appleton looked as though he was about to call out, so Reilly pre-empted him by raising a hand and saying, "We'd prefer to talk to you one at a time."

"Okay, but we'll both tell you the same thing. The last time we saw Lynsey was on Saturday night. But we didn't see her leave the club, and we have absolutely no idea where she went. If we knew something, we'd have called in."

"You might still be able to help," Spiller said. "On Saturday night, did you see how Tony Carter got a black eye?"

"No, that was outside. I didn't go outside until we went home."

"So you must've seen Keith Osborne holding Tony Carter up after he'd been thumped," Reilly said.

"Er, I'd had a few drinks by then, so..."

"You'd still know what your mates were up to though, wouldn't you?" Reilly asked. "Tony claims that Keith brought him back inside. Is that right?"

"Yeah. Sure."

"How did Tony seem to you?" Spiller said.

Eddie smirked, and Reilly clearly didn't approve.

"Something funny, Eddie?"

"No, not really. It's just... Tony was pissed. He couldn't walk straight."

"What about his mood?" Spiller asked.

"He was a mess. He kept going on about Lynsey, about how she'd dumped him."

Reilly raised an eyebrow. "Was he angry?"

"No." Eddie pulled a face. "Bloody hell, I didn't mean anything like that. I told you, he was a mess, a wreck. He was in pieces. The poor sod was practically sobbing. We told him to go home, and he left soon after."

"Did you go with him?" Reilly asked.

"No. I offered, but he said he could look after himself. He wanted to walk and sober up, and we live in different parts of town, so we left him to it. He seemed okay when he set off."

"What time was that?" Spiller asked.

"It must've been going on for one o'clock."

"Fair enough," Reilly said. "But you, Wayne and Keith stayed until chucking out time at two, did you?"

"Yeah."

Reilly smiled. "Thanks, Eddie. We're almost done, but before we talk to Wayne, can you think of any reason why someone might want to harm Lynsey Clifford?"

"No. Lynsey's nice. She's a bit posh but she's... she's a good laugh." Appleton smiled sadly for a split second, but then his mouth tightened as though there was something he didn't want to say.

"It's okay, Eddie," Spiller said. "You can talk to us."

"I was just thinking, it's got to be something to do with her dad. He's loaded, isn't he? Someone could be trying to get money out of him, but I've no idea who would do that."

"Thanks for your time, Eddie," Reilly said. "If you think of anything else that might help, give us a call."

Reilly offered a business card, but Appleton didn't take it. "It's all right," he said. "The number was on the radio."

"Take it anyway," Reilly insisted. "Those are my personal numbers. The appeal line will be busy, and you don't want to get stuck on hold. It's much better to talk to me directly, Eddie. If there's anything at all, call the number on that card. Understand?"

"Yeah. Whatever." Appleton took the card and read it before sliding it into the pocket of his jeans. "Is that it?"

Reilly nodded. "You can get back to your work. Send Wayne through, will you?"

"No problem. Back to the mouldy ceiling." Appleton sniffed, this time producing a tissue to wipe his nose. "See you later."

He strode away as if relieved to be leaving them behind.

"What did he mean by that?" Spiller asked Reilly. "*See you later*. It's an odd thing to say."

Reilly shook his head. "It's just a turn of phrase, isn't it? I say it myself all the time. Nobody takes it literally."

"No, I suppose not," Spiller said. "I don't know what I was thinking."

Spiller looked down at the paint-spattered floorboards, lost in thought. There was something about Eddie Appleton's story that niggled him, but he couldn't pin down what it was.

Before he could ask Reilly if he felt the same, a man stepped cautiously into the room. This, presumably, was Wayne O'Neill. Like his friend Eddie, he wore a T-shirt and jeans, but O'Neill would never be a candidate for a boy band; he was strictly rock and roll. O'Neill's once-black T-shirt had faded to dark grey. The design on the front was cracked and worn, but the words *Def Leppard* could still be read. Everything else about O'Neill's appearance fitted the image, from his long dark hair and handlebar moustache to the tattoos on his neck and forearms.

"Wayne O'Neill?" Reilly asked.

"Yeah," O'Neill replied, and the interview began.

———

SPILLER AND REILLY exited the building, both men breathing deep and exhaling loudly. Spiller blew his nose on a tissue, and Reilly immediately lit a cigarette.

"I tell you what," Reilly began, "you might think ciggies are bad, but I'd rather have a smoke than breathe in that stuff all day. God knows what they're spraying in there."

"Something with chlorine," Spiller replied. "It gets to you, doesn't it?"

"You can say that again. Let's get out of here."

They headed back to the Ford Escort, Reilly puffing away at his cigarette.

"What did you reckon to Wayne O'Neill?" Spiller asked.

"He's got no taste in music, but apart from that, he seemed like a bright lad, and he backed up Appleton's story."

"That's just it. It was almost identical, word for word."

"That's good," Reilly replied. "Usually, witnesses can't agree on a damned thing, and then you've no idea what to believe."

"Yes, but it was all too neat, wasn't it? Too pat."

Reilly wrinkled his nose. "Don't look a gift horse in the mouth, Tim. We've got two solid witnesses who say Carter left the club soon after Lynsey. He might've pretended to be legless, or he might've sobered up once he hit the street. Either way, he could've followed Lynsey home. He had his eye on her old man's money, so when she dumped him, he saw it slipping away. He couldn't stand that. Think of that flash Audi of his. That's not the car of a man who wants to settle down in a two-bedroom house in St Leonards. He wants more than that."

Spiller thought for a second. "What about the noise Carol Whitaker heard? She said it was something like a van door. That could've been the boot of Appleton's Vauxhall slamming shut. Plenty of room to bundle someone into the back of an estate."

"Or Carol might've heard a taxi or just about any other vehicle. But she didn't *see* anything, Tim. She's no help at all."

"So what next?" Spiller asked. "The bouncers?"

"Absolutely. And if you're lucky, I won't smoke on the way."

———

SPILLER HAD COPIED the addresses of the bouncers into his notebook, and he read them out as they drove back across the city. Reilly's mood had improved significantly. He took a detour to avoid the roadworks, cheerfully pointing out various landmarks as he steered the Ford through a series of residential streets.

As far as Spiller could see, the majority of Reilly's chosen landmarks were pubs, but that was fine. Reilly was happy, he'd refrained from smoking, and all was well with the world.

"We'll call on Greg Taylor first," Reilly said. "I know Churchill Road. It's just off Cowick Street. We'll be there in fifteen minutes."

Quarter of an hour later, they rang the doorbell of a terraced house on Churchill Road. The door was answered by a heavyset man with a shaved head: Greg Taylor himself.

Taylor was civil, if not exactly forthcoming. He was not about to invite them in, and he answered most of their questions with a shake of his head.

Taylor had not worked on the door on Saturday night. He'd been stationed on the dance floor, and he'd seen nothing of note. In the darkened room, lit only by flashing multicoloured lights, he hadn't noticed anyone in particular. He'd been looking out for trouble, and he'd seen none. For that, he was grateful, but he couldn't for the life of him say who had been there and who hadn't.

Reilly persisted, showing Taylor a photo of Lynsey, but the man only stared at it blankly before shaking his head.

Reilly handed Taylor a card, then they took their leave.

"Let's hope we have better luck with the next one,"

Spiller said. "Gary Murphy, known as Gaz, lives at 29 Union Street."

It was a short drive to the house, but there was no answer when Reilly rang the doorbell, and the downstairs curtains were closed.

"Maybe he's asleep," Spiller suggested. "He works nights, after all."

"You could be right." Reilly bent down and peered in at the letterbox. "Then again, the place looks deserted."

Reilly tried the bell again, adding a few solid knocks for good measure, but there was no answer.

"We could try the neighbours," Spiller said. "Someone might know where he hangs out."

"No, we don't want to spend all day chasing our own tails. Let's try a different tack. We haven't talked to Lynsey's other friend yet, Mel Parker, and we know where she'll be."

"County Hall."

"That's right, Tim. County Hall."

25

THE OFFICES of Devon County Council weren't quite what Spiller had been expecting. In an ancient city like Exeter, he'd anticipated a venerable stone building with columns and arches, but he was confronted by a boxy, brick monstrosity. A long, three-storey building, its rigid lines and uniform rows of windows were somehow oppressive, and its square clock tower looked as though it might've been built to keep watch over those within.

"It's not an attractive building," Spiller remarked as he and Reilly made their way to the main entrance. "Impressive in a way, I suppose, but it reminds me of a prison."

"An asylum more like," Reilly muttered. "Some might say the inmates are still there, running the place."

Inside, a receptionist checked their ID and made a call. A couple of minutes later, a man in his early thirties came to meet them. Dressed in a subdued suit and a plain blue tie, he might've been trying to look older than his years. He'd cultivated a thin moustache, and his hair was combed and gelled into a neat side parting.

Reilly and Spiller introduced themselves, and the man extended his hand for a shake.

"I'm Victor Tate. I'm the manager of the finance team in the ICT department."

Reilly and Spiller shook his hand, but the man's grip was limp, and Spiller was only too glad for the experience to be over.

"I understand you wish to speak to one of my team," Tate went on.

"That's correct, sir," Reilly replied, "though it's not so much a wish as a necessity."

Tate made his mouth a thin line. He didn't seem to like being contradicted. "May I ask what this is in regard to?"

"Oh yes," Reilly said. "You can ask."

Tate was temporarily speechless.

"Mel Parker may be a valuable witness," Spiller said. "We need to speak to her as part of an ongoing investigation. Time is pressing."

"That's all we can tell you at this stage of the inquiry," Reilly said. "It's a confidential matter, so we'll need to speak to Miss Parker in private."

Tate nodded slowly, an air of resignation in his expression. "There's a meeting room you can use. If you'll come with me, I'll take you up."

"Lead on," Reilly said. "I'm looking forward to seeing how you spend all my poll tax."

"Community charge," Tate corrected him. He looked as though he'd have liked to say more, but one glance at Reilly dissuaded him. Tate was out of his depth, and Spiller tried not to smile too broadly at the man's discomfort.

Tate didn't speak as he led them up the stairs. When they reached a double door, he fed a plastic card into the lock and ushered them through.

The open-plan office was crammed with desks, the area subdivided by fabric-covered screens. At each desk, a CRT monitor took pride of place: the glowing green displays demanding attention, served by an army of industrious employees. Keyboards clacked, the air conditioning hummed, and a dot-matrix printer whirred and whined, chattering out its staccato message.

It was toward this printer that Tate made his way, marching between the desks. Reilly and Spiller followed, attracting semi-curious glances from several employees.

Tate halted behind a young woman with short brown hair. He cleared his throat, and she looked up, her gaze flicking to Spiller and Reilly.

"Hello, Victor," she said uncertainly. "Is something up?"

Tate leaned on her desk and lowered his voice. "Mel, these gentlemen are police officers. They'd like to talk to you. You can use the meeting room."

Mel gestured to her monitor. "But I'm halfway through this amendment, and you wanted it finished by the end of the day. I can't leave it in this—"

"Yes, you can," Tate interrupted. "The sooner you speak to these officers, the sooner you'll be back at your desk."

Mel's expression clouded. "Okay. Give me a sec." Mel rattled off a few keystrokes, then she stood, smoothing her skirt. In a plain lavender blouse and black pencil skirt, Mel might've been dressed in the conservative manner common to her co-workers, but she carried it off with a certain aplomb. Mel had the look of a young athlete, and her attire showed off her slim figure to its best advantage.

Spiller tried not to watch Mel too closely as she led them across the office, but Reilly showed no such qualms, and he flashed Spiller a wolfish grin. Spiller pretended not to get his drift, and they passed the rest of their short journey in silence.

The meeting room was large, its centre occupied by a horseshoe of tables. Mel seemed unsure where to sit, so Reilly indicated a chair near one corner of the tables. He pulled up a chair on the adjacent side so he could face Mel, albeit at an angle. Spiller took his place beside Reilly and, as usual, he readied his notebook and pen.

Mel sat down and faced them quietly, resting her forearms on the table.

"Mel," Reilly began, "is that short for Melanie?"

"Amelia. But no one calls me that, except my mum and dad."

"Were you at The Icebox nightclub on Saturday night?" Reilly asked.

Mel nodded. "Is this about Tony and that man?"

"Why don't you tell us about that?" Reilly suggested.

"Okay, but I didn't see what happened. All I know is that Tony, that's Tony Carter, got into an argument with some man. Tony followed him outside and came back in with his hand over his eye. I heard someone had punched him."

"Did anybody go outside with Tony?" Spiller asked.

"I don't think so, but..." Mel frowned. "When Tony came back in, one of his mates was holding him up."

"Keith Osborne?" Reilly asked.

"Er, yeah."

Now who's asking the leading questions? Spiller thought. Clearing his throat, he said, "You don't sound very sure. Keith is Ashley's boyfriend, but when we spoke to her, she didn't say anything about Keith helping Tony."

Mel blinked in surprise. "You've talked to Ashley? Why?"

"We'll come to that," Spiller said. "If Keith helped Tony, how come Ashley didn't mention it?"

"I don't know. She might've been in the loo or something. It was busy. The place was packed; you could hardly see across the room."

"I expect you're right," Reilly said. "But let's talk about Tony Carter. How were things between him and Lynsey?"

"You'll have to ask him."

"We've already done that," Spiller replied. "We want to get your perspective. How would you describe the way Tony behaved toward Lynsey on Saturday night?"

"I didn't notice anything different. He was just being Tony. He seemed normal to me."

"Is it normal for him to get jealous?" Spiller asked. "Is it normal for him to get angry if he thinks a man is taking an interest in Lynsey?"

"No, but..." Mel hesitated. "He'd had a few, and him and his mates had been letting off steam. You know, they were a bit loud, but they weren't doing anybody any harm. Tony doesn't make trouble, he plays up a bit, but it's all for show. Deep down he's a nice guy."

"I see." Spiller studiously scribbled in his notebook, then he looked Mel in the eye. "Miss Parker, are you in a relationship with Tony Carter?"

Mel shook her head, dropping her gaze, but her blush gave her away.

"That's not what we hear," Reilly said. "We're told you've been seeing Tony behind Lynsey's back."

Mel composed herself before looking up. "What's that got to do with Tony getting into a fight? It was outside and I wasn't there, I didn't see what happened."

"But you *would* have noticed what time Tony left the club, wouldn't you?"

"I might've. Yeah, I think... I think he left quite soon after he'd been hit."

Her blush was in full swing now.

"Mel," Spiller said gently, "did you, by any chance go home with Tony Carter on Saturday night?"

Mel lifted her chin. "What if I did? Lynsey had broken it off with him, and me and Tony like each other. He's got more in common with me than he has with her."

"Far be it from me to judge you," Spiller said. "But we need to know who was in the club and when they left. Did Tony's friends leave at the same time as you, or did any of them disappear earlier?"

"I think the others stayed until the end, but I don't know. I walked home with Tony. He needed someone to make sure he got home okay."

"That's not what he says," Reilly stated.

"I can't help that, but it's what happened." Mel hesitated. "Tony doesn't want people to know about him and me—not yet."

"What about Tony's friends?" Reilly asked. "Are they keeping it quiet as well?"

"Yes. He told his mates not to say anything. We didn't want to hurt Lynsey. I was going to tell her later when everyone's had time to cool off." Mel chewed on her lower lip. "But that night, I stayed at Tony's place, not that it's any of your business."

"At this point, everything is our business," Reilly said. "We're not here for the fun of it, Miss Parker. We're investigating a serious crime, and it'll help if you cooperate, whether you like our questions or not."

Reilly's tone had been stern, and Mel nodded, chastened.

"Do you really not know why we're here?" Spiller asked.

"Isn't it about Tony?"

"Not directly," Reilly replied. "We're here to talk about Lynsey Clifford."

"Oh?"

"Have you seen Lynsey recently?" Spiller asked.

"No, not since Saturday night. She left before I did."

"I presume she said goodbye," Reilly said.

Mel shook her head. "She just left."

"What time was this?" Reilly asked.

Mel thought for a moment. "It was sometime after midnight. It was about twelve when she bought me a drink. We talked for a bit, but when I went to get my round in later, I had to queue for ages. By the time I got back to our table, Lynsey had gone. I wasn't too pleased. I'd bought her a G and T, and it's not cheap in there."

"So what did you do?" Spiller asked.

"I drank it myself. Waste not, want not."

Spiller almost smiled. "No, I meant what did you do about Lynsey? Didn't you go and look for her? After all, one of your friends had gone off on her own. You must've been worried."

"Not really. Lynsey's pretty sensible, and she can afford to take a taxi whenever she wants. We all figured that's what she'd done. To be honest, we weren't that surprised. She hadn't been herself all evening. We'd tried to cheer her up, but it didn't work. She was fed up."

"Something was bothering her, perhaps," Spiller suggested.

"Yeah. She was still upset about something that happened here. It was on Friday. Someone had a go at her."

"You're the second person to mention an argument

between Lynsey and her boss," Spiller said. "This would be Victor Tate, yes?"

Mel's gaze flicked to the door and back, then she nodded. "He can be a bit of a stickler, and Lynsey did something she wasn't supposed to."

"We're going to need the details," Reilly stated. "What happened?"

"If I tell you, are you going to say anything to Mr Tate? I don't want to get into trouble."

"That depends on what you say," Reilly replied. "But if you don't tell us, I might wonder why you'd withhold evidence from a police inquiry, and that's not a road we want to go down."

Mel squirmed in her seat. "Okay. There's a printer in the office, quite near my desk."

"We saw it," Spiller said. "Dot-matrix. Noisy things, aren't they?"

"You get used to it. We don't print a lot of stuff there. All the main reports come off the big laser printers, and they're near the server room. But when we're testing a program, we run off a few pages on the local printer. We like to see whether it's going to come out okay before we run the main print job. Otherwise, we'd waste a lot of resources, and they're very keen on keeping the costs down around here. That's what caused the problem."

Mel paused. "We don't keep the test printouts, so there's no need to use fresh paper. We take old reports, and we flip the paper over and feed it back into the printer. The tests come out on the blank side. It's continuous, you see, each page is perforated and there are holes all along the edges. So long as the holes are okay and not torn or tatty, the printer can feed them through."

"Go on," Reilly said. "How does all this lead to Lynsey getting a dressing down?"

"I went to get a printout, but there were some extra pages, and I saw they had Lynsey's username on the top, so I tore them off and handed them to her. But she didn't know what they were. She hadn't been running any programs; she wasn't even logged on. She had no idea what the printout was for, so we thought there must've been a problem with the print queue."

"Can you explain that?" Spiller asked.

"Print jobs go into a queue and get printed in order, but if there's a problem with the printer or on the network, a job can get stuck, and it might get printed off later."

"Thank you," Spiller said. "So Lynsey had ended up with an out-of-date printout. Was that what got her into trouble?"

"No. Lynsey said it wasn't hers. She had no idea what it was about, but it was blank on the back, so she shoved it in the box to be reused. I forgot all about it, but a bit later, Mr Tate came over, making a fuss and wanting to know where his printout had gone. Lynsey told him about the only printout she'd seen, but when he checked the scrap paper box, it wasn't there."

"Can I check I've got this straight?" Spiller asked. "The printout belonged to Mr Tate, but it had been labelled with Lynsey's name."

"Got it in one." Mel sent him a smile, but it quickly faded and became a frown.

"Something wrong?" Spiller said.

"No, I don't think so. But now I come to say it out loud, I wonder why Mr Tate was using the printer in the first place. He does all the management stuff, hiring and firing and all that, but he doesn't crunch the numbers. That's our job, along with the system analysts and the accounts department."

"What was on this report?" Reilly asked.

"I don't know, but it must've been important. Mr Tate was not happy. He kept going on about confidentiality. He even threatened to get Lynsey sacked."

"That seems very harsh for an honest mistake," Spiller said. "Are you sure he didn't say what was on this printout?"

"Totally sure. He didn't give a reason, he just went ballistic. He kept saying Lynsey must've taken it, but she didn't have it."

Spiller thought of the way Lynsey's flat had been searched. Could she have taken something home from work, something confidential? He glanced at Reilly and saw a newfound interest in his eyes.

As if on cue, Reilly said, "Are you sure Lynsey didn't take any part of the printout?"

"Positive. She put the whole thing in the box; I saw her do it. Anyway, she had no reason to hold on to it. She knew it wasn't hers."

"Perhaps she misplaced it," Spiller suggested. "She might've mixed it up with some other papers, so she kept the one Tate wanted and put something else in the box."

"I don't know for certain, but Lynsey did her best to find it. She went through her desk, and we both looked around in case it had slipped down the back of the furniture, but we had no luck. It was weird. We're talking about big sheets of paper. It's not like they're difficult to see."

"I think we'd better take a look at Lynsey's desk," Reilly said. "Can you show us, Mel?"

"Yeah, I suppose so, but where is Lynsey? She didn't come in today. She is all right, isn't she?"

"We'll talk about Lynsey in a moment," Reilly replied. "Let's go and see where she works."

Reilly stood, and the others followed his example.

"It's this way." Mel led them back into the office and across the room to the desks by the printer. The machine had fallen silent, but Spiller and Reilly took a moment to inspect it. Beneath the bulky printer, the zig-zag folds of continuous stationery snaked up from a white cardboard box. One side of the paper was marked with thin green lines and had been printed with columns of numbers. The reverse side was blank and ready to be used again.

Mel indicated a desk facing her own. "That's where Lynsey sits."

Reilly and Spiller marched around to Lynsey's desk, but there was nothing on its surface save for a CRT monitor and keyboard, their cables disappearing into a hole at the back of the desk. Beneath the desk was a drawer unit. Reilly pulled out the top drawer and Spiller saw a collection of pens and pencils alongside a pocket calculator.

"Excuse me," someone said, and Spiller turned to see Victor Tate homing in on them.

"Those drawers and their contents are council property," Tate went on. "You can't go rifling through them. You can't even look at them without appropriate permission."

Reilly regarded him with a jaundiced eye. "That's not a problem, sir. Under section 17 of the Police and Criminal Evidence Act, we have the power to enter and search any premises in order to save life and limb."

Tate stopped in his tracks. "What are you talking about?"

"Lynsey Clifford is missing," Reilly replied. "And we have reasonable grounds to believe there may be evidence pertaining to her whereabouts in this desk, so we're going to look through it, *sir*."

Spiller bit his lip. Paddy was skating on thin ice, misusing his power to search, and he must know that. *I ought to say something*, Spiller thought, but before he could speak, Mel hissed a curse that made everyone stop and stare.

"Calm down, miss," Reilly said. "Everything's under control."

"It doesn't look like it to me," Mel replied, her voice wavering. "If Lynsey's missing, why didn't you say something before?"

"We had our reasons." Reilly pulled out the swivel chair and sat at the desk, opening the next drawer down. It was stuffed with cardboard folders and sheets of paper, and he pulled them all out together, placing them in an untidy pile on the desk. To Spiller, he said, "Keep the bystanders out of the way. I need to go through these things in peace."

"No problem." Spiller turned his back on Reilly to face Mel and Mr Tate. For a moment, Spiller clasped his hands in front of him, but it made him feel like a bouncer, so he flipped open his notebook and turned his attention to Tate.

"Mr Tate, I understand there was an altercation between you and Lynsey Clifford on Friday."

Tate had been glaring at Reilly, his face white with anger, but he tore his gaze away and focused on Spiller. "What are you trying to say?"

"I'm not implying anything, sir. I simply want to know the facts. Was there an argument between you and Lynsey Clifford last Friday?"

"I wouldn't call it an argument as such, but you have to

draw the line somewhere, and Lynsey breached our strict rules on confidentiality."

"By accident," Spiller replied. "If something confidential was left lying around for all to see, then legally, the person who'd left it there could be considered negligent."

Tate jutted his chin. "How dare you? I did nothing wrong. Nothing whatsoever."

"So what was this information you printed out?"

"It was a financial report, but it's confidential."

Spiller shook his head slowly. "That won't do, sir. We need to know what it was about."

"I can't help you. The whole thing was lost."

"Then you'll need to print it again," Spiller said.

Tate folded his arms and stared at Spiller in open defiance. "We can't. It's gone and it can't be reproduced. It's been deleted from the system."

"Erm."

The sound came from Mel, and the three men swivelled to look at her.

"I can try running the report again," Mel went on. "Everything we do leaves a trail for the auditors, and I can go through the logs. I know roughly what time the program must've run on Friday, and I know Mr Tate's username, so it shouldn't be hard."

"Do not do that," Tate commanded. "If you do, it'll be the last thing you do in this department."

Mel wrinkled her nose. "You say that, but if something has happened to my friend, I'm going to do everything I can to help. Besides, you can't sack me without a warning. I've got rights, and I'm in the NUPE. If you try anything, I'll talk to my rep, and we'll take you to a tribunal. How would you like that, Victor?"

Tate screwed up his features as if working up a head of steam.

"Mr Tate," Reilly began, his tone solemn. "If I were you, I would stay very quiet. You've already been very obstructive, and I've half a mind to arrest you for attempting to pervert the course of justice."

"We'll see about this." Tate turned on his heel and stormed back to his desk where he picked up the phone and began pressing buttons.

"That's got rid of him," Reilly said. "Miss Parker, if you could print out that report for us, we'd be grateful. How long will it take?"

Mel sat down and flexed her fingers. "Give me five minutes."

Reilly and Spiller went to stand behind her, watching in silence.

Intent on her screen, Mel typed furiously on her keyboard, her expression turning from concentration to consternation.

"It looks like he might've tried to hide it," Mel said. "It's not logged under his name."

"Try Lynsey's username," Spiller said. "After all, it was her name on the report."

"Of course. Stupid of me." Mel's eyes narrowed.

"What is it?" Spiller asked.

"I thought Mr Tate had somehow made a mistake, but what if he used Lynsey's username on purpose?"

"Could he do that?" Reilly said.

"He's not supposed to, but he has access to pretty much everything. I just don't see why he'd do that. If he was found out…"

"He'd lose his job," Reilly suggested.

"Definitely." There was more typing, then Mel murmured, "Bloody hell."

"What have you found?" Spiller said.

"There are dozens of jobs with Lynsey's username attached, but I can tell you now, she didn't run most of them. They're all timestamped, and a lot of them were run after five, but Lynsey finishes at the same time as me: half past four."

"Did she ever work late?" Spiller asked.

"Not Lynsey," Mel replied. "On her salary, why should she? She wouldn't get paid for it unless Mr Tate authorised overtime, and that hardly ever happens."

"That is interesting," Reilly said. "But the question is, can you find the report Lynsey lost on Friday?"

"I should be able to." Mel studied her screen. "Yes, I've got it."

"Can you run it for us now?" Spiller asked, watching Mel carefully. They were on the edge of discovering something here, and Spiller's pulse was racing, his senses heightened. But a nagging voice of doubt told him they were going to hit a brick wall. Surely, Mel was about to shake her head and dash his hopes.

But Mel smiled. "Sure. No problem."

Spiller almost cheered.

Mel resumed typing, and a few minutes later, the dot-matrix printer chattered, the paper jerking upward into the mechanism and spewing from the top.

Mel stood and went to watch, lifting the paper's top edge as it emerged. "Yep, this is it."

Mel took the paper as it came, scanning the rows and columns of figures. The process didn't take long. The printer halted, and Mel advanced the paper with the touch of a button before ripping off the folded sheets along a perforated line.

There were a dozen or so pages and she studied them in turn, her brow furrowed. She looked up at Spiller and Reilly.

"What is it?" Spiller asked. "What does it say?"

"I haven't a clue. I'm sorry, but it doesn't mean much to me. I recognise some of the references, but the figures don't look right. I suppose, whatever it is, it's above my pay grade."

Mel's gaze went to something over Spiller's shoulder, and she quickly handed him the printout. "Here, you'd better take it."

Spiller accepted the set of pages just as Tate marched back to join them.

Before Tate could speak, Reilly said, "The report that went missing—why did it have Lynsey's name on it?"

"I have absolutely no idea," Tate replied. "It must've been a technical error, but it's beside the point. It was my report, it was confidential, and she shouldn't have taken it."

"Why didn't you pick it up yourself?" Spiller asked.

"Obviously, I didn't have time. What does it matter?"

"We'll be the judge of what matters and what doesn't," Reilly said. "Please answer DC Spiller's question."

"All right, if you insist." Tate drew a haughty breath. "Mr Roach, the head of ICT, came to speak to me. It was an important conversation and it took priority. We only spoke for a few minutes, but when I came to collect my report, it had gone. Lynsey had already taken it."

"But she didn't keep it," Mel said. "We've been through this."

"Yes, but I didn't believe her then, and I haven't

changed my mind," Tate snapped. "Lynsey was in the wrong."

"No she wasn't," Mel replied. "But you thought you could use her, didn't you? You thought you could do whatever you liked with her username and she wouldn't even know about it."

"I've heard more than enough from you, Miss Parker," Tate said. "You're talking nonsense."

"I'm not so sure about that," Reilly replied. "Mr Tate, as the department manager, I expect you have to work late a fair bit."

Tate grimaced as if dismayed at Reilly's stupidity.

"Answer the question, please," Reilly insisted. "Do you work late, yes or no?"

"Of course I do. All the time."

"There we are then," Reilly said. "All these reports with Lynsey's name on them, apparently printed out after she'd left for the day, could've been produced by you."

Spiller focused his attention on Tate. The man's face was a mask of anger, but there was a flash of fear in his eyes: fear of being found out, fear of being caught in a lie.

Nevertheless, Tate glowered at them as if determined to brazen it out. But then his gaze landed on the printout in Spiller's hand.

"What've you got there?" Tate demanded. "Whatever it is, you can't take it." Turning his glare on Mel, he barked, "What have you done?"

Mel recoiled from the man's anger, but she held her head high. "I've given them your printout and there's nothing you can do about it. Lynsey is missing, for God's sake. We have to do everything we can to help, and whether you like it or not, that includes you."

"Don't lecture me," Tate shot back. "I'll have you

sacked for this." He thrust his hand toward Spiller. "Give that report to me. I've spoken to the head of—"

"Detective Constable Spiller," Reilly interrupted. "Would you say that Mr Tate is attempting to withhold vital evidence?"

"I would, DS Reilly."

"And have we already cautioned him about the consequences if he persists?"

"We certainly have."

Tate's anger tipped over into righteous fury, his face livid, his ears bright red.

"You listen to me," Tate snarled. "You can't barge in and seize confidential data. It's outrageous. You have no idea what you're doing."

"Is that so?" Reilly said. "We'll see about that. DC Spiller, would you do the honours?"

"Happy to." Spiller stepped forward and took hold of Tate by the arm. "Victor Tate, I'm arresting you on suspicion of perverting the course of justice. You do not have to say anything unless you wish to do so, but what you say may be given in evidence."

Tate spluttered in protest, but no one was listening.

To Mel, Reilly said, "Thank you very much for your help, miss." Passing her a business card, he added. "If you think of anything else that might help us find Lynsey, please get in touch straight away. But before I go, I'd better take down your contact details." Reilly produced a notebook and pen, and Mel recited her phone number and address, all the while gazing at Reilly with admiration.

Spiller couldn't help wondering whether Reilly was basking in the young woman's attention a little too much, but Reilly snapped his notebook shut and was all professionalism once more.

"Thanks again, Miss Parker. We'll be in touch," Reilly said. Nodding to Spiller, he added, "Let's go."

Spiller guided Mr Tate through the office, which was now alive with gasps and murmured gossip. More than one person appeared to be hiding their laughter, their heads down and their shoulders shaking.

"This is all a mistake," Tate said loudly. "It's a misunderstanding. Back to work everybody. I'll soon have this sorted out."

I doubt that very much, Spiller thought. *I doubt that very much indeed.*

26

LEEMAN SAT IN HIS BMW, thinking. Earlier in the day, his answering service had registered a call from Francis Clifford. There'd been no message, Clifford knew better than that, but the call could mean only one thing: Clifford wanted to meet.

I'll get hold of him later, Leeman decided. At the moment, a meeting wasn't worth the risk. After the activities of the previous night, the police would be buzzing about like angry wasps.

I blame myself, Leeman thought. After all, he'd killed three men in one evening. The average murderer would've run for the hills by now.

Leeman smiled to himself. He may be a murderer in the eyes of the law, but the word 'average' had never been applied to him.

Even as a child, he'd known he wasn't like other people. He was different, a cut above, and that was fine with him. It was other people who were the problem. They swam in a sea of mediocrity, weighed down by their ridiculous notions of morality, their nagging consciences, their pathetic desire to fit in, to conform, to follow the rules. But the simple truth was, they were weak and he was strong.

He thought back to the night before. Dennis Mankowich had died as he'd lived, mired in weakness. He'd cursed and moaned and yelled, uttering threats at first but finally begging for mercy. He'd died like the pathetic wretch he was. It had almost been too pitiful to watch.

Few tears would be shed for the passing of Dennis Mankowich. He'd been a cruel and vindictive bully: a small-time drug dealer who'd done nothing with his life except create misery. He'd preyed on the vulnerable, taking from those who had so little to start with. The world was better off without him.

There was only one fly in the ointment. Mankowich had known nothing about Lynsey Clifford's whereabouts. He'd admitted to following her outside the nightclub, but she'd rebuffed him and he'd retreated, angry at the world. Lynsey's boyfriend had chosen the wrong time to confront him, and Carter had been lucky to get away with a punch in the face. Mankowich had been reined in by his uncle, and that had been the end of his brief brush with Lynsey's world.

Leeman sighed and looked out the windscreen, gazing up at the ugly brick edifice that was County Hall. Reilly and his partner had been inside for a while now, and that was intriguing in itself. They might be there to investigate a different case, but Leeman's instincts told him otherwise.

There could easily be a connection between Francis Clifford's business and the city council. There was money to be siphoned from the public purse if you knew how to go about it. Perhaps it was time he had another chat with Mr Clifford.

Have you been holding out on me, Francis? Leeman

wondered. *Have you been economical with the truth, my old friend?*

A vision of Francis Clifford cowering before him came to Leeman's mind, but there was no time for daydreaming. Reilly and his partner were trotting down the steps from the main entrance, a man held between them. This was a turn-up for the books. Leeman had parked strategically, as always, and he got a good look at the man's face, memorising it instantly.

So Reilly was getting somewhere with his investigation. That was something, and to give them their due, the police were good for one thing and one thing only: legwork. A couple of cops could knock on dozens of doors in an hour, whereas Leeman's work was often much slower.

My methods might be time-consuming, he thought, *but in the end, my way is so much more effective.*

The policemen bundled their captive into the back of Reilly's showy Ford Escort, and they drove away.

Leeman started the BMW's engine, but he sat for a while, his fingers resting lightly on the steering wheel. The answers he sought were almost certainly within County Hall, but although he had a couple of well-placed contacts, getting hold of them wasn't as easy as making a call. He didn't work that way. Calls could be traced or overheard, and they left too much room for deception. He never spoke to a contact unless he could see the whites of their eyes.

Leeman thought quickly, running through a range of scenarios in his mind. But what was this? A young woman had emerged from the building. Slim and attractive, she seemed distraught, running her hands through her short brown hair. She hurried down the steps and away from the entrance, glancing back over her shoulder as she crossed an area of grass.

A mature tree seemed to be her destination, and she skirted around its broad trunk until she couldn't be seen from the building. The woman rummaged in her handbag, producing a packet of cigarettes and a lighter. Trembling, she lit her cigarette and took a deep drag before blowing out a thin stream of smoke.

Leeman switched off the engine and climbed from the car, making sure it was locked. With his hands in his coat pockets, he strolled over to join the illicit smoker. She turned with a start, eyeing him warily.

Leeman held up his hands, smiling. "It's all right. I won't tell anyone if you don't." He paused a few steps away from her, giving her time to get used to his presence. "Mind if I join you?"

Leeman pulled out his own pack of cigarettes and the woman appeared to relax a little.

"Go ahead."

"Thanks." Leeman moved closer, patting his pockets. "Damn. I've left my lighter in the car. Can I trouble you?"

The woman had been gazing into the distance, distracted, but she looked at him more closely. "What?"

"Could I beg a light? I'm without the necessary."

"Oh, sure. Sorry." The woman retrieved her plastic disposable lighter and offered it to him.

"Thanks." Leeman lit his cigarette and puffed at it, doing his best not to inhale. He didn't smoke, and he had no respect for anyone who did, but there were times when a simple pack of cigarettes served as a useful prop.

He passed the lighter back and copied her posture, leaning his back against the tree.

"I'm supposed to be giving it up," Leeman went on.

"My wife's always nagging me about it, but it's hard when most of your colleagues smoke, and where I work, it's practically part of the job description."

The woman nodded, feigning interest.

"Tough day?" Leeman asked.

"You could say that."

"There's been some trouble," Leeman observed. "That's why I'm here. I'm with the police, following up on a case. Thought I'd grab a fag break before I get started."

The woman was staring at him now.

"Oh, it's all right," Leeman said. "I'm sure you're not in any bother." He paused, flicking ash onto the grass. "My mate DS Reilly was in earlier, along with the new bloke." Leeman frowned as if trying to remember the man's name.

"Spiller," the woman said.

"That's right." Leeman gazed at her as if sizing her up. "You aren't the young lady they mentioned, are you?"

"Probably. We had quite the conversation."

"So I gather. It's a serious business. We need to find Lynsey Clifford as soon as we can. I don't mind admitting, I'm worried about her."

"Me too." The young woman took another long drag on her cigarette.

Leeman held out his hand. "I'm Detective Chief Superintendent Chisholm, by the way." He pulled a notebook from his pocket: another prop. "I was on my way to see you, but we can talk here if you like. It's a bit more convivial."

"Okay."

"Can I just check your name, miss?"

"Mel Parker, and before you ask, it's Amelia, not Melanie."

Leeman consulted the blank page of his notebook. "Ah

yes, that's what I've got down here, but it's always best to double check."

"Well, I really don't have anything else to tell you. They took the report along with Mr Tate, and that's all I know."

"I'm sorry, Reilly did say something about a report, but I didn't get the details. Things have been a bit hectic in the office, what with the murders."

Mel recoiled.

"Oh, sorry, that was a bit tactless of me. It's a different case and probably nothing to do with Lynsey, although I am beginning to wonder what she was involved in."

"Lynsey wouldn't do anything wrong. She's a good person."

Leeman nodded. "I'm sure she is. Nevertheless, this report could be significant, but Reilly didn't tell me what it was about."

"That's because he doesn't know. Hell, I didn't know what it was about, and I run that kind of job all the time. It was... odd."

"In what way?"

"Well, I didn't see it for long, but I've been thinking about it. The figures didn't make any kind of sense." She finished her cigarette and stubbed it out against the tree before stowing the butt in the box it came from. "Best not to leave any evidence. I'm in enough trouble as it is."

"You won't get into trouble over this, Miss Parker. Helping the police is always the right thing to do." Leeman smiled, copying her actions with his own cigarette. They were complicit now, sharing a moment of transgression.

"Tell me more about this report," Leeman went on. "I can see you have a certain insight into these things, and I'd value your input."

"How much do you know about accounting?"

Leeman tilted his head from side to side. "Not much, but I've got a reasonable head for figures. I can follow the graphs on the news, just about."

Mel faced him, gesturing with her hands as she spoke. "The council sets budgets for everything. You name it, there's a budget for it, from buildings right down to paperclips. And there are projections, so you can look ahead and see how much something ought to cost over time. That's what the report seemed to be, but the figures were crazy. One row seemed to be for schools, and their budgets are always stretched tight, but the projections ran to crazy amounts. Victor must've made a mistake." She broke off, shaking her head in disbelief.

"What's wrong?"

"Nothing. But..." Mel looked at him in frank curiosity, her dark eyes boring into his. "If he'd made a mistake, I can understand why he'd cover it up; he didn't want to look stupid. But if that's all it was, a simple cockup, why did he go ballistic when I showed it to the police? And why was he even running that kind of report in the first place?"

Leeman knew the scent of deceit when it was wafted under his nose, and he sensed it now. Here, perhaps, was a possible motive for Lynsey's abduction. When money appeared on the horizon, greed was never far behind, and it brought its bastard cousins, fraud and corruption. Francis Clifford had not received any ransom demands from her captors, and that could only mean one thing: there was more money at stake than Lynsey's father could possibly provide.

Keeping his attention on Mel, he said, "Those are excellent questions, and I aim to find the answers, but before I can do that, I need to find Lynsey and make sure she doesn't come to any harm."

"Yeah, of course." Mel gazed at the ground. "I wish there was more I could do, but I can't think of a thing."

"You've done your best. But I wonder... No. What am I thinking? You'll have covered this already. I don't want to waste any more of your time."

Mel lifted her head wearily. "If there's a chance it'll help, please ask your questions. I don't mind."

"Thank you. I was wondering who else might have seen the report. Might Lynsey have shown it to anyone else?"

"I doubt it. Like I told DS Reilly, Lynsey had no idea what it was. She barely looked at it."

"It must've meant something to somebody," Leeman stated. "Apart from your boss, who else might've understood those figures?"

"I couldn't say, but it doesn't really matter, does it? As far as I can see, the whole thing was nonsense."

"But what if it wasn't?" Leeman asked quietly. "What if these large sums of money were being misappropriated in some way?"

Mel's initial wariness was back. "Is this how you normally do things, Mr... What did you say your name was?"

"DCS Chisholm, but you can call me John. And don't worry. This is just an informal chat. I'm not accusing you of anything, but I think someone else must've known that Lynsey had her hands on that report."

"No. She picked it up by accident. It was nothing to do with her."

"Who else might've seen what happened?"

"Anyone in the office might've seen, I suppose, but we're always pretty busy. I mean, I sit opposite Lynsey, but I didn't know what was going on until Mr Tate started kicking up a fuss."

Leeman examined Mel, his sharp eyes taking in every detail. The tiny muscles beneath her left eye had twitched minutely as she'd spoken. It wasn't much, but it was enough.

"You're lying," Leeman said quietly. "It went like this. She saw something she didn't understand, and she showed it to you. You're her friend, so of course, she asked for your help. You saw something wasn't right, but you kept it to yourself."

"No."

Leeman moved closer to her. "Yes. You pretended not to be interested, but you told someone what you'd seen."

Mel shook her head. "No. That's not what happened."

"Liar."

Mel flinched as though she'd been slapped, but she recovered quickly and stepped back, putting some distance between them. "This is... it's plain wrong. And you never showed me any ID. I'm..."

Mel didn't finish her sentence. She had the good sense to turn and flee, bustling back to the building as fast as she could in her tight skirt.

Leeman watched her go. *I like her*, he decided. *Let's hope I don't have to visit her again.*

Leeman walked back to his car, reasonably satisfied. He'd pushed Mel Parker as far as he could, given their surroundings, and though he hadn't got the answers he'd hoped for, the conversation had been thoroughly worthwhile. Whether she knew it or not, young Mel had given him a lot to think about.

27

BACK AT THE STATION, Spiller joined Reilly at his desk, pulling up a chair while Reilly flipped through the computer printout they'd taken from County Hall. Spiller studied the rows and columns of figures, but they were labelled with abbreviations he didn't understand, and before he could get to grips with one page, Reilly flipped to the next.

Finally, Reilly reached the end and said, "What do you reckon?"

"It doesn't mean much to me," Spiller admitted. "Some of the figures are fairly eye-watering, but I've got nothing to compare them with. For all I know, they might be run-of-the-mill for the council."

"God knows they've had enough cash out of me over the years. Bloody poll tax."

"It pays for public services, Paddy, and that includes us."

Reilly pulled a face. "Up to a point. We're mostly paid by the government. We get a bit from the council but look at the state of our nick and then look at County Hall. It's not hard to see where the money goes."

Spiller glanced around the office. Reilly had a point. The place could do with a makeover. The furniture was a cobbled together collection of desks and mismatched filing cabinets, there were stains on the ceiling and some of the overhead strip lights were on the blink. There'd been none of that in County Hall, and their CRT monitors had all looked brand new, unlike his decrepit computer.

"Ah, sod it." Reilly tossed the report aside. "It's no use staring at this bloody thing. We ought to forget all about it and concentrate on Tony Carter."

"What about his alibi? Mel Parker was with him the whole time."

"I wouldn't put much faith in anything she says," Reilly said. "Mel wants Tony all to herself. She put on a show of being upset, but she's probably glad to see the back of Lynsey. She might even have been in on it."

"That's a bit harsh, isn't it?"

"Is it?" Reilly raised his eyebrows as though genuinely surprised. "Maybe I'm getting cynical, but whatever we think of young Mel, we can't rely on her as a witness. She's involved with Tony Carter, and that would not go down well in court. Any half decent lawyer would tear her to pieces. It's time to move on."

"But I still think this report is important," Spiller protested. "Look at the timing. Lynsey sees it on Friday then she disappears the next day."

"A coincidence; they do happen, Tim."

Spiller fought down his annoyance at Reilly's condescending tone and braced himself for another round.

"What about Victor Tate's reaction? He practically burst a blood vessel when Mel told him what she'd done. And we know he was angry with Lynsey for just picking the damned thing up. Surely that's a connection between

Lynsey and Tate, and we always follow every lead, don't we?"

"Yes, but there's ways and means. Observe." Reilly stood, grabbed the report, and headed over to DI Nicholson's desk. "Ollie. How's it going?"

Nicholson had been furiously writing on a pad, and he looked up from his task with marked reluctance. "What is it, Paddy? I'm up to my neck here. I'm the incident room manager, and I'm trying to get the action book up to date."

"It'd be worth something if you could spare me a couple of minutes," Reilly said. "A slice of cake from the canteen, maybe."

Nicholson looked unimpressed. "What kind of cake?"

"Whatever's biggest, obviously."

"All right." Nicholson pushed the action book away from him with a sigh. "Go on. What do you want?"

"It's about Lynsey Clifford. She works at County Hall, and this was one of the last things to pass through her hands." Reilly showed him the report. "Whatever it is, her boss was very keen to keep it under wraps. He tried to stop us from taking it. He kicked up so much fuss, I had to bring him in."

"Ah, so that was the bloke you arrested for perverting the course of justice." Nicholson shook his head. "I hear you got Tim to make the arrest. You might think you've covered your arse but think again. You were the senior officer on the scene, and you overreached yourself. The guvnor wants a word with you, by the way. He's not best pleased."

Reilly waved Nicholson's words away. "We'll cross that bridge when we come to it. It'll be all right. I'll get Bri to have a word; he'll back me up."

"Don't bank on it. Bri stuck his neck out for you before

and look where it got him." Nicholson glanced briefly at Spiller, before adding, "I'd watch your step if I were you, Paddy. Bri is a changed man. He's doing everything by the book. He knows he's got something to prove, and he's working like a demon."

"He'll understand," Reilly replied. "We had to bring the bloke in. He was trying to put the brakes on my inquiry. Why would he do that unless he had something to hide?"

"I don't know," Nicholson said. "Maybe he's just an idiot. The world is full of them. We can't arrest them all."

"Watch me."

Reilly laughed but Nicholson didn't join in. Instead, he said, "You've landed yourself in trouble, Paddy, and you know it."

"I might've overstepped the mark a tiny bit," Reilly admitted. "But I'll be in the clear if I'm right. This report might be the reason someone took Lynsey. The problem is, we can't make head nor tail of it."

Nicholson nodded slowly. "So this is where I come in, is it? I'm supposed to bail you out, am I?"

Reilly smiled. "All I'm asking is for you to have a look at it. You're good at this sort of thing, Ollie, much better than anyone in the nick. If there's something to find, you'll see it."

Nicholson narrowed his eyes, but his gaze lingered on the report in Reilly's hand. "I suppose I could have a look later on, after the end of play, but, and this is a big but, only if someone plies me with a pint of Guinness."

"Sure, I'll get you a pint." Reilly gestured to himself and to Spiller. "*We* will. Two pints. And a packet of crisps. Salt and vinegar. That's better than cake any day of the week."

"Oh, I want the cake as well. I'll have that now; beer and crisps later."

"Bloody hell," Reilly muttered. "You drive a hard bargain."

"Well? What's it to be?"

"Cake, beer, crisps, whatever you want." Reilly placed the report on Nicholson's desk. "You've got to have a proper look, mind. You can't just give it a once-over and say that's it."

"I'll sort it, don't you worry." Nicholson pulled a battered leather briefcase from beneath his desk and tucked the report inside. "Now, what would go well with that cake is a nice mug of tea."

"Sure. Whatever." Reilly made for the door, but before he left, he called out, "Tim, make Ollie a mug of tea, will you?"

Spiller was about to reply, but Reilly was already out the door.

"I'll put the kettle on," Spiller said. "Thank you for helping us out, Ollie. We were getting nowhere fast." He hesitated. "I suppose I'll get a bollocking for making that arrest."

"Oh, yes," Nicholson replied. "But I'd bet a tenner you were only doing what you were told."

Unsure what to say, Spiller shuffled his feet.

"I thought so," Nicholson went on. "Don't worry about it, Tim. You won't get far in this job without getting a bollocking now and then, not unless you're a complete non-entity. To be honest, it shows you're willing to stick your head above the parapet. The trick is to know when to duck."

"And when to wear your helmet," Spiller replied.

Nicholson smiled, seeming to see Spiller anew. Nevertheless, he shooed him away. "Go on, young man. Where's my tea? Milk and one."

"I remember." Spiller strolled over to the kettle, smiling to himself. Nicholson might be warming to him, and that could only be good. But as the tea brewed, Spiller glanced back at Nicholson and a thought struck him. The DI looked like a man who could put away a fair few pints of an evening. How many free beers would he demand?

It's all very well for Reilly to make promises, Spiller thought. *But some of us are still waiting for our first CID pay cheque.* Still, he could stand his round, so long as the others didn't go mad and demand large whiskies. *It'll be worth it,* Spiller decided. *It had better be, or Sheila will kill me.*

———

After a hasty lunch in the canteen, Reilly wolfing down sausage and mash while Spiller self-consciously munched on his homemade sandwiches, the pair reconvened at Spiller's desk.

"Here you go," Reilly said, handing over a stack of paper. "One for each call to the hotline. Enjoy."

Spiller set to work, quickly realising that most of the calls could be set to one side. Not everyone had listened carefully to the appeal before phoning in, and Spiller soon found himself muttering under his breath as he sorted the wheat from the chaff.

"What's up?" Reilly called from his desk. "Nothing decent coming in?"

"Not yet," Spiller replied. "We've had reports of teenagers mucking about, including a number of girls, one of which *might* be Lynsey. Someone else saw a woman making a noise in the street on Saturday night, and she *might* have had brown hair, but she was the wrong age, by the sound of it. Another caller saw a woman with brown hair sticking her head out of a car window and shouting as she passed by. That was probably the best one so far, but do we know when this happened? No we do not. All we know is, it was on a road called Summer Lane." Spiller sighed. "I don't know. Everything I've seen so far has been too vague to be useful."

"It's always like that. Some people don't need much of an excuse before they call in. They see something they don't like the look of, and they happily put two and two together. Some of them are lonely or they've got nothing better to do; they want to feel useful." He paused. "I'm interested in the woman seen shouting from a car, though. Chase it up. It could be the best lead we get."

"There's an address. Shall I pop over and see what they say?"

"Phone first. It's the same routine for any promising leads. Try to get an idea if the person is reliable, then you can start to prioritise. We can't go chasing after every possible sighting. Pick the best ones and take it from there."

"Will do. How are you getting on?"

"Not bad. Background checks are done, but there's nothing earth-shattering so far. I drew a blank on the PNC, so neither Carter nor his friends have been on our radar. But we still need to tick Keith Osborne off our list. I've lined up an interview, so we'll see what—"

Reilly halted abruptly as Detective Chief Inspector Wendell marched into the room, a smartly dressed man in his wake.

"Bugger it," Reilly murmured.

Spiller sent him an inquiring look, but Reilly simply shook his head, a warning in his eyes.

"There you are," Wendell called out, crooking his finger at Spiller and Reilly. "You two, here, now."

"Yes, sir." Spiller jumped to his feet, and a beat later, Reilly followed suit. They trudged over to Wendell like reluctant schoolchildren, their gaze hovering somewhere near the carpet.

"This is Mr Pike," Wendell said, "a solicitor acting on behalf of Mr Victor Tate."

"I know Mr Pike," Reilly began, but that was as far as he got.

"Perverting the course of justice?" Wendell growled. "Are you two out of your minds?"

Neither Spiller nor Reilly replied.

"For God's sake," Wendell went on, "have you any idea what you're doing?"

Reilly took a breath, flaring his nostrils. "With respect, sir, Mr Tate was trying to conceal evidence, and we had reason to believe he'd already been obstructive. He'd lied to us from the start."

"Good lord," Pike murmured, his cultivated accent making the two words sound like particularly damning criticism. "If, Detective Sergeant, you had reason to believe you'd find significant evidence at County Hall, can you tell us why you didn't seek a search warrant for the premises?"

"Because, sir, we did not know about said evidence until we'd spoken to Miss Parker. She's a colleague of Lynsey Clifford: a young woman we're searching for as a matter of urgency."

"Tell me, DS Reilly," Pike began, "have you heard of the Police and Criminal Evidence act? Does it ring a bell at all?"

Reilly said nothing, though it looked as though he would dearly like to.

"You seized a document without the proper authority," Pike went on. "What has become of it?"

"It's been entered into evidence," Reilly stated. "We're looking at it closely to establish whether it's relevant."

Pike peered at Reilly as though inspecting a rare specimen of humanity. "Evidence of what, DS Reilly? No, don't answer that. You must know you could never present it in court."

"Even so, we believe the report may help us to understand what happened to Lynsey Clifford."

Wendell thrust out his hand. "Let's have a look at it."

"I'm afraid we can't give you the report at the moment, sir." Reilly offered a regretful smile. "One of my colleagues has taken it for analysis."

Wendell and Pike stared at Reilly, wordless.

"I'll be happy to return it to County Hall at the earliest available opportunity," Reilly went on. "In the meantime, I can see no reason why Mr Tate can't be released without charge."

Mr Pike rocked back on his heels and Spiller glanced down at the man's pristine black shoes. *Handmade Oxfords*, Spiller thought. *Italian leather, most likely.*

"Well, well, well," Pike said. "A rare outbreak of common sense." He bestowed a smile on Wendell. "It seems as though today's visit will be brief, Brian. Perhaps, if the formalities could be concluded quickly, I'll be able to escort my client from the building."

"Of course," Wendell replied. "I'll see to it myself."

"Thank you, but..." Pike's gaze settled on Reilly. "I'd like him to do it."

"We don't generally take requests," Wendell said. "But in this case..." He hooked his thumb toward the door. "Go on, DS Reilly. Get Mr Tate out of the cells. Snap to it, and while you're down there, offer him a polite apology. That way, we might not end up with an official complaint landing on our desks."

"I think we can safely agree to that," Pike replied. "In my view, it would be best if this sorry incident were to be forgotten entirely. Unless, that is, we have further reason to meet again in regard to this matter." He looked expectantly at Reilly.

"I'm sure we needn't trouble Mr Tate again," Reilly said. "Unless he gives us good cause, that is. None of us are above the law, Mr Pike."

"Indeed." Pike's smile put Spiller in mind of a Great White Shark.

"I'll take you down," Reilly said with a smile of his own. "To meet your client, I mean. I'd hate for you to think I was making a threat."

Pike didn't reply, but his eyes sparkled as though he'd enjoyed Reilly's play on words. Wendell's gaze, on the other hand, burned with repressed fury, and as soon as Reilly and Pike had left the room, he turned his glare on Spiller.

"I know you're new, Spiller, but you've been in uniform, and you ought to know where to draw the line. There are ways and means of doing things. We have procedures and we follow them. What we *don't* do is sling around allegations without evidence. That's not how we work, Spiller. It's not good enough."

"Yes, sir. Sorry, sir." Spiller's apology was sincere, but he looked Wendell in the eye and accepted his punishment. He could stand to be corrected, but he'd be damned before he'd be bullied.

Wendell held his gaze, but he seemed to realise there was no more entertainment to be had at Spiller's expense.

"Don't just stand there, man," Wendell snapped. "Get back to work."

"Yes, sir," Spiller said, but Wendell was already storming from the room.

Spiller stood for a moment, recalling Ollie Nicholson's earlier advice. If taking a bollocking really was a sign of progress, he was already doing well.

28

SPILLER REPLACED the phone's receiver and marked a tick beside the last name on his list of taxi firms. *Probably another dud*, he thought. *Just like the others.* No taxi driver, it seemed, had picked up a woman on her own near The Icebox club on Saturday night. Still, he'd asked each firm for a complete list of pickups in the area between midnight and three o'clock, along with the destination of each taxi. After all, Lynsey may have stayed later than her friends thought, or she may have shared a taxi with someone else.

Spiller had doggedly recorded every detail. After his brush with DCI Wendell, he was determined to show what he could do. Even so, he was far from satisfied. *We've left it too long*, Spiller decided. *We should've done this yesterday.*

Memories were unreliable, and the records kept by taxi firms weren't exactly comprehensive. It would've been better to talk to them sooner, speaking to every driver in person. It would've taken time and resources, but it would've been worthwhile. Unfortunately, that decision hadn't been his to make.

Paddy must've had his reasons, Spiller thought. *He knows what he's doing.*

As if reading Spiller's mind, Reilly came over to join him.

"Any luck, Tim?"

"Not yet."

"Let's have a look."

Spiller handed him the list and Reilly perched on the edge of Spiller's desk while he scanned it. "You've been busy," Reilly went on. "You'll be ready for a change of scene. Keith Osborne's just come in for an interview. Do you fancy sitting in?"

"Yes I do. Anything to get off this chair for a bit. I'm starting to feel like I'm welded to it."

Reilly laughed. "Ah, you're that kind of copper."

"Go on," Spiller replied wearily. "You're going to poke fun at me anyway; we may as well get it over with."

"Don't get me wrong, Tim. I wasn't taking the mickey. Some coppers like to keep their feet under a desk all day. They want to stay inside where it's warm and dry, and there's tea and biscuits. But I reckon you're more of an old-fashioned, hit-the-streets kind of copper, and there's nowt wrong with that. I'm the same. I recognise a fellow sufferer, you might say."

"I'll take that as a compliment." Spiller stood, grabbing his jacket from the back of his chair and arching his back. "That chair is an instrument of torture. It's playing hell with my back."

"We'll get you a better one, eventually."

"What about a better computer? I notice everybody else has an HP, but I've got this old Olivetti. The keyboard's a bit sticky and the *D* doesn't work properly. What good is that?"

Reilly stifled a grin. "If it's sticky, it's because it used to be Ollie's. He's always eating, that man. Give the keyboard a wipe down and shake the crumbs out of it. But you can do that later. We've got a witness waiting, and he should be nicely on edge by now. Leave him too long and he'll tip over into annoyed and uncooperative, and we don't want that."

Spiller followed Reilly down to the lobby. Behind the desk, Sergeant Colin Goodwin greeted them with a nod. "Your visitor has stepped outside. He was getting a tad impatient, so I should grab him quick if I were you."

"Cheers, Skip," Reilly said, adding to Spiller, "Can you fetch him? I'll wait here."

"No problem."

Outside, a man in a pale-grey, double-breasted suit paced the tarmac, smoking a cigarette and inhaling hard enough to make the tip glow bright.

"Mr Osborne?" Spiller called out.

The man halted abruptly and faced him, his features wrinkling in annoyance as he took the cigarette from his mouth. Spiller immediately thought of a baby being deprived of its dummy, and he couldn't help but smile.

"Yeah, that's me," Osborne replied. "Who are you? You don't sound like the bloke I talked to on the phone."

"I'm Detective Constable Tim Spiller. You spoke with Detective Sergeant Reilly. He's inside waiting for you."

"It took him long enough." Osborne threw his cigarette to the ground and extinguished it with the sole of his shoe. He made to climb the steps, but Spiller wasn't having that.

"Excuse me, sir, but littering is an offence."

"What?"

Spiller pointed to the cigarette stub. "If you could pick it up, sir, we'll say no more about it. There's a bin inside."

"Bloody hell." Osborne retrieved the butt, holding it between finger and thumb as he marched up the steps.

As he drew closer, Spiller saw what might be a bruise on the man's right cheek: an oval of reddish skin below the cheekbone. He made a note to ask about it later, but for the meantime, he led Osborne inside.

Reilly stepped forward and introduced himself, shaking Osborne by the hand.

"We'll go through to an interview room, Mr Osborne. It's nice and quiet in there, and we won't be disturbed."

"It's all the same to me."

"It's this way." Reilly marched along the corridor, opening the door to Interview Room 1 and extending his arm to usher Osborne inside.

Osborne entered slowly, his gaze taking in the spartan room.

"Christ, what a dump." He pointed to a chair beside the table. "Do I sit there?"

"Yes please, sir," Reilly replied cheerfully, and Spiller had to respect his ability to remain polite and friendly. Osborne was instantly unlikeable, but that wasn't a crime. Unless the situation changed, Osborne was a member of the public and entitled to professional courtesy.

However much of a prat he is, Spiller thought, but he plastered a smile on his features and joined Reilly, who'd taken a seat facing Osborne across the table.

"We'll be recording the interview, Mr Osborne," Reilly said. "It's just a formality, but it saves us taking notes and then we can concentrate on our little chat."

"Do I have a choice?" Osborne asked.

"Don't be like that, Keith," Reilly replied. "Do you mind if I call you Keith? We're all friends here. You've taken the time to come and help and we appreciate it. This is just routine."

Without waiting for any further comment, Reilly started the recording and announced who was present.

"Okay, Keith," Reilly began, "can you confirm your address for us?"

"No. I can tell it to you, but I can't confirm something we haven't already said, can I?"

Reilly's smile lost some of its humour. "You know what I mean, Keith. We have an address for you, but I'd like to hear it from you. Where do you live?"

"Kingsley Avenue. Number eight."

"Very nice," Reilly replied. "You live there on your own?"

"Yeah."

"Nice neighbourhood," Reilly said. "You must be doing all right for yourself."

"I do okay." Osborne seemed to be trying for a nonchalant smile, but it didn't convince Spiller.

"Buying or renting?" Spiller asked.

"If you must know, I rent. Satisfied?"

"For now," Reilly replied. "You know why you're here, don't you, Keith?"

Reluctantly, Osborne said, "Yeah. Lynsey's gone missing. I saw it on TV. It was on the news."

"That's right," Reilly said. "I understand you were with Lynsey at The Icebox on Saturday night."

"Sort of. I was there with Tony Carter. I think I saw Lynsey."

Reilly frowned. "You either saw her or you didn't, Mr Osborne."

"All right, I saw Lynsey. She was with my girlfriend, Ashley. They're friends."

"Did you talk to Lynsey during the evening?" Spiller asked.

Osborne made a show of thinking. "We said a few words. I can't remember what we talked about. Nothing much, I shouldn't think."

"How did she seem?" Reilly asked.

Osborne shrugged. "All right. A bit quiet, maybe."

"Is that it?" Spiller asked. "Nothing else struck you at all?"

"No." Osborne stared at them, sullen insolence in his gaze.

Reilly tutted. "Now then, Keith, you can't expect us to believe that. We've seen a photo and Lynsey's a looker. You're a red-blooded young man; I reckon you took more of an interest in her than you're letting on."

"Not really. Lynsey was going out with Tony, and Tony's a mate. I wouldn't eye up his girlfriend."

"Okay, but you did notice her," Reilly insisted. "You would've seen, for example, if she went outside during the evening."

"No. I was with my mates, having a good time. I talked to Ashley, but that's different. She's my girlfriend. If I don't pay her a bit of attention, she gets moody. But that's women, right?"

Spiller held his tongue.

Reilly, on the other hand, simply switched tack. Pointing at Osborne, he said, "How'd you get that mark on your face?"

Osborne seemed startled, his hand going to his cheek, but he recovered quickly, folding his arms. "It was Tony. He got into a bit of a fight with some bloke. Tony didn't mean anything by it, but his mouth runs away with him when he's had a few. Anyway, he's a mate, so I was trying to keep him out of trouble, but the silly bugger wouldn't listen. I had to hold him back, and he didn't like it. He gave me a slap." Osborne laughed. "He apologised afterwards, but it was nothing. It didn't even hurt. He was too far gone to throw a decent punch, the poor lad."

"When was this?" Spiller asked.

"Saturday night, outside the club."

Spiller looked Osborne in the eye. "Are you sure, sir?"

"Yeah. I'm not going to forget something like that, am I?"

"No," Spiller replied. "You're not likely to forget, so you must remember who Tony got into a fight with."

"Er, it was just some bloke. Tony reckoned he'd been ogling Lynsey, so he went out and said something."

"Did he do that kind of thing often?" Reilly asked.

"Not really. Tony's not a troublemaker. He just gets a bit jealous, that's all."

Reilly nodded wisely. "Jealousy makes people do bad things—terrible things. I've known men kill for it."

Osborne let out a muted laugh as though he wasn't sure whether Reilly was joking.

"This is no joke," Reilly went on. "Is Tony Carter like that? Does he have a temper?"

"No. He's a good lad, but that night, he was in a funny mood. He said Lynsey chucked him, but I don't know if that was for real or if they were having one of their *rows*."

The way Osborne emphasised the last word made Spiller sit up a little straighter. "Did they argue a lot?"

"No, not like you're thinking."

"Is that so? And what am I thinking, Keith?"

Osborne waved a hand in the air as if shooing away a troublesome fly. "You're trying to trick me. You want me to make out like Tony's a bad bloke, but he isn't. He's not an angel, but he knows where to draw the line. He'd never get rough with a girl."

"It's funny you should say that," Reilly began, "because we didn't say anything about Tony getting rough with Lynsey. Where did that idea come from?"

"You see! You're twisting what I say."

"Set us straight then," Reilly said. "Tell us about Tony and Lynsey, and we'll listen."

Osborne looked unconvinced, and Spiller thought he was about to clam up, but Osborne drew a breath and said, "Okay, I'll tell you how it is. Tony worships the ground that girl stands on. They had their little rows, the same as any couple, but it was nothing serious. Usually it was because they didn't want to do the same things, but they always figured it out. Tony might be out with the lads one night, but he'd stay home with Lynsey the day after. Give and take, you know?"

"I think there was more to it than that," Spiller said. "We've heard reports of them shouting at each other."

"So what? Ashley yells at me, but she doesn't mean it. As far as I know, it was the same with Tony and Lynsey. We all thought they were solid. We thought they'd be getting married before long, so maybe you can see why Tony was in such a state when she broke it off with him. Any bloke would be the same."

"Maybe so," Reilly said. "But this isn't any bloke and any girl. It's your mate Tony and his ex-girlfriend, who happens to have disappeared."

"Yeah, and I'm worried about her, but I don't know where she's gone, and I don't know why. All I can say is, Lynsey can be very headstrong. She might have taken it into her head to get out of here for a few days. It wouldn't surprise me at all. She can afford it."

"Why would she do that?" Reilly asked.

"I don't know. Maybe..." Osborne shook his head as if changing his mind. "Maybe she was fed up, wanted a holiday."

"What were you going to say just now?" Reilly said. "Something about Tony, perhaps? Something about him cheating on her with Mel and Lynsey finding out?"

Osborne's face fell. "Tony might've had a bit on the side now and then, but it was nothing serious. Lynsey was the only girl he cared about."

Reilly drummed his fingers on the table, the sound reverberating in the bare-walled room. He seemed distracted, looking away as if deep in thought. Spiller wasn't sure whether to say anything, but Reilly suddenly looked up and said, "Where do you work, Keith?"

"In town. An office on Barnfield Road."

"What kind of office?" Reilly asked.

"ABM. We're building contractors."

Reilly raised his eyebrows. "You're dressed very smart. It must be a posh builder."

"It's a big company. We're not house builders. We do big projects: commercial, industrial, that sort of thing."

"And what do you do, Keith?" Reilly asked. "What's your job title?"

For the first time, Osborne looked uncomfortable. "I'm only an assistant at the moment. I deal with the paperwork, but I'm learning on the job. I'll get a promotion soon."

"Paperwork, eh?" Reilly said. "That doesn't sound like much fun for a young man."

"It's steady and it pays the bills, which is more than you can say for a lot of jobs these days."

"That's true enough," Spiller replied. "This building

firm you work for, do they have anything to do with Mr Clifford's company?"

Osborne's lip curled in disdain. "We build things, we don't knock them down."

"I know," Spiller said. "But sites need clearing before you can build, and Mr Clifford runs a demolition and salvage business."

"Yeah, but they're small fry. They get the crumbs from the table. Besides, I hear they're not doing so well."

"Where did you hear that?" Spiller asked.

"I dunno. It's common knowledge." Osborne shifted his position on the chair. "Look, you said you wanted to ask about Lynsey, not her old man. She's missing, and we're talking a load of old bollocks. Let's get on with it."

Spiller and Reilly shared a look. Osborne was keen to change the subject away from his work, but why?

"Something bothering you, Mr Osborne?" Spiller asked.

"No." Osborne drew a steadying breath. "I'm just worried about Lynsey. I want to help, so let's talk about her."

"All right, then," Reilly said. "Let's get back to the club on Saturday night. What time did Lynsey leave?"

"I don't know. Like I said before, I wasn't hanging around with her but..." Osborne sighed. "If I had to make a guess, I'd say she must've left before one o'clock. It was about that time when Tony got thumped, and I'm pretty sure she'd left by then." Osborne's expression brightened and he clicked his fingers. "Yeah, Ashley said something about it. Mel had bought a drink for Lynsey, but she'd already gone. Mel wasn't too happy about it."

Osborne grinned, and something in his manner made Spiller want to push him further.

"What kind of drink?" Spiller asked.

"Eh?"

"It's a simple question," Spiller said. "What kind of drink had Mel bought for Ashley?"

"Er, I think it was gin." Osborne pulled a face, "I can't stand the stuff myself. Give me a whisky any day."

"Same here," Reilly said. "How long have you been going out with Ashley?"

"A couple of years, give or take."

"It's a long-term thing, then," Spiller said. "In all that time, you must've been to Lynsey's flat more than once."

"No, why would I?"

"You're going out with one of Lynsey's friends," Spiller replied. "Lynsey must've invited you both to her place."

Osborne shook his head firmly. "The girls go to each other's houses sometimes, but me and the lads usually meet down the pub. We don't do spaghetti bolognaise and bottles of plonk. If we want something to eat, we grab a curry. I expect you're the same; you don't look like dinner-party types."

"Perish the thought," Reilly replied, but Spiller said nothing. He was busy studying Osborne. The man's last remark had been an attempt to close the subject, to steer the discussion away from Lynsey's flat.

Making sure he had Osborne's attention, Spiller said, "Keith, I hope you don't mind me asking, but how did you get on with Lynsey?"

Osborne tensed. "She's all right. I was sorry to hear she'd gone missing. It's a damned shame."

"With respect, that's not what I asked," Spiller replied. "Are you avoiding the question? Is that because you don't like her?"

"No. Me and Lynsey, we get on okay, but..." Osborne

hesitated. "I know this sounds bad, but you're right, we're not exactly friends. To tell you the truth, she's never liked me. I tried to be friendly at first, mainly for Ashley's sake, but right from the start, it was obvious what Lynsey thought. She barely spoke to me, and sometimes she'd look down her nose at me, like I was something the cat dragged in, you know?"

"I see," Reilly said. "Thanks for being straight with us, Keith. It helps to build up a picture."

"If you say so."

"We do," Reilly replied. "But let's talk about you for a sec. What kind of car do you drive, Keith?"

"Flipping heck, you go around the houses, don't you? What's that got to do with anything?" Osborne held up a hand. "Never mind. I'm not going to argue; it's not worth it. I drive a Vauxhall Cavalier. New."

Spiller sucked air over his teeth, impressed. "Very nice, but not cheap."

"It's a company car."

"What colour did you go for?" Reilly said. "I saw a nice one the other day: polar white."

Osborne wrinkled his nose. "Get a white car and people think you're a cop. No disrespect, but I don't want that. I went for midnight blue, charcoal interior. It's the new GSI model. 150 BHP."

Reilly nodded, but he seemed to take this information badly, and he looked downcast. Perhaps he was thinking that, despite his years of service in the police, there'd be no brand-new company car for him. On that score, Osborne was already ahead, even though he was young and only an assistant.

As if reading Reilly's body language, Osborne said, "Is that it? Can I go?"

"Yes, you can," Reilly replied, "I reckon we're done for now. Thanks for your time, Keith."

"No problem. I don't see how it helped, but I suppose you have to talk to everyone."

"We do," Reilly said. "We also have to say that if you remember anything that might be useful, or if you see or hear anything that might help us find Lynsey, please get in touch."

Reilly handed over a business card and Osborne stowed it in his jacket pocket.

"I hope you find her soon," Osborne said. "Tony's going spare."

"You've spoken to him?" Spiller asked.

"Yeah, he gave me a call at work. He said you'd been to his house and chased him down the street. I told him it was his own stupid fault for running away. It made him look guilty, the silly bugger."

"Indeed, it did," Reilly said. "I'm glad you've got more sense than your mate. Anyway, unless there's anything else you want to tell us, we've finished."

"No, there's nothing I can think of." Osborne checked his watch. "I've got to go. They're expecting me back at work."

"Fine," Reilly said. "DC Spiller, could you show Mr Osborne out? I've got to deal with this tape."

"No problem." Spiller headed for the door, and Osborne followed. They didn't talk on the way, and as soon as Spiller opened the main door for him, Osborne marched off without a backward glance.

It was only then that Spiller realised he'd missed something. *He lied about that bruise*, Spiller thought. *It can't have happened on Saturday night*. The bruise had been red, not blue, and that meant it was fresh, probably from earlier that same day.

On its own, it didn't amount to much, but it showed that Osborne wasn't to be trusted.

I ought to tell Paddy, Spiller decided. *But I know what he'll say*.

If they pressed Osborne on the subject, he'd easily conjure up some excuse, saying he'd walked into something or tripped over his shoelace. There was no other evidence to link Osborne with Lynsey's disappearance, and several witnesses had said that Osborne helped Tony Carter after he'd been thumped. That fight, such as it was, had occurred sometime after Lynsey left the club.

Osborne had an alibi, and what was more, he'd voluntarily come in for an interview; that was a point in his favour. There was no clear motive for Osborne to harm Lynsey, but with a steady job and the prospect of promotion, the man had plenty to lose. He was in the clear.

Spiller made his way up to the CID office, a deep sense of unease making itself at home in his mind. It was as if the events of Saturday night were taking on a solid form around him: an encircling wall of testimony with each witness adding new bricks. But there was one crucial piece missing from the foundations: no one was talking about Lynsey.

Oh, they referred to her, they mentioned her, but there was little substance in what they had to say. She was independent, they'd said, she could look after herself. So they'd left her to go home alone.

Was Lynsey even real to these people, to her parents, to her so-called friends?

She's real to me, Spiller thought. *And she's real to someone else*. To the person who took her, Lynsey was everything;

she was the difference between wealth and need, between success and failure, between freedom and a life behind bars.

It was up to him to bring Lynsey into focus, but how was he to do it?

There's one good way to break down a wall, Spiller decided. *You find a weak spot and you shove it as hard as you can.*

There'd be an inconsistency in the evidence; there had to be. All he had to do was find it.

29

The Horse and Groom pub sat on a corner; the quiet of Church Street on one side and the bustle of Fore Street on the other. Spiller followed Reilly and Nicholson in through the front door and felt instantly at home. This was a good old-fashioned boozer, with none of the loud music and garish lighting that had spoiled so many pubs.

Nicholson spied a vacant nook, separated by frosted glass partitions on either side, and he made a beeline for it, calling over his shoulder, "A pint of Guinness, lads. And don't forget the crisps. Salt and Vinegar."

Spiller headed for the bar, but Reilly laid a hand on his arm. "I'll get these, Tim."

Spiller started to protest, but Reilly held up a hand to stop him. "What'll you have, lager?"

"Please, but I'd better have a half."

"You will not," Reilly replied. "I'll get you a pint and no arguments. You go and keep Ollie company before he starts chewing on the beermats, but don't let him start without me. If he says anything about the report, distract him. Ask him about his kids. Okay?"

Without waiting for a reply, Reilly marched to the bar and was immediately served.

Nicholson had stowed his briefcase beneath the table and was making himself comfortable, loosening his tie and sitting back, gazing expectantly around the room. Spiller sat facing him and smiled, looking forward to his beer.

"Heard you copped an earful from Bri," Nicholson said. "Don't say I didn't warn you."

"Water under the bridge," Spiller replied. "I hope so, anyway."

Nicholson waggled a hand in the air. "Bri's okay, but he's a hard man to please since his you-know-what. I'd keep your head down if I were you."

"Sounds like good advice. To be fair, he was totally right. We were out of order when we brought in Victor Tate. I should've thought it through at the time, but it all happened so fast."

"Thereby hangs a tale," Nicholson said. "Don't get caught up in the heat of the moment. Next time you feel the urge to arrest someone, think of the paperwork. It's like a cold shower. It gets me every time."

"I'll remember that."

They sat in silence for a moment, then Spiller said, "Why was DCI Wendell suspended?"

Nicholson puffed out his cheeks. "Are you sure you want to ask that, Tim?"

"Yes. The guvnor said something about him being made a scapegoat, but that can't be right, can it?"

Nicholson nodded toward the bar. "Ask Paddy. He'll explain it better than me."

Reilly was already approaching the table, three pint glasses held in front of him.

"Here we go, lads. Fresh from the pump." Setting the

glasses on the table, Reilly pulled three packs of crisps from his jacket pockets, tossing the snacks on the table as he sat down.

Nicholson and Spiller thanked him as they picked up their drinks, but while Spiller sipped his lager, Nicholson took a long draught as if determined to drink the glass dry in one go.

Spiller watched him from the corner of his eye, almost envious of the man's ability to put the stuff away. At this rate, a quiet drink after work would turn into something else entirely.

Thankfully, Nicholson restrained himself after a few long gulps, wiping his mouth with the back of his hand and emitting a heartfelt sigh.

"That's better, eh?" Reilly said. "Three coppers in the pub, and all is well with the world."

"Amen," Nicholson said, tearing open a packet of crisps. "Tim was just asking about a certain DCI, wondering why he was kicked into touch for a while."

Reilly's smile slipped. "Oh? Why?"

"I was curious, that's all," Spiller said. "But we don't have to talk about if you don't want to. I mean, he's back at work, so it must all have been cleared up."

"That's right, lad," Reilly replied. "There's no use raking over the ashes, that's what I always say, but..." He leaned his elbows on the table and Spiller copied him, bringing their heads close together.

In a stage whisper, Reilly added, "That's why I lost my job as a fire inspector." Reilly cackled and sat back, slapping his leg, and Nicholson cracked up, crumbs of crisp flying from his lips. Spiller had to join in the laughter.

"You got me fair and square," Spiller admitted, and he took a drink, hiding his chagrin behind his pint glass.

Apparently, the topic of Wendell's suspension was out of bounds, so he tried not to dwell on it.

"So, Tim, your wife didn't mind you coming to the pub then?" Reilly asked.

Nicholson gawped at Spiller. "You're married?"

"Yes. There's no need to look so surprised."

Nicholson held up his hands in mock surrender. "It's just that you're young, that's all. Good luck to you. You'll need it."

"Ollie and his wife are separated," Reilly explained.

"It's a *trial* separation," Nicholson protested. "Only a trial. It's not like we're getting divorced or anything. We're trying to work things out, for the sake of the kids as much as anything."

"How are the kids doing?" Reilly asked.

Nicholson's expression lit up. "Oh, they're great, thanks. Did I tell you Ben was top of his class in maths? Not that they shout about it in school, you know, so they don't put the other kids off, but he scored higher than anyone on the last test. And Clara's doing well too. She can spell better than I can, that's for sure."

Nicholson rattled away on the subject for a minute or so, though it felt longer to Spiller as he nodded and smiled.

"Amazing," Reilly said as Nicholson's narrative dwindled to a halt. "Ben must get that from you, Ollie, being good with figures and such. Speaking of which, how did you get on with that report?"

Nicholson grinned. "Smoothly done, Paddy. And you must get the gift of the gab from your folks back in the old country, eh?"

Much to Spiller's surprise, Reilly didn't rise to the bait. Instead, he chuckled along with Nicholson, clapping him on the back.

"Ready for another pint, Ollie?" Reilly asked.

"Not yet. No sense in it sitting there while we talk." Nicholson took a sip, then he set down his glass and put it out of the way, making room in front of him as he pulled the careworn leather briefcase from beneath the table. He extricated the sheets of computer printout and laid them flat on the table before shoving his bag back down by his feet.

Smoothing the paper, he began.

"So, lads, what we have here is a set of budget projections, and if you ask me, it's either a complete cockup or something very fishy is going on."

Reilly and Spiller craned their necks to get a better view. But when Spiller saw what Nicholson had done, he let out a muttered curse.

"What's up?" Nicholson asked.

"You've written on it," Spiller replied. "That could be evidence, but you've written all over it."

"Don't worry about it. I'm sure we can get hold of another copy if we really need to. We can force the council to hand over as much info as we need. Anyway, I had to draw a few lines and notes and so on; it was too hard to interpret otherwise."

"It'll be fine, Ollie," Reilly said. "Tell us what it all means."

Nicholson ran his hands over the rows and columns as he spoke, tapping figures with his fingertips for particular emphasis.

"These are cost centres, you see, and—"

"Hold on," Reilly interrupted. "I don't know what that is."

"A cost centre is something that doesn't bring in a profit directly, but it costs money to run," Spiller said, and when Reilly and Nicholson stared at him in surprise, he added, "I did business studies at college, for a while, anyway."

Robbed of his chance to explain, Nicholson looked put out.

"Can you run that past me again?" Reilly asked. "In plain English, if you don't mind, Ollie."

"Okay." Nicholson steepled his fingers. "Look at it like this. When you buy a new shirt in M&S, you don't really think about it, but they must have accountants and secretaries and a personnel department. Those people all need wages, they need desks and chairs, they need pens and paper and computers. Those things are cost centres. They all cost money, but they haven't got much to do with your new shirt."

"I get it," Reilly said. "But we're talking about a county council. They don't make a profit, so it's not the same."

"Not exactly, but they have an income, and not just from the poll tax," Nicholson replied. "They get funds from central government, and unlike a business, those funds roll in year after year, whatever happens."

"Okay, so what's fishy about it?" Reilly asked.

"The final two columns are the key. One is labelled maintenance, and the other is a total. For every row, the total is three hundred times the maintenance. What does that tell you?"

Reilly pulled a face. "Come on, Ollie, skip the maths lesson and get to the point."

"All right. Three hundred is twenty-five times twelve, so—"

"A monthly amount for twenty-five years," Spiller blurted.

Nicholson smiled. "Give that man a gold star."

"But what's it all mean?" Reilly demanded. "I'm not hearing anything worth getting het up over."

Nicholson pursed his lips for a moment. "How do you maintain a curtain?"

Spiller and Reilly shrugged.

"You can wash it, I suppose," Spiller suggested. "Or take it to the cleaners maybe?"

"Okay," Nicholson replied, "but how could that cost nearly ten thousand pounds?"

"You mean for lots of curtains," Reilly suggested. "Like, all the curtains in a block of flats, say."

Nicholson shook his head firmly and raised a finger. "One. One curtain in one school is going to cost almost ten thousand pounds, but that's not to buy it. No, that's a whole different figure. It costs hardly anything to buy it; this is to *maintain* that curtain."

Spiller frowned. "That's more than half a year's salary for me, but they blow it on a curtain?"

Reilly grimaced then he took a gulp of lager.

"Here's a few more to think about, all of them to do with schools," Nicholson went on. "Twenty-five thousand pounds to maintain a few outdoor sunshades, nearly eight thousand pounds for a deep-fat fryer, over five thousand pounds to install a socket and remove a ceiling light; *one* ceiling light. Then we get closer to home. Almost a grand to maintain a chair in a police station. Remember, that's not to buy the bloody thing, it's to somehow look after it, though why you'd spend a thousand quid to look after a chair is beyond me. You'd be better off buying a new one."

Reilly nodded. "Which begs the question, why would they want to spend all that money?"

"I don't know," Nicholson replied. "But they haven't spent it yet. These are projections, remember. The point is, if these figures are right, somebody is going to sign some very big deals, then sit back and siphon public funds into their bank account, year after year, for the next quarter of a century."

"That could add up to hell of a lot of money," Spiller said. "All the cost centres in all the schools and police stations."

"And libraries and council houses," Reilly put in. "Not to mention County Hall and any other public buildings you can think of. It makes you wonder, doesn't it?"

Nicholson drained his glass, setting it down heavily on the table. "It was two pints you promised, wasn't it?"

"I'll go and get it." Spiller stood. "Paddy?"

Reilly nodded. "Cheers, Tim."

"I won't be long." Spiller crossed to the bar. He hadn't made much progress with his own pint, so he bought himself a half. *That'll keep the cost down*, he thought as the barmaid readied their drinks. *Costs*, he thought, his mind spinning with the figures Nicholson had reeled off. Whenever he heard news of public finances, they always seemed to be in dire straits. Public services were always being shut down or stripped back. Kids went to schools where there weren't enough books, families were crammed into damp flats that weren't fit to live in, community centres had leaky roofs, and across the public sector, staff were being laid off. So how on earth could anyone squander thousands on a single item?

Mel Parker knew something was up, he thought. *She said the numbers didn't look right.* But again, Spiller came back to Victor Tate and his attempt to hide the report. Why would he do that unless the figures were correct?

Spiller paid up and thanked the barmaid before returning to the table, where Reilly and Nicholson were engaged in a heated debate. They paused long enough to accept their drinks, both men watching with dismay as Spiller topped up his pint glass with the half he'd bought.

"Seriously, Tim, what are we going to do with you?" Reilly asked. "You know she gave you that in a ladies' glass, don't you?"

Spiller hadn't paid much attention to his half-pint glass, but Reilly was right, its sides were curved and it had a short stem. "It doesn't matter," he said. "I tipped it out."

"But what if someone had seen you?" Nicholson demanded. "Plenty of uniforms come in here, and you know what they're like. Think of our reputation. You're a detective now, Tim; you've got to drink like one."

"I'll do my best." Spiller manfully took a gulp of lager. "Anyway, what were you two arguing about just now? Public fraud or corruption in high places?"

"Actually, no," Nicholson admitted. "You hadn't touched your crisps, so I was going to open them, you know, to help you out, but Paddy said we couldn't, and we had a serious disagreement."

Spiller looked from Nicholson to Reilly and back. Surely they were pulling his leg. He waited for their laughter, but none came. Slowly, he picked up the remaining packet of crisps and opened it carefully, all the while keeping an eye on his companions. They watched in respectful silence as he laid the open packet on the table.

"Help yourself," Spiller said with a straight face. "I prefer cheese and onion."

"Ta." Nicholson took a crisp, inspecting it before posting it into his mouth and chewing. He shared a look with Reilly then they both laughed.

"You were on to us that time," Reilly admitted. "Well played, Tim. We were, as you guessed, arguing over this thing." He tapped the report with his index finger. "I reckon it must be right, but Ollie said, what was it, garbage out, garbage in?"

"The other way around," Nicholson replied. "Garbage in, garbage out. If your data is no good, the results don't make sense. That's what could've happened here. Otherwise, someone's going to rip off the taxpayer for years to come, and they wouldn't get away with it."

Reilly started to argue, raising his voice, but Spiller talked over him, and his stern tone stunned them both into silence.

"What if nobody's supposed to find out?" Spiller demanded. "What if all this was kept off the books somehow?"

"That's no good, Tim," Nicholson replied. "It's far too much money. Something this big, you can't just put it down as expenses and hope no one notices. It would have to be kept under wraps for twenty-five years, and that's a long time. How could they hope to get away with it?"

"I don't know," Spiller admitted. "But that's what my instincts tell me. Someone's found a loophole and they're going to exploit it. They've found a way to get their claws into public money, and they're going to latch on, like a parasite, like one of those tapeworms that can get into your gut. They don't kill you. They don't even do you much harm; not at first. They need to keep you alive, so they hold tight for a long time, safe and warm, feeding from their host."

Nicholson paused with a crisp halfway to his mouth, then he grimaced and placed it on the table. "Bloody hell, Tim, you've put me right off."

"I'm sorry, but we've got something here," Spiller said. "I can feel it. It's all coming together. Lynsey Clifford picks up a report. She doesn't know what it is, but Victor Tate knows she's seen it. Lynsey might not know what it's all about, but her father is in the salvage business, and he'll understand it right away. Francis Clifford has a high profile in this city. People listen to him. And if Lynsey were to tell him what she'd seen, the whole scheme could've come out in the open. They couldn't allow that to happen, so the very next day, Lynsey was taken, but there was no ransom demand. Why? Because all they really wanted was that report. They searched her flat, but of course, they didn't find anything. Lynsey didn't take it home. She didn't even keep it."

"So where is it?" Reilly asked.

"That, I don't know," Spiller replied. "But if Lynsey can't give them what they want, God knows what they'll do to her."

A brief silence settled over the table.

Nicholson shook his head slowly. "That's one hell of an imagination you've got there, Tim. You make a good case, but it doesn't stack up. Kidnap is too risky. It wouldn't be worth it. Besides—"

Reilly raised his hands. "Wait a second, Ollie. Over twenty-five years, what would all these costs add up to? Are we talking about hundreds of thousands or what?"

"Millions," Nicholson stated. "Maybe hundreds of millions. And that's just for Devon. If it could work here, it could work anywhere, so if you look at the whole UK, a scheme like this could bring in billions."

"That's more than enough to attract organised crime," Spiller said. "Slip a few backhanders to the right people, sign up some juicy deals, then sit back and count the money. It's easier than smuggling drugs, safer too. What do you say, Paddy?"

Reilly seemed to be studying his pint, deep in thought. After a moment he said, "I'm not sure about the organised crime angle, we've no evidence of that, but you might be on to something, Tim."

"The more I think about it, the more this says organised crime," Spiller insisted. "Ollie's right, kidnap is risky. But it's nothing to an organised gang. Put yourself in their shoes. With that much money at stake, would you kidnap someone if they got in your way?"

Reilly looked up from his pint. "I would. If I were in a gang, I'd kill for that much money. I wouldn't think twice about it."

Spiller nodded, his expression grave. Picking up his drink, he said, "We've just found our motive. Now we have that, we're one step closer to figuring out who's behind it."

He held out his glass, and the others clinked their glasses against his in a silent toast.

To Lynsey, Spiller thought. *To bringing her home.* And despite his renewed determination, a whispered voice in the back of his mind added three ominous words: *Dead or alive.*

30

LEEMAN SIPPED at his glass of neat vodka. It was filthy stuff, no better than the muck you'd find in any supermarket, and it had been desecrated by the addition of too much ice, but what could one expect in a dump like the Horse and Groom?

He'd eked out his drink for as long as possible, occasionally taking a tiny sip as he'd listened and listened. *God, policemen are dull*, he thought. *They think they're amusing with their weak-minded jokes and inane banter, but it's enough to drive a person mad.*

Still, his patience had repaid him in full. The flat-foots had somehow stumbled onto something significant. Whether they understood it or not was another matter. The youngest of the trio—they'd called him Tim—must be the detective constable mentioned by Mel Parker. Spiller. He was interesting. He had a spark of zeal that was missing from most policemen.

It might be worthwhile to keep an eye on DC Spiller. An enthusiastic detective could be useful in any number of ways. Compared to his jaded colleagues, Spiller had potential.

A number of delicious scenarios presented themselves immediately. Spiller was married and that opened up a whole world of vulnerabilities. How good it would be to take a young detective in harness, staying with him as he rose through the ranks. It would be a long game, but as it played out, there'd be new possibilities, new advantages to be pressed home. Every ounce of effort would be worthwhile.

Leeman was so lost in thought that he drained the last of his drink without tasting it. Strange. It wasn't like him to allow his attention to slip. *Detail is everything*, he reminded himself. *Lose focus, and you're finished.*

He put his plans for DC Spiller to one side and reflected on what he'd just heard, comparing it to the news he'd received from Francis Clifford. They'd met that afternoon, but the picture was only now becoming clear.

Remarkably, Spiller had chanced upon the truth. The financial report they'd retrieved was almost certainly the document the kidnappers were looking for. Thwarted, they'd resorted to an alternative strategy, using Lynsey as leverage, forcing her father to sabotage his own business.

That won't be enough for them, Leeman thought. *They want more than to take down a bit player like Francis.* The kidnappers still didn't have what they were looking for, and they weren't the kind of people to take no for an answer. So what would be their next move?

Whatever the answer, it wasn't going to come to him in the dismal pub. He'd already learned enough from the policemen. It was time to go.

Leeman stood, picking up his coat and draping it over his arm, smoothing the creases with deft strokes of his hand. That task accomplished, he strolled to the door. He vowed to keep looking straight ahead as he passed the policemen, but he couldn't resist a quick peek at the trio of gossiping coppers. Surely, they wouldn't notice him; people tended not to.

But as Leeman glanced at the men, he inadvertently locked eyes with DC Spiller. It was only for a moment, but Spiller's frank gaze was alive with curiosity. Leeman kept walking, and he didn't stop until he reached his BMW.

Oh yes, he thought, *that young man has something about him*. He'd cross swords with DC Spiller before too long, and it was going to be the most tremendous fun.

WEDNESDAY

31

STANDING OUTSIDE 12 RALEIGH ROAD, Spiller and Reilly paused on the pavement to look up at the building where Lynsey had made her home.

"Are you sure this is worth it?" Spiller asked. "The SOCOs will have found everything worth finding, won't they?"

"Don't bank on it," Reilly replied. "They do their best, but they were only called in on Monday, and you know what happened that night."

"The murders," Spiller said. "But the team won't have just upped and left, will they?"

"They'll have done the basics, lifting prints and fibres and such. They would've released this place before now, but they've been too busy. They've got three murders in two different locations; the poor buggers must be working night and day."

Spiller heard the regret in Reilly's voice. "You'd rather be working that case than this one."

"Wouldn't you?"

"I'm not so sure. Lynsey could still be alive. We have to do our best for her. We have to give it our best shot."

Reilly sent him a look. "Hark at you. You've only been here five minutes, and you've got the bit between your teeth. We all start out with fire in our belly, I suppose. The question is, can you keep it up?"

"I'll do my best."

"Time will tell." Reilly nodded toward the building's entrance. "Let's make a start."

They headed for the entrance, but as they approached, the door opened and a young woman stepped out.

Smartly dressed in a plain skirt and a belted raincoat, she wore her long, black hair tied back. In contrast to her dark hair, her skin was pale, and her eyes were a striking shade of pale blue. She glanced at the policemen, smiling as though faintly amused, but she didn't speak as she made to pass them by.

"Good morning, miss," Reilly said, and when the young woman turned to acknowledge him, he added, "Could we talk to you for a minute?"

The young woman halted, her hand going to the strap of the colourful fabric bag she wore slung from her shoulder. Her gaze darted from side to side, perhaps gauging whether she was at a safe distance.

Reilly produced his warrant card, and once he'd made the introductions, the young woman relaxed.

"Oh," she said, "I thought you were..." She left her sentence unfinished, instead saying, "Never mind. What can I do for you? Only I haven't got much time. I'm a bit late for work as it is."

"We won't keep you long, miss," Spiller said. "Do you live here or are you visiting?"

"I live here. The ground-floor flat."

"Ah, we called on Monday, but you weren't in," Reilly said. "What's your name, miss?"

"Jem."

Notebook and pen in hand, Spiller said, "Like a precious stone?"

"I wish. It's short for Jemima. Jemima Tussell." She frowned. "But why were you here on Monday? Was it about Carol?"

Spiller and Reilly shared a look.

"Why would we be visiting Carol?" Reilly asked.

The rush of blood to Jem's cheeks was plain to see. "Oh, nothing. I was guessing, that's all. I didn't mean anything." She hesitated. "Why *were* you here?"

"We'll come to that in a minute," Reilly replied. "Some of our officers knocked on your door a few times that day, and we couldn't help but notice the curtains were closed. Have you been away from home?"

"Yes. I went to Dorset for a few days. I left on Friday evening, and I came back late last night. Why do you need to know? You still haven't said."

"I'm surprised you haven't heard," Spiller replied. "Your neighbour, Lynsey Clifford, hasn't been seen since Saturday night. We're all worried about her."

Jem's hand flew to her mouth. "Poor Lynsey. What's happened?"

"That's what we're trying to establish," Reilly said. "Do you know Lynsey well?"

"Yeah. Lynsey's great. She comes in for a coffee and a chat sometimes. She likes my work."

"Work?" Reilly asked.

"I'm an artist." Jem seemed faintly embarrassed, adding in a flurry of words, "Well, that's what I really want to do, but I've got to do something to keep the lights on, so I'm temping at the moment. I'll be stuck in Argos today, grabbing boxes in the storeroom and taking them through to the shop. I'll be bored silly, but what can you do?" She shook her head as if to ward off a reply. "Sorry, I didn't mean to go on. I still haven't taken in what you said about Lynsey. I can't get my head around it. I can't believe no one told me."

"Your other neighbour didn't mention anything?" Spiller asked.

"Carol?" Jem's eyes widened. "She doesn't give me the time of day."

Something in her tone told Spiller the feeling was mutual. He sensed an untold story, but he wasn't sure whether it was worth pursuing; they weren't here to arbitrate in a dispute between neighbours.

While Spiller hesitated, Reilly said, "When did you last see Lynsey?"

"Friday, after work. She popped in, and I gave her a glass of wine. She seemed upset."

"Any idea what might've been bothering her?" Reilly asked.

Jem rolled her eyes. "The usual: her work, her boyfriend, her family."

Spiller's ears pricked up at the mention of Lynsey's work. Making sure he had Jem's attention, he said, "Did Lynsey say anything about her job at County Hall?"

"Not a lot. She was grumbling about her boss. He's obviously a total... Well, I won't say what he is."

She offered a wry smile and Spiller found himself returning it. Jem's openness and honesty was instantly engaging. It was good to feel that, at last, he was meeting someone who'd been a true friend to Lynsey.

"Did she say anything specific about her work?" Reilly asked. "Was there a particular incident?"

Jem shook her head. "She was fed up, but we all get like that by Friday, don't we?"

"Oh yes," Reilly replied. "Was there anything else that was worrying her?"

"Not that I can recall, but we were just having a girly chat. Once she'd had a glass of wine, Lynsey seemed fine. We had a laugh, but she didn't stay long. I was heading out, you see. I had a train to catch." Jem smiled sadly. "If there was something upsetting Lynsey, she didn't tell me about it. It's awful to think she might've been struggling with something on her own. If she couldn't talk to me, then who did she have? That boyfriend of hers wouldn't be much help."

"You've met Tony Carter?" Spiller asked.

"Once or twice. The last time was on Lynsey's birthday. She invited me up for a drink, but... I only stayed for a little while." Jem looked away.

"You didn't like him," Spiller suggested.

Jem shook her head, but her gaze remained fixed on something in the distance.

"I've heard Tony described as having a roving eye," Spiller went on. "Does that sound like a fair description to you?"

Now Jem faced him, a flash of anger in her eyes. "Roving hands, more like. He went past me in the hall, and... you can guess what he did. I'd have slapped him if it wasn't for Lynsey. She obviously couldn't see what he was like. I felt like saying something, but I didn't want to interfere, not on her birthday. I couldn't do that to her." She paused, recovering her composure.

"So no, I didn't like Tony, and I didn't think much of his

friends either. But if you want to know about them, maybe you should—" Jem clamped her lips shut tight, her expression suddenly guarded.

"Go on," Spiller said. "What were you going to say?"

"Nothing. I meant you should just ask around. Try the pub, The Mount Radford, I think they go in there."

"We might just do that," Reilly replied. "Thanks for your help, miss. We'll let you get to work." He smiled. "Argos, eh? I went in the other day. I was after a CD player for the Escort."

Jem's brow furrowed.

"For my car, I mean," Reilly went on. "But there were tons of people waiting, so I gave it a miss. They're always busy in there, aren't they?"

"Yeah. All the more reason for me to get a move on. I'm late as it is. I hope you find Lynsey soon. I wish I could help more, but I don't know what else I can do." She gazed at them in turn, her eyes filled with sadness. "You'll do everything you can, won't you? You won't just forget about her."

"Of course, we'll do our very best," Reilly said.

"Good. Only, you hear stories, don't you? People go missing, and they're not found for years, or maybe never..." Jem pressed her fingertips against the edge of her eyes, fending off the tears already forming. "I'm sorry. I'd better go."

Jem made to move away, but Spiller raised a finger. "Just a moment, miss, if you don't mind."

Jem halted. "What is it?"

"A couple of things," Spiller began. "This might seem an odd question, but there's a bike in the hall. Do you know who it belongs to?"

"Not exactly. It's something to do with Carol, I think.

It's a pain in the neck, actually. I'd ask her to move it, but there's no point. She won't listen to me."

"That must be annoying," Spiller said.

Jem watched him expectantly. "Is that it?"

"Not quite," Spiller replied. "A minute ago, when we were talking about Tony Carter's friends, you stopped yourself short. What you were going to say is that we ought to ask Carol. That's right, isn't it?"

Jem stared at Spiller like a rabbit caught in headlights.

"I'd like an answer, please," Spiller went on. "What is it you're not saying?"

"Nothing. But... I hear things through the ceiling, and Carol seems to have a lot of visitors. Men." Jem raised her hands. "I'm not saying she does anything wrong."

"But that's why you thought we were here," Spiller said. "When you found out we were police officers, you thought we'd come to talk to Carol."

Jem chewed on her lower lip, then she nodded. "I thought somebody might've complained, what with all the cars coming and going at all hours. It's a quiet street usually, but Carol has a lot of *visitors*."

"Ah," Reilly said. "What my dear old mam might call *gentlemen callers*."

"Something like that."

"Including Tony Carter's friends?" Spiller asked.

"I'm not sure, but I think they're friendly with her. That's the impression I get, but I don't really know."

Reilly nodded slowly. "I see. Thank you for being so frank, Miss Tussell. We needn't hold you up any longer. I hope we haven't made you late for work, but if your boss complains, tell him you were unavoidably detained. Show him this." Reilly held out a business card, and Jem took it, reading it carefully before sliding it into her shoulder bag.

Reilly issued the usual reminder about getting in touch if she heard anything about Lynsey, and Jem took her leave, an urgency in her determined stride.

"Interesting," Spiller said. "We need to have another chat with Carol Whitaker."

Reilly tore his gaze from the departing figure of Jem Tussell and sent Spiller a world-weary look. "Why? Carol was at work when Lynsey was at the club. I phoned The Mount Radford, and they confirmed what she told us. She worked until closing time, then she headed home at about half past eleven."

"That leaves her unaccounted for at the time Lynsey disappeared."

"Yes, but I've no reason to believe she lied," Reilly said. "She was at home and in bed after working a long shift in the pub. She told us about the vehicle she heard. She wouldn't have mentioned that if she had anything to hide."

"Even so," Spiller began, but Reilly didn't want to listen.

"Even so nothing," Reilly said. "You don't approve of young Carol, I can see it in your face, but that's neither here nor there. She's an adult, so if she likes to play the field, it's no business of ours. You've got to be objective, Tim, and I don't see what Carol's love life has to do with Lynsey's disappearance. They might be neighbours, but they barely knew each other. Where's the connection?"

"Carter and his friends?"

"I wouldn't set much store by what Miss Tussell had to say. She was guessing. She as good as admitted it. The truth is, she doesn't like Tony and his mates, and she doesn't think much of Carol. Her *impression* that they're friendly doesn't amount to anything." Reilly shook his head. "Until we can dig up a better lead, we'll focus on Lynsey's flat and see what we can find."

"You're the boss."

Reilly smiled. "That's the spirit. But before we get started, I need something to sharpen me up." He pulled out a pack of cigarettes and lit up before crumpling the empty pack and shoving it in his pocket.

"You're not going to smoke inside, are you, Paddy?"

Reilly shrugged. "Why not? The SOCOs have finished, and once we stopped guarding the scene, it doesn't really matter what we do. Anything we find won't be much use as evidence; it could've come from anybody at any time."

"I know, but it seems a bit…"

"Don't worry about it, Tim. It'll be fine. Anyway, there's more to an investigation than forensics. If we're lucky, we'll find something that'll point us in the right direction. God knows we could do with a fresh lead." He took a drag on his cigarette then ejected a jet of smoke from the corner of his mouth. "I'll tell you what. I want to look at the place on my own for a few minutes. I need a bit of quiet while I concentrate."

Spiller tried not to look too put out. "Okay. Do you want me to wait on the landing for—"

"No, no," Reilly interrupted. "I need to think, and I can't do that with you hovering outside the door. Why don't you do me a favour? Nip to the shop around the corner and grab me a box of ciggies. Twenty Benson and Hedges, okay?"

"Erm…"

"Go on, Tim. It'll give you something to do, and besides, you could do with the exercise."

"I beg your pardon."

Reilly pointed to Spiller's stomach. "You're getting a paunch. Too many home cooked dinners, lad. Too much hotpot. That won't do, you know. DCS Boyce likes us all to keep fit."

Spiller bridled, but deep down a sense of embarrassment stirred. The truth was, the move to Exeter had disrupted all his old habits, and apart from chasing after Tony Carter, it had been some time since he'd done any real exercise.

"Go on," Reilly said. "It'll only take you ten minutes."

Spiller wanted to argue, but this wasn't a battle worth fighting. He held out his hand. "I'll need some money."

"I'll pay you back later."

"Fine," Spiller said from between clenched teeth, then he turned on his heel and set off down the street. He'd expected a bit of give and take when it came to fitting in with his new colleagues, but so far, he seemed to be the only one giving.

He'd better not find anything without me, Spiller thought. *That'd be the last straw.*

32

Lynsey moaned and curled into a foetal ball on the bed. From behind her, she heard the door opening and footsteps on the bare concrete.

"You needn't bother carrying on like that," he muttered in his low, guttural drawl. "You don't fool me. It's the oldest trick in the book."

Without looking around, Lynsey said, "I'm not pretending. I'm not well. It's that muck you've been giving me. You put something in my water."

"If you'd stay quiet, maybe I wouldn't need to."

Lynsey turned now, rolling over to face him. He'd shut the door, and there was no light in the room except for the thin beam slipping through the tiny gap below the door. In the gloom, all she could see of him was a vague dark shape.

"I threw up," she stated. "Look in the corner if you don't believe me."

The man sniffed. "I don't need to; I can smell it from here. But you made yourself do that, didn't you? You shoved your fingers down your throat."

"Of course I didn't. I'm ill. I've got a temperature. Put your hand on my forehead. I'm burning up."

He didn't reply.

"Please, you have to listen to me. I don't know what you've been giving me, but it's killing me. I just know it. I'm begging you, please call a doctor. If I don't get help, I'm going to get worse and worse. For all you know, I could die. Is that what you want? Do you want to be guilty of murder? Do you want to spend the rest of your life in prison?"

He stepped closer to her. In the darkness, he loomed over her.

He can't see me properly, Lynsey thought. *His eyes haven't had time to adapt.*

The man might not be used to the dark, but she was.

Slowly, Lynsey raised her fist. When the man didn't react, she lowered her voice, wheedling. "Please, you've got to help me. I need you. Without you, I'm not going to make it."

"No, you'll be okay," he murmured. "If you stay quiet, you won't get hurt."

She made her voice a croaky whisper. "Please, I need your help. I need it."

He was even closer now, bending as if to see her better.

Lynsey pulled back her arm and punched out hard, aiming low, guessing for where his groin might be.

Her fist met soft flesh, the physical contact sickening, but the man let out a grunt and staggered back. It was all Lynsey needed.

She jumped to her feet and kicked out, putting all her strength into it, hoping to hit his knee. Her foot hit muscle and bone, and the man cried out, but it wasn't enough to bring him down.

Lynsey darted past him and made for the door. She

turned the handle, hardly daring to believe it wasn't locked. And it opened. For a split second, she froze, then she was out and up the stairs. There wasn't much light, but even so, she had to shield her eyes.

At the top of the stairs was a bare corridor. There were no windows, but pale shafts of light from the skylights cut through the gloom. The place looked industrial, like an old warehouse, but all she cared about was the door at the far end. She charged along the corridor, but already there were footsteps behind her.

Shit! Lynsey ran her heart out, her arms pumping, her breath coming in ragged gasps, her heart beating against her ribs. It wasn't long since she'd thrown up, and she was light-headed, running on empty.

His footsteps were closer now, thudding against the floor, reverberating all around her, the sound filling her ears. The door was five paces away. Four. Three.

And then he was on her, sending her sprawling face down on the floor. He landed on top of her, crushing the breath from her body.

Lynsey screamed, letting out a long, drawn-out wail of anguish, but then his hand was over her mouth and she couldn't speak, couldn't breathe.

He wrapped his other arm around her, lifting her to her feet as easily as if she were a child. Lynsey struggled, kicking out and twisting her body, trying anything to be free of his grip. But it was no good. He had her, and he dragged her backwards, cursing and complaining as he did so.

Lynsey was deaf to his words. All she could think about was the door at the end of the corridor. She kept her gaze fixed on it, but the door grew smaller and smaller, as step by step, she was taken further and further away.

33

SPILLER'S MOOD had recovered by the time he stepped into the SPAR on Magdalen Road, and he took in the scene with interest. After all, Francis Clifford had said that Lynsey was a regular customer.

It was one of those small shops that seemed crammed beyond its natural capacity. The narrow aisles between the overcrowded shelves were not wide enough for two people to pass, and the place put Spiller in mind of a maze. Somewhere within its multicoloured labyrinth, shoppers skulked, their presence advertised only by the shuffling of shoes on the scuffed vinyl flooring.

Thankfully, Spiller didn't need to go hunting for food, so he turned his back on the array of canned goods and brightly illustrated packets, and marched up to the counter.

The man behind the counter bore a badge identifying him as Hazeem. Spiller knew that a man by that name had already been questioned during the door-to-door inquiry. Nevertheless, it didn't hurt to check.

Spiller identified himself, and yes, Hazeem was the store manager.

Showing the photograph of Lynsey, Spiller said, "Do you recognise this woman?"

Hazeem nodded sadly. "Yes. I didn't know her name until the police officers told me, but she came in all the time. I was asked about her the other day. Twice."

Spiller frowned. "By police officers?"

"Yes. The first one was in uniform. The second man was in plain clothes like you. A detective."

"Do you recall their names?"

Hazeem furrowed his brow. "Do you not already know this yourself?"

"Yes, but I'd like to check, please, sir."

"Okay, let me think. The first man was a constable, but he wasn't here long, and I can't recall his name. He was not polite."

"I'm sorry to hear that, sir. I'll see if I can find out who it was. I'll have a word with him."

Hazeem gave a resigned shrug. "Don't worry about it. Some things never change. But the detective who came, he was much better. Very nice manners. He was quite senior, I think, a superintendent. We spoke for some time. He was very polite."

"Detective Superintendent John Chisholm?"

Hazeem nodded. "That sounds right. Yes. Definitely."

"Thank you, sir," Spiller said, doing his best to keep surprise from his voice. "Do you recall what the detective superintendent asked?"

"Not really. He asked about the young woman, and I said I'd seen her on Saturday. She bought a few basic items: bread, milk. You know, the usual things. And I'm sure she bought some meat. She said something about making a meal on Sunday." He looked down at the counter. "I was very sad to hear she was missing. She always smiled and said hello. She was well brought-up, I think."

Spiller asked a few more questions, but Hazeem had nothing more to add.

"Thanks for your time, sir," Spiller said, and he might've walked away, his mind on the case and his errand forgotten, but he spotted the packs of cigarettes on the shelves behind the counter. He requested a packet of Benson & Hedges, and Hazeem handed them over, naming a price that made Spiller's eyebrows shoot upwards.

Reluctantly, Spiller took out his wallet and handed over a five-pound note. Pocketing the change, he thanked Hazeem again and turned to leave, but he found himself face to face with a familiar figure.

"I didn't have you down as a smoker," Carol Whitaker said, studying him with a twinkle in her eye. She held a wire shopping basket, and Spiller noticed a large loaf of wholemeal bread and a plastic bottle of milk nestling alongside a jar of Nescafe instant coffee and a packet of cheddar.

"Oh, they're not mine," Spiller replied, hurriedly jamming the cigarettes into his pocket. "They're for someone else."

"That's all right then. I'll let you off." Carol wrinkled her nose. "I can't stand the smell of the damned things. I get sick of it at work. By the time I go home, my clothes stink of smoke. It's horrible, but in my line of work there's no getting away from it."

"I suppose not." Spiller thought back to the well-used ashtray he'd seen in Carol's flat. Evidently, it was there for Carol's visitors, and that fitted with what Jem had told him. Another memory nudged at the edge of Spiller's consciousness, but before he could pin it down, Carol interrupted his train of thought.

Lifting her wire basket and nodding toward the counter, she said, "Do you mind? This is getting heavy."

"Oh, sorry."

Spiller moved aside and Carol plonked the basket on the counter with a sigh, smiling at Hazeem and returning his cheery hello.

Spiller lingered for a moment, toying with the idea of asking Carol a few questions, but he recalled what Reilly had said about focusing on Lynsey's flat rather than on her neighbour. Besides, Carol seemed to have forgotten he was there. She was chatting with Hazeem as her meagre supply of groceries were loaded, one by one, into a plastic carrier bag.

"Bye for now," Spiller said, then he walked away. He opened the shop door and glanced back. Hazeem had turned around, and he plucked an item from the shelves, adding it to Carol's plastic carrier bag. Carol produced her purse and began sorting through it.

That's odd, Spiller thought. As far as he could recall, the shelves on the back wall had been stocked only with cigarettes. Indeed, a couple of minutes ago, he'd watched Hazeem go through exactly the same motion to select the packet of Benson & Hedges.

An elderly gentleman halted on the pavement outside, and he squinted up at Spiller. "Excuse me, son. I need to get in."

"Of course. Sorry, sir." Spiller held the door open and stepped back.

"*Sir,* eh? That's nice, I must say." The man stepped in past Spiller and tipped him a wink. "Well done, young man. You'll go far."

"Good manners cost nothing," Spiller said with a smile.

"Quite right, son. Quite right. Cheerio."

Spiller had already loitered by the door for too long, so he made his exit and marched back to 12 Raleigh Road.

When he arrived at the front door, he found it locked, so he rang the bell for Flat 3 and waited. And waited.

He looked back along the street. Perhaps Carol would appear with her bag of shopping, but she hadn't necessarily been on her way home. For all Spiller knew, she'd popped into the shop before heading elsewhere. At any rate, the pavement remained empty.

Spiller rang the bell again, and half a minute later Reilly appeared, frowning.

"Keep your hair on, lad," he grumbled. "No need to ring twice. I heard you the first time."

Then why didn't you let me in? Spiller thought, but he simply held out the packet of Benson & Hedges and said, "Your cigarettes."

"Ta." Reilly pocketed the cigarettes, then stepped back to allow Spiller inside. "Come on. You can give me a hand."

Without further explanation, Reilly made for the stairs and Spiller followed.

Inside Lynsey's flat, Reilly headed straight for the bedroom. Spiller joined him, surprised to see that the corners of the carpet had been lifted and rolled back as far as the furniture would allow.

Reilly went to one end of the chest of drawers and took hold of it. "Give us a hand with this."

"Should we be doing that?" Spiller asked.

"Yes." When Spiller didn't immediately come forward, Reilly pointed to the middle of the floor. "Stand there."

"Why?"

"Just do it, Tim. Trust me."

"Okay." Spiller stood on the spot indicated. "Now what? Is there supposed to be a secret trapdoor or something?"

"Don't talk daft. Just move around a bit. Shift your weight."

Feeling ridiculous, Spiller did as he was told, and was rewarded with the creak and groan of a loose floorboard.

"There," Reilly said. "You see?"

"It's an old house, Paddy. I'd be surprised if the floorboards weren't a bit dodgy."

"Go with it. She might've hidden something down there."

"And then she put the carpet back and moved the chest of drawers on her own?" Spiller asked.

Reilly gazed at him in the manner of a teacher waiting for the class to quieten down, and Spiller gave in. Together they moved the chest of drawers, then they rolled up the carpet and underlay as far as the bed.

Reilly studied the floorboards. "Look. This section has been sawn, and there are no nails."

"Probably lifted by a plumber or an electrician," Spiller said.

"We'll see." Reilly knelt and produced the largest pocketknife Spiller had ever seen. It was an ugly thing, its body made from dull grey metal, and from its side, Reilly unfolded a heavy-duty metal spike.

"This will do the job," Reilly said, jamming the steel spike into the gap alongside the loose floorboard. "It's a marlin spike."

"It's an offensive weapon, is what it is."

"No, it's an antique: a soldier's jackknife from World War II. It belonged to my dad. It's no use as a weapon, but it comes in handy, I can tell you."

For what? Spiller wondered, but he kept his reservations to himself.

Reilly soon had the loose board levered out of its home, and he set it to one side. Spiller kneeled down to join him in peering into the void below.

Spiller saw several grey cables meeting in a plastic junction box, but nothing else save for dust and a few dead woodlice.

"Bugger it," Reilly muttered. "Waste of bloody time."

The phrase, 'I told you so,' was not far from Spiller's tongue, but he bit it back, instead saying, "Never mind. It was worth a try. Once you'd had the idea, you couldn't have let it lie. You had to check."

Reilly exhaled noisily. "True enough, lad. True enough. Let's put it all back."

It didn't take them long to replace the floorboard. Relaying the carpet was more problematic, and it ended up looking rucked and untidy, but Reilly said it would have to do, so they replaced the chest of drawers and left it at that.

Reilly brushed his hands together. "Right. What's next?"

"I'm not sure." Spiller hesitated. "Paddy, when I was in the SPAR, I talked to the manager."

"A guy called Hazeem. Uniforms interviewed him. Not much to say from what I recall." Reilly lifted his chin. "Has he remembered something?"

"Not exactly, but it was odd. He said he'd been interviewed by Detective Superintendent Chisholm."

Reilly's face remained immobile for a moment, then he laughed. "No, the bloke's made a mistake. The guvnor doesn't go around knocking on doors, much as he'd like to. He's stuck at his desk, day in, day out."

"Hazeem was pretty sure about it, although he did say

the detective he talked to was very polite; he made a point of it. I'm not being funny, but..."

"It doesn't sound like the guvnor," Reilly suggested.

Spiller nodded. "He can be a bit brusque."

"Brusque? That's one word for it. Most would say he's a bit of a bastard, but that's okay because he's our bastard. The guvnor's on our side and don't you forget it."

Spiller held up his hands. "You don't have to tell me. I've got a lot of respect for the man."

"Glad to hear it."

"But what's been going on? Hazeem was certain that a superintendent came to see him."

Reilly sent him an austere look. "Did he give you the guv's name or did it come from you?"

Spiller groaned inwardly. "I might've mentioned it first, and he said he recognised it. He caught me unawares. I didn't have time to think."

"There's *never* time to think, Tim. You've got to stay sharp. When we make mistakes, people get hurt, or their lives get turned upside down. You don't want that on your conscience, believe me."

"Point taken."

Reilly's expression softened. "Don't take it so hard, lad. You're still new to the job. When I was in your shoes, I didn't know my arse from my elbow, so I'd say you're doing all right." He smiled. "Don't worry about the shopkeeper. I'll check with the guvnor, see if anyone else has been poking their nose in."

"Somebody from another nick?"

"That's one possibility."

Reilly's tone gave Spiller pause. "Are you thinking it could've been someone from Complaints?"

"It crossed my mind."

"Who would've complained? We're doing our best."

"Think about it," Reilly said. "I'll bet Francis Clifford isn't too pleased with our lack of progress, and he has friends in high places. He might even be a Mason. A funny handshake and a quick word over drinks in the golf club, and the next thing you know, we've got the rubber heels breathing down our necks. All the more reason to do our job properly, so no more chitchat. Let's get on."

"Okay." With a new sense of purpose, Spiller scanned the room. "Did you find anything while I was at the shop?"

"No, you didn't miss much. Mainly, I was walking around the place, getting a feel for it. It's good to put yourself in someone else's shoes for a bit."

"Victimology. Find out how someone lived, and you might figure out how they died, or how they disappeared."

"That's right, lad." Reilly gestured to the door. "Go ahead. Give it a go."

Spiller nodded, then he walked slowly back into the living room.

"There's no need to creep about," Reilly said. "Act natural. Do what she'd do."

Spiller hesitated. Was Reilly being serious or attempting to make a fool of him?

"Go on," Reilly urged. "You don't have to pretend to be her. I'm not expecting you to dance around singing 'Deeply Dippy' or whatever. Use your intuition."

A tense silence filled the room as the two men stared at each other, narrow-eyed.

"Do you think," Spiller began, "that Lynsey's a fan of Right Said Fred?"

A snort of laughter burst from Reilly's lips and Spiller joined in.

"Deeply Dippy," Reilly said. "I don't know where I got

that from, but I reckon Lynsey's more into Nirvana. Anything to annoy her old man."

Spiller's smile vanished as Reilly's words hit home. *Anything to annoy her old man*, he thought. *It makes sense.*

People with Lynsey's background didn't live in one-bedroomed flats and take poorly paid admin jobs at the local council. They didn't hook up with unimpressive lads like Tony Carter, and they certainly didn't spend their evenings in dingy nightclubs like The Icebox. No. Everything Lynsey had done with her life was an act of defiance, an attempt to dash the hopes and dreams of her ambitious father.

"She hates him, doesn't she?" Spiller said.

"That would not surprise me one bit." Reilly said. "But let's focus on the job. Lynsey comes in from work. She's had a bad day. What does she do?"

"She puts her keys somewhere."

"Show me."

Spiller crossed the room to the entrance, then he turned around on the spot. There was no hook to hang a key on, nor any shelf within reach. Spiller scanned the room, then he headed for the kitchen.

"Why in there?" Reilly asked.

"Things get shifted about in a living room. It's too easy to lose your keys down the side of the sofa or under a magazine, and I think Lynsey's careful. She likes things neat."

In the kitchen, Spiller turned to his right and ducked his head to peer at the underside of the wall-mounted cabinet. Sure enough, a small brass hook had been screwed into the underside. The hook was empty, of course; Lynsey would've had her keys with her when she went out.

"She hung her keys here," Spiller said, "then she went

to make a drink." He started toward the kettle then changed his mind. "She'd had a rotten day, and we know she likes wine." He opened the fridge and closed it, then he opened the wall cabinet above. There were four wine glasses, none of them matching, alongside a few cheap tumblers. The glasses bore the traces of black fingerprint powder left behind by the SOCOs.

On the second shelf, an assortment of crockery had been stored neatly. It was hard to see what was on the third shelf because it was too high, but Spiller recognised the edge of a sandwich toaster, and there was a ceramic casserole with a floral pattern. And something else.

Protruding a few millimetres from the top shelf was a right-angled sliver of transparent plastic, perhaps the corner of a plastic bag. Spiller almost didn't notice it, but it caught the light.

He reached up and plucked the bag from the shelf, pinching the plastic between finger and thumb. And when he saw what he'd found, a sinking feeling settled on his shoulders.

Reilly came to his side. "What've you got?"

"This." Spiller held up his find so Reilly could have a proper look.

The small ziplock bag was transparent, and the yellow pills within were easy to see, each one embossed with a smiley face.

"Ecstasy," Reilly said. "She really did have a bad day, didn't she?"

"We don't know she took them," Spiller said.

"Don't we? Maybe this was why she was prescribed Valium. The E left her jittery. She needed something to bring her down."

"But the bottle of Valium was almost full."

Reilly grunted under his breath. "Those are just the ones we know about. And her friends said she wasn't herself on Saturday. Mopey, one of them said. Dopey, more like. Taking E one minute and downers the next, all washed down with gin. That's not a good combination, but it could explain a lot."

Spiller frowned. What was Reilly trying to imply? Did he think that Lynsey was somehow responsible for what had happened to her?

Before he could ask, Reilly said, "You can't blame the SOCOs for missing that bag. They were looking for fingerprints, bodily fluids and fibres. They weren't going to find any of that on the top shelf, were they? Plus, they were pushed for time."

"But before they left, they ought to have—"

"They were called away," Reilly interrupted. "There were three bodies, two of them in a park, for God's sake. With a murder, every second counts. The SOCOs will have done their best, and that's all you can ask."

"We'll see about that."

"Oh aye. What's that supposed to mean?"

"It means I'm going to say something to the guvnor. The SOCOs have been asleep on the job, and God knows what else they've missed. It's not good enough, especially if we've got the Complaints Authority on our backs."

"That's a big *if*," Reilly pointed out.

"Maybe, but we don't want this to come back on us, Paddy. We ought to cover ourselves. I'll talk to the guvnor when we get back."

"Oh no you won't, lad. Listen, the SOCOs are on our side, and sooner or later you'll want them to pull out all the stops. When that day comes, you do *not* want to be in their bad books."

"So when they cock things up, what are we supposed to do? Accept it?"

"No, but there's no point in throwing your toys out of the pram. You don't want everyone to think you're a pain in the arse. Take it from me, Tim, a quiet word goes a long way, but only if it comes from someone who's earned a bit of respect."

"You'll deal with it?"

"Leave it with me."

Spiller puffed out his cheeks and felt his sense of outrage ebbing away. "I suppose you're right, but what do we do with this?" He waved the plastic bag in the air. "If it's not admissible, do we still enter it into evidence?"

"Definitely." Reilly produced a plastic evidence bag from his pocket. He held it out and Spiller dropped the small bag of pills into it. Reilly sealed it and took out a pen. As he wrote on the bag's label, he said, "Always carry a few evidence bags and a marker pen. Gloves are good too. We ought to have worn them two days ago when we first came in, but we didn't know what we were walking into. Even so, we should've been prepared. That's on me."

Spiller offered a rueful smile. "I didn't think of it either. I guess we're none of us perfect."

"You're not wrong there, lad. We're not even close."

34

LEEMAN FOLLOWED the woman at a distance. He'd been watching her since she'd left the building where Lynsey Clifford lived. Reilly and Spiller had almost spoiled things, but Leeman knew his craft, and there'd been no real danger of being spotted by the policemen.

Similarly, the woman was oblivious to his presence as he dogged her footsteps. She glanced back once, looking around before crossing the road, but her gaze skimmed past him. She'd been too busy fussing with her bag, rearranging the straps on her shoulder.

She wasn't bad looking, if you didn't mind them a bit tarty, but she wasn't to his taste. He preferred his women to be more sophisticated.

A fleeting image of Francis Clifford's wife, Diana, came to mind, and Leeman allowed himself a moment's reflection. Diana was a woman to be admired. He'd only met her once, but he'd seen her at a distance many times. It was important to keep an eye on a man like Francis, and in this case, the task came with certain benefits.

Everything he'd seen of Diana confirmed his high

opinion. She was clever, refined, well-bred, and she was wonderfully courteous. She'd only spoken to him for a minute, but she'd made him feel like the most important person in the room. Her smile was like a thousand-Watt bulb in a darkened room, a blazing fire on a cold night.

But she wasn't always so happy and contented. *Francis doesn't look after her*, he thought. *I may need to have a word with him about that.*

His dream of Diana was dispelled by a very different mental image. It wouldn't be hard to break a man like Francis. He might've been tough once, but the trappings of wealth had weakened him until he was little better than a child.

Leeman repressed a sigh, turning it into a long, slow breath. It was time to focus. In front of him, Lynsey's neighbour headed for a cafe and marched inside.

Leeman strolled past, taking his time. The place was called The Concorde Cafe, though there was nothing to evoke the glamour enjoyed by the airliner of the same name. *Cheap* was the word that came to Leeman's mind, describing everything from the tatty furniture to the dim lighting.

From the corner of his eye, Leeman watched the woman as she hurried to a table where a man was waiting. *Interesting*, he thought. He walked a little further, then he turned and headed back, stepping into the cafe and marching up to the counter as if he were a regular customer. The woman behind the counter favoured him with something like a smile.

"What can I get you, m'dear?"

Leeman was about to order coffee, but he spied the glass jug keeping warm on top of the machine, half full.

The brown liquid within was distinctly murky, and it might well have been sitting there for some time.

Adopting a patient smile, Leeman said, "I don't suppose you can offer an espresso, can you?"

The woman's brow wrinkled in confusion.

"Never mind. Tea will be fine. Black, please. English Breakfast if you have it."

"We've got normal tea. I don't know what brand it is."

"I'm sure that will be fine."

The woman went to work and soon loaded a tray with a stainless-steel teapot, a cup and saucer, a teaspoon and a small jug of milk.

What part of black tea did you not understand? Leeman thought, but he simply smiled and paid, almost chuckling at the laughably low asking price. "Put the change in there," he said, patting the charity collection pot for the RNLI.

"Thank you very much, m'dear." Finally, the woman had figured out how to smile.

Leeman took his tray and manoeuvred his way through the eclectic collection of rickety tables. The woman he'd followed was deep in conversation with a man who was perhaps a year or two older than her. They looked like a couple, their heads close together as they spoke in hushed tones.

Leeman found a spot not far from the couple, and he sat down, setting his tray on the table with exaggerated care. As he'd expected, the table wobbled, but it would have to do.

Leeman poured himself a cup of tea and sipped it while he pretended to gaze out the window. The woman was conversing with the man in hushed tones, and when Leeman glanced in their direction, he saw her caress the man's cheek. It was a tender gesture, but the man roughly pushed her hand away, and she shrank from him, almost cringing.

As if realising he was being watched, the man's head snapped around, and he locked eyes with Leeman. He scowled, but Leeman didn't react.

That's right, Leeman thought. *Let me have a good look at you.*

The woman touched her friend's arm and said, "Don't."

The man's nostrils flared, but he looked back at her and his expression mellowed.

Leeman let his gaze drift back to the window, but he listened carefully. The cafe was quiet, and he quickly tuned in to the couple's voices.

"How's your coffee, love?" the woman asked.

"All right." The man took a sip and sniffed. "I needed it. I'm sick of being... you know."

"It won't be for much longer though, will it?"

"God knows. Nobody tells me anything."

A pause before the woman replied: "Maybe that's for the best. The less we know..."

The man grunted. "That doesn't help. It's not..."

Leeman sensed the man was looking at him, so he busied himself by pouring more tea from the pot.

When the man spoke again, his voice was lower, his tone more urgent. "I can't go on like this. It isn't worth it."

"It will be," the woman replied. "It'll be worth it for us, for our future."

"There'll be no future if I'm... if I have to go away. And that's where this is headed. I can feel it."

The woman shushed him. "Don't say that, love. We'll be all right. It'll all work out, you'll see."

"I bloody well hope so." A pause and then: "Did you get that stuff for me?"

"Yeah."

Leeman heard something rustling, and he risked a quick look. The woman had her shoulder bag open on her lap, and she pulled a carrier bag from inside it.

"There's coffee, milk, cheese and a loaf of bread," she said. "I got wholemeal."

"I asked for white."

"Sorry. It was all they had. It's Hovis."

"What about the fags? You did get them, didn't you?"

"Yeah, I got Embassy. The ones you like." The woman sighed. "Sorry about the bread."

"It's all right. It's supposed to be good for you, isn't it?"

"That's what they say."

"It's better than nothing, anyway." The man sniffed and blew his nose.

"What's up, love? Are you getting a cold?"

"Nah, it's just that place. It's damp."

"You poor thing," the woman said. "It's not right."

"No. None of it's right. It's all..."

Leeman heard a chair scrape back, and he looked around.

The man was standing. He was taller than Leeman had realised and more physically imposing.

He stared at Leeman, hard-eyed. "All right, pal?"

"Yes, thank you," Leeman replied. "Are you?"

The man's eyes narrowed, but confusion showed in his gaze. He obviously hadn't expected a reply.

"Yeah, I'm all right, but you want to mind your own business, mate. Know what I mean?"

"Yes, that's sage advice. I'll do that."

"Right. Good." The man looked down at his girlfriend. "I'll see you tomorrow, okay?"

The woman nodded enthusiastically. "Yeah, same time and place?"

"No. It'll be somewhere else." The man glanced meaningfully at Leeman before adding, "I'll call you."

"Sure. Bye."

"See you." The man headed for the door.

Leeman found himself the object of the woman's curiosity.

"Sorry about that," she said. "He's not usually so grumpy. He's not been well. But what he said... he didn't mean anything by it."

Leeman tilted his head to one side. "Yes he did. He wanted me to feel intimidated, but I'm afraid he fell short. It didn't work." He sent the woman a smile. "Not one bit."

The woman's laughter was nervous. "Well, that's okay then, isn't it?"

"Yes. Hunky dory, as my mother used to say. Well, I must be going. It's been nice meeting you, miss..."

The woman smiled. "Never give your name to strange men, that's what *my* mother used to say."

"Touché. Have a nice day." Leeman stood and made for the door, straightening his jacket as he went.

Outside, the man was striding away, the carrier bag swinging against his legs. Leeman set off after him, but suddenly, the man broke into a run, and with a surge of horror, Leeman saw why.

A dozen strides ahead of the man, a bus was pulling up at a stop. It growled to a halt, and a couple of passengers stepped down to the pavement. The doors started to close, but the man put on a burst of speed, and perhaps he was noticed by the driver. The doors jerked back open with a hiss, and the man leaped aboard the bus.

Leeman started running, but it was hopeless. There were no other passengers to pick up, and Leeman wasn't near enough. The doors swung shut and the bus pulled out, joining the stream of traffic and rumbling away.

Leeman jogged to a halt. *Never mind*, he thought. *It's not the end of the world.*

Leeman memorised the service number on the back of the bus. It wouldn't take long to find the route, and that would narrow his search. He knew that the man had been holed up somewhere damp, somewhere where he'd needed a few basic supplies. It wouldn't take much effort to join the dots. The man had Lynsey hidden away somewhere, but who was he? And who did he work for?

There was an easy way to find out. Leeman turned around and strolled back toward the cafe. Before he reached it, Lynsey's neighbour emerged and set off without a backward glance. With a bit of luck, she'd be heading for home. It was always so much easier to talk when you were behind closed doors.

I just hope the policemen are safely out of the way, Leeman thought. He hated to be interrupted while he worked. If Reilly and Spiller were still hanging around, he'd have to hang back and bide his time. But that was fine. He could afford to wait a little while, at least. It wouldn't take him long to tackle the woman. She didn't look like the sort to put up much resistance. Which, all things considered, was something of a shame.

35

SPILLER AND REILLY stayed in Lynsey's flat for a while, hunting out places the SOCOs might not have looked, but Reilly's efforts were half-hearted at best. He mooched around the place, occasionally lifting things up and replacing them with barely a glance underneath.

As far as Spiller could tell, finding that bag of ecstasy had changed everything for Paddy. From the moment he'd seen the drugs, his enthusiasm had dimmed. Reilly hadn't said it aloud, but he'd more or less given up his search for the missing report.

Spiller was peering at the underside of a table lamp and wondering if anything could've been hidden inside it when Reilly strolled up to him, his hands in his pockets.

"We won't find anything else," Reilly said. "We may as well head back to the station."

Spiller replaced the lamp carefully. "I hate to go back empty-handed."

"We're not. You found the pills, and that's the biggest lead we've had so far."

"What about the report?"

"She probably took it with her when she left town."

Spiller wanted to protest, to say they mustn't give up too easily, but he had no evidence to back his argument, and Paddy's mind was clearly made up.

"It's your call," Spiller said. "I'm happy to stay longer if—"

"We'll go now," Reilly interrupted, and they headed back to the car, locking up Lynsey's flat as they left.

While Reilly drove them away from Lynsey's home, Spiller stared out of the Ford's side window. Reilly began a rambling anecdote about a dawn raid he'd taken part in, but Spiller wasn't paying attention.

In his mind, he was replaying the moment when he'd found the bag of ecstasy in Lynsey's flat, but no matter how many times he ran through it, he couldn't stop it from bothering him. *It doesn't fit*, he thought. *It's out of character.* True, he'd never met Lynsey Clifford, but that didn't mean he hadn't formed an idea of her habits, her personality, her way of life.

Lynsey was a well brought-up young woman. She had principles. She wanted to forge her own way in the world. She was a hard worker. Somebody like that didn't throw their lives away on the empty promises offered by drugs.

Come on, man, Spiller chided himself. *You're not being objective.*

Lynsey was young, free and newly single. She had no ties, few responsibilities and she liked to go clubbing with her friends. Looked at in that light, she was exactly the kind of person who might experiment with ecstasy.

Which was the real Lynsey? At this rate, he'd never find out.

Paddy wants this case done and dusted, Spiller decided. *I'll have to talk him around.*

There seemed to be no pauses in Reilly's tale, but as Spiller waited patiently to get a word in, he spotted a familiar figure on the pavement.

"Ah, there she is," he murmured.

"Who?"

"Carol Whitaker," Spiller said. "We just passed her. She's probably on her way home from somewhere. I saw her in the shop earlier. I told you about it."

"So what?"

Spiller was about to reply, but Paddy added, "You haven't been listening to a word I've said, have you?"

"I have, but..." Spiller's imagination failed him. "To be honest, I haven't been taking it in. Sorry, Paddy. Tell me about it another time. I'm not in the mood right now. My mind's on the case." Spiller hesitated. "I want to talk to Carol again."

"We've been through this, Tim, she hardly—"

"I need to be doing something," Spiller interrupted. "And there are a couple of questions I want to ask her. I may as well strike while the iron's hot. Can you stop the car?"

"Now? We're on our way to report in."

"You go on if you like, but I want to get this done."

For a moment, Reilly didn't reply, then he pulled the car over to the side of the road. "Go on then. You'll have to find your own way back to the nick."

"Fine. I'll catch a bus."

Reilly pulled a face. "No. It's quicker to walk, lad."

"We'll see. Can I have the keys to Raleigh Road?"

"Why not?" Reilly rummaged in his pocket and retrieved Francis Clifford's bunch of keys. Handing them over, he said, "Watch your step, Tim. Don't go getting yourself into trouble. Talk to Carol and then head straight back."

"I will. Thanks, Paddy." Spiller hurried from the car and set off. From behind him came the roar of the Ford's engine as Reilly sped away.

It didn't take Spiller long to walk back to Raleigh Road, and he relished every step. This was more like it: pounding the streets, chasing up a witness, feeling the pavement beneath the soles of his shoes.

He let himself in at the front door of Number 12, then hot-footed it up to Carol's flat. Spiller took a breath and ran a hand over his hair, but as he raised a fist to knock on the door, he heard something from within: voices, one of them male.

Spiller listened for a second, but he could only pick out a few isolated words, and they meant nothing to him. He rapped his knuckles firmly on the door, and the voices fell silent. After a moment, the door opened a crack and Carol peeped out.

"Oh, hello, officer," Carol said. "Erm…"

"Sorry to bother you, Miss Whitaker," Spiller replied. "I was hoping to have a word."

Carol's lips twitched as though she was having difficulty choosing her words.

"Is this not a good time?" Spiller went on.

"No, not really. A bad time. A very bad time."

"I see. Unfortunately, we need to do this now, but it needn't take long. Two minutes at most."

Carol paled. Again, her lips moved but no words emerged. Was she trying to mouth something? If so, he couldn't make it out.

"Are you all right, miss?"

"Yeah. Fine."

"It's just that you seem rather nervous, but you needn't worry. You're not in any trouble."

"Right. Well, I'm not nervous. I'm fine. I'm a bit tired, that's all."

"Is someone with you?" Spiller tried to see past Carol, but she was blocking his view.

"No. I'm on my own. I... I had the radio on. Maybe you heard that."

"That would explain it." Spiller offered a smile. "Since we're talking anyway, I'm going to go ahead and ask you a couple of questions, okay?" Without waiting for a response, Spiller said, "In the shop, you were asking for something from behind the counter. What was it?"

"I don't remember."

"It wasn't long ago. Come on, Carol. It was cigarettes, wasn't it?"

"Oh, yeah. That's right. What about it?"

"You told me you didn't smoke, so who were they for?"

"My friend. He doesn't like to take them home. His dad thinks he doesn't—"

"His *dad?*" Spiller interrupted. "How old is your friend, exactly?"

"What?"

"Forgive me. I didn't mean to sound rude, but what you've described... well, it sounds like the sort of thing a teenager might do. Is your friend too young to buy cigarettes, is that it?"

"No, it's... it's not his dad he's worried about. I meant to say girlfriend."

Spiller frowned. "If you don't mind me saying so, that's an odd mistake to make."

"Yeah, it is, isn't it?" Carol blurted. "I don't know what I was thinking. Sometimes, my mouth runs away with me. I don't know what I'm saying half the time."

Spiller studied her for a second. Carol had been nervous at first, but while they'd been talking her anxiety had grown steadily worse. She was agitated, practically trembling, unravelling before Spiller's eyes.

Making his voice gentle, he said, "Carol, can I step inside for a minute?"

"No. No, no, no. Not right now. I'm... I'm expecting someone. A man."

"Does this man have a name?"

"No. I mean, yes, of course he does. But I'd rather not say."

Spiller thought back to what Jem had said about the male visitors to this flat. And he recalled the way Tony Carter had cast aspersions on Carol, questioning how she managed to pay the rent.

"Miss Whitaker," Spiller began, "the man you're going to meet, is he going to pay you?"

Carol flinched as though she'd been slapped. "I beg your pardon."

"Please don't take offence, but certain allegations have been made to us, and we're obliged to follow them up. So I'll ask again: When men come to your flat, do they pay you in any way?"

"No, they bloody well don't." Carol opened the door wider, standing with her hands on her hips. "Who's been saying that? Go on, tell me. Who was it?"

"I'm not at liberty to—"

Spiller was interrupted by someone pulling the door wide open from within, and a man stepped to Carol's side.

The man was smartly dressed and well groomed, his

hair preternaturally neat. Something about the man seemed familiar, but Spiller couldn't place him.

"Hello," the man said with a wide condescending grin. "How may we help you?"

"That remains to be seen," Spiller replied. "You are?"

"My name is Boothby. Gerald Boothby. Or to give me my proper title, the Reverend G. Boothby. I do believe that the correct forms of address are important, don't you, Detective Constable?"

"Er, yes." Spiller blinked in surprise, but he quickly pulled himself together. "Sorry, I wasn't expecting a clergyman. Nice to meet you, Reverend Boothby. You're not wearing your..." Spiller gestured to his own throat.

Boothby chortled. "Ah, the old dog collar. No, one doesn't always wear it. It isn't mandatory, you know, and there are times when discretion is the better part of valour. By the way, it's *Mr* Boothby, please. We don't use the term Reverend on its own, not on this side of the Atlantic, and saying *The Reverend* all the time becomes wearisome. *Mr* is more appropriate."

Spiller wasn't sure how to reply. The rug had been well and truly pulled from beneath his feet.

As if sensing Spiller's discomfort, Boothby lowered his voice and said, "I visit some of my parishioners on a less formal basis. We find that it breaks down the barriers. After all, joy shall be in Heaven over one sinner who repenteth, more than over ninety-nine just persons which need no repentance. In your business, I expect you have a different view of those who transgress."

"You're right there," Spiller said, thankful to be heading for firmer ground. "People can repent all they like, but we'll arrest them just the same. The courts can take remorse into account, but we leave that to them. It's not for us to decide, thank goodness."

"That is a shame. Repentance, true repentance, is so important. But perhaps there's room for a little forgiveness in your daily work. Would you arrest a poverty-stricken woman who found a five-pound note and used it to buy food for her children?"

"No, of course not."

"There we are then. There's hope for you yet, Detective Constable. Let the good book be your guide; you could do a lot worse."

"I'm sure you're right, sir. But while I'm here, I do have a few routine questions to ask." Spiller took out his notebook and pen. "That quote; whereabouts in the bible does it come from?"

"The Gospel According to Luke, Chapter 15, Verse 7." Boothby grinned. "Was that one of your questions?"

"No, it was purely for my own interest. My questions are for Miss Whitaker, so if you don't mind..."

Boothby held out his hands. "Go ahead. I'd never stand in the way of an officer doing his lawful duty."

"Thank you, sir," Facing Carol, Spiller said, "When I asked you about the cigarettes you bought, you didn't give me a straight answer. Who were they for?"

"I can answer that," Boothby replied. "Alas, they were for me. I know I should give them up, but I rely on the occasional cigarette." He clasped his hands together in a display of contrition. "I'm not proud of it, and I don't like to be seen buying them in the local shop, so I asked Carol to act on my behalf. It's a weakness, and for that, I am guilty as charged."

"I see," Spiller intoned. "Do you call on Miss Whitaker often?"

"No, but I stop by when time allows. I do what I can."

Boothby was a charismatic speaker, and he had a curiously intense gaze, but Spiller forced himself to focus on Carol.

"You told me you don't like cigarette smoke, but when DS Reilly and I came in the other day, your ashtray was full. Was that all from Mr Boothby?"

Carol shook her head.

"So you have other visitors who smoke," Spiller went on. "Were any of them with you on Saturday?"

"No. I was on my own."

"What about on Sunday? Any visitors then?"

"No."

"Monday morning?"

Another shake of the head.

"Are you sure about that?" Spiller asked. "Your ashtray was full on Monday, but if you hadn't had any visitors over the weekend, you must've put up with the smell for several days."

"I expect I got used to it."

Spiller nodded thoughtfully. "Either that or there's someone you're not mentioning, someone who's been in your flat recently."

"No, no one's been here."

Spiller studied her in silence for a second. Then: "The bike in the hallway; it belongs to a friend of yours, doesn't it?"

Carol lowered her eyebrows. "Er, yes."

"And what's his name?"

Boothby held up his hand. "That, too, is my doing. I find it a convenient way of getting around, but it needs repairing. I must get it seen to. It's been there too long."

Spiller searched Boothby's expression but saw no sign

of dishonesty, nor could he imagine why the man would lie about such a thing.

"My dear fellow," Boothby went on, "I believe we've answered your questions. Meanwhile, Carol and I have spiritual matters which require our full attention. Time is always pressing. When I've finished here, I'll be visiting the sick and the dying. For those poor souls, time is precious, but I must conclude my conversation with Carol first. I'm sure you understand."

"Yes, but if I could just—"

"I'm afraid not," Boothby said, already swinging the door shut. "Goodbye, Detective Constable. It was lovely speaking with you. Farewell and Godspeed."

Spiller was left staring at the closed door, but the image that stayed with him was his last glimpse of Carol. She'd stared out at him, mute, her eyes dark with some untold emotion. It was as if she'd been trying to tell him something, but what?

Carol hadn't seemed frightened. It was more as if something was eating her up from the inside. Was it guilt he'd seen in her eyes? No.

It was desperation, Spiller decided. *She's landed herself in trouble and she can't cope.* Perhaps that explained why Carol had consulted a clergyman. She'd sought out spiritual help in her hour of need; she wouldn't be the first.

Spiller thought of the biblical passage Boothby had quoted. When he'd talked about one sinner repenting, had he been referring to Carol? It made sense.

Spiller headed for the stairs and descended slowly to the street. It would take some time to get back to the station, and he'd find Reilly waiting, wanting to know what he'd found out.

The square root of naff all, Spiller thought. *So much for following a hunch.* He left Raleigh Road behind and trudged along Magdalen Road. There were several bus stops along the street. Reilly had told him to walk back to the station, but that had been a wind up, hadn't it? *Send the new boy on a wild goose chase,* Spiller thought. *Not today.*

Spiller set his jaw in determination and marched along the road. All he had to do was figure out which service would get him back to Heavitree. How hard could it be?

36

THREE BUSES, Spiller thought as he stomped up the stairs to the CID office. *Three bloody buses!* To be fair, the driver of the first bus had tried to make him see the error of his ways, but Spiller had stuck to his guns. If there was one thing he hated more than asking for directions, it was admitting when he got lost. Sheila had pointed this out to him often enough, but still, he never learned.

On this occasion, the cherry on the top was that Reilly had been telling the truth from the outset. If he'd turned around on Raleigh Road and walked in the opposite direction, he'd have been back at the station in a few minutes. But no, he'd been bloody minded, and he'd wasted a great deal of his own time. Ridiculous.

When Spiller stormed into the office, he found it busy, the triple murder investigation in full swing. Every desk was full, and there were at least a dozen people Spiller didn't recognise, some of them standing in huddles, their voices urgent. The air was filled with the background buzz of activity.

Spiller's steps faltered, but he spotted Reilly beckoning to him from his desk.

Spiller made an effort to look cheerful as he went over to join him, but he stopped in his tracks beside his own desk; it was already occupied.

The woman, dressed in plain clothes, was about the same age as him, although it was hard to be sure. She had youthful features and wore her hair short. She looked up at him and said hello, then she went back to work, tapping on the keyboard of a computer. A *new* computer. A computer that, by rights, ought to have been his.

"Over here, lad," Reilly called out to him. "Hurry up. You're making the place look untidy, standing there like a lemon."

"Okay, Paddy. I'm coming."

Spiller trudged toward Reilly's desk, searching in vain for a spare chair.

"Perch on the desk, lad," Reilly said, and when Spiller did as he'd instructed, he added, "What took you?"

"I... had an interesting talk with Carol. I was there quite a while."

"What did she come up with? Anything other than speculation and gossip?"

"Erm..." Spiller glanced pointedly across the room. "Who's that sitting at my desk?"

Reilly leaned closer and said, "That vision of loveliness is DS Claire Baintree, drafted in from Plymouth and assigned to the Major Investigation Team."

Baintree looked up sharply. "Taking my name in vain, DS Reilly?"

"Certainly not," Reilly replied with a smile. "I was just introducing you to our newest DC, Tim Spiller."

"Good to meet you, Tim," Claire said. "Are you with the MIT?"

"Not as yet," Spiller admitted. "I'm working on a MisPer."

Baintree's brow furrowed. "Wow. I'd have thought... never mind."

"It's an important case," Spiller said. "There were indications of foul play."

"Although there's some doubt about that now," Reilly put in. "We found drugs at her flat."

Baintree nodded wisely. "You think she might just have taken off?"

"It looks that way," Reilly said. "You know what these people are like. Chaotic lifestyles. Who knows what nonsense was going through her head? She made some bad choices and suffered the consequences. She ditched her friends and dumped her boyfriend, then went home to snatch a few clothes. She was in a rush, so she made a mess, then she headed off into the night."

"We don't know it happened like that," Spiller protested. "Until Saturday, Lynsey was holding down a job and paying her taxes. I don't see her as a habitual user. It was only a few ecstasy pills we found, not heroin or cocaine."

Reilly shrugged. "Another little rich girl going off the rails. We've seen it all before. Truth be told, if her old man didn't support certain charities, we would never have spent so much time on this case."

Spiller stared at Reilly in horror.

"I'm only saying what everyone else is thinking," Reilly went on. "We ought to be working on the murders, Tim. There's a nutter on the loose, but we're chasing after a girl who's buggered off for no apparent reason; a girl who ought to have known better."

"Surely, that's for others to decide," Baintree said. "Someone must think your missing person is worth chasing up."

"Exactly," Spiller replied. "This is our case, and I'm going to see it through."

Baintree smiled. "Good for you, Tim. Stick to your guns. But I have a lot to be getting on with. We'll talk later."

"Sure," Spiller said. "Definitely."

Baintree went back to work, leaving Spiller and Reilly to eye each other in uncomfortable silence.

"Is that what you really think?" Spiller asked.

"Yes. Okay, I might've gone a bit OTT about the drugs, but the chances of us finding Lynsey were slim to start with, and it's only going to get harder. We've done our best, but we've hit a wall, and nobody's about to turn up with a ladder. I can tell you one thing for certain: we're not going to get any more resources. Everyone else is tied up. We may as well call it a day, then we can join the MIT and do something that might actually make a difference."

"I don't see it like that," Spiller insisted. "I meant what I said. I want to see this through. I'm not going to give up."

Reilly looked him in the eye. "Don't misunderstand me, Tim. I never said anything about giving up. As long as I'm on the case, I'll have a good crack at it. But I've already talked to the guvnor, and I didn't sugarcoat it. I told him where we are and what I think."

"You did that without me?"

"Yeah. You weren't here, and we haven't got time to waste. If you'd come back with me, you could've fought your corner, but you were off chasing after God knows what, so I went ahead. I had no choice." Reilly pointed to his own chest. "I'm an experienced DS, Tim. I'm needed on those murders. I can't sit around like a spare part when there's real work to be done."

"I know that, Paddy, but you could've—"

"No, I couldn't," Reilly interrupted. "I said what had to be said. The guvnor's going to talk to Boyce. By tomorrow, I expect we'll be reassigned."

It took a moment for this to sink in, then Spiller said, "So we've got until tomorrow."

"Most likely."

"Okay." Spiller took a breath. "We can still do it. I'm going to that meeting with Ronny tonight. Something might come of it."

"I doubt it. In the meantime, you'd better catch up with your paperwork. Get everything in order; that's what I'm doing. If we're told to tie this case up tomorrow, and that's probably what's going to happen, I want it done quickly, okay?"

Spiller nodded. "There's only one problem. I've got nowhere to work."

Reilly gestured to the office in general. "Find a corner, Tim. It doesn't matter where."

"Okay." Spiller headed toward his desk. There were a few bits and pieces he needed to collect from the drawer, and if he happened to have a chat with DS Baintree, that would be no bad thing. Perhaps she might even have a few words of advice for him.

At least she listened to me earlier, Spiller thought. *I could do with somebody on my side.* He wanted to hold on to Lynsey Clifford's case until the bitter end, but it wasn't going to be easy. He was a lowly DC, in over his head, and there was some logic in everything Reilly had said.

The industrious activity in the room exuded a sense of common purpose. Everyone was working hard to catch a triple murderer; they had no time for anything else.

The tide is against me, Spiller thought, and if he was going to swim against it, he'd have to give it all he'd got.

37

LEEMAN WATCHED Carol very carefully as she made the call, his head pressed close to hers, a knife held in front of her face where she could appreciate the proximity of the blade.

Apparently, Carol's little friend, her partner in crime, could only be reached by phone at a prearranged time, so Leeman had been forced to wait. That was okay. He had the patience of a statue, and the time had passed without incident. So far, Carol had been good. She'd even made him a cup of tea.

But now, the hour was at hand, and everything was about to change.

Leeman breathed deep as he listened to the electronic tone pulsing from the phone's receiver. The fragrance of Carol's hair tickled his senses. Her shampoo was evidently something cheap and floral, but he detected muskier notes that were uniquely hers, and they were really quite intoxicating. It was a shame he wasn't going to have more time with Carol. Given the right circumstances, she could be quite—

Leeman's thoughts came to an abrupt halt as the phone

was answered. Leeman heard the man's voice, sullen and ungracious: "Hello, who's this?"

"It's me, Carol."

"Are you all right? You sound a bit—"

Leeman nudged her, and Carol said, "I'm all right. But listen, I need to meet you. Tonight."

"I can't come out. I've got to... you know. I've got to babysit."

"I could come there. Where is it?"

A pause. The oaf on the other end of the line muttered something Leeman couldn't hear, then he went quiet.

"Are you still there?" Carol asked.

"Yeah. I'm here. But what's going on? Are you on your own?"

"Of course I am."

Another pause. "Carol, if the cops are on to you, just say *I understand*. Got it? Just those two words."

"Yes, but they're not. A policeman called earlier, but I sent him away. I didn't let him in."

"What did you say to him?"

"Nothing. I just said I didn't know anything about it. I told him I was at home that night, fast asleep. I said what we agreed, and he went away."

"Good. That's good, Carol. But what's all this about? You know I can't take you to where she is. It's for your own good."

Pressing his lips very close to Carol's ear, Leeman murmured, "Tell him you can help to look after her. Some things need a woman."

Carol parroted his words, and Leeman smiled. She was shaping up to be much more useful than he'd initially supposed. Biddable and yet not entirely stupid, Carol saw which way the wind was blowing and went with it.

But the man was speaking again, his voice low, and Leeman had to concentrate to hear him.

"To be honest, she isn't doing too well. She's been a bit poorly. Maybe... maybe you could come with me. You'll have to come to my place first. I'm not going to tell you where she is."

"Right." Carol glanced at Leeman.

He nodded.

"Okay," Carol said. "What time?"

"Eight. On the dot. You can't be late. I won't wait for you."

Carol looked to Leeman, and once again, he nodded.

"That's fine," Carol said. "I'll see you at eight. Bye."

She hung up, and Leeman stepped back from her, pocketing his knife.

"Well done, Carol. That was a good job. Thank you."

Carol swallowed. "What are you going to do? You're not going to hurt him, are you?"

"That depends on how cooperative he is."

Carol started to protest, but Leeman held a finger to his lips, and it silenced her instantly.

In a low voice, he said, "All I care about is getting Lynsey safely back home. I'm not interested in you and lover boy. You are merely pawns in the game. You were only doing what you were told, weren't you?"

"That's right. I didn't even know what was going to happen. It's all too much. I never wanted this. You've got to believe me."

"Well, you're in it now, Carol. We'll have to see how it plays out, won't we? And if you help me, if you play your part, maybe you and your friend can go free. But if you don't behave yourself, or you try to get away from me, you won't live to see tomorrow. If you don't do as I say, I'll make it painful for you, Carol. Painful and slow. And it'll be worse for him. Much worse. Do we understand each other, Carol?"

Carol nodded.

"Good," Leeman said. "Now, while we wait, let's pop into the kitchen. I fancy another cup of tea."

38

SPILLER DROVE past the Green Gables Inn, slowing the Volvo until he found a parking space at the side of the road. The evening was dark, but the pub on Buddie Lane hadn't been difficult to find, not least because of its distinctive front gable which, Spiller noted with a smile, was dark green.

Spiller checked his watch. It was quarter to seven, so he was in good time. He'd popped home briefly after work, wolfing down the spaghetti bolognaise Sheila had lovingly prepared. She'd wanted to talk, particularly about finding somewhere better to live, but Spiller had been in a rush. He'd agreed to go house hunting at the weekend, then he'd given her a kiss and headed out. Sheila, to her great credit, had not complained.

I'll make it up to her, Spiller told himself as he climbed from the car and looked around. *Not a bad place to live*, he thought. The brick-built houses were in short terraces of three, each with its own front garden. Sheila wanted semi-detached, but an end-terrace would do just as well, wouldn't it?

For a moment, Spiller wondered whether the murders

of Dennis Mankowich and two of his associates would bring property prices down, but he pushed the idea from his mind. He couldn't move to this neighbourhood. Bringing Sheila to a place tainted by his work would be a poor foundation for their new life in Exeter.

Spiller headed for the pub, thinking of his colleagues in the MIT. Over the last few days they would've made their presence felt in the surrounding streets, pounding the pavements, knocking on doors and asking questions. How did the local community feel about that? Would they be reassured? Or were they angry that a horrible crime had been allowed to happen so close to their homes?

I'll find out soon enough, Spiller decided, and he suddenly felt very alone. Despite their differences, it would've been good to have Reilly by his side. Spiller had mentioned the meeting before he'd left work, but Reilly had simply repeated the excuse he'd given to Ronny. He had something on, apparently, and that was that.

He never said where he was going, Spiller thought. *I wonder why?* It was hard to figure Reilly out. At times he was every bit the solid copper, keen to get the job done, but earlier in the day he'd shown another side: jaded and disillusioned, too keen to dismiss a case and blame the victim. In other words, exactly the kind of policeman Spiller didn't want to become.

Sometimes you had to stick your head above the parapet, Ollie had told him, and Spiller couldn't agree more.

Squaring his shoulders, Spiller marched in through the pub's front door. The bar was busy, the room full. Some sat at tables, deep in conversation, while others stood in small groups, busy talking while they cradled their drinks.

In one such group, a very recognisable figure stood: a

man who, at their last meeting, had dressed Spiller down in no uncertain terms.

Detective Chief Inspector Brian Wendell was being spoken at by a middle-aged couple. The pair gesticulated angrily, the man making karate chop movements with his hand, the woman wagging her finger in the air. Wendell's head was slightly bowed, and he nodded as though taking in everything they said.

But then he lifted this gaze, his stare finding Spiller, and a cold light of anger flared in the man's eyes.

Bloody hell, Spiller thought. *I've put my foot in it this time.* Of course they'd sent a senior officer to the meeting. It made perfect sense, but Spiller hadn't thought of it. Paddy had warned him not to come, and he'd ignored that advice. Wendell was not going to be happy with him for stepping out of line. All he could hope for now was to save face.

Spiller made his way to the bar, mentally framing a reasonable excuse for his presence. He'd come along to help, he'd say. He was here to offer his support, to show a united front to the public, officers of all ranks working together.

It sounded trite, even to him, but before he had a chance to come up with something better, Wendell strode toward him.

"Spiller," he growled, keeping his voice low. "What the bloody hell are you doing here?"

"I thought I might be able to help. Can I get you a drink, sir?"

"No, I'm not going to be drinking in front of all these people, and neither are you."

"No, of course not, sir. A soft drink, then?"

Wendell's eyes narrowed to slits. "Are you taking the piss?"

"No. It was—"

"I'm not here for a night out," Wendell snapped. "I'm here on police business. We're supposed to be professionals, and the way we present ourselves to the public is part of the job. We can't have officers turning up just because they feel like it, especially an officer who hasn't been assigned to this case and hasn't been briefed. We work hard at community outreach, but a word out of place can ruin years of effort. This is serious police work, Spiller, and I'm beginning to wonder if you're cut out for CID."

A cold knot of anguish twisted tight in Spiller's gut, but he said nothing.

"You know, I approved your application," Wendell went on. "I'd heard good things about you, and I thought you were the man for the job. Did I get that wrong?"

Spiller stiffened his spine. "No, sir." Swallowing the lump in his throat, he added, "I ought to have checked before I turned up. It was my mistake, sir. I'll do better in future."

"I should bloody well think so, but I'm getting tired of your excuses and apologies. They're starting to sound like a familiar tune." Wendell let out a sigh of exasperation. "I hardly know what to say. Did you tell anybody else you were coming?"

"Erm, I'd rather not answer that, sir."

Wendell looked him in the eye. "It was Reilly, wasn't it? He knew you were going to come, but he let you blunder in with your size nines. His idea of a prank, I suppose. It beggars belief, it really does."

Spiller kept his lips closed tight.

Wendell glanced around the room, then he checked his wristwatch. "Listen, Spiller, the meeting starts soon, so I haven't got time for this. Fortunately, I caught you before you did any damage, so there's no harm done. Consider it a lesson learned and bugger off home. We'll talk tomorrow, *if* I have time. But I'll leave you with one thing to ponder. You're very lucky to have met me and not DCS Boyce. If he'd been here, he would've hung you out to dry. But he doesn't need to know about this, okay? Tell Reilly you changed your mind. Say you didn't turn up, and maybe we can forget about it."

Spiller nodded. "Understood, sir. Thank you."

"Go on then. Get out of my sight. I've got to get ready to face the music. Half the people in this room would happily put me in the stocks, and the other half aren't so good-natured. If I'm not in the office tomorrow, send a search party."

With that, Wendell strode into the crowd.

"Yes, mate," the barman called out to Spiller. "What can I get you?"

Spiller offered a regretful smile. "Sorry. I've got to go."

"Please yourself." The barman moved on in search of better customers, and Spiller made a swift exit.

Outside, Spiller stood and threw back his head, sending a plume of misty breath into the cool evening air.

"Been banished, have you?" someone said from behind him, and Spiller wheeled around with a start.

A figure emerged from the shadows at the pub's corner. The young man was not tall, but he swaggered toward Spiller with a sense of purpose in his stride, his features concealed by a hoodie.

Spiller fixed his stance, ready to fight if need be.

"Take it easy," the man said, and this time, Spiller recognised his voice.

"Ronny?"

"Who else?" Ronny pulled back his hood as he drew nearer, and Spiller allowed himself to relax.

Ronny grinned. In his pristine white trainers and faded jeans, his hair styled and gelled, Ronny no longer looked like a man who wiped tables in a burger bar. The shadows threw the young man's cheekbones into sharp relief, and with Ronny's broad grin and bright eyes, Spiller could imagine him being a big hit with the girls.

He's a chameleon, Spiller thought. *He knows how to blend in, but he can stand out when it suits him.*

Aloud, Spiller said, "I wasn't banished, but I didn't want to intrude. I thought it might be better if I left."

"Is that right?" Ronny halted in front of him. "I was there, Mr Spiller, as close to you then as I am now, but you didn't notice me. I heard pretty much every word your boss said. He wasn't a happy bunny, was he?"

"You've got me fair and square. It's not my day, is it?"

"Why do you say that?"

Ronny's frank curiosity was impossible to ignore, and Spiller found himself saying, "I made a cock-up. I should've checked with my boss before I turned up."

"We know why that is, don't we? The high-ups don't want anyone speaking out of turn. They're scared somebody might tell the truth."

"No, it's not that."

"Isn't it?" Ronny demanded, moving closer. "Look at your man, Wendell. Suspended for corruption."

Spiller tried not to react, but the shock must've shown.

Ronny pointed at him, laughing. "Your face! Bloody hell, you didn't know, did you? Your own boss, in it up to his neck, and nobody told you."

"That's because it was all sorted out," Spiller bluffed.

"DCI Wendell was cleared or he wouldn't be at work, would he?"

Ronny grinned but stayed silent, as if determined to enjoy Spiller's discomfort for as long as possible. Finally, he said, "Go on. Ask me."

"Ask you what?"

"Did he do it? Is Wendell bent?"

"There's no need to ask," Spiller replied. "I already know the answer."

"Bloody hell, they've got you hook, line and sinker, haven't they?" Ronny inclined his head to one side, appraising Spiller with a measured look. "You know what? I'm going to tell you anyway; put you out of your misery. He didn't do it. Wendell might be a dick, but he's straight."

"That's what I've just said."

"Yeah, but you don't know the whole story, do you, Mr Spiller? And you want to. You want to know everything."

Spiller hesitated. "You're right about one thing. I don't know the details, but—"

"A drugs bust went wrong," Ronny interrupted. "It was just around the corner. Do you know what that means? Do you know who lives around here, or I should say *lived?*"

"Dennis Mankowich."

"Got it in one, Mr Spiller. Poor old Mank was almost in trouble. Your mob showed up and battered down a few doors. They grabbed a whole load of blokes and dragged them away, but do you know what your mates found in those houses?" Ronny formed his fingers into the shape of a zero.

"I see," Spiller said. "That's unfortunate. Someone must've made a mistake."

"Oh, this wasn't your everyday cockup. This was big. Your mates hit half a dozen houses at once, but they didn't get a single thing. You don't have to be a genius to figure it out. The dealers were tipped off. They knew the cops were coming and they knew exactly when."

"Not necessarily. It could've been bad timing."

"No way. It was all too neat. Afterwards, the cops had to let everybody go. How they kept it out of the news, I'll never know. But then, that's what happens when there's a bent copper, isn't it? It gets covered up. It's always the same."

"I'm not having that," Spiller protested. "Give me a name, and I'll see they're investigated."

Ronny pursed his lips, gazing at Spiller with undisguised interest. After a moment, he said, "Not yet."

"Why not? If you know, you have to tell me."

"I don't have to do anything, Mr Spiller."

Spiller opened his mouth to argue, but Ronny swept on regardless.

"It's all about trust; you've got to earn it. Maybe you'll be all right, but you might turn out to be just like the others. You'll cover your back, look after your own."

"No. I've got no time for that. We're not above the law."

Ronny grunted in contempt. "The trouble is, there's one law for your lot, and another for everybody else."

"This is getting us nowhere," Spiller said. "You didn't follow me outside for a debate on law and order."

Ronny nodded slowly. "There's someone you need to meet. He wants a word."

"And who might that be?"

"You'll see. He's inside."

"In the meeting? I can't—"

"He doesn't go in for meetings," Ronny interrupted. "That's not his style. He's upstairs, waiting."

Spiller took a moment to consider. Every instinct, every

routine drilled into him during his days in uniform told him to wait, to call for backup. But this was a make-or-break moment. The person waiting inside wasn't going to hang about while Spiller followed protocol. Whoever it was, he'd sent a messenger to summon Spiller. He wanted to show who was in charge, who was making the rules.

Taking a breath, Spiller said, "Okay. Lead on."

"I'll take you up, but then I'm going down to the meeting. I won't be in the room with you, so behave yourself, Mr Spiller. Go in with an attitude, and you'll get nothing. But play nicely and you might learn something. That'll be good for you, and it'll help that girl who's gone missing, okay?"

"I understand."

"I hope so. Come on."

Ronny led him back inside. The bar was almost empty. Only a few stragglers were still making their way through a door that presumably led to the public meeting. But Ronny took Spiller along a short hallway and through a door marked *Staff Only*. Beyond it, a set of carpeted stairs led upward.

They climbed the stairs in silence, then Ronny halted outside a white-painted door.

"Wait a second," Ronny said. "Let me check." He knocked and slipped through, emerging a moment later and closing the door behind him. "Go ahead, Mr Spiller. I hope it helps."

"Thanks. Hang on. Let me..." Spiller produced his wallet, but Ronny held up his hands to stop him.

"Not now. Maybe another time, but we'll see how it goes. Maybe you're okay, but maybe you're not. I only take money from people I trust, and you..." He waggled his hand in the air. "You're not quite there."

"Fair enough." Spiller returned his wallet. "But if this isn't about money, why are you getting involved?"

"You saw the crowd downstairs. The people around here wouldn't normally come to a meeting, but they're angry, frightened. This is my neighbourhood, Mr Spiller. I want something done. If you find that girl, it won't solve everything, but it'll be a start. Have I come to the right man?"

Spiller nodded. "But what about the person on the other side of that door? What are they getting out of it?"

"You'll have to ask him yourself. I can't speak for him. I'm just the messenger."

"Oh, you're more than that," Spiller said. "You've set this up, and the middleman always gets a cut. Since I'm not paying, you must be getting something from the man I'm here to meet. Is it cash, or will he owe you a favour?"

"No comment."

"I see. If this turns out to be useful, Ronny, I won't forget."

"You know where to find me." Ronny stepped away from the door. "Go on in, Mr Spiller. They're waiting for you."

"They?"

Ronny smiled. "It's all fine. You'll see."

"Right. Well, I'll catch you later."

"No, you won't." Ronny chuckled and headed down the stairs, leaving Spiller to face the white door alone.

39

LYNSEY LAY on her back and stared up into the darkness. She was drained, empty, cold. It was as if she was shrinking, fading to nothing, her whole body trembling while she wasted away. Soon she would be gone, but so what? To rest, to sleep, to drift into the darkness; anything would be better than this room, this bed, this misery.

The door opened, but Lynsey didn't even turn her head.

"Go away," she murmured. "You're not going to help me, so why don't you just leave me alone?"

The man didn't reply, but his footsteps came closer. A light shone in her face, and she closed her eyes, raising a hand to protect herself from its blinding glare. He was shining a torch at her. He hadn't done that before.

"What's the matter with you?" he said, and his voice sounded odd. "You look ill."

"I am ill. I've already told you. Now leave me alone."

He placed his hand on her forehead, and she recoiled. "Don't touch me."

"Bloody hell," he muttered, but at least he took his hand away.

The light flicked off, and a green afterglow flooded Lynsey's field of vision.

"You're burning up," he said.

"I'm dying. I know it."

"Jesus Christ," he murmured. "This isn't..."

She heard his feet drag on the floor as if he was backing away. And a tiny spark of hope glimmered into life. He was frightened. He didn't want her to die, so maybe he'd do something about it. Maybe...

Summoning her last reserves of strength, Lynsey cried out: "Please, help me. Please."

The man cleared his throat as if about to speak, and Lynsey held her breath, listening, hoping with all her heart.

But the door opened and closed, and she was left in silence.

That's it, she thought. *It's too late.* Her last chance had just slipped away. It was over.

40

STANDING in the stairwell of the Green Gables Inn, Spiller placed his hand on the door handle. *I'll be fine*, he told himself, then he squared his shoulders and marched inside.

The room was a lounge, perhaps for the use of the landlord. There was a sofa, a TV and a Hi-Fi system along with a shelf of vinyl albums. To Spiller's right, at the far end of the room, two men faced him, silently waiting. The older of the pair sat in a wing-backed armchair. In his sixties and lean as a whippet, the hollows of his cheeks lent him a hungry look, and his eyes burned with a cold indifference.

The man standing beside him was much younger, perhaps in his twenties. His hair was cut short, and though not broad across the shoulders, his upright bearing portrayed a certain physical confidence.

The three men examined each other for a moment, and then the older man jutted his chin and said, "Close the door, please, DC Spiller."

The man had an Eastern European accent, but his voice was that of a lifelong smoker, dry and painfully hoarse. The hushed, rasping whisper set Spiller's nerves on edge, but he kept his expression neutral and did as he was asked.

"That is much better," the old man went on. "Now we can talk in a civilised manner."

"Go ahead," Spiller said. "You already know my name. What's yours?"

"Ah, straight to business. Good." The man's smile was grim. "My name is Arnulf Mankowich. I am, or was, grandfather to Dennis."

"Oh, I'm sorry for your loss."

Mankowich tilted his head in acknowledgement. "Dennis was a good boy. He did not deserve to die like that." He heaved a rattling sigh. "I didn't want him to get mixed up with drugs. I told him no good would come of it, but he was young, headstrong..." Mankowich's voice trailed away and he shook his head.

"Forgive me," Spiller began, "but I'm not sure how I can help. I'm not assigned to the team investigating your grandson's case, but I'm sure my colleagues are doing their best to—"

"Are you?" Mankowich interrupted. "Are you really so certain of that, Mr Spiller?" He grimaced in disgust. "What is the death of another drug dealer to them? Nothing. *Less* than nothing. They are glad of it."

"No, we don't work like that," Spiller insisted. "We have a duty to investigate every crime, and we don't want a killer walking the streets any more than you do."

Mankowich sneered. "Whoever did this, he'd better hope you find him before we do. But even then, he won't be safe. We'll get the bastard, one way or another."

"Then we'll have to come looking for you," Spiller said. "Is that what you want, Mr Mankowich, to see out your days in a prison cell?"

"I've known worse. There's nothing you can threaten me with, Mr Spiller. I was fourteen years old when the Nazis took me and my family. Nothing could be worse than that, believe me."

Unsure what to say, Spiller let his gaze settle on the other man present. "You haven't introduced yourself, sir. Are you a relative of Dennis?"

The man's only reply was a narrowing of his eyes.

"We'll come to him in a second," Mankowich said. "He is why you are here. But I need you to understand first." He drew a breath, his thin shoulders rising and falling. "People talk, Mr Spiller. Rumours. Gossip. They know a girl has gone missing, a girl Dennis met. Then they find out he was killed, and they say the two things must go together. That is what they whisper to each other when they think I can't hear. But none of this is true. Dennis talked to the girl that night, but he had nothing to do with what happened to her."

"And what did happen to her?" Spiller asked.

"I don't know. I hope she will be found, but I do know that Dennis was not involved. He would never do anything to harm a woman, and I will not have his name blackened like this, do you understand?"

Spiller nodded. "For what it's worth, Mr Mankowich, I believe you. But I can't stop people from gossiping."

"No. But you can find this young woman, and then the truth will be known, yes?"

"Yes, it could work out that way. If there's anything you can do to help us find Lynsey, I'm listening."

"Good." Mankowich indicated the man at his side. "This is Gary. Gary Murphy. They call him Gaz."

Spiller looked at the man with renewed interest. "You're the bouncer at The Icebox?"

Murphy nodded.

"We've been trying to talk to you for days," Spiller said. "Why didn't you come forward?"

Murphy glanced at Mankowich, and Spiller understood. A good foot soldier, Murphy would not talk to the police unless he was told to do so.

"Go on," Mankowich said. "Tell him what you saw."

"Okay." Murphy focused on Spiller. "I was on the door on Saturday night. It was quiet until the pubs turned out, then I was busy for half an hour or so. After that, most people were inside, and they stayed until we turfed them out at two. But there was one young lady who came out, and it sounds like she's the one who's gone missing."

"Her name is Lynsey," Spiller said. "Did you see her leave?"

"Yes. I saw her walking away."

"When was this?"

"About quarter to one, give or take."

"Did Lynsey say anything to you?"

"Yeah. I thought she was looking a bit unsteady, so I asked her if she wanted a taxi. I said I'd call it for her, but she said not to bother. At least, I think that's what she said. She was drunk. She wasn't making much sense."

Spiller fought down a surge of anger rising from his gut. This information would've saved so much time. Given half a chance, he would gladly drag Murphy back to the station in handcuffs, but that wasn't going to happen. All he could do now was squeeze as much information as possible from this reluctant witness.

Keeping his voice level, Spiller said, "What happened next?"

"Well, I think she got a taxi anyway."

"I need to be sure. What exactly did you see?"

"There was a car, and she was standing next to it. I thought she might be talking to somebody through the window, but it was at the far end of the street, so..."

Spiller's hands wanted to go to his notebook, but that wouldn't go down too well. Instead, he said, "Tell me about the car. Make and model? Colour?"

"I couldn't tell you the make, it was too far away, but it was a saloon. I think it was black. There was no light on the top, so I figured it was a minicab."

"Did you see Lynsey actually get in?"

"Yeah. I think so."

"That's not good enough, Gary. It's a yes or no type of question."

Murphy lowered his eyebrows. "All right, mate. I'm trying."

"Try harder," Mankowich said. "Answer the man's question."

"Okay. No, I didn't see her get in. She was too far away, and I was working. I must've been distracted for a second, and when I looked again, the car was driving away."

"Did you see anyone with Lynsey?"

Murphy pushed out his lower lip. "Not that I can recall."

"What about before she left? Did you see anyone talking to her outside the club?"

"Yeah. Earlier on, Dennis came out and had a word with her, but only for a minute, then he went back inside."

"Any idea what they said to each other?"

"Not exactly. I think, maybe..." He looked to Mankowich and received permission in the form of an impatient wave.

"It looked like Dennis was chatting her up," Murphy went on. "She's a pretty girl, but she obviously wasn't interested, so Mank, I mean Dennis, gave up and left her alone. He wasn't the sort to try it on, if you know what I mean."

"I do," Spiller said. "How about Lynsey's boyfriend, Tony Carter, did you see him?"

"We all know Tony. He came out a couple of times. He said something to the young woman, but she told him to get lost. I couldn't hear it all, but she laid into him, called him all sorts of names. He didn't like that, but he wasn't going to do anything about it. He was broken up. His face was a picture. He went back in with his tail between his legs. I must admit, I had a laugh once he'd gone."

"You said he came out twice," Spiller prompted.

"Yeah, he turned up at the door a bit later and made a nuisance of himself, but it was all taken care of. The young woman had gone by then."

"What happened?"

"Not a lot. Dennis and his uncle were having a chat by the door, and Tony came out, shouting his mouth off. He had a go at Dennis and got what he deserved. It was only a tap. If he'd been sober, it wouldn't have knocked him down, but the daft sod was legless. He went down like a sack of spuds."

"You didn't need to step in?"

Murphy smiled as though the idea was ridiculous. "It was all over before it began. Mank's uncle told him to leave it, so that was the end of it. I picked Tony up and handed him to one of his mates. A guy called Eddie."

"Not Keith?"

Murphy shook his head. "I don't know a Keith. Tony's mates are Eddie and Wayne. Anyway, I told Eddie to take his mate home. Tony left, but he was with a girl. Pretty, short, brown hair. She was holding him up."

"When was this?"

"About one o'clock, give or take."

"Almost everybody else said the same thing, more or less," Spiller said. "But Tony Carter reckons he stayed until closing time, and so does the barman, Freddie Hall."

"They've got it wrong. Tony was in no fit state. If he'd tried to stay, I would've kicked him out. To be honest, the bloke wouldn't have known what day it was, never mind what time. And Freddie was rushed off his feet behind the bar. He didn't have time to keep an eye on the door. That's my job."

Spiller was about to move on, but something made him pause for thought. "I keep hearing this. The barman was busy, there was a long wait for drinks. But Freddie wasn't on his own that night, was he? There was a barmaid, Lucy Proctor."

Murphy shook his head. "Lucy works some nights, but she wasn't there on Saturday."

"What? Are you sure?"

"Positive. On Saturday it was Carol. She came down after her shift at the Mount Radford."

"Hang on," Spiller said. "This is Carol Whitaker, Lynsey's neighbour?"

"Yeah. Well, I didn't know she was—"

"What time did she get there?" Spiller interrupted. "And when did she leave?"

"She turned up around quarter to twelve, and she worked until closing time."

Spiller's heart beat a little faster as he formed his next question. "But she wasn't there the whole time was she? That's why Freddie was so busy."

"Yeah, that's what I heard. She sloped off for a bit, but I

didn't see her go. She must've slipped out the back. There's a yard where we get deliveries. It's usually locked but—"

"Carol could get hold of the key," Spiller said. "I expect the keys are behind the bar."

"In the office, but yeah, Carol could go and get them any time." Murphy looked to Mankowich. "Carol can't have done anything to that girl. She's not like that."

"We will soon know the truth," Mankowich replied, his voice edged with pure malice.

"Hold on, Mr Mankowich," Spiller said. "This case has nothing to do with what happened to Dennis."

"That may be so," Mankowich replied. "But one way or another, I will have Dennis cleared. Again I say it: We will soon know the truth."

Spiller tore his gaze away from Mankowich's icy stare and focused on Murphy. *This is it*, Spiller thought. *I'm so close.* He was almost certain that Carol was involved, but who'd driven the car that took Lynsey away?

"You sound as though you know Carol fairly well," Spiller said. "Is she religious at all?"

Murphy seemed thrown by the change in direction, and he almost laughed. "Carol? Do me a favour, pal."

"I thought not. Have you ever seen her with a man who looked a few years older than her?"

"All the time."

"The man I'm talking about is very distinctive," Spiller said. "He's smartly dressed and neat, his hair combed in a side parting. He's clean shaven and quite softly spoken. He sounds educated."

"That's not ringing any bells. Carol's *friends* tend to be a bit rough around the edges: middle-aged men with one thing on their mind."

"These friends, does she seem especially close to any of them?"

"Not really." Murphy hesitated. "I've heard there's one bloke who keeps buying her drinks. Freddie pointed him out. He reckoned the bloke wanted Carol all to himself."

"What's he called?"

"Now you're asking." Murphy screwed up his features in concentration. "Sorry, I don't remember. All I know is, he's a flash git, always mouthing off. He hasn't been coming for long. He used to turn up on his own, but these days he's in Tony's crowd."

Spiller's mind worked fast. "This man, does he smoke?"

"Like a chimney. He flicked a fag end by the door once. I had to have a word with him."

Keith bloody Osborne, Spiller thought. *It has to be him.* Osborne had lied about the bruise on his cheek, and he drove a dark blue saloon that might, in the glare of the streetlights, be mistaken for a black minicab. But he wasn't a recent friend to Tony Carter; that didn't fit. He'd been going out with Lynsey's friend Ashley for a couple of years.

But Ashley never said how long they'd been going out, Spiller thought. *I've only got Osborne's word for that.*

And the word of a liar meant nothing.

Spiller saw it all in a flash, his mind working overtime.

When they'd interviewed Osborne, he'd steered them away from the subject of Lynsey's flat because he wanted to hide his connection to Carol in the flat below.

But what was his motive for taking Lynsey? Was it sexual? Ashley had described him as having a roving eye, but that wasn't enough. Money then. Reilly had wondered how Osborne could afford to live in a nice neighbourhood. Yes, Osborne was only renting, but Spiller knew from bitter experience how expensive that could be. Perhaps there was money to be made by exploiting the report Lynsey had handled at County Hall. After all, Osborne worked for a building company.

"You know the man we are looking for," Mankowich stated. "I can see it in your face."

"I have my suspicions," Spiller replied. "I'll go and find him now." To Murphy, he added, "Unless there's anything else you can tell me."

"No, that was it," Murphy said. "If what I said helps, that's good. I... I should've said something before. I suppose I'll be in for it."

"Don't worry about it." Spiller pulled out his notebook and found Osborne's address. "Do either of you know Kingsley Avenue?"

"Yeah," Murphy said. "It's off Summer Lane."

Spiller ran a hand over his brow. Of course, there'd been the witness who'd called in. She'd seen a young woman shouting from the back of a taxi in Summer Lane. He'd followed up by phone, but the witness had added nothing new.

I'm an idiot! Spiller scolded himself. *I should've seen her in person.* He'd wanted to go, but Reilly had told him to call instead. That had been a mistake, but it was time to put it right.

"I'm going to go now," Spiller said. "Thanks for your help." He marched away without waiting for a response. He had to pull Keith Osborne in for questioning, but he didn't want to do it alone. As Spiller stomped down the stairs, he made his decision.

Finding the back room, he strode through the door. In the assembled audience, every head turned to stare, and from a chair at the front, DCI Wendell glared at Spiller, his jaw clenched.

"I'm sorry to interrupt, sir," Spiller heard himself say. "But I'm going to need your help."

41

LEEMAN SMILED. "GET UP," he said. "Now."

The man cowering in the corner of the room covered his face with his hands, whining.

"For God's sake," Leeman muttered. "You've seen a bit of blood before, haven't you?"

The man snivelled, wept.

Leeman picked up a cushion and wiped the blood from his knife. He examined the knife carefully, turning it so the blade caught the light, its cutting edges perfectly honed. It was important to look after the tools of your trade.

Satisfied, he threw the cushion to the floor and folded the blade away, stowing the knife in his pocket.

"Time to go."

Stepping around the blood on the carpet, Leeman crossed the room and leaned over the pathetic specimen in the corner. Grabbing the man by both arms, he hoisted him to his feet and held him there. The man complied, all trace of resistance gone.

"You killed her," the man whimpered. "Why?"

"Why not? It worked, didn't it?"

The man's gaze dropped to the blood-soaked carpet. "You... you didn't have to do that."

"Didn't I? Oh well. Under promise and over deliver, that's the mantra of our times, isn't it?"

The man stared at him, his eyes round and dark with abject terror. Thankfully, it seemed that he'd run out of feeble-minded remarks.

Leeman released one of the man's arms, but kept his hand clamped firmly on the other. Making his voice bright, he said, "Let's go. I'll drive, darling."

The man bleated something or other, but Leeman wasn't listening. Keeping a tight hold on his captive, Leeman led him across the room and made for the door.

Thank God, Leeman thought. *This is almost over.*

42

STANDING outside the Green Gables Inn, DCI Wendell remained impassive while Spiller outlined his case, and then he nodded.

"Bloody hell, Spiller," he said. "You don't take defeat lying down, do you?"

"I hope not, sir."

Wendell almost smiled. "Okay, we'll pull Osborne in, but we'll play it by the book."

"Sir, it's—"

"Urgent, I know," Wendell interrupted. "But we can't go off half-cock. This needs a proper raid on his address, and if we don't think ahead, any number of things could go sideways. We can't afford to make mistakes."

He studied Spiller for a moment then added, "Listen, if you're right and Osborne has Lynsey, we'll have to take him fast. If he has time to react, he might kill her to stop her testifying, or he might use her as a hostage, and we don't want that. And what if he gets away? If Lynsey isn't there, if he's hidden her somewhere remote, she might never be found."

Reluctantly, Spiller said, "I can see that, sir. It's just that we're so close. I want to get this done."

"And by sending it up the chain of command you've gone the right way about it. I'll lead the raid myself. Osborne won't know what's hit him."

"I'd like to be there, sir."

Wendell pursed his lips. "Not this time. You haven't had the experience or the training. Sit this one out."

Spiller started to protest, but Wendell gestured for him to be quiet.

"I need to call this in," Wendell said. "When I get back to the nick, I want a team ready and a search warrant for Osborne's address. We'll move as soon as we can." He paused. "I know you're keen, but you can go home, Tim. You've done all you can. And as it goes, you've done okay."

"Thank you, sir," Spiller said, but the words tasted like ash on his tongue.

Wendell headed off, and with nothing else to do, Spiller returned to his car.

Sitting behind the wheel, Spiller looked out onto the deserted street. The silence seemed wrong. He should be at the station, getting ready, and he definitely should be there when they took Osborne. But what choice did he have?

The chain of command wasn't an optional extra; it was sacrosanct. And Wendell was right to be cautious. He was a senior officer, and he knew what he was doing.

Spiller opened the glove box and retrieved his A-to-Z map of Exeter. Sure enough, Kingsley Avenue could be reached via Summer Lane, which was just off Pinhoe Road. *A fifteen-minute drive*, he thought. *Less if I put my foot down.*

In the time it took Wendell to get a search warrant, Spiller could be at Osborne's house. Once there, he wouldn't have to actually do anything. He could just keep an eye on the place. Where was the harm in that?

Osborne might spot me, he thought. *That would ruin everything.* Yes, caution was the best principle here. Procedures were there for a reason. He should sit back and let Wendell do his job.

"Sod that," Spiller muttered. He started the engine and pulled the Volvo out into the road, the tyres emitting a screech that would've made Reilly proud. He was on his way.

The streets were quiet, and he made good time, but he slowed the car to a more sedate speed before he pulled into Kingsley Avenue. The houses here were semi-detached bungalows, most with front gardens, though some lawns had been gravelled over to house the family car.

Spiller counted off the houses as he drove, but as he approached number eight, his mouth went dry. There, on the pavement, stood Keith Osborne. And by his side, standing very close, was the man who'd introduced himself as the Reverend Boothby.

Spiller dropped his gaze and hunched his shoulders, trying to shrink into his car seat as he kept driving. In his rearview mirror, he saw Boothby guiding Osborne into the passenger seat of a white BMW.

They're working together, Spiller thought. *I'll have to follow them.*

The avenue was short, ending in a turning circle, and Spiller turned his car around, taking his time. He mustn't appear hurried. He drove forward slowly, then he spotted a vacant driveway and reversed onto the gravel, switching off the Volvo's headlights. His car was partially hidden by a low wall and an evergreen shrub, and Spiller risked a look, peering along the road.

Boothby stood beside his car, turning his head slowly, scanning the road. Spiller sat stock still, trusting to the gloom within his car.

But it was no good. Boothby was staring in his direction. Something had attracted his attention.

Oh hell! Spiller caught a glimpse of movement in his wing mirror. Someone in the house behind him had opened a curtain, no doubt wondering at the unannounced visitor in their driveway. A middle-aged woman appeared at the window, backlit by the cosy glow of a front room. She raised a hand beside her face, the better to see out. Was she going to make a fuss? Was she going to bang on the windowpane, or even worse, come out and complain?

Spiller froze. Both the woman and Boothby would be wondering why someone would park and then stay in their car. Spiller half-turned in his seat, pretending to unfasten his seatbelt, and that seemed to do the trick. The woman backed away from the window, letting the curtain fall back into place, and along the street, Boothby lost interest. He climbed into the BMW, and its headlights came on. Spiller let out a slow breath.

Spiller glanced over his shoulder to check the house. The front door opened, a man standing on the threshold, the woman close behind. The man folded his arms and looked ready for an argument, but Spiller was already flicking on the headlights and pulling into the road. He sent the couple a cheery wave as he drove away.

Boothby drove carefully, sticking below the speed limit, and Spiller had to make his car crawl or he'd get too close. There was no traffic at the first junction, but Spiller hung back, letting the BMW pull away from him. He counted to five and then followed.

The next junction was busier, and once the BMW had

taken the turning, Spiller allowed three cars to pass before joining the stream of traffic.

The road was well lit, and the white car stood out clearly, but Boothby drove smoothly and fast, taking one turn after another, leading Spiller on a winding journey through backstreets. Spiller thought of calling in, but following the BMW without being seen took all his attention.

Before long, the traffic thinned and the streetlights were further apart. They were nearing the edge of the city, and Spiller slowed down as the cars between his Volvo and the BMW turned from the road.

Spiller gripped the wheel tight, ready for anything, but although the BMW accelerated, Boothby hardly exceeded the speed limit. Soon they were driving along a road with no street lighting, and Spiller hung back further. He'd be fine so long as he kept the BMW's taillights in sight.

Spiller reached for his radio, but the BMW suddenly braked hard and took a left turn, disappearing into a narrow side road.

Spiller forgot about the radio. He had to make a split-second decision. If he followed the BMW, he'd almost certainly be the only other car on the narrow side road, and Boothby would notice. It wasn't worth the risk.

He kept driving, fixing the junction in his mind as he passed. Spiller counted off the seconds, and when he reached five, he pulled in, chose his moment and executed a U-turn. An oncoming car flashed its headlights, the driver sounding the horn, but Spiller took no notice.

Spiller found the junction easily, his heart beating faster as he guided the Volvo slowly into the narrow side road. The BMW was nowhere to be seen, and Spiller cursed his luck. The place looked like some kind of industrial estate with rows of squat concrete buildings, each one surrounded by pointed metal railings or a chain-link fence. Any one of those grimly anonymous buildings could easily conceal a car.

Narrow alleys led off into the darkness between the buildings, but neither the alleyways nor the buildings bore any signs, and the only light came from the Volvo's headlights.

I stand out like a sore thumb, Spiller thought. *They'll see me coming from a mile off.* But he couldn't spot the BMW, no matter which way he craned his neck as he drove.

Ahead, the road led to a car park, and Spiller turned the car around on the cracked tarmac, ready to try again. His headlights swept across a long, low building, and at each window, the beams reflected back from jagged shards of broken glass.

So that was it. The place was abandoned. He should've realised earlier.

Spiller brought the car to a halt and took stock. He was alone, in an unknown location, and he'd lost sight of his suspects. There was only one thing to do.

He grabbed his personal radio and called in, giving his position as best as he could, describing the industrial estate and the last major road he'd passed. That done, he sat in silence, waiting while his radio hissed gently.

They'll tell me to hold my position, Spiller decided. *They'll tell me to wait for instructions.* But that wasn't good enough.

Spiller flung his radio onto the passenger seat and drove back the way he'd come. A muted message crackled from his radio, matching his prediction almost word for word, but it was too late. He'd already crossed the point of no return.

Spiller guided the Volvo into the first alley he came to,

winding down the window and listening as his car crawled along the lonely way between dark buildings. The tarmac was badly pitted, the potholes filled with water. He picked his way through, but one of the front wheels found a deep hole and the Volvo's suspension bottomed out with a thud. Spiller cursed under his breath and halted the car. Had he made too much noise? Were Osborne and Boothby already making themselves scarce?

Spiller waited, listening, his nerves taut. And a sound came from his right: a solid metallic clunk. *That was a car door*, he thought. *A solid, German car door*. He set off slowly, taking the next right turn and driving at a snail's pace. He hunched over the steering wheel, peering into the gloom, but there was nothing.

The seconds stretched out. But then, as he passed a large car park, Spiller glimpsed a white shape in the distance. He pressed hard on the brakes, put the Volvo into reverse and crept the car backwards. Yes. He'd almost missed it, but sitting at the far end of the car park was the white BMW.

Spiller switched off the Volvo's headlights and killed the engine, then he retrieved his trusty torch from the glove box. The aluminium-bodied torch had been a friend when he was in uniform, but when had he last changed the batteries?

Covering the lens with his hand, he flicked the switch on and off. Good. The bulb still shone as bright as ever.

Spiller climbed from the car, closing the door very slowly, then he stood for a moment, listening, allowing his eyes to grow accustomed to the dark.

The faint whisper of distant traffic was the only sound, so Spiller set off on foot toward the BMW. Surely, Boothby would've parked near the building he intended to enter.

When he reached the car, Spiller hunched beside it. Should he let down its tyres? It would prevent the man from getting away, but it would make a noise and betray his position. And what if the car had an alarm?

Spiller looked over to the nearest building. It wasn't far away; his best bet would be to get inside and see if he could pick up the trail. In a half crouch, Spiller dashed across the car park, placing his feet as carefully as he could. Even so, grit crunched beneath the soles of his shoes, the sound reverberating across the empty space, unnaturally loud.

At any moment there would be a shout, the beam of a torch, a scream. But he made it to the building safely. He spotted a dark recess that looked like a doorway, and he headed toward it.

The door was unmarked but it seemed promising. Spiller stayed close to the wall, holding his breath as he pushed the door handle down. The catch emitted a faint squeak, and he felt the door shift slightly as the mechanism disengaged. Good, it wasn't locked. A heartbeat, then Spiller swung the door open and darted through, moving to one side so he wouldn't be outlined in the doorway. Ahead of him, a long windowless corridor stretched out, the darkness barely touched by the faint glimmer from the skylights.

And Spiller heard voices: two men, one of them pleading, his voice wavering. The other sounded like Boothby. *I'm almost there*, Spiller thought. He was so close.

Spiller shut the door gently, then he crept forward. He risked a flash from his torch and saw four doorways ranged along the corridor. One was open, its door hanging lopsided from its hinges, but the other three were closed. There were no tell-tale slivers of light beneath any of the doors.

He heard the voices again, echoing eerily along the corridor. Spiller turned his head, but it was impossible to tell where the sounds were coming from.

Spiller's mouth was dry, but a strong sense of purpose took root in his mind. Lynsey was here, her plight so much worse than his, and he'd set her free if it was the last thing he did.

Keeping one hand on the wall, Spiller felt his way along, listening at each door. Nothing.

And then he saw it. At the end of the corridor, on the left, a faint flickering light filtered up from somewhere below. Spiller edged along the wall, one arm stretched out in front of him to feel his way, not daring to use his torch. His fingers found a hard edge, and he understood. This was the top of a stairwell that led down below ground level. There must be a basement or an underground storeroom.

Spiller peered around the corner and found the source of light. At the bottom of the steps, a metal door hadn't been closed properly, and shifting beams of light escaped from within. Whoever was inside, they had torches of their own. They might not notice if he used his, but still, he daren't risk it.

Spiller eased around the corner, but as he placed his foot on the top step, Boothby's voice rang out, steely edged: "Don't move."

Spiller froze, but the door below did not open, and he heard another man breathe one word: "Okay."

That had to be Osborne. He and Boothby were clearly arguing, and that was all to the good. With their attention on each other, they wouldn't hear him approach.

Spiller took the steps one at a time, transferring his weight slowly from one foot to the other. He was only six steps from the door when he heard something that made his blood run cold.

There was no mistaking the sharp crack of a gunshot, and Spiller's instincts told him to turn and run. Alone and in the dark, armed only with a torch, he was in no shape to tackle a gunman. But before he could react, the door flew open and a man dashed out, launching himself at the stairs.

Spiller saw only a silhouette, but he charged at the man, his arms outstretched. They collided, and the man stumbled, but he didn't fall. Spiller wrapped his arms around him and lunged forward, pinning his captive against the wall.

"Police!" Spiller yelled. "You're under arrest!"

The man stiffened, then he planted his hands on Spiller's chest and shoved hard, pushing him away, breaking his grip.

Spiller's feet slipped on the smooth steps, and he had to stagger back to regain his balance.

"Run," the man urged. "Get out of here!"

Spiller's mind reeled. He knew that voice. "Paddy?"

He flicked on his torch and saw Reilly's frightened face.

"Just go!" Reilly shouted, then he ran, haring up the stairs.

Light flared from below and Boothby stepped into the doorway, his hands raised, one holding the torch, the other a gun. In the confines of the stairwell, the shot was almost deafening.

Reilly's body jerked, but he kept running. The second shot brought him down, and he fell hard, landing on his front, his body meeting the concrete stairs with a sickening thud.

Spiller turned to face the gunman. Boothby stood, rock

steady, the gun and the torch now pointed directly at Spiller's face.

"Put the gun down," Spiller said. "I called for backup. They're on their way."

Boothby's laughter echoed in the stairwell.

"Put the gun *down*," Spiller said again. "There'll be firearms officers, dogs. You won't make it out of here unless you give yourself up."

"Now that, Mr Spiller, is simply incorrect. I'm going to walk away, and you are going to do what you're told."

"No, Boothby, you can't—"

"For God's sake, that's not my real name, you idiot. My name is Mr Leeman. You'd do well to remember that."

Spiller stared. This man would not have given up his identity unless he intended to leave no witnesses. *What I wouldn't give for the sound of sirens*, he thought. *Even one car would do.* It was his only hope, but it was almost certainly in vain. His colleagues would arrive too late. He was somewhere beyond the city, reached by a road with no name, standing in an unmarked and unlit building that was one of many.

Still, it wasn't over. Not yet.

"I'm going to back away," Spiller said. "I want to see to Reilly."

"No. Stay there."

"But he might still be alive."

"So what? Let him die."

"I can't do that." Spiller gathered his courage and backed slowly away, his feet finding the steps with difficulty.

"Oh, all right," Leeman muttered. "You can check his pulse, but that's all. You'll be saving me a job."

Spiller knelt beside Reilly. With only torchlight to work

by, he could barely make out the bullet holes in Reilly's coat, and there wasn't much blood on the steps. But what little he could see of Reilly's face was deathly pale, his eyes closed. Spiller searched for a pulse at his throat. It was there, but it was weak, unsteady.

"Paddy, stay with me," Spiller said. "Help is on its way. We'll get you to a hospital."

Reilly didn't raise his head, but a thin, wheezing breath escaped from his lips, and his arm twitched, his hand tapping against Spiller's leg.

"Don't try to move," Spiller said, but Reilly's hand knocked against him again. *He wants me to hold his hand,* Spiller thought, but when he reached down, something metallic was placed against his palm.

The jackknife.

Reilly's grip was weak, and Spiller took the knife, concealing it in his fist.

"It's okay, Paddy," he said. "I understand."

Once more, the beam of Leeman's torch shone on Spiller's face.

"That's enough," Leeman called out. "Stand clear, Spiller."

"Not yet." Without looking down, Spiller slipped the knife into his jacket pocket. "I need to stay with him."

"No, you don't. Stand up and move away, or you'll die by his side."

Spiller shook his head, but Reilly's hand pushed against him.

"Go," Reilly wheezed. "Now."

He's right, Spiller thought. *If I can get away, I can bring help.*

"Okay," Spiller said. "Take it easy, Leeman. He's a police officer and he's still alive, but if he dies, you'll go down for life." Spiller stood, inching back from Reilly while keeping his eyes on Leeman. "Think about it. You'll be locked up until the end of your days."

Leeman didn't reply, but he turned his torch on Reilly, the beam centred on his head.

Spiller felt rather than heard the gunshot, the sound shuddering through him like a punch to the chest. He didn't want to look at Reilly, but he had to. Reilly was dead.

Spiller turned his glare on Leeman. "You bloody animal. He was a good man."

"I think not. He deserved to die."

"No. He was here to save Lynsey. He would've taken you in."

"Don't you get it, Mr Spiller? He was in on the whole thing."

"That's not true."

Leeman sighed. "I'm afraid it is. I wasn't expecting to find him, but he was here when I arrived."

"He'd found her. He was going to—"

"For God's sake," Leeman interrupted. "Can you really be so obtuse? Reilly knew where Lynsey was, but he did nothing to help. As if that wasn't enough, Osborne told me one thing before he died. He didn't know who was in charge, but he knew they had a policeman in their pocket: a corrupt detective who could sabotage any case. I've put an end to that. You should be thanking me."

Spiller shook his head, his mind a whirl. But he held on to one thought, one burning question. "Is Lynsey all right?"

"She's alive, but she's not in great shape. They've been doping her with something; God knows what."

"Lynsey?" Spiller called out. "Are you all right?"

A plaintive moan came from beyond the open door.

"She needs help," Leeman said. "But you are going to take her to a hospital."

"What?"

"It's very simple. Miss Clifford needs medical attention, and I'm delivering her into your care. All you have to do is take her to the nearest hospital."

"I can use my radio. It's in my car. I can call an ambulance."

"No radio. You'll do as you're told. Do you understand?"

"You want time to get away." Spiller hesitated. "What about Osborne? Is he...?"

"Dead. He had it coming. You must've figured out what he did. He took Miss Clifford with the help of his little tart. And before you ask, she's dead too. She deserved it every bit as much as he did. She worked at the nightclub, and she drugged Lynsey's drink, then she found the poor woman outside and made sure she got into Osborne's car. She told me everything in the end, but it didn't do her much good. I left her in Osborne's house."

"You're..."

"A monster?" Leeman suggested. "Insane?" He chuckled darkly. "No, I'm just doing my job. I was paid to resolve this issue, and I have done so."

"Paid by who?"

"By *whom*," Leeman replied. "But I'm not going to answer. All you need to know is we're on the same side, you and I. That's why I'm letting you live."

"You were paid to find Lynsey?"

"And to make sure the guilty parties suffered. Yes."

"So when I saw you with Carol..."

"I got to her before you did. You asked some good questions, by the way, but I couldn't allow you to get ahead. That would've been very inconvenient."

"I should've realised," Spiller said. "You used my rank, but I hadn't given it."

"Ah, a slip of the tongue on my part. You know, for a policeman, you're really not that stupid. You've never been far behind. I'd be impressed, but I fear you might become a nuisance."

"I'm going to take you in."

"You see? There you go, Mr Spiller, true to form, even though I'm the one with the gun."

"I'm not talking about today. It might take a while, but I've seen your face and I know your name. I've memorised the registration number of your car. I'll track you down."

"No, you won't. But we've talked for too long. It's about time we took Miss Clifford out of here. We owe it to her to be pragmatic, yes?"

"For her sake, yes. I agree."

"Good. In that case, you can come down, but please, don't even think about upsetting me. My track record speaks for itself."

Leeman backed into the room and Spiller trod the remaining steps with a heavy heart. This was all wrong, but what could he do? If Leeman was telling the truth, Lynsey needed help, and his first duty was to protect life.

Spiller took a steadying breath and stepped into the room, his torch in his hand.

Keith Osborne was sitting slumped on the floor, his back against the wall and his head lolling forward, his chin on his chest. The top of his head shone wetly, his hair matted with blood and fragments of splintered bone. One glance was enough for Spiller; Osborne was beyond earthly help.

Against the opposite wall a bed had been set up, and a figure lay curled on the thin mattress, unmoving. *Lynsey!*

He forgot about Leeman and went straight to her. In the light from his torch, Lynsey's face was ashen, a sheen of sweat on her skin. Her eyes were shut tight, her brow creased in pain, and she let out a low, murmuring moan.

"It's all right, Lynsey," Spiller said gently. "I'm a policeman. I'm going to make sure you get to a hospital. You're going to be okay."

Lynsey blinked and he moved the beam of his torch from her face. She turned her head to look up at him.

"Really?"

"Yes. I'm going to take you out of here. Do you think you can stand?"

"I don't..." Lynsey shifted, wincing as she stretched out her legs.

"Are you hurt?" Spiller asked.

"No. I just feel awful. I can't..."

"Here. Let me help." Spiller leaned over and wrapped his arm around her shoulders, easing her into a sitting position.

Lynsey wiped her eyes with the backs of her hands. "That's better. I think I can stand, but don't let go."

"I won't," Spiller said. "I'll hold on for as long as you want me to, okay?"

"Yes."

Spiller set down his torch and helped Lynsey to her feet. She clung to him for dear life. Lynsey was light as a bird, but she was unsteady and they made slow progress up the steps, taking them one at a time. Leeman followed close behind, using his torch to light the way.

When they reached the corridor, Leeman tapped Spiller on the shoulder.

"This is too slow," he said. "Let me take her."

"No, I can manage."

"This isn't a discussion. Time is precious, but you're tired, and I'm fresh. It will be quicker this way."

Leeman stowed his gun in his jacket, then he held out his torch to Spiller. "Take it."

Reluctantly, Spiller did as he was told, and Leeman swept Lynsey up in his arms, carrying her easily as he set off along the corridor.

Spiller walked beside them. One hand held the torch, but he slipped the other into his jacket pocket, his fingers closing around Reilly's knife. He had a weapon, but could he use it? It might serve as a threat, but Leeman was a killer, and he seemed to have no fear. He wouldn't be cowed by the sight of an old jackknife.

But what was the alternative? If he waited for a chance, he might be able to overpower Leeman, but it wouldn't be easy. He'd need to take him by surprise.

Spiller thought of the knife's marlin spike. What force would it take to drive the steel shaft into Leeman's back? And even if he managed it, would one blow be enough to disable him? The man had a gun, for God's sake.

I have to bide my time, Spiller told himself. *I'll only get one chance.*

In the car park, Leeman carried Lynsey to Spiller's Volvo, and together they guided her onto the back seat. Lynsey was able to sit, and Spiller put Leeman's torch on the seat before fastening her safety belt.

When he straightened up, Spiller slipped his hand into his pocket, his fingers finding the knife, unfolding the brutal metal spike.

Leeman faced him, holding out his hand.

"What?" Spiller asked.

"You have my torch."

Spiller nodded. "It's in the car on the back seat. Get it yourself."

Leeman smiled. "You have a knife, and up until now, you've been wise not to use it. If you'd tried, it would've ended badly, both for you and for Miss Clifford."

"No, you're wrong." Spiller let go of the knife and showed his empty hand.

Leeman locked eyes with him. "It's in your pocket, Mr Spiller. You took it from Reilly."

For a long moment, the men eyed each other, then Leeman gestured to Spiller's car.

"Hand me the torch, then you can go. The sooner you get to a hospital, the better it will be for Miss Clifford."

"All right."

Spiller retrieved the torch and Leeman took it from him.

"Thank you. Good luck, Mr Spiller. Goodbye."

With that, Leeman turned and walked away.

He's right, damn him, Spiller thought. *All that matters now is Lynsey.*

Spiller didn't watch Leeman go. He climbed into the Volvo, and when he looked around, the white BMW had gone. Leeman had slipped away, his job done. Only the chaos he'd left in his wake remained.

Spiller retrieved his radio and requested an ambulance, arranging to meet it at the junction with the main road.

Swivelling in his seat, he said, "They're on their way, Lynsey. We'll go and meet them. They'll look after you."

Lynsey nodded, then she stared out the side window, her eyes vacant.

"We'll get going," Spiller said, then he drove from the car park, taking care to avoid the potholes.

As he drove, Reilly's last moments came unbidden to

his mind: the way he'd fallen, the pallor of his face, the wheezing of his breath. And then there'd been the horror of Leeman's gunshot. It was no way for a policeman to die.

What the hell had Reilly been doing there? Had Leeman spoken the truth? Was Reilly involved in the plot to kidnap Lynsey?

Reilly had been in control of the investigation, and it wasn't hard to think of times when they might've made more progress. Instead of taking part in the door-to-door inquiry, they'd been on a series of errands that had yielded very little.

Reilly had been blinkered, focusing on Tony Carter even though there'd been no real evidence against the man. He'd even delayed talking to Dennis Mankowich until it was too late.

Had all this been deliberate mismanagement on Reilly's part? And what about the sudden appearance of drugs in Lynsey's kitchen? Reilly had been in the flat on his own, so he could've planted them there with ease. And what about the failed drugs bust Ronny had talked about? He'd said that DCI Wendell was in the clear, hinting that someone else in CID was to blame.

It was Reilly, Spiller thought, and the realisation stirred a deep anger in his chest. Reilly's treachery was a bitter pill to swallow, but Spiller forced it down.

He had to think of Lynsey now, of her and nothing else. Soon she'd be in hospital, her ordeal over. Only when she was safe and being cared for, could he allow himself to return to the case. And return to it, he certainly would.

THURSDAY

43

In the Royal Devon and Exeter Hospital, Spiller found Lynsey's ward and was directed to wait until a doctor could be found.

He took a seat and looked around, watching the bustle of activity, listening to the strange conversations between staff members, much of it consisting of acronyms and abbreviations.

Finally, a woman in a white coat marched up to him and said, "I'm Doctor Mishra. I understand you're here to see Lynsey."

"That's right." Spiller jumped to his feet and showed his warrant card as he introduced himself.

The doctor studied his ID then nodded as if satisfied.

"How is Lynsey doing?" Spiller asked.

"She's very tired. She's been through an ordeal. We're still running some tests, and in the meantime, she needs rest."

"But what's the prognosis?"

"It's good. We're getting the drugs out of her system,

and she's responding well to treatment. We expect her to make a full recovery."

Spiller had been holding his breath, and he let it out slowly. "That's great news. Thank you."

"Thank *you*, DC Spiller. I hear that it was you who called the ambulance."

"I was just doing my job. The paramedics did the hard work. They were fantastic."

Doctor Mishra smiled. "We're all in it together." She paused, her expression becoming more sombre. "I expect you want to interview Lynsey."

"Only if she's feeling well enough, but it won't be a full interview; just a quick chat."

"That might be possible, I suppose, but Lynsey's father may be with her at the moment. He's hardly been away from her side."

"I'm sure Mr Clifford will understand," Spiller said. "He'll want justice for his daughter just as much as I do, and I only want to speak to Lynsey for a few minutes."

"A few minutes? That's what you policemen always say. But I can't have Lynsey upset in any way."

Spiller held up his hands. "I understand. All I want is the chance to ask a few simple questions, nothing more."

Doctor Mishra pursed her lips while she scrutinised him, then she nodded. "I can see it's important, but I'll have to come with you, and I'll only let you stay for five minutes at most. If Lynsey becomes distressed, you'll have to leave. Is that clear?"

"Perfectly. Thank you."

"It's this way. Lynsey has a side room."

The doctor set off with a determined stride, Spiller trailing behind her.

Lynsey's room was bigger than Spiller had expected,

and nicer too. Light flooded in from the windows, and two bouquets of flowers had been arranged in vases on the bedside cabinet. Lynsey was sitting up in bed. She'd been reading a magazine, but she let it fall to her lap when she saw them come in.

By the window, Francis Clifford turned around as though he'd been looking at the outside world. He'd aged since Spiller had last seen him, the lines on his forehead deeper and his eyes less bright than before. He acknowledged Spiller with a brief nod, then his gaze went to the doctor. "Is everything all right?"

"Yes," Doctor Mishra replied. "This is Detective Constable Spiller. He'd like to ask Lynsey a few questions."

"We've met." Clifford looked to Lynsey. "What do you think, darling? We can ask him to come back later if you like."

Lynsey clasped her hands in her lap. "No, that's all right. I'd rather get it over with."

"Are you sure?"

"Yes. Why don't you go and get a coffee or something? You look like you're tired."

Clifford gazed at his daughter as if at a loss.

"Please, Dad," Lynsey went on. "Why don't you go for a walk? The fresh air will do you good."

"That's my daughter, always thinking of others. You get that from your mother." Clifford's voice had grown hoarse as he'd spoken, and he cleared his throat. "I suppose I could do with a coffee." Looking to Spiller, he added, "You won't be long, will you? You mustn't upset her."

"I'll do my best," Spiller replied. "And perhaps you and I could have a quick chat afterwards."

"Yes, of course."

"Go on, Dad," Lynsey said. "And don't worry. I'll be fine."

"Okay, but I'll be right back. I won't go far." Clifford made for the door, letting himself out without a backward glance.

"Poor Dad," Lynsey said. "He can't stand hospitals. Ever since Mum..."

"This must be hard for him," Doctor Mishra said. "But he must be very relieved you're on the mend."

"Yes." Lynsey smiled sadly.

"You're looking remarkably well," Spiller said. "How are you feeling today?"

"Much better." Lynsey plucked a tissue from her bedside cabinet and dabbed at her eyes. "Sorry. I keep crying every time anyone's nice to me. I can't help it."

"That's perfectly understandable," Doctor Mishra said. "Lynsey, are you okay to answer a few questions for DC Spiller?"

"Yes, I think so."

"Okay, but I'm going to stay in the room," the doctor said. "If you feel tired or upset, just tell me, okay?"

Lynsey nodded. "I'll do my best. I want to help."

The doctor gestured to a chair beside the bed. "Have a seat, DC Spiller, but don't get too comfortable."

"Thanks." Spiller sat down, pulling the chair around so he could face Lynsey. "The flowers are nice. Are they from your father?"

"One bunch is. The other's from Tony." She sighed. "He can be sweet sometimes, but..."

"But you don't see a future for your relationship," Spiller suggested.

"That's right." Lynsey seemed to see him with fresh eyes. "You're very perceptive, for a man."

Spiller affected a show of modesty. "I get these tips from my wife. When we watch the TV, she likes to pick things apart. She can usually figure out the plot twists before I can, and she always spots the villain. She'd have made a very good detective."

Lynsey laughed, tears springing to her eyes.

Spiller took the box of tissues and offered them to her.

Lynsey dried her eyes and said, "That sounds lovely, watching the TV together. I can imagine the pair of you settling down with a mug of cocoa."

"And that's very perceptive of *you*. We do like a hot mug of cocoa. It's a quiet life, but it suits us."

Lynsey lapsed into silence, staring into the middle distance.

"For what it's worth," Spiller began gently, "I'm sure you'll have plenty of happy times yourself. This might sound like a cliché, but you really do have your whole life ahead of you. One day, all this will be a distant memory."

"I hope so." Lynsey looked at him. "But right now, you need to sort out what happened, don't you?"

"I'm afraid so. We need to make sure that the people who did this are brought to trial so they can never hurt anyone again."

"But they're all..."

"Some of the people responsible were killed, yes. But we still need to understand exactly what happened in case others were involved."

Lynsey took a deep breath and let it out slowly. "Okay. Go ahead."

"Thank you." Making his tone soft, Spiller said, "Lynsey, when you left the Icebox club on Saturday night, what happened?"

"I was stupid. I got into a car. I thought it was a taxi,

but I didn't really know what I was doing. After my last drink, I was out of it."

"Can you recall who served you that drink?"

"Carol. She lives in the flat downstairs." Lynsey frowned. "I heard..."

Spiller nodded. "This is going to be upsetting to hear, but you deserve the truth. I'm afraid Carol was killed."

Lynsey nodded very slowly, her gaze losing focus.

Spiller glanced at Doctor Mishra and saw the concern in her expression.

To Lynsey, he said, "Are you okay to go on? If you are, I'd really like to know what happened outside the club that night."

"Yes, of course." With an effort, Lynsey composed herself. "The car pulled up and the driver called my name. I thought I recognised his voice, but I couldn't see into the car properly. I was going to say something, but Carol came out of nowhere. She said it was okay. I think she got into the car as well. She said she'd help me. But I don't remember what happened after that. It's like there are gaps in my memory. It's a horrible feeling."

"I understand. Did you have anything else except alcohol that night?"

"Like what?"

"Drugs. Pills."

Lynsey grimaced. "No. I don't do drugs. Never."

"Are you sure about that? You won't get into trouble over it, but we do need to know."

"I'm positive. I hate all that kind of thing. A few drinks is my limit."

"There was a bottle of Valium in your flat. Your name was on the label."

"That was from ages ago. My parents fuss over me, and

they got it into their heads that I was anxious. They convinced me to see a private doctor, and I went along with it. But I never took the pills. I'd have thrown them away, but you're not supposed to do that, are you? You're meant to take them back to the chemist, but I kept forgetting."

"What about ecstasy? We found some in your flat."

Lynsey stared at him. "Where?"

"They were in one of your kitchen cupboards."

"Are you sure?"

Spiller nodded. "I found them myself."

"That's not right. I would never take pills. Maybe Tony put them there, but I doubt it. Even he's not stupid enough to mess around with drugs. It was the one thing we agreed on."

"Okay. Now, I'm sorry to have to ask about this, but we need to talk about the place you were being held. Is that okay?"

"Yes, but I didn't see much. It was dark."

"Did you see any of the people who were keeping you there?"

"Not properly, but..."

"Go on," Spiller said. "When you're ready."

"There were two men. At first, there was just one, but later on, not long before you found me, the second man came, and he wasn't so bad. He didn't threaten me or say anything horrible. I think he was worried. He saw I was ill, you see."

"Did you get a look at him at all?"

Lynsey shook her head. "It was dark, and I was feeling pretty bad. He shone a light at me, then he went away for a bit." Lynsey pointed to the water jug by her bed. "Would you mind?"

"Of course not." Spiller poured a glass of water and

passed it to Lynsey. Her hand trembled as she held the glass, but she took a few sips and seemed to rally her strength.

Setting the glass down, she said, "That's better. Thank you."

"You're welcome. Do you want to stop?"

From the corner of the room, Doctor Mishra said, "I think you could do with a break, Lynsey."

"In a minute. There's something I want to say." Focusing on Spiller, she said, "You've got a Midlands accent. Is that where you're from?"

"Yes. Telford."

"Ah, where they built the bridge. The Industrial Revolution. I always liked history at school. It was my best subject."

"That's right," Spiller said. "The first iron bridge was built near my hometown. You have a good memory."

"For some things." Lynsey paused. "The second man had an accent. I think he was from Yorkshire."

Reilly, Spiller thought, his heart hardening.

"After a while he came back, and then everything was very confusing," Lynsey went on. "I was dizzy, and I felt weak, but someone else came in, so there were suddenly three of them, and..." Her voice trailed away.

"Take your time," Spiller said. "The third man, had you seen or heard him before?"

Lynsey shook her head. "It was that one time. He..." Her lower lip quivered. "He came in and... it was awful. I can't even..."

"It's okay, Lynsey," Doctor Mishra said. "You don't have to go on."

"Yes, I do. Because he had a gun, and he shot the man who took me. In a way, he saved me. Who was he?"

"He said his name was Leeman. We don't know his first name."

Lynsey's lips moved as if she were repeating the name silently.

"He carried me to your car." Lynsey's gaze found Spiller's. "I have got that right, haven't I? It doesn't seem real."

"Yes. He carried you part of the way." Spiller hesitated. "But that doesn't make up for what he did. We're still looking for him."

"Of course. I think he might've shot the second man too. I heard it, and when you took me out, I saw someone lying on the stairs."

"That's right. Let's talk about the man who took you; the man who drove the car. Do you have any idea who he was?"

"No. It was always dark, and he kept his voice quiet, like a whisper. He was trying to scare me."

"You could be right, but it's possible he was altering his voice so you wouldn't recognise him."

"I don't understand."

"Lynsey, we believe the man who took you was Keith Osborne."

Lynsey's eyes grew round. "Ashley's boyfriend?"

"Yes. Did you know him?"

"Not really. They hadn't been going out long, and he never spent much time with her, at least, not as far as I could see. To be honest, I've hardly spoken to him. He's only been hanging around with Tony for a few weeks."

"That's what we thought," Spiller said. "When I found you, Osborne was in the room. He'd already been shot."

"Christ," Lynsey murmured. "All this, for... for what? Were they trying to get money from my dad?"

"Not directly," Spiller replied. "Someone was trying to influence him, and they were also looking for a document you'd inadvertently handled at work."

"He kept asking about that. I told him I didn't have it, but he wouldn't listen." Lynsey shook her head. "Keith," she muttered in disbelief. "How could he? How could he do that to me?"

Lynsey put her hand on her brow, covering her eyes, and her shoulders started to shake.

Doctor Mishra started to speak, but Spiller was already getting to his feet.

"I'm going to go now, Lynsey," he said. "Thank you very much for your help, and I'm really sorry all this has happened to you. Please, get some rest. The only important thing right now is for you to get better."

Lynsey sobbed quietly, and the doctor went to her side.

"Goodbye," Spiller said. "Take care." To the doctor, he added, "Thank you."

Spiller made his exit, and he almost didn't recognise the man sitting in the corridor. Hunched over in the hard chair, his gaze fixed on the plastic cup he held in both hands, Francis Clifford had removed his jacket, and his crumpled white shirt seemed too big for him. He looked up at Spiller and blinked as if waking from a dream, then he made to stand.

Spiller gestured for him to stay sitting. "It's all right, Mr Clifford. I'll come to you."

"Thanks." Clifford sat up and took a sip from his cup. He winced and then looked around searching for somewhere to dispose of his cup. Finding no table, he set the cup carefully on the floor.

Taking the seat beside him, Spiller said, "That bad, is it? The coffee, I mean."

"Cold. I must've been out here longer than I realised."

Spiller waited for Clifford to meet his gaze, then said, "How are you holding up?"

"Me? I'm fine. It's Lynsey we're all worried about." He hesitated. "I should've thanked you, by the way. For everything you did. Lynsey said you were very kind. I won't forget that."

"I was doing my job. I only wish I could've found her sooner. But there was someone else who got there before me. A Mr Leeman."

Clifford didn't react.

"Do you know anyone by that name?" Spiller went on.

"No. It doesn't mean anything to me."

"That's interesting, because Mr Leeman claimed that someone had hired him to find Lynsey."

"Well, it wasn't me," Clifford replied. "It sounds far-fetched. He was probably one of the kidnappers, feeding you a story to save his own skin."

Spiller nodded slowly as if considering this, all the while watching Francis Clifford. The man showed no emotion. If he was lying, he was making a good job of it.

"Are you looking for him?" Clifford went on. "What was his name again? Leeman?"

"That's right, Mr Clifford, and we certainly are looking for him. He killed a policeman, and he claimed to have murdered several other people, although we're still looking into that."

"He sounds like a dangerous criminal. I wish you luck. We can't have people like that on our streets." Clifford sat up straighter, regaining some of his poise. "I shall say as much when I next meet with the Chief Constable. We go back a long way, and he'll listen to me. I'll tell him, in no uncertain terms, that you must have whatever support you need. For too long, the police in this city have been underfunded, and that has to change."

"We appreciate your support, sir, but—"

"No buts," Clifford interrupted. "You do a difficult job, but without the proper resources, it becomes next to impossible, am I right?"

Clifford was a charismatic speaker, and Spiller found himself thinking of his clapped out computer.

"I can see that you agree," Clifford went on. "I'll do what I can. I'll make some calls, set up some meetings. I'll knock some heads together if I have to, but I'll get this done." He clapped his hands together as if relishing the prospect of a confrontation, his eyes bright.

He's back in business mode, Spiller thought. *Just like that.* The tenderness of a distraught father had vanished, replaced by a hard-nosed businessman. Was Clifford capable of hiring a killer? *Oh yes*, Spiller decided. *He wouldn't think twice.*

"Mr Clifford," Spiller began, his tone level, "I hope you don't think that your offer of support will, in any way, influence our inquiries."

Clifford's only reply was a piercing stare.

Spiller gave as good as he got. Unblinking, he said, "If I find a connection between you and Leeman, I will bring you in. That will be my lawful duty."

"You won't find a connection," Clifford stated. "Take it from me."

"That's almost a denial," Spiller replied, "but not quite." He got to his feet. "Take care, Mr Clifford. You know what they say about supping with the Devil; make sure you use a long spoon."

With that, Spiller walked away. Francis Clifford was in it up to his neck, but sometimes you had to pick your battles. *I laid my cards on the table*, Spiller thought. *What else could I have done?* The games of power and influence were never fought on a level field, and all too often, it was people like Clifford who set the rules.

If Clifford had hired Leeman, he would've been careful; it wouldn't be easy to prove a link. Leeman, on the other hand, had left a trail of slaughter in his wake, and that meant fingerprints and fibres, minute particles and blood spatter patterns. If they were lucky, there might even be DNA. Forensic evidence had a way of stacking up.

Leeman might well have fled, but he wouldn't stay quiet for long. He'd kill again, and when he did, Spiller would be ready.

Meanwhile, the people who'd ordered Lynsey's kidnapping were still at large. The image of Lynsey crying in her hospital bed came to Spiller's mind, provoking the memory of a different bed, and Lynsey lying helpless, her spirit almost broken. *That poor woman*, he thought. *Somebody has to pay for what they did to her.* He would make sure of it. He'd stay on this case, even if he had to fight for it. When the culprits were caught, he would be the one to put them in cuffs. He had to see this through to the bitter end.

44

Spiller stood to attention, waiting. Detective Chief Superintendent Boyce, meanwhile, sat upright in his chair, regarding him in silence.

After a long moment, Boyce said, "Sorry I didn't get to you earlier, Tim. As you can imagine, it's been a busy day." He paused. "How are you holding up?"

"I'm fine, sir. I've been debriefed by DCI Wendell, and I've been carrying on with my work. I've been assigned to the MIT."

"Good. You're in safe hands there. Brian's a solid officer."

"Yes, sir."

"I understand you were able to visit Lynsey Clifford in hospital."

"Yes, sir. She's recovering well. The doctor said she was fit for questioning, but only for a few minutes."

"Good. Was she able to tell you much?"

"She did very well. She's keen to help, and her account confirms everything I was told by the man who called himself Leeman."

"Ah yes. Leeman. In your report, you seem to attach a great deal of weight to what he had to say. Remember, he's a self-confessed murderer, Tim, and he killed a serving police officer. You saw that with your own eyes."

"Yes, sir. It's not something I'll ever forget."

Boyce nodded, his expression solemn. "When we come to DS Reilly, we must tread carefully. When this comes out, it's going to be difficult for all of us, but especially for you." Boyce allowed his words to hang in the air before going on. "I'm a great believer in openness and transparency, Tim, but there are times when it doesn't work in anybody's favour. Are you following me?"

Spiller's frown spoke volumes.

"Let me put it to you another way," Boyce went on. "When the public hear bad reports about the police, it undermines the trust they place in us. It leaves the public feeling vulnerable and unprotected: frightened, even. So it's not good for them, and it's not good for us, because if people don't have faith in us, we can't do our jobs properly. We can't police by consent if the public feel we're not to be trusted."

"I can see the difficulty, sir."

"Then you'll understand, Tim, that this is your chance, your last chance, to decide how we interpret recent events."

"*Interpret*, sir? I was there. I know what I saw."

"Quite so. Nobody's doubting your word, Tim, but let's weigh everything up and see which way the scales tip, shall we? For instance, it's true to say that DS Reilly was working on the Lynsey Clifford case with you, yes?"

"Yes, sir."

"You were both doing your best to find Lynsey, so perhaps DS Reilly simply beat you to it. He got there first."

"I don't believe so, sir."

"How can you know for sure? We can't ask Reilly, now can we?"

Spiller took a moment to choose his words. "Sir, the evidence suggests—"

"The evidence is not clear cut," Boyce interrupted. "Is it not possible, say, that Reilly was attempting to free Lynsey when he was gunned down by the kidnappers?"

"With respect, I don't believe we can say that, sir. When Reilly was shot, the kidnappers were already dead."

"That's assuming you believe this Leeman character you encountered."

"Yes, sir. It also fits with what Lynsey told me this morning. As far as I can tell, Leeman was not one of the kidnappers. He'd been hired to find Lynsey and punish the perpetrators."

Boyce frowned in disapproval. "I think that's unlikely. It's more probable he was one of the gang. They argued among themselves, you said so in your report, and Osborne was killed. Reilly burst in and was threatened at gunpoint. He made a bid to escape, and you got in his way. As a result, Reilly was killed in the line of duty."

Spiller ran his tongue over his dry lips. "Again, with respect, sir, I can't agree. Leeman let me leave with Lynsey. He helped me to take Lynsey to the car."

"That's the oldest trick in the book. How many times have we seen criminals pretending to be helpful to throw suspicion onto someone else?"

"I understand what you're saying, sir, but I believe Reilly was involved in the plot to kidnap Lynsey; maybe not at the outset, but he was definitely in on it."

"Prove it," Boyce said.

"DS Reilly mishandled the investigation from the start."

Boyce raised an eyebrow. "In what way?"

"He deliberately led at least one witness in order to give Keith Osborne an alibi. When we talked to Carter's friends, Eddie Appleton and Wayne O'Neill, Reilly fed them Keith's name, and they went along with it. I knew something wasn't right at the time. Their stories were too pat, but Reilly went easy on them. We ought to have brought them in for a proper interview."

"Hardly conclusive," Boyce said.

"No, sir, but I've been doing background checks, and both Appleton and O'Neill are subcontractors for the firm where Osborne worked. In effect, Osborne was their boss. When Reilly suggested that Osborne had helped a friend, they were happy to agree. Either that or Osborne had already told them what to say."

"Pull them in, Tim. Interview them under caution, and let's see if they change their story."

"Yes, sir. But there was something else. When we talked to Mel Parker, she said Tony Carter had been helped by one of his mates after he'd been in a fight, but she didn't give Osborne's name; that came from DS Reilly. He planted the idea in her head, and she agreed. By influencing three different witnesses, DS Reilly placed Osborne in the club at a specific time, but it wasn't true. Osborne wasn't in the club when Carter got into a fight. He was driving away with Lynsey in the back of his car." Spiller paused.

"There's one more thing. I believe Reilly planted the drugs in Lynsey's flat, because he wanted to stall the investigation and throw us off the scent completely. Lynsey says she's never taken ecstasy, and I believe her."

"She's hardly likely to confess to having a controlled substance in her flat."

"Maybe not, sir, but she also said that more than one

man came into the room where she was being kept, so we know Osborne had an accomplice."

"Yes, that must've been Leeman."

Spiller reined back his frustration. Keeping his voice level, he said, "I doubt that, sir. Leeman is softly spoken and he sounds educated, but the man Lynsey heard had a Yorkshire accent. That points to DS Reilly." Spiller hesitated. "Then there was the way Reilly searched an office in County Hall and seized evidence. We were explicitly asked to stop and get permission, but Reilly went ahead, potentially making any evidence we found inadmissible."

"Not to mention the arrest of Victor Tate," Boyce said, his voice stern. "You were the arresting officer; not Reilly."

"Yes, sir. I ought to have known better, but I won't make excuses. I'll accept the consequences. I've made my report and I stand by it."

"So be it. This is going to be tough on you, Tim. There will have to be a full and complete investigation, and that means the Police Complaints Authority. When they arrive and start asking questions, you're not going to be popular in CID. Reilly was well-liked, but you're new here, and your colleagues might blame you for upsetting the apple cart."

"I can stand up for myself, sir."

"I can see that. If anyone can weather the coming storm, it's you. If I were a betting man, I'd put money on it."

Thanks seemed inappropriate, so Spiller simply nodded in acknowledgement.

"There's one more thing we need to talk about." Boyce opened a desk drawer and pulled out a plastic evidence bag, laying it on the desk then averting his gaze as if he didn't want to acknowledge what the bag contained.

Spiller knew why. Through the transparent plastic he saw Reilly's jackknife.

"In your report, you said that Reilly carried this item on his person," Boyce went on. "That reference should be removed. It's not relevant."

"Sir, the murders in the park... those men were stabbed."

"With a short and very sharp pointed blade," Boyce replied. "Nothing like an old pocketknife, and certainly not a marlin spike."

"I'm glad to hear it, sir. For a second, I thought..."

"That Reilly was some kind of gangland enforcer?" Boyce shook his head. "Our erstwhile colleague was many things, but not that. If, as you suggest, he was involved in covering for Osborne, he would've been drawn in against his will. Someone must've had some kind of hold over him. And who knows? If things had played out differently, he might've freed Lynsey. He didn't get the chance."

"Yes, sir."

"So let's take that knife out of the picture. It had no bearing on the case, but the media love that kind of detail, and it makes the man look like a thug."

"When you put it like that, sir, it seems best not to mention it. I'll change that part of my report."

"Good, but that leaves one small problem. Reilly's ex-wife was listed as his next of kin. I've spoken to her, but she doesn't want Reilly's personal effects, so what can we do with this?" Boyce pushed the evidence bag away from him. "I could have it destroyed, but perhaps you'd like to take it as a reminder. Not to carry, but to keep somewhere at home."

"I'm not sure that's appropriate, sir."

"I am. Paddy was a good policeman at heart, but we're

all human, Tim. We all have our weaknesses, and we can all be tempted. So take Paddy's old knife, and whenever you catch sight of it, say to yourself, there but for the grace of God go I."

Spiller nodded sadly, then he stepped forward and picked up the evidence bag without a word, stuffing it into his pocket.

Boyce eyed him levelly as if weighing him up, then he seemed to reach a decision. "You'll be all right, Tim. There'll be fallout in the days to come; there's no getting away from it. You didn't follow protocol, but you did your best, and you got Lynsey home. If you hadn't put yourself in harm's way, we might never have found her in time."

"Thank you, sir."

"I want you to tie up the loose ends. Somebody was telling Osborne what to do, and I want you to find out who. This will be in addition to your work in the MIT."

"On my own, sir?"

"Yes. Liaise with me where necessary, otherwise, follow up every lead. You can start with that report from County Hall. It may not have evidential value, but that doesn't mean we can't use it as a source of intelligence. I can bring in a financial expert to go through it. Pass the report to me, and I'll see to it."

"Yes, sir. Erm..." Spiller took a quick breath. This was the moment he'd been dreading, but he had to press on and get it over with.

"I'm sorry to say that there's a problem with our copy of the report. DI Nicholson says he returned it to DS Reilly, who was supposed to deliver it to the evidence store, but he never actually did it. I've checked the records, and I've searched through the store, but DS Reilly hasn't deposited any evidence recently, and no one else has brought in a computer printout or anything resembling one."

"That's a shame, but it's not the end of the world. Presumably, we can get another copy from County Hall."

"Actually, sir, I've already tried. I went to County Hall this morning."

"You have been busy."

"I prefer it that way, sir. Unfortunately, I didn't get past the front desk. I was told that the man who originally created the report, Victor Tate, was taking an extended period of leave and would not be back for several weeks. He's supposedly visiting a sick relative in Australia, but I have my doubts."

"You've checked the flights," Boyce said.

"Yes, sir, and he wasn't listed."

"There could be a legitimate reason for that, I suppose. Still, there must be someone else at the council you can talk to."

"You'd think so, sir. I asked to speak to the person in charge of finance, but I was told to submit my request in writing. I've done as they asked, but it could be a while before I hear back from them."

"Let me have a go, Tim. They won't fob me off."

"Thank you, sir. That ought to do it."

"Let's hope so, but we can't count our chickens just yet. Somebody, somewhere, didn't want that information to see the light of day. They were worried enough to commit a kidnap rather than have it leaked to the outside world. So what's the betting that all those figures have been made to go away?"

Spiller nodded. "The thought had crossed my mind, sir."

"Nevertheless, we'll chase it up, Tim. I'll do my best to

get you that report, but I smell corruption, and I fear we may be up against it. All we can do is keep plugging away, looking for new leads until we find a way in."

"Yes, sir. That's fine with me. I'm like a dog with a bone."

"Good man," Boyce said. "I'll let you get on with it."

"Thank you, sir." Spiller marched from the room and went in search of a free desk. Everyone in the MIT was hard at work, and suddenly, losing himself in ordinary policework was very appealing.

———

AT THE END of the day, Spiller visited Raleigh Road. Once there, he strode up to the front door and rang the bell for flat one.

Jemima Tussell was wearing jeans and a sweatshirt when she answered the door.

"Hello again," Spiller said. "I was hoping you'd be back from work by now."

"Yes. I haven't been back long." Jemima hesitated. "I heard they found Lynsey. Is she going to be all right?"

"Yes. I'm pleased to say she's doing as well as can be expected."

"Thank God for that. When I saw you, I thought..."

"Don't worry. I haven't come with bad news. Actually, there's something you can help with."

"Oh?"

"Yes. I've been doing some background checks, and it turns out there's something you didn't mention when we talked the other day."

"I don't think so. I've nothing to hide."

"That's not entirely true, Miss Tussell. When we spoke, you said you were going to work in Argos."

"I was. It was my first day."

"Exactly. It was a new job, but you didn't point that out at the time."

"Didn't I? I suppose it didn't come up."

"Maybe not, but the fact remains that during the previous week, you were working at County Hall."

"I did a few shifts. It was admin."

"Mainly in the post room," Spiller said. "And one of your tasks was to deliver internal mail. I'm assuming you had access to most of the building."

"Yes, I had to push the mail around in a trolley. It wasn't a bad job. Better than Argos, anyway."

"I can imagine. But when you were in County Hall, pushing your trolley around, I expect most people didn't pay you much attention. Some jobs are like that. It's as if the people doing them become part of the furniture: always there, but never noticed."

"It was a bit like that," Jem said. "People were busy, and they didn't always say please or thank you, but most of them were okay."

"How about in the ICT department? What were they like?"

Jem shrugged. "They were all right."

"Did you see Lynsey while you were there?"

"Oh yes. Every time I went up there." Jem frowned. "You don't think I had anything to do with—"

"No, no," Spiller interrupted. "As I said, you've nothing to worry about, but I wonder whether you might've taken something from that department; something that didn't belong to you."

The corners of Jem's lips turned down. "Oh. I know I

probably shouldn't have, but it wasn't... I mean, it was nothing."

"We're talking about a computer printout, yes?"

Jem nodded. "It was scrap paper. It had been used already, and it was only a little bit. They used to chuck it in a box, so every now and then I liberated a few pages. It's not exactly a crime, is it?"

"We needn't get into that. The thing is, we'd like to have that printout back."

"Oh."

"Is there a problem?"

"Yes. I'd help if I could. It's still here, sort of, but... I'd better show you."

Jem led Spiller inside and showed him into her flat. On the table was a sculpture: a figurative piece that unmistakably represented a giraffe. For some reason, it had been painted a metallic gold colour.

Jem gestured to the sculpture. "It's in there."

Spiller furrowed his brow. "Inside the giraffe?"

"No. It's literally *in* the piece. It's papier mâché. I tear up paper into small pieces, then I glue them onto a wire form. That's why I needed so much paper, and that stuff was good quality. It was a shame to see it go to waste. They'd have shredded it eventually, but I used it to make something beautiful. That's justifiable, isn't it?"

"Erm..." Spiller looked from the sculpture to Jem. "You used all of it? The whole report?"

"Yes. That's why I said it's still here. It is, but it's been torn into tiny pieces, so I can't give it back. I'm sorry, I really am."

"So am I," Spiller said. "So am I."

45

SPILLER WAS SITTING on the two-seater sofa with Sheila, ostensibly watching the evening news, but neither of them were paying much attention. Sheila was telling him about a house she'd seen advertised for rent, and Spiller was all ears. But something on the news caught his eye, and he stood quickly, crossing the room to turn up the volume.

"What did you do that for?" Sheila asked. "I was trying to talk to you, and it's only the blooming chancellor again, droning on about nothing."

"Sorry, love, but I want to listen for a minute."

"Oh, all right. I'll go and make some cocoa. Do you want one?"

"Yes please, love," Spiller said automatically, his attention fixed on the screen.

Norman Lamont, the Chancellor of the Exchequer, was saying, "I'm today announcing the Private Finance Initiative. This bold new strategy will release public funds for a range of new developments across the nation. New schools, hospitals and other public buildings will be built with the help of private companies. As a government, we are delivering on our promises without placing the burden on the taxpayers. This will pave the way for a whole range of exciting new projects, revitalising our cities, our towns and our communities."

It sounds too good to be true, Spiller thought. *So it probably is.*

Sheila came in with a tray and set it down on the coffee table, retaking her seat.

"Thanks, love." Spiller joined Sheila on the sofa and picked up his mug. "That was quick."

"I had everything ready. Biscuit? I got some of your favourites. Chocolate digestives."

"You spoil me." They shared a smile as Spiller took a biscuit from the proffered plate. There was no taking food straight from the packet with Sheila; she frowned on such things.

Spiller sipped his cocoa, and the news coverage switched back to the studio, where a correspondent was explaining how the new scheme, branded PFI, was expected to work:

"The government are hoping to keep capital costs down by offering contracts to big businesses. Private companies will provide the public buildings and be reimbursed by contractual payments over time. In other words, the companies will build new schools and hospitals and so on at a low cost, but they'll have contracts to maintain them in the future. This will free up public funds which can be used elsewhere."

"That sounds all right," Sheila said. "It's about time somebody did something about the schools. They're always complaining about leaky roofs, aren't they?"

"Yes," Spiller replied absently, adding, almost to himself, "How do you maintain a curtain?"

"You wash it, or if it's the wrong kind of fabric, you take it to the cleaners. Why?" Sheila glanced at the window. "What's wrong with the curtains? They'll do for now, won't they?"

"The curtains are fine," Spiller replied. "I was thinking of something else. But never mind, love. Never mind."

EPILOGUE

Barry Leeman paused to take in the splendour of his surroundings, breathing deep and filling his lungs with the sweet air of the Lake District.

Stunning, he thought. *Simply stunning.*

The vista was made even better by the fact that Francis Clifford was paying for this trip. That was one good thing about Clifford; he always paid his bill on time. The man may have had his troubles, but he was a fighter to his core.

Clifford kept company with fat cats and bureaucrats, but it wasn't always thus. He'd cut his teeth on deals made in backstreets and smoke-filled pubs. In those days, he'd gathered a different circle of friends, none of whom would be welcome in the golf club. Some of those old associates still owed Clifford a favour or two, and like him, they were the kind of men who always settled their accounts.

With friends such as those, Francis Clifford would be all right.

Leeman walked on, his hands on the straps of his rucksack, and his sturdy boots making short work of the uneven, rocky path. Soon the slope of Scafell Pike rose above him, its crags and crooked pathways inviting him onward.

When the slope grew steeper, he pushed on, his leg muscles working hard, his heart rate rising. This was fantastic; exactly what he needed.

I should do this more often, he decided. *God knows, I've no excuse.* Back in Devon, Dartmoor was on his doorstep, and Exmoor wasn't far; both had their hills and challenging terrain. True, there was nothing in Devon quite like Scafell Pike, but he could explore the moors whenever he wanted, provided he could find the time.

Free time was always a luxury, but especially today. He had a task to complete, and time was very much against him.

Leeman spotted a small group approaching him: two adults with a young girl walking between them, the child clinging to the man's hand.

Leeman stopped to consult his OS map and compass.

"Hello," the man called out cheerily as he drew near. "Lovely day for it."

"Yes," Leeman replied. "Perfect."

The woman glanced meaningfully at Leeman's map. "You're not lost, are you?"

"No, but I like to check now and then to make sure I'm on the right path. It's beautiful here, isn't it?"

"Oh yes," the man replied. "I could live here at the drop of a hat."

"And how would you manage without shops nearby?" the woman asked. "And what if you wanted to go to the cinema or the theatre?"

"Where there's a will, there's a way." The man offered a conciliatory smile to the woman, but she didn't return it.

Definitely married, Leeman thought. Aloud, he said, "Have you been to the top?"

The woman lifted an eyebrow. "I wish. Not with these two in tow."

"Two?" Leeman smiled at the young girl. "You haven't left someone behind, have you?"

The girl chuckled. "No. My brother's up there." She pointed to the man's back, and Leeman realised that what he'd taken for a large rucksack was actually a contraption for carrying a small child.

"Very heavy he is too," the man said. Looking to his partner, he added, "Could you pop him down for a bit? I'm sure he can walk from here."

"Okay."

Leeman watched with interest as the woman retrieved a small boy from her husband's back, setting the youngster on the ground. The boy immediately grasped the woman's hand, and he gazed up at Leeman with frank curiosity, his grey eyes bright.

"That's a fine boy you have there," Leeman said. "Full of mischief, I'll bet."

"He's good as gold," the woman said. "He's no trouble at all."

As if to contradict his proud mother, the boy pointed at Leeman and said, "Another funny man."

"Darling, don't be so rude," the woman scolded, her cheeks flushing.

"That's all right," Leeman said. "I expect I do seem a bit odd to him, marching along on my own."

The man ruffled his son's hair. "It's my fault. We passed someone earlier, and I might've described him as a funny man. He was a bit... less than friendly."

"Not everyone wants to stop and chat," the woman said. "I expect he was in a hurry to get to the top."

"As am I," Leeman said. "But manners cost nothing, as my mother used to say."

"Mine too," the man replied. "But we'd better let you get going while the weather's good. You never know what it's going to do up there. It can change in a second."

Leeman was about to say that he was well equipped, but the young boy had another pronouncement to make. Pointing this time at Leeman's feet, he called out, "Boots. Shiny boots."

"Well, well, he does have sharp eyes." To the boy, Leeman said, "Yes, my boots are new, that's why they're so shiny."

"I know," the boy replied, and Leeman laughed.

"Sorry, our son is rather precocious," the man said. "He's always noticing little things like that."

"He's a smart lad," Leeman replied. "He'll make something of himself one day." Turning to the girl, he said, "As will you, young lady, I'm sure."

The man's smile became guarded, as if he didn't approve of this stranger's sudden interest in his children. "Well, we'd better head off. Enjoy your walk."

"Thank you. You too."

Leeman watched the family for a moment as they wended their way down the path. The young boy half turned to look over his shoulder at Leeman, and the woman, still holding the boy's hand, said, "Look where you're going, Dan."

A nice family, Leeman thought. *Informative too.*

He'd been almost certain that his target was ahead of him, but it was nice to have it confirmed. *Unless there's another man walking up here on his own*, Leeman told himself. But when he scanned the rocky path ahead, he saw no one. Besides, it was getting late and encountering more than one lone walker at this time of day seemed unlikely.

Leeman marched onward, redoubling his efforts, and the time passed quickly. But as he gained height, soft curls of mist swept in from nowhere, softening the craggy slope above. Cold droplets of moisture prickled Leeman's face, and he paused to grab a coat from his rucksack.

In the minute it took him to don his waterproof coat and replace his rucksack, the mist grew thick enough to obscure the surrounding landscape, removing the reference points Leeman had been keeping an eye on. *That's no problem*, he thought. *I know exactly where I'm going.*

He could still see the path that lay at his feet, and that was all he needed.

He resumed his journey, taking care with each footstep, partly to guard against accidents, and partly to avoid any loose stones that might crunch underfoot. He must be nearing his objective, and while the mist would shield him to some extent, it would do little to dampen the sound of his footsteps.

Leeman's route led him along a ridge, and he peered into the mist-clad depths below. He was no more than a hand's width away from an unseen void, and he smiled to himself.

But he didn't have time to enjoy the moment. A figure emerged from the mist, hurrying down the path toward him, his head down, hiking poles in each hand.

There he is, Leeman thought. *Right on cue.* Aloud, he called out, "Hello there."

The man halted, looking up with a start. "You made me jump," he said. "Are you okay?"

Leeman strolled closer. "I'm fine, thanks. You?"

"Yes, I'm okay, but..." The man lifted one arm to gesture hopelessly at the mist. "It came in so quick."

"Quickly," Leeman said.

"What?"

"Forgive me for being picky, but I think you meant to say, it came in so *quickly*. It's a common error."

"Right. Well, if you'll forgive *me*, I'll make tracks. I need to get down before the weather gets worse. If I were you, I'd do the same."

"I'll head back soon, when I've achieved my goal."

"If you really want to make it to the top, that's your prerogative, but it's not a good idea. It would be much better to come back another day and try again."

Leeman nodded thoughtfully. "Thanks for your advice. My name is Leeman, by the way. Barry Leeman." He stepped even closer to the man, his hand outstretched. "You are?"

"Tate. Victor." Fumbling with the strap of his hiking pole to release his hand for a shake, Tate looked down. His gaze left Leeman for only a fraction of a second, but it was enough.

Leeman grabbed Tate by both arms and spun him around, keeping hold of his right wrist and forcing it up behind his back, at the same time wrenching the metal pole from his grip.

Tate yelped and lashed out with his free hand, the hiking pole waving wildly in the air, but a swift kick to the back of his legs sent him to his knees.

Leeman planted his foot on the pole, trapping it against the ground, the loop of its handle still around Tate's wrist. Tate struggled to get his hand free, but he was too slow.

Leeman already had his left arm around Tate's throat,

and he squeezed hard, pressing against the man's windpipe, constricting the arteries in his neck.

Tate gagged, fighting for air, his face turning puce. His left hand finally free, he clutched feebly at Leeman's arm, but it was a pathetic effort and futile.

Leeman leaned in, his mouth close to Tate's ear. "Now we can talk properly. Who have you been working for, Mr Tate?"

Tate spluttered, attempting to speak, and Leeman relaxed his grip just enough to let the man have a little air.

Tate gasped rapidly, every exhalation whining in his throat.

"I need an answer," Leeman went on.

"I don't…" Tate's voice faltered, and he coughed. "I don't know what you mean."

"Come on. We both know you're not the brains of the operation. You haven't got it in you."

Tate was breathing easier now, his cheeks returning to their former colour, but his voice still shook as he said, "I don't know what you're talking about. Let me go."

"I expect Lynsey Clifford said the same thing. But then you weren't there, were you? You didn't have the guts to face the consequences of your actions. You let others do the dirty work."

Tate didn't reply.

"I'll ask one more time, who were you working for?"

"I work for the council. I'm only a—"

"No," Leeman snapped. "I've had enough of this nonsense. So I'll tell you what we'll do. We'll go back to your hotel and discuss it there. Your wife could join us. Jane. That's a nice name. Simple. She looks like good company. I'll enjoy getting to know her."

Tate struggled briefly to get free, but he didn't stand a

chance. He let out a whimper of frustration, but then he seemed to recover, and when he spoke his voice was steadier.

"There's no need to bring my wife into this. She knows nothing. Nothing."

"That may be true, but she must've had an inkling. The nice car, the four-star hotel, the exclusive restaurant where you dined last night. They're all rather pricey for a public servant such as yourself. A woman notices these things, but for some reason, she hasn't put two and two together. That's wilful ignorance, and it makes her complicit. She'll have to pay for your mistakes; it's only fair."

"Fair? What the hell are you talking about? There's nothing fair about this."

"Don't you think so? It's all a question of perspective."

"For God's sake! I don't care what you do to me but leave my wife alone. She's completely innocent."

"No one is *completely* innocent." Leeman heaved a sigh. "I suppose Jane might be spared any unpleasantness, but only if you tell me the truth. Who's been giving the orders, Victor? Give me a name."

"I... I can't. They send me instructions, but I never know who they come from."

"How do you get these instructions?"

"They call me at home on the phone. Someone tells me where to go, usually a cafe or a bar, a different one each time. They give me a false name to use. I sit down, and someone will come over, a waitress usually, and they ask if I'm Mr Smith or whatever. When I say yes, they say someone left a message for me, and they hand me an envelope."

"Clever. How did they get their hooks into you, Victor?"

"I... Oh God."

"Come along," Leeman said. "Confession is good for the soul."

"All right. I'm doing my best." Tate coughed and took a long breath. "There was a woman. I was at a conference, and on the last night I had too much to drink, and I... went to her room. I suppose they set me up. When I got home, a photograph came in the post. If Jane had opened it..." Tate swallowed. "I was so ashamed. I'm not that kind of person, I'm really not."

"The evidence says otherwise, Victor. I'm disappointed in you."

For a moment, no one spoke.

"What are you going to do?" Victor said.

"At the moment, your fate hangs in the balance. I can see how it might be useful to have you on my side."

"Yes. I could help you. I could find out who's involved. It won't be easy. They're organised. They have people everywhere. That conference was in London, but they still got to me. They have a lot of resources, a lot of money. I'm sure I wasn't the only one working for them. There were others. Important people."

"I suspect you're right. We'll talk some more, Victor, but let's get you to your feet. Your knees must be killing you."

"Yes. They are pretty painful."

Leeman released Tate's throat and guided him into a standing position, holding tight to both of his arms.

"Thank you," Tate murmured. "For what it's worth, I never knew what they were going to do to Lynsey. I didn't want any of that to happen, but it was beyond my control."

"Oh dear."

"What? Why do you say that?"

"Turn around," Leeman said, and he let go of Tate completely, taking half a step back.

"Okay." Holding his hands to shoulder height as if in surrender, Tate turned to face him.

"When I said your fate was hanging in the balance, I meant it," Leeman said. "But then you had to go and make that foolish remark. It was beyond your control, was it, Victor? Do you expect me to swallow that?"

"You know what I mean. I couldn't—"

"You could've helped the police," Leeman interrupted. "You knew Lynsey had been kidnapped long before the police figured it out. You could've phoned in and tipped them off, but did you help her? No, you did not." He advanced on Tate, forcing him to take a faltering step back.

"Look, I'm sorry," Tate said. "I didn't know what they were going to do to her. I was getting data for them, that's all. But when I told them what had happened, they were furious. Then Lynsey went missing, and I panicked. I didn't know what to do. But I can make it right. I can help you."

"Yes, you can," Leeman stated. "You can give her family a kind of closure."

"How? Tell me what to do."

"It's easy."

Leeman rubbed his hands together, his gaze hard, implacable.

Tate took another step back, looking down as he left the path and found himself standing on uneven ground.

"Face me like a man," Leeman said. "Look me in the eye and tell me you're sorry."

Tate kept his head bowed, but he lifted his gaze enough to peer at his tormentor. "I'm sorry," he began, and Leeman lunged forward, placing his hands on Tate's chest and shoving hard.

Tate's arms flailed in the air, and then he was gone, tumbling backwards over the ridge's edge and disappearing into the mist.

Leeman listened, and after a gratifying delay, he heard one muffled thud and then another.

Leeman brushed his hands together and then he set off down the path. He smiled, recalling the first words Tate had uttered when they'd met just a short time ago: You made me jump.

So I did, Leeman thought. *So I did.*

———

Thank you for reading Lawful Duty. I hope you enjoyed it.
What becomes of Tim Spiller?
Meet him in the present day in my contemporary series,
The Devonshire Mysteries.
Here's a handy link to the first novel, Valley of Lies:
Find Valley of Lies on your favourite store

Visit: books2read.com/valleyoflies

GET FREE EBOOKS

WHEN YOU JOIN THE AWKWARD SQUAD - THE HOME OF PICKY READERS

Visit: michaelcampling.com/freebooks

AUTHOR NOTES

ARE THE LOCATIONS REAL?

Yes. Unlike the Devonshire Mysteries, which blend real and fictional locations, the settings in this book are almost exclusively real. I use the names of real streets, neighbourhoods, pubs, cafes and so on. It's important to note that while the settings are *inspired* by real places, all locations are used in a fictionalised way. There is no implication of real-life wrongdoing in any of the locations mentioned.

The Icebox is a fictional nightclub, but there were a couple of nightclubs on the quayside in Exeter during the 90s. Similarly, while Safeway was a supermarket chain in the UK, there wasn't a branch in the location I used.

The police station at Heavitree was abandoned some time ago. The empty building is still there, so I used its real location, but I felt free to use my imagination when it came to descriptions of the interior. Funnily enough, I met a uniformed police officer who told me that, back in those days, he visited the CID office at Heavitree because it was the only room in the building where he could smoke. A curious coincidence.

ARE THE POLICE PROCEDURES REAL?

I research these details as much as I can, but there's always room for fictional interpretation. The story and characters have priority over legal accuracy.

Setting the story in the past brought its own challenges. Some details are well documented and easy to find, e.g. you may notice that the formal caution was different from the modern one. Also, the salary of police officers in 92 was published online. Other details were harder to find amidst the wealth of present-day information, so I did my best.

I tried to steer away from some of the well-worn cliches that feature in a lot of crime fiction, and I even have a little joke about some of them, e.g. the idea that officers would refer to a superintendent as 'Super'.

If you'd like to delve into the reference material I used, please see the note below headed 'Can I see some of your sources?'

HOW ABOUT COUNTY HALL?

County Hall in Exeter is a real building, and I've described its appearance from my perspective, but I have never been inside. The office is based on my experience of working in corporate IT in the 90s. We called it ICT in those days, the C standing for communications. I have vivid memories of my CRT monitor and keyboard. There was no PC; all my work was on a mainframe. Behind my desk was a wide-carriage dot-matrix printer, and we used it for small test runs. We fed it with old printouts, printing on the reverse to save paper. It was a hideous old thing, and the noise drove me mad. I was glad to see the back of it when we moved to a new building.

WHAT'S GOING ON WITH ALL THE SEXISM?

I was interested in the banter and camaraderie between officers, especially since political correctness was still scoffed at by many during the 90s. You'll notice a distinct laddishness among the male characters. Sadly, that was par for the course in those days. Hopefully, we've moved on as a society, but there's still a long way to go.

In the story, Lynsey wouldn't put up with any sexist nonsense, and neither would Mel, so I hope their strength and independence provides a counterpoint.

In retrospect, I would've liked to bring in a female police officer at an earlier stage and given her a more important part to play. In fact, I wish I'd provided a more diverse cast. Hindsight is a wonderful thing, and if there are more books in the series, I'll do better.

WAS PFI REAL?

Definitely. The Private Finance Initiative was set up by a Conservative government and embraced by successive governments as a way of keeping expenditure 'off-balance-sheet'. In 2018 the Chancellor of the Exchequer, Philip Hammond, announced that PFI, and its successor PF2, would no longer be used, but the existing contracts are still running.

PFI contracts are shrouded in secrecy, and some of them are being disputed to this day. Hard-pressed public services are burdened by huge debts, but they find it hard to negotiate new terms when the private companies refuse to be transparent.

Hundreds of billions of pounds of taxpayer money have been poured into these schemes, and a search for 'PFI scandal' will point to many reputable sources.

The figures that Ollie quotes for the so-called maintenance of various items were real, taken from an article on the website of the *i* newspaper. Here are the figures in more detail, all the below were for schools:

£25,471 for three sunshades

£5,180 to install a single socket and remove a ceiling light

£9,736 for a dividing curtain

£8,695 for a deep-fat fryer.

And in a police station, £884 for a single chair.

These are the current costs. To see these figures through the eyes of Spiller and his colleagues, here are some typical cost-of-living figures from 1992:

- Pint of milk: 34p
- Loaf of bread 55p
- Pint of beer: £1.49
- Petrol: 43.4p per litre
- Average annual salary: £12,088.

None of this is to say that organised crime gangs were involved in PFI contracts. It is possible that it happened, but I have no evidence that it did, so that part of the story is purely fictional. That said, there are questions over whether PFI contracts were ethical or justifiable.

A PFI funded hospital, for example, might have to close wards and make staff redundant to save money, but it cannot default on the payments it makes to the private company who built it.

For further reference material, please see my shared online notebook of sources below.

CAN I SEE SOME OF YOUR SOURCES?

Yes, you can. When I'm researching a book, I compile an online notebook using a program called Notion. The list is not exhaustive, but there's a lot there, from the cars used by Spiller and Reilly, the pubs and cafes they visit, police salaries, Leeman's push dagger, articles on PFI and much more.

Here you are:
michaelcampling.com/lawful-duty-notes

———

Thanks for coming back with me to the nineties.
I hope I'll have the pleasure of your company again very soon.
All the best,
Michael Campling
Devon, 2024

ACKNOWLEDGMENTS

I'm especially grateful to everyone who has supported me recently by sending me a mug of tea via Ko-fi.com. To name a few: Lara, Alonza, Clairey, Cynthia, John, Diane, Lesley, Chriss, Pat, Barbara, Nana, Violet, Barbara and Elizabeth.

Special thanks go to these keen-eyed advance readers: Helen, Christopher, Bev, Gary, Doreen, Arthur, Pat, Pauline, Dave, Jean, Saundra, Annemarie, Linda.

This book was edited by Michael-Israel Jarvis.

ABOUT THE AUTHOR

Michael (Mikey to friends) is a full-time writer living and working on the edge of Dartmoor in Devon. He writes stories with characters you can believe in, and plots you can sink your teeth into. His style is vivid but never flowery; every word packs a punch. His stories are complex, thought- provoking, atmospheric and grounded in real life. You can start reading his work for free with a complimentary mystery book plus a starter library which you'll receive when you join Michael's readers' group, which is called The Awkward Squad. You'll receive free books and stories, plus a newsletter that's actually worth reading. Learn more and start reading today at: michaelcampling.com/freebooks

facebook.com/authormichaelcampling

x.com/mikeycampling

instagram.com/mikeycampling

amazon.com/Michael-Campling/e/B00EUVA0GE

bookbub.com/authors/michael-campling

ALSO BY MICHAEL CAMPLING

One Link to Rule Them All:

michaelcampling.com/find-my-books

THE DEVONSHIRE MYSTERIES

A Study in Stone (an Awkward Squad bonus)

Valley of Lies

Mystery at the Hall (an Awkward Squad bonus)

Murder Between the Tides

Mystery in May

Death at Blackingstone Rock (an Awkward Squad bonus)

Accomplice to Murder

A Must-Have Murder

THE DARKENINGSTONE SERIES:

Breaking Ground - A Darkeningstone Prequel

Trespass: The Darkeningstone Book I

Outcast—The Darkeningstone Book II

Scaderstone—The Darkeningstone Book III

Darkeningstone Trilogy Box Set

Printed in Great Britain
by Amazon